# THE TOWER OF THE GLADE

# R.L. AIKEN

Copyright © 2017 R.L.Aiken

All rights reserved.

ISBN

978-0-6485683-2-2

*For my mother, Margaret, who gave me her reading gene*

*For our girls
Linzi, Hayley, Bonnie, Crystal, and Carley*

*And for our William River*

*With love*

The Traders Series

Book 1
*Shaeli of Purple Leaf*

Book 2
*The Thrower's Apprentice*

Book 3
*The Tower of the Glade*

# ACKNOWLEDGMENTS

As always, there are many people to thank ~ my family, my friends, and my husband ~ but most of all I'd like to thank you, the reader. After all, it's you who this story was intended for all along; you who I thought about every step in this long journey; you who love to read, who want to "live a thousand lives, instead of just one". And while it makes me sad to finish it at last, I'm so happy to hand it over to you... and it may not be the end really; it's a big world, and I may have to visit it again sometime, just to see what's been happening without me...

.

# PROLOGUE

In the city of Palveron on the Land of Zirrus, people prepared for the Wintering as usual, yet behind closed doors and in shadowed street-corners, they whispered. They whispered about the scourge of the guard sweeping the countryside, and of the rebels who met them at every turn. They whispered about the true heir rumoured to be somewhere in the World, the child of King Tenelon and his queen, Irinesta, and what it could mean. In muffled tones they talked of the papers that had fluttered from the tower of the Glade and the body of the old woman who had followed the papers to the cobbled stones of the courtyard, and they looked warily up at the gates of Great Court, closed to the city for the first time in memory. Yet they did nothing more than whisper, and even that was done as little as possible. They had learned who stood with the queen and who did not, and if they valued their comfortable lives they would not speak of these things among many; but when people were sure of their companions, sure their words would not be repeated, then they whispered, and they whispered with hope-tinged fear.

If Queen Virrisian knew of such whisperings in the castle, no one knew, but if she did, they were sure that she cared very little. The courtiers and servants had walked carefully around the queen since the day the old woman fell to her death, more so since the gates had been closed – her temper was ever-present and only the very brave or the very stupid drew attention to themselves. They spoke loudly about the madness of the old maid, and the absolute right of the queen to her throne, in public at least, but there were few who did not privately wonder at the truth of such a thing. Many dreaded the captive Moons of the Wintering in the castle, but, to the great relief of the entire court, something had happened to soften the queen's mood. These past days had seen her grow less terse, her smile easing the hearts of those who served her into relieved reticence – though all knew better than to relax completely. Yet the queen continued her good-humour, bestowing gifts on those she favoured and merely ignoring those she did not. What had happened to bestow this benevolent mood upon her was also unknown, though many wondered, yet they merely enjoyed the respite from her temper and watched the final days of autumn drift across the Land.

If they had known, both townspeople and courtiers, what the new year would bring, perhaps they would not have been so complacent.

\* \* \*

Far across Zirrus, Shaeli, Tarkoda and Kirrit stood outside the tunnel that came from the cave of the Zoi, looking out into the vastness of Cave. Behind them came two men, Flin and Spotjaw; two drell, Blenny and Wendll; three Ammerr, Ishaan, Cheval, and Olando; and two elves, Williver and Llianas. The tiny jevvi, Ebony, was on Shaeli's shoulder.

Together with the companions collected along the way, the three young traders had endured the Poisoned Marshes, the queen's guard waiting for them at every step of their journey across the Land and the sea; they had lived through the coming of the black ship and the attack by the giant eels in the lake far below the mountain; they had endured this and more. They had run laughing into Cave, expecting warmth and smiles and the wide arms of safety. Instead they were met with silence and ruins and the stench of smoke.

It was dark, a few lamps hanging here and there, the red glow of the fire-pits casting dull light into the amphitheatre.

The old ones' huts were a crumpled mess, squashed into piles like kindling, yet it was the sight of the Traders that broke their hearts.

They lay in crooked piles, tossed together as if by a giant wave. There was hardly a balloon to be seen whole; these slack and torn, barely floating above their ships. Here and there, blackened piles showed where some ships had burnt, and the air was filled with the stale, acrid smell of it.

They could hardly tell one ship from another, and they were stopped instantly by the sight of the wreckage of their homes. The laughter caught sharply in their throats like fine bones.

"What's happened?" whispered Kirrit.

"I... I don't know," said Tarkoda. "Smells like a fire."

Their companions, coming from the shadows, gasped at the sight of the devastated Cave.

A few figures could be seen moving through the pile that had been the old ones' huts. The place where the bolt tunnel should begin was a mound of stones. A few more people could be seen kneeling beside the spring stream. The shape of the great tunnel that led out to the mountainside was different, a pile of rocks beneath it covering the path.

Shaeli was suddenly very afraid. She looked at the jumble where Purple Leaf should be moored, and could not tell which one it was. She looked at her brother, her face ashen, and then back down at Cave.

She could not see Almarnoch's little hut, but she could see more people moving about down near the fire-pits. She started to run.

\* \* \*

# CHAPTER ONE

The black ship had come three days before with the setting of the sun – a distant shadow in the greying sky to the south-east.

A work party returning from the Lea saw it first. It swept up from the Valley of Stones and across the Long Lea with amazing speed, and by the time they reached the path it had already gone over their heads and entered the tunnel.

Andos was with the work party. He was one of the first to reach the path, one of the few to see the ship slide soundlessly into the tunnel mouth. With him were Rhubic and Rennan from Shaeli's cave year, and Tajindi, Kirrit's brother.

They raced up the path and were about to cross the stepping stones when the ground shook and a great muffled explosion shuddered through the air. They were almost knocked from their feet by the force of it, and cries of distress came from the others on the path behind them. Moments later a great cloud of dust billowed from the tunnel.

They took the stepping stones two at a time. Rhubic and Rennan entered the bolt tunnel, Andos and Tajindi on their heels, when a second, smaller rumble sounded from inside Cave. The bolt tunnel was engulfed in another cloud of dust that sent them coughing and choking back outside. The others from the work party had reached the ledge as they leapt back over the stepping stones. Andos shouted to them to see to the cave of the animals, and then he turned and followed the other three into the main tunnel.

The dust was starting to clear, but they still could not see far. The familiar tunnel seemed foreign territory, and they slowed their pace, marking the places between lamps at a slow jog. As they neared the entrance to Cave, they smelt smoke and heard screams.

\* \* \*

Mareesha was with Eenis in the big room on Purple Leaf when the first explosion rocked Cave. The Trader shuddered.

Eenis dropped a bowl, screaming, and looked as if she was going to bolt. Illen came running from the front of the Trader, her eyes the same as Eenis', wild and wide. Both looked at Mareesha. All colour had fled from her face.

"The twins," she breathed, and she ran down the hall and up the steps.

Eenis and Illen heard her footfalls on the deck above. They looked at each other, swallowed their fear, and followed Mareesha outside.

\* \* \*

Almarnoch was loading his fireplace with rocks. He could feel the Wintering in his bones this year and he did not appreciate the sensation. He was just saying as much to Llevvis when the first explosion thundered through Cave. He took up his staff and was through the door before Llevvis had gained his feet.

\* \* \*

Jarris and Baroz were helping Baroz's mother, Bydi, repair the tiny veranda at the front of her hut. Jeth and Qiren had provided a great deal of instruction and very little practical help during the afternoon, and Wyshka had just taken them to inspect her cracked kitchen bench, seeing, she said, as they both knew so much.

As Jarris watched them go up his mother's steps, someone screamed down near the tunnel. He supposed someone had been the repository of a glow worms' rejects, and turned with a smile on his face. The twins were by the spring-pool, and he called down and asked them what the fuss was about. Neesha opened her mouth to reply when the screaming began again, only this time it did not stop. The screams went on and on, and then the side of the tunnel mouth exploded into Cave.

\* \* \*

Shanna and Neesha were sitting by the spring-pool with some of the other young people. They heard the scream and Jarris' question, but before Neesha could answer, another scream cut the air. Neesha turned her head in time to see a woman run from the main tunnel, her mouth wide with the unending scream, and then there was a thud, a flash of red light, and the side of the tunnel exploded.

The rock belched out, great boulders of it, and they fell onto the path and the screaming woman in a cloud of dust. The scream abruptly ceased. Dust from the fall of rocks flew in a rolling cloud that dimmed the brightness of Cave almost instantly.

It was hard to see the shape of the thing that followed the dust-cloud into Cave. It was a black mass, indistinct in form, flying through the main tunnel into Cave like some grotesque parody of a Trader.

The children scattered while Neesha watched, fascinated, as the black shape flew into Cave. She heard her father's shout behind her, and then Shanna grabbed her hand and began pulling her up the slope towards the huts of the old ones.

\* \* \*

Andos, Rhubic, Rennan and Tajindi slowed their pace even more as they came around the last bend. The air was full of dust, the smell of smoke grew stronger with each step, the shouts and screams grew louder. They crept forward, smoke in their eyes and dread in their hearts.

\* \* \*

Mareesha was hit by the dust as she crossed the deck. She ran to the rail, coughing, and looked out across Cave. The sight of the black ship drifting slowly into Cave stopped the breath in her throat, but she forced her eyes away from it, to the spring-pool. She saw the children scattering, saw Shanna's head turn; watched as she grabbed Neesha and the two of them began to run up to the old ones' huts. She saw Jarris run towards them, and then a red light lit Cave. It came from the black ship, and she saw the light of it fall on her running children. She cried out, and her cry was echoed by Eenis, who had come with Illen, unnoticed, to stand by her side. There was a flash of light from below, and she looked down to see Almarnoch, staff raised, striding across the ground towards the black ship.

\* \* \*

Llevvis watched Almarnoch move across the floor of Cave as if there were wings on his heels. His staff trembled when he saw what was in their Cave, and he gripped it tighter as the great red eye opened on the black ship and trained on running figures. His view was blocked by a white flash from Almarnoch's staff, and he did not see it hit its target. What he did see was the red light travel over the figures on the path, and then a flash of red threw itself across Cave and demolished the opening of the bolt tunnel.

Another flash from Almarnoch's staff flew across Cave, and Llevvis followed it with one of his own. The red light turned towards them.

\* \* \*

The twins were bathed in red light as Jarris ran down the path. He reached them, grabbed at their hands, meaning to drag them up and out the bolt tunnel to safety, but the light passed over their heads and a ball flew from the black ship and slammed into the bolt tunnel. The rock exploded outwards, and Jarris threw the girls down and covered them as best he could. He did not see the boulders fly into the huts of the old ones, but he heard Bydi scream. He did not see the rock flying towards his head, either, and after that he heard nothing.

\* \* \*

Neesha felt the thud, and then her father slumped over them. They lowered him to the ground, saw the wound on the side of his head, and they looked at each other over his still body. Around them was dust and chaos and screaming, and then the red light blazed. It was answered by Almarnoch's white and beams from Llevvis and Demeris. Together they pulled Jarris towards the amphitheatre, dragging him behind a rock. Shanna ripped off a piece of her skirt and wrapped it around Jarris' head. The cloth was soaked with blood in a moment.

"We have to fetch Mam," said Shanna.

Neesha nodded and took her hand.

* * *

When Andos came close enough to see the mouth of Cave, it looked odd, and he saw the side of it was shattered across the path, the debris tumbling down to the edge of the spring stream. A foot, small and pale, protruded from beneath one huge boulder.

The four edged their way along the wall towards the mound of rocks. Flashes of white and red came from inside Cave, smoke and noise filled the air, but the thudding of their hearts seemed loudest.

* * *

Mareesha saw the red light slam into the mouth of the bolt tunnel, and it disappeared in a cloud of dust. Huge chunks of rock flew out, thudding into the old-ones' huts and down onto the amphitheatre. She saw the rock fly towards where Jarris and the twins huddled, and the blow it gave him. The sight of it thudded into her heart.

As the Warlocks drew the black ship's fire, she saw the girls drag Jarris' body out of sight. The next time she saw them, they were running beneath the old one's huts, towards the back of Cave, towards her. She bolted for the Landing.

* * *

Almarnoch threw bolt after bolt at the hovering black ship. Though he had drawn its fire, he could not seem to penetrate it and he narrowed his light, but still he could not mark the ship's surface. He could barely make out its surface, nor determine its exact lines – its edges seemed to shimmer at the edge of vision – but he knew why it was here, and he would not let it have what it wanted. He fired again, and saw a red flash to his right.

Qiren had drawn his wand and was firing at the ship. The red eye turned towards the elf.

* * *

Jeth turned from the window where he and Qiren had watched the black ship enter Cave. Wyshka peered between their shoulders, and she screamed as the bolt tunnel disappeared. Cries were heard from the neighbouring huts.

"Take the old ones to safety," said Qiren, pulling the wand from his belt.

Jeth nodded and dragged his mother out the back door where the old ones were milling between the huts and the rock wall, and he led them as quickly as could towards the back of Cave.

Qiren left the hut in time to see the twins leave Jarris' side and run towards him.

"Go back," he yelled down at them, and he threw a blast at the side of the black ship.

It turned its light towards him, and he leapt down as the huts took a blast that demolished what the rocks had not. Qiren prayed that Jeth had gotten the old ones to safety as he fired again. He saw the girls run back towards the amphitheatre, out of danger. Or so he thought.

* * *

Shanna and Neesha skidded to a halt when Qiren yelled at them, and by the time the old one's huts had been torn apart, they were halfway back to the amphitheatre. They could see Taffka standing in the middle of the melee, yelling for buckets, for someone to take the children to the store-caves, for calm, but they thought only to help Jarris.

"That way," yelled Neesha, pointing across the open space between the fire-pits and the landings.

"No," cried Shanna. "We'd go near the *thing*," she said, looking up at the hovering ship.

"We'll go behind it," said Neesha. "It's not going to worry about us."

Shanna thought for the briefest moment, and she nodded. She took her sister's hand and they ran.

* * *

Andos and the three others reached the distorted end of the main tunnel in time to see the black ship destroy the last of the old ones' huts. Qiren leapt down to the floor of Cave as the huts crumpled, and then he was up and running to join Almarnoch and Llevvis, short bursts leaping from his wand as he ran. Neither the light from his wand nor the beams from the Warlocks' staffs seemed to touch the surface of the black ship.

The four young men clambered over the rocks covering the path, and jumped down into Cave. A dozen children cowered nearby, and Andos told Tajindi to take them back over the rocks to the cave of the animals. Tajindi nodded and began to help the children over the rock pile.

All around was chaos. People ran past with buckets, more leapt from their ships down stairs, away from landings lit by flame, Taffka stood yelling orders to the frightened, confused traders. The colours of the balloons glowed strangely.

To their right stood Demeris, firing up at the ship, the light of his staff growing increasingly paler. A bolt from the black ship flew at him, slamming into three Traders behind him. The balloons were ripped apart, two of the ships crashed together, destroying the landing between them, and then they dropped to the ground. One of the Traders fell with a crack and began to burn.

"Look," yelled Rhubic, and Andos turned to see his cousins running across the open space towards the Traders.

The two girls ran in a half-circle beneath the rear of the hovering ship. One of them – Andos couldn't be sure which in the smoky haze, but he thought it was Shanna – hesitated as the Traders fell to the ground beneath shredded balloons, but the other pulled her on. Suddenly the black ship above them spun around and a series of short bursts slammed into the

Traders near Purple Leaf, but Andos had only a moment to fear for his mother before another light leapt from the black ship.

This light was different. It came from the belly of the ship, a white light with swirling stripes of purple-black running through it. It shone on to the floor of Cave, illuminating the running figures of the twins.

\* \* \*

Mareesha's feet barely touched the boards going down the stairs. She ran beneath the Traders, her heart a drum in her chest. To her left were a score of ships already on the ground, a few on fire, and a dozen more sinking. As she ran, two more thudded to the ground, and to her right she could see the old one's huts were gone and Qiren was running towards Almarnoch and Llevvis, but she could not see the twins in the chaos. Ahead Demeris was firing valiantly from a fading staff, and beyond, Andos and three others were clambering down the mound that was the main entrance, and then she saw the twins. She saw them as they began the dash from the fire-pits, across the floor, beneath the black ship.

She ran screaming at them to go back, knowing they could not hear her in the madness that had swept through Cave, but screaming anyway, and when the ship spun around and fired above her head, she did not see the bolt destroy Purple Leaf's landing and a Trader behind her. All she saw was the light spew from the belly of the ship and fix on her running children.

\* \* \*

Almarnoch kept the white fire in his staff aimed at the shapeless black ship, but he was unable to penetrate it. His light seemed almost absorbed by the thing, and he was tiring. He could feel the strength draining into his staff, feel the exhaustion of Llevvis beside him, Qiren also.

The elf threw light after light, concentrating his red beams on the destructive red light of the ship, thinking if he could not damage the ship itself, at least he could stop the light from destroying every Trader, yet it seemed little use, he could not touch it.

When the ship swung around, its sudden burst took out a half-dozen balloons and Traders, and the white light snapped on beneath it.

Almarnoch stilled the fire in his staff. He saw the twins cowering between the swirling purple-black lines as the ship continued to swing back towards the entrance. He and Qiren both leapt towards the girls.

Across the Cave floor they ran, Llevvis just behind them, and through the haze and the swirling white beam they saw the girls were screaming, and yet they could not hear them.

\* \* \*

At first, they weren't sure what had happened.

One moment, they were running across the floor of Cave amid smoke and chaos, the next they were surrounded by white light and lines of swirling purple and black, and they weren't running any more, somehow they had stopped, though they didn't remember stopping, and the sound of panic around them was gone, as if it had never been. Between the moving lines the members of the Fleet still ran and screamed and Traders still burned, but they could hear none of it.

One voice they could hear, and then an answering voice. The voices came from above. They looked up, hands held tightly, and when they saw what lay above them, they began to scream too.

\* \* \*

Andos saw the twins freeze in the white light. He saw them look up and their mouths open in a silent scream. He ran forward, Rhubic and Rennan on his heels.

\* \* \*

Mareesha had almost reached the end of the Traders when someone grabbed her from behind and dragged her backwards.

She flailed and fell back onto whoever had grabbed her, and she struggled, incensed at being stopped, but before she could move, a great piece of burning balloon fell to the ground in front of her and a Trader dropped down beside it with a mighty crash. If she had not been stopped, she would have been beneath it.

She turned and saw Eenis struggling to her feet. Mareesha helped her up, squeezed her hand in gratitude, knowing what it must have taken for Eenis to follow her, and then she turned and ran on. She dodged the burning balloon and its fallen ship, racing into the space where the black ship still hovered overhead.

She was there in time to see Almarnoch reach the circle of light in which the girls were imprisoned. There in time to see their feet lift from the ground.

\* \* \*

Almarnoch, Qiren and Llevvis reached the light surrounding the twins as their feet lifted. The High Warlock could see them screaming, yet still he could hear nothing of their voices. The cries around him grew quieter as the Fleet watched the twins drawn higher. Almarnoch squinted up but he could see nothing against the intensity of the light.

Qiren tried to leap through the wall of white light. One arm disappeared through the wall and then he was thrown back, his body thudding to the ground.

Andos, Rennan and Rhubic ran up, the three circling the light as if looking for a door. They flung themselves at the light and were also thrown back.

Mareesha came from nowhere and threw herself at the light wall with a scream. She, too, was thrown to the ground, but she scrambled up and would have thrown herself again at the light if Andos had not grabbed her. Rhubic tried again to penetrate it and was thrown. He got up and again ran at the thing that was dragging the twins out of reach, and again he was thrown back, his heavy body slamming into the ground.

They looked up, helpless, as the girls floated higher and higher, their bodies swallowed by the light, and then they were gone.

Something dropped from the ship, and then the circle of light disappeared. The black ship began to drift towards the tunnel. Mareesha screamed and followed it.

\* \* \*

The last thing the twins saw before they were swallowed by the light was their mother throw herself at them. They saw her bounce off as she were no more than a drop of rain on a window; saw her fall to the ground, and then they saw no more. The light was too bright, and all they could hear were the voices; one gritty, one gleeful, and another soft and slow.

\* \* \*

# CHAPTER TWO

Shaeli didn't know when she began to shout for her parents, only that she was calling for them, for Almarnoch, for Shanna and Neesha, for Andos, Eenis, Jeth, for *someone* to answer her.

Beside her ran Tarkoda and Kirrit. People started to emerge from the shadows, looking across at the shouting, running figures.

Almarnoch's little hut rose out of the gloom, and she almost cried with relief at seeing it whole, untouched, but the Warlock did not emerge with her cries and she ran on. She was almost at the fire-pits when he emerged from behind a broken Trader. She looked up and realised it was Purple Leaf, its balloon deflated, leaning oddly on its crooked bottom. Almarnoch's face was weary, but his eyes lit up when he saw her. She slid to a halt and looked at him, afraid to ask the question.

"My child," he said, his eyes darting from the three of them to the company that followed. "Where did you come from? How did you get here?"

"Where are they, Almarnoch?" she said, brushing away his questions with the ones she dreaded asking. "Where's Mam and Da? Where are the girls?"

A voice spoke from the shadow behind the Warlock. It was her mother's.

"Shaeli? Shaeli, is it *you*? And Koda? Oh, thank the *gods*." She came forward in a rush, arms outstretched. "We're alright, Shaeli," she said. "Da and I, but..." Her eyes were dull and her voice shook as she continued. "But it's taken them. It's taken the twins." And then she began to cry.

Shaeli held her as she sobbed. Tarkoda put his arms around her, too, and together they held their mother until she had finished.

\* \* \*

Mareesha's tears did not last long. She kissed their cheeks sniffing, and Kirrit's also, questions spilling from her as she dabbed at her eyes.

"Where did you come from? Who brought you to Cave?"

Almarnoch echoed them. "If my mind was not playing games with me, it seemed that you came from the *back* of Cave," he said.

"We did, Almarnoch," said Tarkoda. "And we didn't come alone."

"So I see," Almarnoch said, looking at the others who were coming more slowly across Cave. His eyes narrowed when he saw Ishaan among the group.

"But what happened, Almarnoch?" said Shaeli. "Mam, where's Da?"

"He's alright. Don't worry," she said. "He's injured, but he will recover." She said the words staunchly, as if they would disagree with her.

"Was it a fire, Mam?" asked Tarkoda.

"No, my son. Not fire," Mareesha said. "'Twas the black ship, and it has taken your sisters. I don't know how it knew them, but it did, and it's taken them."

"*Taken* them?" Tarkoda's voice echoed the words as if he did not understand their meaning.

"Mam, *no*," cried Shaeli. "But when? How?"

Mareesha began to answer, but was stopped by a voice nearby. Knots of people had gathered around, and pushing through them was Delphi.

"Where is she?" she was saying. "Where's my Kirrit?"

"Mam," cried Kirrit, rushing into Delphi's strong arms.

"There you are, you wicked girl," said Delphi, tears running down her wide face. "Making me worry about you all these Moons."

"I'm sorry, Mam," Kirrit said, patting her mother's back. "But I'm alright, really I am." A gaggle of siblings bolted up, surrounding Kirrit in a sea of auburn heads. She kissed each of them and then looked around, over their heads. "Where's Da?" she asked, expectantly. "He's not injured, like Jarris, is he?"

Delphi's face crumpled like an old handkerchief. "No... he... he..." she started, but she could not go on.

Tajindi put his arm around Kirrit's shoulder. Shaeli saw he was taller than his sister now.

"Da is with the gods," Tajindi said. "He and Bydi died when the black ship came."

Kirrit stared at him, her face draining of colour, then her eyes moved to her mother. Delphi's face was buried in her apron, a stony-faced Maize comforting her. The boys stood solemnly staring at their feet. Mimsy cried silently with her face pressed into her mother's back.

"No," said Kirrit, shaking her head. "Not *Da*. Not *dead*," she said, and she kept on shaking her head as her eyes filled. Her face contorted and she began to sob. "Not Da, *no*," she repeated, over and over as Tajindi held her. "Not my Da." She turned to her mother, and sobbed with her sisters, her mother's dark head bowed within the circle of red. Kirrit raised her head and looked back at Koda and Shaeli. "My Da," she said. "My *Da*."

It was Tarkoda who moved first. He went to her with his arms open, and Kirrit fell against his chest, sobbing.

Shaeli followed him, wiping tears from her face, for she could not see. Her throat ached for Kirrit and her family, for the kind and gentle Baroz, always so quick with a smile, a strong arm or a hug, whichever was needed. They held Kirrit, and Shaeli looked over to where Almarnoch stood.

"How many?"

His gaze did not waver. He knew exactly what she meant. "Seven and twenty dead," he said. "Scores more injured."

"Seven and..." she said. She stopped, swallowed hard. "Who? Who else?"

"Four old ones, Ennan one of them," he looked at Kirrit. "Bydi also. And Olver was badly injured. Wyshka has not left his side," he said. "Teila of Silver Hawk. Young Bryl of Blue Dolphin. Driss of Blue Snake, Tylo of Sky Lark." He shook his head. "These and more. Three young lads are still missing."

Shaeli could not comprehend such a thing. Baroz? Bydi? Rennan's grandfather? Little Bryl? And Driss, who had been her childhood friend? All dead?

"Oh, Almarnoch," she breathed. Her eyes grew huge and shone with fresh tears. "But *why*?"

Her mother answered. "Your sisters, Shaeli," she said. "It wanted your sisters."

She had not yet fully realised this fact, that her sisters were gone, and the sudden explosion of the knowledge in her mind hit her in the stomach and she crumpled, as if from a blow. Another voice lifted her head.

"Is it true? Is it really them?"

Eenis rushed through the knots of people, Andos and Jeth just behind her. She praised the gods as she rushed at them, kissing them and Kirrit, giving her condolences on the loss of Baroz.

"You should be proud of him. He died trying to save his mother's life," she said. "And who are these people?" she added, looking past the circle of traders.

Their companions had stood quietly in the background, but now with Eenis' question, they stepped forward. Tarkoda introduced them to his Fleet, causing the murmur among the traders that he had anticipated, yet the delight he had also anticipated did not accompany it. He held out an arm to his friends, introducing them as he had rehearsed so many times in his mind.

"Spotjaw, master juggler. Flin, master of skylights. Williver and Llianas, elves of Lythnori. Lord Blenn and Wendll of the Drell Mountains," here he paused a moment, as he had so often planned he would in those long dark hours beneath the mountain. "And Olando, Cheval and Ishaan, Ammerr of Qorientae."

Each bowed as Tarkoda spoke their names, the enjoyment they also would have felt at the gasps they caused among the traders erased with the devastation they had found. They faced the Fleet solemnly, compassion etched on each face. Through the crowd came Illen and Qiren, and the Fleet was again astonished as Williver and Qiren greeted each other as cousin. Then Eenis, ever practical, spoke again.

"I'm sure all this can wait," she said. "There are more greetings to be made and tales to tell, but this company must be tired and hungry and in need of a good cup of tezz. Jarris will be most anxious to see them, I'm sure. Andos, run and tell Taffka what is happening. Let him decide where the tales are to be told."

\* \* \*

There was no familiar little landing, only the stairs leaning crookedly against the side of the Trader. Beside Purple Leaf, Pink Swan floated still, but the top deck was missing.

Tarkoda and Shaeli left their packs and bundles on the ground, and rushed up the stairs to see their father. Kirrit had been taken by Delphi to be hugged and cried over, and the others waited for them at the bottom of the stairs under the curious eyes of Almarnoch.

They walked across the deck and down the stairs. Everything sloped slightly to one side, but down here, all looked much the same. The door to Shaeli's room was open, her little bed all made up, and it was all she could do not to just crawl into it and pull the covers over her head.

Their father lay in a darkened room, swaths of bandages covering his head and arms. The circles beneath his eyes were red-purple with bruises.

Mareesha sat beside him and lay a hand against his cheek. He stirred and opened his eyes. They drifted round the room and settled on Mareesha's face.

"My eyes grow cloudy," he said, the words slightly slurred. "I thought I saw the faces of my children in the shadows."

"Your eyes see true," she answered, softly. "They are home. Koda and Shaeli have come home."

She stood and he saw the two of them standing in the doorway, their childish faces shimmering beneath the grown ones. Both felt ten Winters old as they fell to their knees beside the bed and felt the bandaged-swabbed hands on their heads. They cried as if they were children again.

* * *

"It took until the next morning to put out all the fires," Taffka said. "Most of the injured are in one of the store-rooms so the Faunists can work more easily, and we've cleared the path of the main tunnel. The bolt tunnel is more difficult and we have not managed to clear it yet." He passed a hand across his eyes. "As to the Traders, there are few undamaged. Nine we lost to fire, dozens more are unsound, but it is the balloons which have sustained the greatest damage. Many are burnt, dozens torn, some far beyond repair. If we have thirty ships ready to fly by the year it will be a miracle."

He told the story in the amphitheatre. Eenis had fed them and then they had gone to meet Taffka.

The entire Fleet had heard of the arrival and the rumour they had come from the cave of the Zoi, and most were there to watch. Taffka related the story for the sake of the travellers, yet he spoke so they could all hear. The Fleet had remained silent, faces grim, as he had recounted the coming of the black ship, but now, though they had known the devastation to their ships, hearing Taffka say that most of them would not fly out into the World the next year caused them to begin calling out questions.

Taffka was weary, Shaeli could see it, and she knew he would have barely slept since the black ship came. He limped as he walked before his Fleet, his old wound obvious, and she saw Renn watching him anxiously as he answered questions as best he could. He held up his hands for calm as voices began to rise, and while most did as he asked, a few began to ask questions about Shaeli and her companions.

"Is it true they came through the Zoi cave?" yelled one.

"How do we know the birds will fly next year?" cried another.

"What damage have they done?"

"How did they get there?"

The crowd took up the question and passed it among themselves.

"The cave of the Zoi is unharmed. The birds of Purple Leaf saved our lives."

Ishaan's voice was not loud, but it carried over the shouts. He was known to all the old ones and the children of Shaeli's Cave year, and the story of his arrival and departure were fast becoming Fleet legend. All turned to listen to his words.

"We have come this way only through necessity," he said. "Shaeli and her companions were also attacked by the black ship in the Straits of Nebillonia, their ship sunk beneath them." There were gasps from the crowd at this. "'Twas only by the grace of the gods that my people were there to save them, and four of us joined them. We travelled inland, to Lythnori in the elven lands, and then we went beneath the mountains." He drew a breath and looked among the faces of the Fleet. "We have travelled a long way, we know not how many days, beneath the mountains, through deep tunnels. Far below lies a great cavern holding a vast lake, and therein resides a beast, a giant eel and its brethren, who are lit with stinging light, and have teeth like spines."

The people were silent as Ishaan told of the coming of the Zoi, of the battle with the giant, and the help they had received from the birds. He told of the punt and the battle on the beach and they looked at Shaeli and Tarkoda with admiration as he told how they had saved the female lead of Purple Leaf, and they were silent with eagerness as he told how they had gone through the Zoi cave.

"What was it like?" cried out a voice.

"What lies therein is a wondrous sight, but 'twas clear the birds were not impressed with our passing through their cave," Ishaan said.

Shaeli shook her head at Ishaan's understatement, remembering the raised talons of the Zoi.

"But again, the birds of Purple Leaf escorted us through. Yet what lies in the cave of your Zoi should remain as it has always been, a mystery, a forbidden place, for the birds will not welcome you, and I'm sure your leaders will wish it so." Ishaan looked at Taffka and Almarnoch, who both nodded their agreement.

"But why were you there in the first place?" came another voice. "Why not come through Meoro Pass?"

Flin answered the question. "We intended to," he said. "But when our boat was sunk, we had no other way, except to travel inland, first through the Ammerr's homeland and then through elven lands. Ishaan and Williver thought it possible to travel beneath the mountains, and so it was, but the way is a grim one, and we lost one companion to the beast in the lake below."

"But where did you start?" came another voice. It was Lunn of Sky Lark, whose temper had been bad since he and his ship had been damaged in a storm many Winterings before. His wife had been killed when the black ship came, and now his anger was edged with grief. His daughter, Crylla, who had shared Shaeli's Cave year, sat beside him.

"We began our journey from the cave of the lost dragons," said Williver. There were gasps as the words rolled through the crowd. "My people are caretakers of the dragons' lair. They keep the mountain from plunder, in case the dragons should one day return," Williver said. "With their permission we went through the lair to the tunnels below."

"'Tis impossible," cried Lunn. "They lie."

"I think not, Lunn." Almarnoch spoke for the first time. "They have come through the cave of the Zoi, and besides, what reason could they have for lying?"

"Who knows?" answered Lunn. "Elves and Ammerr, if they are really Ammerr as they say, have always been in league, and it is certain there is much afoot here that the Fleet has not been told. Why did the black ship come? Why did it attack them in the Straits? Why would it take two girls of the Fleet? Why has it pursued Shaeli and these strange companions? 'Tis time to tell us the truth."

There were cries of agreement through the crowd, and again Taffka held up his hands for silence, but it was long in coming. When the uneasy quiet came it was Almarnoch who spoke.

"Lunn is not wrong," he said, waiting for the murmur to ripple through the crowd before he continued. "There are things happening within the Fleet that most of you are unaware of." Again the murmur of discontent. "But these things are also happening in the World outside, and I will tell you that much is at stake, for the Fleet, and for the World. We are caught in a storm, my friends, a dark storm, and we must fight together if we are to survive. More than this, I cannot tell you, but I will ask you this: will you trust in me, trust in Taffka, for we need you behind us if we are to weather the storm. Will you? Will you trust us?"

From most there was a cry of agreement, but from a few, Lunn amongst them, there were stony faces and lowered brows.

"So we are not to know why our ships were destroyed?" called Lunn. "Why those we loved died?" Beside him Crylla sat with her head bowed, her hands clenched tightly in her lap.

"Is it not enough that it is so?" Almarnoch said gently. "Is it not enough that they are gone? Is it not the time to turn our thoughts to renewal? We grieve with you Lunn, for Tylo and all those we have lost, but we must repair our damage, and go on. For the Fleet, for those who rely on us in the World outside, and for those with the gods; we *must* go on. There is nothing else to do."

"But..." began Lunn.

"No, Lunn," said Almarnoch. "'Tis for others to take care of. Our job is to take care of the Fleet."

Lunn pursed his lips.

"Almarnoch speaks good sense," said Taffka. "And rest assured, we ourselves do not know what all this means, but when we do, you will be told. I promise you this."

Shaeli squirmed uncomfortably. She knew that Taffka and Almarnoch only sought to protect her and her family, but she thought the Fleet should know the truth. She looked at Crylla's tear-washed face, then she sought her mother's eye, imploring her with a look.

Mareesha stared back for a moment, then she squared her shoulders and nodded at her eldest daughter. Shaeli took a step forward, avoiding Almarnoch's eye.

"I'm sorry, Taffka," she said. "There are things the Fleet should know, as Lunn says, and I think they deserve the truth." Taffka looked at her, much as her mother had, and then he nodded. Shaeli looked around at the Fleet. So many faces, so well known. She took a deep breath. "A lot of this is my fault," she said, and the crowd murmured again. Her hand clutched her amulet, as always drawing strength from the familiar weight of it. "Some of you might remember that I found an old wand when I was young," she began. A few nods and murmurs. "It seems this wand was once a powerful thing, and it is wanted by whoever is in the black ship. And whoever it is inside that thing is in league with the queen, for her soldiers followed us on land and sea."

"Why should they want you so badly?" cried a voice.

Williver answered. "Because Shaeli is a great magician," he said. "Her power with the stones is stronger than any man, or any elf, alive."

Shaeli closed her eyes for a moment at his words, still unable to grasp the concept, yet she opened them again and returned her eyes staunchly to the traders. "I don't know why it wants me, but I know it seeks the wand," she said.

"How does it even know that you have the wand?" came another voice.

"I don't know." Shaeli shook her head. She had asked the question herself, many times, and found no answer. "But this is one of the reasons why Purple Leaf was pursued. And you must know this: whoever is in the black ship is with the queen. Before the black ship came, it was *her* soldiers who sought us; it was the queen's guard who attacked Purple Leaf under false claims of treason." She raised an arm to the broken ships. "It is *she* who has done this. And it is she who has taken my sisters." Again she looked at her mother, and Mareesha met her gaze unflinchingly. She drew another breath. "And she has taken them because one of them is the child of King Tenelon and Queen Irinesta, and rightful heir to the throne."

There was silence at her words for long moments. Comprehension flickered slowly through the crowd. All had heard the rumours of what had happened at Great Court when the old maid had fallen from the tower of the Glade, some had seen the scraps of paper Taffka had brought back from Palveron. They knew that the queen had sent out heralds decrying her pity for the mad, unfortunate old woman, driven to insanity by confinement, who had concocted this fantasy unbeknown to the old Queen Irinesta, and then jumped from the tower. Everyone on every Land had speculated about that day – everyone but Shaeli and her companions – but each trader knew the close bond that had been between Mareesha and the old queen, that the twins had been born at the same time as old King Tenelon died and his queen had given birth to a stillborn child. All eyes turned to where Mareesha sat in the front row. She met their eyes with her shoulders square and her chin high.

Shaeli sought to turn the gazes away from her mother. "The black ship thinks we died in the Nebillonia Straits," she said. "Now it has my sisters. The *queen* has my sisters, and as soon as I can, I'm going to try and get them back. They're very young," she said, and her voice began to crack. "And they must be so frightened." Her voice broke then, and she could not go on. She dropped her head, and covered her eyes. Suddenly she was very tired.

Taffka came and put an arm around her shoulders. He looked around at the crowd. "The Wintering is very close," he said. "Navez has prepared lists of work for everyone. The weavers and tailors will work in shifts, day and night, repairing and creating balloons. Everyone else will be working on repairing the Traders, those least damaged first. Those irreparably damaged will be stripped and used in the rebuilding, for wood will be our greatest need, besides the balloons. And a work party will be delegated to rebuild the huts of the old ones."

Navez stood. "I have spoken with the old ones, Taffka," he said. "They do not wish the huts to be rebuilt immediately. They wish only that their possessions, what remain of them, be found, but the wood should be used for the ships. We have all found beds, and we would not take the strength of the young for our own needs. There will be time later to rebuild the Wintering huts, but for now, the need of the Fleet is greatest." He sat down and Sahli'en patted his hand.

Taffka was silent as his eyes sought those of each of the old ones, his feeling at the gesture laying plain upon his face, and then he spoke again. "Then let the renewal begin," he said. "The Wintering will not seem long, I fear, and the World will have need of us when first thaw comes, perhaps now more than ever."

The crowd began to disperse, and Almarnoch watched them go. Most were happy to trust in him and in Taffka, but there were some with the curdle of discontent lining their mouths. He would do well to watch them. He turned to Shaeli and her companions.

"I'm sure your companions will wish to wash the journey from them, Shaeli," he said. "I suggest you take them to first terrace. 'Tis a little chilly perhaps, but I'm sure you would all like to see the sun."

"We would," she agreed. "What hour is it, Almarnoch?" she asked. "We have no idea."

"'Twas just after sunrise when you arrived," he said. "It was the reason there were few to see your entrance. The sun should be shining nicely outside, though the air is cold."

"It will not matter," she smiled. "To see the sun and breathe cool, fresh air will be wonderful."

"I shall join you shortly," said the High Warlock. "There are things I would know, my friend, but I must speak with Taffka first."

They gathered their bundles and went through the dim main tunnel, passing the new rock pile that had so altered the shape of the mouth, and on around the familiar bends. Around the last bend the light shone, and as they walked through the entrance they were blinded. Squinting against a sun they had not seen in many days, they walked out onto the ledge and turned their pale faces up, just as they had turned them up as they stood on the ledge outside the mouth of that other tunnel, the tunnel so far away on the Dragons' Mountain, before their descent into the dark recesses beneath it. The sun was not yet high over the mountains, and its light was thin, but each of them revelled in its warmth, just as they had then.

Before them the Lea spread out. The spring stream ran through the middle, the hall and the huts were all shuttered, the fields empty but for dry grass. Far down, the orchard's rich green was etched against the grey of the Valley of Stones, and Shaeli drank in the sight. At least everything was the same out here.

Their companions admired the sight as they had not been able to admire the inside of Cave. Tarkoda led them down the path to first terrace, and across to where the shallow pool churned. The water was as cold as Almarnoch had predicted, yet they did not mind. They scrubbed at their bodies, their hair, the grime of the journey staining the froth grey, the grimy suds floating to the edge and tumbling over to the Lea. Ishaan, Olando and Cheval disappeared beneath the bubbling water for long periods, and each time they surfaced there was more colour in their faces, more brightness in their eyes.

They were watched from above by dozens of children, curious faces following every move, gasping as the Ammerr immersed themselves, pointing and whispering at the elves ears, the drell's size. As they dried themselves off, revelling in the feeling of pale sunshine on paler skin, Spotjaw, fumbling about in his pack, came up with an old shoe.

"I think this is yours, Blenny," he said, loudly. "I believe you've been making me carry your things on our journey." He tossed the shoe at Blenny.

Blenny caught it deftly, tossed it high with one hand, and caught it in the long fingers of the other.

"I think not," he said, the shoe dancing on its toe in his hand. "'Tis me that's been carrying for you." And he tossed back the shoe and followed it with his pipe.

Spotjaw threw back the pipe, the shoe, and his frypan, and so began a routine much like the one they had performed on Purple Leaf for Koda's birthday many Winterings before. Somehow they juggled and bantered their way up the path to the awe-struck children, who became a delighted part of the act. Soon they were giggling and shouting as Spotjaw and Blenny stole shoes and hats and mittens from them, tossing them in the air and catching them at an ever more furious pace. As the pace reached a frenzy, the jugglers' hands blurring in the air, each shoe and hat and mitten flew back unerringly to, if not its owner, then another delighted pair of hands. Shaeli, watching from below, could see and hear the relief in the faces and voices of the children that there should be fun and laughter again in their lives.

Almarnoch and Llevvis stood at the top of the path watching the impromptu show. The High Warlock had a smile on his face, Llevvis was laughing out loud as Spotjaw and Blenny finished throwing stolen items back to the delighted children. The children followed them back to the path, begging for more. Almarnoch stopped them.

"You have been given a rare treat," he said, the smile still on his face and his voice gentle with it. "I must speak with them now and you must give us our privacy." There were disappointed groans, but Almarnoch silenced them. "Forget not, these guests will be with us for the Wintering, and I'm sure you will see more of them. And do not forget also," he said. "We have a master of skylights among us. Perhaps she and her teacher will show you some of their magic also." There were awed looks cast down at Shaeli and the others. "Along with you, now."

In moments the ledge was clear of children, and Almarnoch had joined them on the terrace. Shaeli hugged Llevvis warmly, and then Almarnoch spoke.

"You all look better, I see," he said. "Water and sunshine replenish all souls." He looked at Shaeli. "'Tis time to tell me of your journey, and all you can about the black ship."

"But Almarnoch, shouldn't we go somewhere more private?" she said. "And there's other things I need to talk to you about." She stopped. "Perhaps I should speak with Mam first."

"You have *more* to divulge than you have just told the whole Fleet?" he asked, his lips curving beneath his whiskers.

He chuckled. "There is no need to speak with Mareesha first, my child," he said. "She has told us all that happened the year your sisters were born. There is no need for you to be wary." Shaeli looked startled and he patted her cheek. "We have taken steps to secure their safety, but I will tell you of this later. As to being overheard, I wish not to meet behind closed doors. Walls and shadows have ears, and here there is none but the wind to hear us." He smiled. "So, my child, I know all that happened until Purple Leaf left you on the north coast of Zirrus, in a village west of Conroi. Tell me of your journey, and how you came to gather such strange companions." He looked across at the others listening nearby. "We should make ourselves comfortable," he said. "For I think the tale will be a long one."

It was hard to begin. To Shaeli, the chase through the forest after they had left Purple Leaf at spring's end seemed so long ago, but the others helped, and soon she was telling of Trilby and pulling the bangle from her pack. Almarnoch turned it over in his thin hands, his face as inscrutable as ever, and then he passed it back to her. Next, she told of the journey through the mountains on the horses, and the chase through the Lakes' country. Blenny told of their meeting, what he had seen in the smoke, and taking them into drell sanctuaries. Llevvis' face followed every horror of the journey through the Bad Lands and the Poisoned Marshes, and beyond to the Drell Mountains. The ships that had set upon them in the seas to the north was quickly told, but the coming of the black ship in the Straits of Nebillonia seemed too close, too raw, and Ishaan helped her through it. The journey to Lythnori took little time, but the demands of its leaders took longer. Then came the journey beneath the mountain, the might of the lair on the far side, the bones of long-dead dragons and the fugue state which had come upon her. She told him of what she had found in the bones of the dragon beneath the mountain, yet she did not draw the stone from her pack, fearful still of unseen eyes, but she opened it and Almarnoch looked in.

She could see the not-so-inscrutable quiver in his brows when he saw what lay inside, but he did not linger over it, he merely closed the pack and pushed it back to Shaeli.

The rest of the journey was told quickly, he had heard much of it inside Cave, and when she was telling of the black lake and the eels, she suddenly knew what the thuds they had heard were, what the tremors that had trembled through the cavern had been; it had been the black ship decimating her home. When she had finished she couldn't help but give voice to the emotions that churned within her.

"And it's all been for *nothing*, Almarnoch. The black ship has destroyed the Fleet, and the twins are gone. I thought we would be safe when we reached Cave – that everything would be alright. But nothing is right, nothing at all." She stood up. "We should be getting ready to leave again. We should be finding a way of following them. We should be finding my sisters."

"'Twould do no good to leave now, my child. We know not where they go, and the Wintering would stop you anyway." Almarnoch said the words quietly, and Shaeli's eyes filled. "Yet do not lose hope. We have not been idle this year."

"But the *twins*, Almarnoch," she cried. "My sisters."

"They'll not be harmed, Shaeli," he said.

"How can you be sure?" she said. "Even now they may be..." She could not finish the sentence.

"I *can* be sure, Shaeli, because they have told us," he said. "Because there is something they want much more than the twins. Something they will give anything to have."

"What?" she asked, but before the word left her mouth, she knew. It lay in a bag at her feet, and somewhere inside Cave. She changed the question. "*How* do you know, Almarnoch? How did they tell you?"

"They left a message, Shaeli," he said. "When the black ship took your sisters it dropped this before it left." He pulled a small scroll from his robes and unrolled it. The script inside was stamped with the queen's seal. "Basically, it says that at Autumn's Eve the twins will be exchanged for the wand. All claim to the throne will be publicly renounced by Tenelon's heir, then, they say, the girls will be returned."

"But why in public?" she said. "Why should they want the People to know anything?"

"Because the People already know," he said. "And they will not be happy until their questions are answered."

"The People *know*?" Shaeli was incredulous. "They know about Tenelon's heir? But how?"

"You must ask your mother," he smiled, and looked up at the path.

Mareesha stood looking down at the group gathered on first terrace. She looked at them for a long time, this strange group of companions who had gathered about her daughter, and then she came down and joined them.

"'Tis time for your part in the story," Almarnoch said, as she walked slowly over to them.

"I thought as much," she said. She looked at her children and their companions again for a moment, and then her eyes drifted out over the Lea, and she began to speak.

"Many Winterings have passed since I lived at Great Court," she began. "But my friendship with Tenelon and Irinesta was undiminished by time. Irinesta gave me a gift when I left to marry Jarris, a rare and magical gift with which we could speak to each other at any time. With the gift came a vow, a vow that I never show anyone the gift, nor reveal knowledge of such a thing, and I kept that vow. I did not even tell Jarris, not until this year.

"When Tenelon was first taken ill with Green Fever, I was of the first to know. When it became clear he would not survive, Irinesta asked me to do her a service, and I could not refuse, for her fear was for her child. Between us we hatched a plan. The gods had blessed us with children at almost the same time, and the solution seemed simple. Many times we spoke in the days before Tenelon died, and when we were certain, when all hope was gone, I told her which herbs to use. I took the same ones, so the babes would come into the World at the same time. The child was delivered to us, and we took her as our own."

Mareesha still looked out across the Lea, her gaze fixed on the memory of that night beside the town of Zuen, of Irinesta's face, so pale, so forlorn, but she did not speak of it. She had not spoken of it to anyone; she and Jarris had never even discussed it. It was too impossible.

"When we heard that Tenelon had died, I tried to contact Irinesta, wanting to reassure her of the babe's safety, yet... yet something happened. Something was in the way, in my head, and it took me." Her face was torn with the remembering, her eyes looking at something long past.

"The black wind," breathed Shaeli.

Mareesha's eyes moved back into the present and over to Shaeli. "Yes," she said. "The black wind." She shuddered at the memory, as if trying to shake it from her. "And if it had not been for the quick wit of my very small, very brave daughter, the wind would have taken me," she said.

Shaeli smiled at her, and after a few moments, Mareesha smiled back.

"Yet it was not so," she went on, "and we were safe. At least, after a few Winterings I felt safer. But I never tried to contact Irinesta again, for I think it was her gift that brought the black wind to me. I still don't know how long it roamed in my thoughts, or how it could not find me, but I never used the gift again. Not until we returned to Cave this year." She looked over at Almarnoch, and he nodded encouragingly before she went on. "When we returned, we had been pursued every step of the journey, the last time they tried to take Purple Leaf was at Serrat. Jarris and I decided it was time to tell Almarnoch and Navez. Almarnoch thought it safer for the twins if the World knew that Tenelon's heir lived, and so I contacted Irinesta, for there was no other way. It was she who told the World." She told them about the papers that had fluttered from the tower, but not of the body of old E'Nith that had followed them; she could barely bring herself to think of it, let alone speak the words; she had known the kindly E'Nith many Winterings. "Taffka said that before he left Palveron, Great Court had closed itself off from the city. Queen Virrisian has not been seen since word spread throughout the Lands that Tenelon and Irinesta have a living child."

"So that's what you meant when you said you had taken steps to secure their safety, Almarnoch?" asked Williver.

"It is," said Almarnoch. It was he who told them that after the rain of paper had come from the tower of the Glade, it had been followed by the body of the old queen's maid. Mareesha closed her eyes against the words. "It has been said by the queen's herald that the papers were dropped by this maddened old woman, unbeknown to the old queen, but there are still rumours, suspicions. The other Lands would not take too kindly to anyone harming the child. No matter what the might of Zirrus or the extent of Virrisian's ambition, she'll not want to estrange them."

"What *is* this gift, Mam?" asked Shaeli, ever curious. "How can you talk to the old queen in Great Court? I've never heard of such a thing."

"They are calling stones, and there are few in the World," Mareesha said. "I know how to use the one Irinesta gave me, but apart from that, I know little."

Blenny spoke. "Calling stones are an ancient magic. Stones identical, or cut perfectly in two, each side a mirror of the other," he said. "Once, the magic used to create them was not uncommon, but the gift died out. Those calling stones that remained in the World were lost or broken, until few pairs remained, as your mother says." He looked at the amazement in the eyes turned towards him. He pulled the pipe from his pocket and shrugged at them. "Drell have been here a long time," he said, stuffing the pipe. "Our memories are long."

"Did you bring it, Mareesha?" said Almarnoch.

"As you asked," she nodded. "Yet I should have more privacy when I tell her such terrible news."

"Go beneath the overhang, Mareesha," said Almarnoch. "We shall stay out here, and see no one approaches."

Mareesha looked at a space beneath the ledge. Beside the pool, a rocky outcrop created a dark corner, a spot generally favoured by young lovers looking for some privacy. She looked at Almarnoch and nodded.

"Come with me, Shaeli," she said, a tight grin doing little to hide her fear. "In case I need a good hard kick."

They walked over the dry, late-autumn grass and into the shadow beneath the ledge. Mareesha knelt, pulled a cloth from beneath her apron, and unravelled it. Inside there was another cloth, this one of gold velvet, and Mareesha unwrapped something and lay the cloth on the ground. Onto the cloth she placed a short thick candle and a small rock, a crooked half-sphere, half the size of her fist, its inside hollow. When her mother asked her to light the candle, Shaeli saw that the rock was lined with the tiniest of crystals. The minute crystals were perfectly formed, nestled on the inside of the small half-rock, dozens of them, jammed so close together that not a space was to be seen inside the hollow. Shaeli was enchanted, and wanted to look more closely, but she stepped back as her mother lowered her head and began to chant quietly.

The chanting was soft, either wordless or so murmured that Shaeli could not understand it. It went on for a short time, and then the tiny crystals began to shimmer and produce light. Brighter they grew, and Mareesha kept chanting until her face was bathed with silvery light. She leant over the glowing stone and the chanting slowed, and then stopped. Mareesha spoke a series of words unfamiliar to Shaeli. From the rock came a click, like the turning of a key, and then Mareesha spoke. Shaeli's heart leapt when a soft voice answered. The voice came from the rock.

"Irinesta," Mareesha said. "I bring grave tidings. Cave has been struck by a black ship and much of the Fleet is damaged, but worse, much worse is..."

The voice from the rock stopped her. It was a soft voice, trembling with emotion. "Worry not, my friend," it said. "I know all."

"You *know?*" said Mareesha. "How could you...?"

Again the voice of Irinesta interrupted her. "They are *here*, Mareesha," she said. "They are here and they are safe." The voice cracked. "And they are *so* beautiful. I wish E'Nith could have seen them. Here, speak with them." And then incredibly, they heard the voices of the twins.

"Mam, are you there?" Neesha.

"Is it really you, Mam?" Shanna.

"Yes, it's me," said Mareesha, her own voice breaking. "Are you alright? Did they hurt you?"

"No, we're alright," Shanna said.

"But we want to come *home*," Neesha said.

"We'll find a way," Mareesha said. "I promise we'll find a way. You're safe with Irinesta, trust her, and do as she says. We love you so much."

"We love you too, but Mam, they said, on that thing, that ship... they said that Shaeli was dead."

Neesha's voice held the plaintive note that Shaeli knew so well. She could not help it. She leant forward.

"Not a chance," she said.

"*Shaeli*," they cried together.

"I'm here," she said, her own throat working now. "I'm coming for you," she said. "Don't you worry. I'll be coming for you soon."

From the stone came a thud, and Irinesta's whisper.

"The soldiers are coming back," she said. "They watch us closely. But worry not, they are safe for now. But Mareesha, which is...?"

Abruptly the light went out in the little rock, and they knew it was over.

Shaeli said nothing as her mother blew out the candle and rewrapped it and the small rock in their cloths.

"Come," she said, holding out her hand to her eldest daughter. "We must tell them the news. The twins are safe with Irinesta at Great Court." Her eyes were bright with relief, but then her brow clouded. "For now."

\* \* \*

First snow came to the edge of the World as they slept their first night beneath the roof of Cave, and the next day, three Traders arrived, the last of the Fleet, flying miraculously whole into Cave. Seven days later, the blizzards turned the Lea white overnight, and all hope of following the twins was dashed like the sleet against the ledge. The Wintering curtailed any other plan – even should they go back beneath the mountains, the blizzards would stop them reaching the safety of Lythnori – and in those first days Shaeli drove herself to lifting rocks and beams and anything she could until exhaustion took over and she could sleep.

She turned her emotions to the clearing of the bolt tunnel the day after they arrived, lifting boulders out through the main tunnel and rolling them across the ledge onto the Lea until the way was clear. Amazingly, the three lads who had been missing were found trapped in the bolt tunnel, in a space between two rock falls. They were dirty, hungry and badly in need of water, but they were alive and their return had been cause for celebration.

If she was not working or sleeping, she could be found sitting beside her father, coaxing him to eat a little something or exercise weak muscles. The injury to Jarris' head healed as the days passed, but the bruising inside it had addled his senses and they had to show him how to accomplish the simplest of tasks. Mareesha, Sahli'en, and the other Faunists were unsure how long it would take for him to regain himself, or indeed – as some of the more pessimistic believed – if he ever would. Shaeli spent every moment she could with him, and they made sure someone was with him at all times, feeding him, helping him stand and walk, reminding him of his life, and slowly, as the long days passed, he began to improve.

One day as she sat helping him with a bowl of broth, he stopped eating to stare out the window. He seldom moved from Purple Leaf, the sight of the broken Traders, the ruin of the old ones' huts, the absence of so many balloons caused him such agitation they kept him below, and he did not seem to notice much, content to sit and stare at the walls, yet this day his eyes suddenly took on some focus, the spoon stopped halfway between bowl and mouth, and he jerked upright in his chair.

"Where are they?" he asked. "Where are the girls?" He looked at her frowning, struggling with his mind. "Something happened, Shaeli, something that is out of reach. I can't... I can't seem to remember." He spoke slowly, slurring a little. "What happened? Shaeli, tell me."

She did not know what to say, but she knew he could not comprehend the truth, would not understand.

"Everything's alright, Da," she said. "The twins are fine, they're just not here right now. You'll see them soon," she soothed.

"No," he insisted. "Something's wrong, I know, I just... just can't *remember*." He dropped the spoon and pushed the bowl away. "Tell me, Mouse, why won't you tell me?"

He grew more agitated, began to cry, to shout, calling for the girls and begging Shaeli to tell him what had happened, to help him remember. Mareesha came and soothed him, wheedled him into taking a drink in which she had mixed a sleeping draught, and she held him until he relaxed, still muttering to himself, and then he finally slept.

Shaeli, watching from the corner, had crumpled as soon as he fell asleep, her father's broken mind almost the worst thing of all. She had waved a hand at her mother when she'd asked if Shaeli was alright, words caught in her swollen throat, and she had stumbled from the room. Eenis had found her later, huddled in the store room where she'd hidden so many years before after kicking her mother, and she'd held her, murmuring words of comfort. Finally she'd drawn Shaeli to her feet and smoothed the hair from her face.

"Come now," she said. "Your father has always looked after us, been strong for us, now it is our turn. You must face what comes with your head high, and with faith." She smiled gently. "I know what it is to lose faith, to lose hope, and it is not the right way. I'll not lose faith nor hope again, and I'll not let you either. We must go on, as he would want us to." She straightened her apron and squared her shoulders. "Wipe your eyes now, and come and help me in the kitchen. That old chicken is not going to flavour himself, and I know you're much better with herbs than I."

She smiled her tight little smile and went to turn away, but Shaeli pulled her back and hugged her. Eenis hugged stiffly back and patted her shoulder.

"Thank you Eenis," Shaeli said. "You're right, I know. I'll do my best."

"I'm sure you will," she said. "And the gods can ask no more than that, now, can they?"

"No," said Shaeli. "No, I don't suppose they can." But as she followed her aunt to the kitchen, she wondered, would it be enough?

\* \* \*

Days passed, long days of hard work and worry; longer, restless nights, full of fear and imaginings turned to nightmare stretching interminably between them. Everywhere Shaeli went people stared at her, whispered behind their hands or avoided her completely. She walked around in a curious mixture of daze and determination, trying to ignore the whispers, the averted eyes, but having little success; the out-loud accusations that came her way from some members of the Fleet were the most difficult to ignore. Lunn of Sky Lark did not lower his voice when she passed, did not avert his eyes when she chose to meet them, and worse, Crylla would not speak to her either.

"My mother is dead, Shaeli," she said, the one time Shaeli had cornered her, "and though my father may not be right to blame you entirely, I agree that you must take some of the responsibility. You could have warned us, could have told the elders, anything, but you chose to put your family ahead of the whole Fleet, and now... now my mother is dead, and I cannot call you friend any more." She swiped at her eyes. "I don't ever want to talk to you again. Seeing you only reminds me of what I have lost, so just leave me alone."

She had pushed past Shaeli, eyes swollen, and although Kirrit tried to comfort her, she shrugged her off and went to work.

While most did not blame Shaeli, there was a contingent of the Fleet who regarded her and her companions with suspicion, who would walk away when they approached, who refused to work beside them, and Shaeli felt this burden weigh on her shoulders with all the rest, another thing to trouble her heart and her mind. Each day she struggled, seldom talking of those things that weighed so heavily upon her, shrugging off the questions of her family and friends, each night staring for long hours into the darkness until the blessed peace of sleep overtook her, yet then came the dreams, and these she could not escape as she escaped from the questions, the whispers, and the averted eyes.

\* \* \*

Shaeli was dreaming. Dreaming of a dream. A wind blew through her mind. A black wind.

She saw her memories flash past like the pages of a book – the pages falling open on the day she'd first seen her sisters; the day she'd found the wand; the day she'd met Ellirra; the day she'd found Nol's family; other moments in her life... and then she was on the tiny boat with the wind and Ebony tearing at her hair, and she wanted it all to be gone – she didn't know what, just *gone* – and she felt the bumps beneath the boat and rain on her face, and she heard Williver and Ishaan and Ebony, their voices all mixed up, and she focussed on the jevvi, because she was closest, she was *there*, and then... then there was a thud, and a light in her face. She heard voices. One deep, a man. The other soft, high, like the voice of a child.

"Who is it, M'zena?" came the voice of the man.

"I know not," answered the child's voice. "But the seas of Xyros have given us a life to save, boy. Two if you count the jevvi. And save them we will." There was nothing but the pounding of the waves for a moment, and then the voice came again – quiet, almost begrudging. "This'll be the one who wants to know the way in," it said.

"The way in?" asked the man's voice, puzzlement coiled in the words. "In where?"

"Nowhere, lad," said the child's voice. "That is to come later. Bring her in now, and..."

Shaeli heard no more, but was swept away into deeper sleep. Yet she remembered snatches of the dream: her mind turning like the pages of a book; the black wind in her head; the voice of a child.

*The seas of Xyros have given us a life... the way in...*

And when she woke the images were still there. She went to wake Williver. And Almarnoch.

* * *

For Shaeli, the first Moon of the Wintering had passed in agony, each day, each blizzard bringing more questions about the girls. Even sleep had deprived Shaeli of respite, her dreams were dark and jumbled, but when *this* dream came she knew it was something. She wasn't sure what yet, but she knew it was *something*.

Now, the morning after, she found Almarnoch, Tarkoda, Ishaan, Blenny, Flin and Williver, and they sat in the High Warlock's little hut. They all knew about her dream and being taken by the black wind at Flin's on the Starisles, but she began there anyway, and then she told them of *dreaming* about the night the black wind had sent her out onto the sea, and of remembering the voice of the man, the voice of a child, and the words they had spoken.

"I remember a few things after that. A fire. A warm blanket. Being fed soup. Landing back on the wharf at Flin's. Not much else. But I remember her saying 'the seas of Xyros'. Almarnoch, what does it mean, 'Xyros'?"

"Xyros is the name given to the Starisles in the old tongue, child," he said. "Not many know the word, it has been lost with the passage of time. But why should it mean so much to you?"

Shaeli's face glowed with excitement. "She said something about 'the way in', Almarnoch," she said, breathless in her eagerness. "Don't you know what that means? Don't you see?" She swallowed, took another breath, closed her eyes, and recited. "It's something like, 'Let those who would rule know their time is short. The old one knows the way in. Seek for her on Xyros'." She opened her eyes and looked at him, willing him to know, willing him to see.

Almarnoch frowned, and then his eyes widened, his shoulders rose as if with the shedding of a burden. "My child," he said. "You think of the prophecy."

"Yes, Almarnoch, *yes*," she said. "I *knew* you'd see."

"Well, *he* may," said Williver. "But I see nothing."

"I'm lost, too," said Flin. "What are you talking about?"

"The old king's prophecy," Shaeli said, her face excited for the first time since they'd reached Cave. "King Tenelon said that his child would be saved by its brother and sister, that those who would rule should know that their time is short. That the others run with the wind and metal birds seek them."

"Traders run with the wind," said Flin. "And they have been sought by a metal bird."

"Yes," cried Shaeli. "And there was more... that the old one knows the way in, to seek for her on Xyros, and something about birds saving someone, I forget what."

"Like the Zoi saving us, you mean?" asked her brother dryly.

Shaeli looked at Tarkoda, seized on his words. "Of *course*. They did, didn't they? But, don't you *see*?" She took a breath and her voice scurried on. "Everyone thought it was the Green Fever talking, for Tenelon's child *had* no brother or sister. People everywhere believed that he was just maddened and his words meant nothing." She looked at them, her eyes shining. "But don't you see? Tenelon's child *does* have a brother and a sister, *two* sisters, and if *that* part of the prophecy is true, then maybe the rest..." She left the words hanging, her face alight and smiling, her lip trembling behind the smile, her eyes filling with tears.

"Maybe the rest is true, too," Almarnoch finished.

\* \* \*

# CHAPTER THREE

Two Moons later, with the last of the Wintering still gathered along the horizon to the south, Shaeli sat beside the dock at Meoro Village, her eyes scanning the first ships of the year.

She would see him. She knew she would. He was the only one they could trust.

The journey through the Valley of Stones was the stuff of nightmare; dropping from the Trader between the stony grey monoliths, then following the path taken by Ishaan five or six Winters earlier; the spring run-off a force to be terrified of; the memories of ice-cold water, clinging to a short log, Ebony clinging to her hair as she had during the trial in the Starisles; and then finally Serrat. Her childhood friend, Meri, had secured their release from the city. Meri's father, Billit the baker, had survived the assault on Purple Leaf – barely – yet Meri had risked a great deal to secrete them in a wagon bound for Meoro Village, and the good will of the gods and the slackness of Virrisian's soldiers guarding Meoro Pass had given them clear passage to the Village. Now all they could do was wait. They could not afford to approach strangers, and while Shaeli watched, the others lay in hiding nearby.

She stroked Ebony's coat as she waited. The jevvi lay beneath the folds of her cloak, and Shaeli took comfort from the warmth of the creature. She knew the others could see her; that it would only take a bolt from Flin's stone – or her own, for that matter – to secure her safety, yet her heart thumped too high in her chest, and she struggled to control her breathing, and to blend easily, casually, into the crowd around the wharves. She wondered when it had become an easy thing to throw a bolt at someone.

She had found a spot where she could see the ships docking, between bales of wool waiting for the bigger ships to come. For now, with the clouds of the Wintering still edging the southern sky, only the smaller, lighter ships would brave the waters of Nebillonia Straits, and every moment she sat there, she willed him to come. Her worst fear was that she would see him sailing past, and she had envisioned his ship sailing past her through the Straits so many times, that when she finally saw it docking, she thought she had fallen asleep and was dreaming.

She saw him on the deck, calling orders and laughing with his men. She dare not wait too long in case he was only docking for water, yet she lingered, praising the gods, then she pulled the hood over her hair, tucked Ebony beneath it on her shoulder, and went down to speak with him.

* * *

They were on board within the hour. They came in twos and threes, trying their best to look inconspicuous. It was still very cold and it was easy to muffle themselves into cloaks and scarves. By midday they were watching Meoro Village fall behind them and Shaeli's heart began to beat its normal rhythm.

They had done it: they were on board *The Painted Lady*, Captain Mahi's ship, bound for the Starisles.

* * *

They had spent the Moons of the Wintering working, and planning for this day.

Repairing the damage done to the Fleet had continued ceaselessly throughout the long days of the Wintering. Their companions had worked tirelessly beside the traders, those of the Fleet who did not lay the blame on Shaeli's doorstep soon lost all awe of the visitors – some the stuff of fantasy – working and joking with them. Work on the ships had continued from early morning to long into the night, and while the workers slept, teams of weavers and tailors continued to work on balloons through the night. Silk from the glow-worms cocoons had been stockpiled for decades, used only as a new Trader was built, or to repair large pieces of balloon torn in an accident, but while there was much in the store-rooms, the need was greater; balloons were designed and colours allocated carefully, balloons too damaged to repair were used like patchwork to mend others; Purple Leaf had a patch sewn high up on the top of the balloon where a bolt from the black ship had torn a hole. The old ones' huts were demolished, and the place where they had always stood looked bare for a long time, and when they realised they'd grown used to the sight, the sadness came again. Three more people died of the wounds they had sustained when the black ship came, but the rest recovered as the days crept by.

Shaeli's company helped wherever they could. The Ammerr fished debris from the spring stream; Blenny and Wendll used their mining abilities to help with the rock falls; the elves lithely climbed balloons to replace ropes, and when the mood of Cave grew heavy, Flin, Qiren and Shaeli sent skylights to dance around the roof. The whole Fleet worked tirelessly, even the children were given jobs sanding boards or carrying food and water to the workers; a whole band of women spent their time cooking, feeding the workers. Timber, as they had known, was the thing most in demand. Traders too ruined to ever fly again were stripped of their wood, piece by careful piece, even the nails were straightened and re-used; store caves were scoured for anything useful. When first thaw came their expectations were exceeded, for almost half the Fleet were able to fly out into the World. Taffka had headed straight for Serrat and then Palveron, Purple Leaf on its tail, to push whatever diplomatic buttons they were able. Shaeli and her companions had flown three-quarters of the way down the Valley of Stones with Purple Leaf, but, fearing the guard at Serrat, had left the Trader and traversed the route taken by the spring stream. It was well they had, for Meri had told them each Trader had been searched before it was allowed to continue, and Purple Leaf had continued its journey to Palveron with a dozen soldiers on board. If they had stayed on the Trader, it was sure they would not be considered dead any longer; even if Shaeli was not known, those of another race would have given them away.

As they had waited at Serrat, several Traders flew into the town, and each one was searched by Virrisian's guard. Soon, all Traders that were able would fly down the Valley of Stones to Serrat and on into the Lands; some to gather wood and ferry it back to Cave. All but one. One that had flown north, into the mountains.

Now, on Captain Mahi's ship, Shaeli looked at her companions, their numbers altered since she had arrived at Cave.

Williver stood up on the bridge, talking to the first mate who held the huge wheel, both laughing at Ebony's antics in the rigging. The mate, Piet, was a new crew member since Shaeli had last been aboard, and he seemed an amiable man. He guffawed loudly at the jevvi, declaring over and over he'd, "never seen a thing like it in me life".

Kirrit, sitting near Shaeli on the deck, was calling encouragement to Ebony as she glided from rope to rope. She had had a difficult time convincing her mother to allow her to go with Shaeli again – the loss of Baroz had made Delphi tearful and clingy – yet Kirrit had told her gently that she was going, was far too old to have to ask permission anyway, and wisely, as her father would have done before her, she nudged Delphi's sense of propriety by saying if she didn't, Shaeli would be alone with a group of males. Delphi had finally agreed.

They were now far from Meoro Village, yet Flin still braved the rocking of the ship on deck. Shaeli could tell by the now-familiar green tinge on his face that he was unwell, but he had wisely eaten nothing since early morning, and he stood staunchly watching the craggy coastline of Zirrus go by. He wanted to see the place where the black ship had destroyed their boat, the place where Qorientae lay hidden behind the walls of jagged rocks, and Shaeli, too, scanned the rocks, reliving that dark night as she sat in the warm rays of the afternoon sun. Ishaan nodded at the spot as they went by, but there was nothing to be seen, only ugly rocks and a dark, towering cliff face, and when it had passed, Flin went on unsteady legs below deck.

Shaeli smiled fondly at his disappearing back, and then sought out their other companion, the only one who had not been there on the night the black ship had destroyed their boat.

Almarnoch stood talking to Captain Mahi as they sailed over the spot where the remains of the little boat lay. He had surprised them all by insisting he would accompany them and he would not enter into a discussion of the matter. If they were going to the Starisles and then to Palveron to try and enter Great Court, then he was going with them, and Shaeli had not bothered to argue with him: he would do as he would. Yet she smiled at the memory of him in the Valley of Stones, perched calmly atop the packs strapped to a make-shift raft, completely confident that Williver and Ishaan would guide him safely through the rough water. And guide him they had, until they had reached the outskirts of Serrat and snuck into the town in the small hours of the night. Then the High Warlock had veiled himself and become just another bearded old man.

Shaeli looked forward. The Straits stretched on, their waters broken by Xenel Island ahead. Beyond lay the Starisles, and perhaps someone who knew a way into Great Court.

\* \* \*

The journey to Pa'laidiz was uneventful. There were only two other passengers on board, a just-wed couple who had eyes only for each other and who spent much time in their room.

They'd meant to hire a smaller boat to complete the rest of their journey when they reached the Starisles, but Captain Mahi, on finding they intended travelling back to Palveron almost immediately, insisted on taking them to their destination, so they could return with him. They spent two nights in the calm harbour at Pa'laidiz, loading the goods for the return journey.

The second night, Shaeli couldn't sleep. She was full of imaginings; trying to find the one who knew the way into Great Court — if that's what it even meant — sailing back to Palveron with Captain Mahi; sneaking in and taking back her sisters; it all seemed to unravel so easily in her mind. It seemed to her that it was about time that something was easy; everything until now had been so difficult.

She finally gave up tossing beneath the blankets, and slipped from under them, taking care not to disturb Ebony who was curled up at the end of the bed, or Kirrit, who was asleep in the other bunk. Throwing her cloak around her shoulders, she went up on deck. Thick socks made her passage soundless, and she crept to the front of the ship to look at the lights along the waterfront.

It must have been very late, for only a few lamps burnt along the shuttered docks, the bustle gone with the lateness of the night. She looked down the docks to the empty Landing, wondering when Blue Dolphin would arrive for its first cargo of salt. She had seen it before she'd left Cave, its balloon sporting a dozen new seams, its wood patched, but ready for the year.

She also wondered if the guard here would search the Traders as they had on Zirrus, and she frowned at the bland building that housed the queen's guard. Even on the Starisles, the scarlet and black of Virrisian's standard had permeated. It was here that Purple Leaf had been challenged last year, and now it seemed that the queen's guard had established a permanent base. As she watched, a figure emerged from the dark shadows around the building.

The figure came down towards the docks, slipping from shadow to shadow as smoothly as molasses. She wasn't sure why, but something made her lean back into the shadows and pull the hood of her cloak down.

He went through the light of the last lamp quickly, but it was enough for her to see his face. She shrank into the shadows as he came on board, willing him not to see her. She needn't have worried, all his concentration was given to sneaking unheard back onto the ship.

She knew they should have all been aboard already, Mahi had ordered it so in preparation to catch the early tide, and she watched, frowning, as Piet removed his shoes and disappeared below.

She sat for a long time in the shadows, her thoughts in turmoil until the cold drove her back to her bed. She followed the first mate below, but it was a long time until the chill left her bones and her thoughts.

* * *

She woke while the sky still held remnants of night to the west. Again she slipped from the blankets, threw her cloak about her and went out into the passage, yet she did not go on deck. She tapped quietly on a door, and without waiting for answer, she opened it and went in.

Moments later she followed a tousled Flin back out into the passageway. He was pale, but two days in the harbour had him almost recovered from the journey. He ducked beneath the low beams of the passage, and like Shaeli, when he reached his destination, he knocked lightly and went straight in. Shaeli, after taking a look at the dim, empty passage, followed him.

Flin explained quickly and if Mahi were surprised he did not show it, nor did he speak for a long time.

"It may be that he has only disobeyed orders," he said finally. "Perhaps he thought to visit a tavern, or one of the ladies who…" He stopped, glancing at Shaeli. "He is new, and, though he came highly recommended, this offence alone speaks ill of his character. I have always taken my own counsel when it comes to the judging of character, and besides," here, a smile played around the corners of his mouth, "besides, if I listened to what is said about the treasonous nature of Flin, Master of Skylights, and his apprentice, who are considered to have died a fitting death in the Straits, I would have turned you in at Meoro Village, now wouldn't I?" He let the smile loose with the looks on their faces. "I come from Palveron, my friends, and spent much of my Wintering in warm places listening to people talk, and you are one of the things they talk about; you, the rebels, the taxes. The thing they talk most of is the finding of Tenelon's heir." Shaeli tried to keep her face neutral but Mahi did not look at her, he kept speaking to Flin. "The People sing your praises, though not within earshot of the guard," he said. "But I shall tell you more of this later. For now, we have the matter of the first mate." He thought for a moment. "I think it best if we leave before the turning of the tide," he said, and he smiled again. "I shall blame the impatience of my passengers for the change of plan."

Before the sun had left the horizon, they were sailing from Pa'laidiz. Shaeli had watched Piet as he went about readying the ship. He had said little about the change in plan, but his brow was lowered, he worked slowly and kept glancing over at the building housing the guard. As they untied the ropes and the sails filled, Shaeli knew her instinct had been right. From the guard's building came a troop of running soldiers, but run were all they were able to do.

Piet saw them coming and at last his face showed panic. He looked up to where the captain stood glaring at him from behind the wheel, and before anyone could move he ran to the side of the ship and dove into the water. They watched as he surfaced and began to swim back towards the wharf and the guard who ran uselessly to their empty berth. By the time the guard reached the wharf, Piet was dragging himself out of the water, Mahi's ship was striding across the bay, and the soldiers could only watch as it cleared the harbour and headed out to sea. They knew then that it was going to start again, but they did not speak of it, they merely turned their faces east to the islands ahead.

\* \* \*

# CHAPTER FOUR

They passed many islands, some small and sandy, others large and verdant in the clear blue ocean, their white sands shimmering in the morning sun. The water seemed depthless, its clarity belying how far below the fields of brightly-coloured coral lay, how deeply the patterned fish swam. The wind blew gustily from the west, pushing them further out into deeper water, bouncing them over the waves towards the Endless Sea.

They watched the sun and most of the islands disappear behind them. Ahead lay only a few more islands, and Shaeli strained her eyes against the dying light to see the one she sought – the last island before the Endless Sea. She heard the orders given by Captain Mahi to drop the anchor near a tiny island, uninhabited by the sparse look of the vegetation and the lack of smoke or light coming from it, and she tried not to be disappointed. Mahi had told her he would sail Nebillonia Straits blindfolded, but would not sail his ship through darkness in unfamiliar waters, and she spent the night sleepless with anticipation.

They were away and sailing into the rising sun, yet the soft breeze of sunrise did not lift with the sun and the sails moved sluggishly through the morning. By noon they could see the last few islands growing hazily out of the sea, and tantalisingly, there they stayed through the afternoon as the breeze dropped to an occasional puff.

Ishaan provided the only respite from the frustration. He dived overboard into water still chilly from the Wintering, and came up with interesting shells and some fine crustaceans for their dinner. Finally, as the sun was falling towards the western islands, a breeze filled the sails, the gusts strengthened with each passing moment and they began to scud across the water. By the time the sun touched the islands to the west they were dropping the anchor in the tiny half-moon bay of the last island before the Endless Sea.

They could see a man standing on the white beach looking across at them, one hand shading his eyes against the last rays. Behind him, above the beach, a few buildings sat huddled at the base of a small hill. Across the water came the lowing of a cow, and from one of the huts there came a figure. A figure so small it could only be that of a child.

\* \* \*

Mahi lowered a boat and bid his crew to ready the ship for the trip back to Palveron at first light. They nodded at Mahi's orders, watching from the rail as the captain accompanied the others to shore.

Neither figure on the island moved as they rowed across the tiny bay, and Shaeli leant forward, anxiously looking for something that would trigger a memory, yet there was nothing; it was if she had never been there before. She looked at Ishaan.

"Are you sure this is the place?" she said.

"I'm sure," he nodded.

"Does nothing look familiar?" asked Williver.

She shook her head.

"I believe that man is the one who brought you back to Pa'laidiz," said Flin, squinting across the water. "In fact, I'm sure it is."

"Really?" said Shaeli. "Good. I don't think I ever thanked him."

"Maybe the other one is his daughter or his sister," said Kirrit, and Shaeli looked up to where the other figure stood outside the little hut.

The last of the sunset lit the beach, turning the white sand to gold, but the figure outside the hut stood in shadow and was impossible to see clearly.

The man hailed them as they neared and caught the rope Williver tossed him. He tied it to a faded trunk embedded in the sand and turned to greet his visitors.

Mahi and Ishaan pulled the boat up on the beach, and Almarnoch and Flin stepped out. Flin put out a hand to help Kirrit and Shaeli, and her feet touched the sand as the man turned. His smile of greeting faded as he looked at Shaeli. His eyebrows rose and his mouth dropped open.

"*You*," he breathed. "You're back."

Shaeli looked up at him. He was tall, his shoulders broad, his hair curling thickly upon his collar. His hands were large and work-brown, the fingers long and slender. His eyes were deeply brown and a memory rose to the surface of her mind. A memory of those eyes, their brown depths filled with concern.

"You gave me soup," she said slowly. "You took me home."

"Yes," he nodded. "I gave you soup." A wry smile curled his lip. "You look a great deal better than the last time we saw you," he said, and seeing Ebony peaking out from beneath her hair added. "So does your jevvi."

Shaeli found herself hugging the man without any memory of planning to. He stood, surprised, as she squeezed him around the chest, thanking him over and over, and then he patted her shoulder and eased back. Realising she had embarrassed him, she began to add apologies to her thanks, looking up at him through shimmering eyes.

"Thank you," she said again. "Thank you so much."

"A pleasure," the man said, his voice brusque. "Anyway, 'tis not to me you owe your thanks, but M'zena," he said, looking up at the figure outside the hut. "'Tis she who did the saving of you and the little jevvi. I only sailed you home." He smiled a little, his lips curving into the same wry grin. "And fed you the soup."

"Is she a Faunist?" asked Kirrit, glancing up the beach.

The man looked at her, and shook his head. "A Faunist?" he smiled more widely, as if amused by the idea. "No. She just... knows things." He looked back up at the hut, but the figure was no longer there. "Come," he said, throwing out an arm, and walking up the sand. "She'll have the tezz on by now.

We shall introduce ourselves before the fire." He looked at Shaeli as they left the beach. "You see, I still don't know your name. You were... unable to tell us the last time you were here."

"Shaeli," she said. "My name is Shaeli. I'm afraid I remember very little about my last... um, visit. I don't know your name, either."

He laughed. "'Tis Ezebar," he said, "and it's pleased I am to welcome you to our home."

They had reached the door. No light spilled out. Only the red glow of a fire gave outline to the doorway.

"M'zena?" Ezebar called. "Where are you? We have guests."

"They're not guests, lad," came a voice from inside. It was light, like a voice fashioned from tiny golden bells. Like the voice of a child. An angry child. "Not *guests*," it repeated. "They're change. Change that comes like a thief in darkness and I am not *ready*." This last was said petulantly, and then there came a sigh as light as mist. "Yet it will come as it will. Bring them in, Zeb, so I can see what shape the gods have chosen for this last great change."

Ezebar looked back out at them, a frown creasing his brow, suspicion narrowing his eyes. "Come, then," he said, his voice holding none of its previous welcome. He turned and went into the hut.

Dusk had turned to night as they had walked from the beach and the hut was filled with deep shadows, these only pushed back by the small fire on one side. Ezebar moved around lighting lamps, and as he did the room came alive, one corner at a time. A tiny kitchen beside the fire, a curtained off corner, an open doorway where they could see the corner of a bed covered in a patchwork quilt. Opposite the fire, across the room, was a tiny cot, and near it was a thickly padded armchair and a rocking chair, its back turned towards them. The chair was rocking furiously.

Shaeli knew the cot. She saw herself propped in it, looking over at the fire. She saw Ezebar, sitting in the armchair, spooning soup into her mouth, and wiping her chin, and she saw herself looking over at the rocking chair. The chair had been rocking gently, then.

Sitting in the rocking chair had been a woman who spoke comforting, meaningless words in a voice like a song.

Shaeli glanced at Almarnoch, and then she went forward, around the furiously rocking chair. She knelt down and looked up at the person who sat in the chair. She was looking into the oldest face she had ever seen.

\* \* \*

She was tiny, almost as small as a child. Her face was as wrinkled as a tezz seed, and as dark. Shaeli could see straight away that she was of the race from across the sea, the Irikai; her eyes were as black as Ebony's, the hands folded tightly in her lap were the colour of dark ale.

Her lips were pursed and she would not look at Shaeli when she knelt at her feet, and Shaeli saw there was anger in the pursed lips, fear in the diverted eyes, but she knew that this was the woman who had saved her life, and any other thought was driven from her mind. She put out a finger, touching the old one's clasped hands – all soft wrinkles and thick knuckles. The furious rocking stopped. Shaeli lay her head on the woman's knee.

"Thank you," Shaeli whispered, the tears thickening her throat as she cupped the gnarled hands with her own. "Thank you."

After a moment a hand came out and patted Shaeli's back.

"There, there, child," the old woman said, all trace of anger gone from her voice. "No need for that, now. We do only as the gods mean for us to." There came that sigh again, the one like mist across water. "And we must follow the path given us, ready or no."

\* \* \*

They had all found somewhere to sit and been given the promised cup of tezz. They listened as M'zena spoke of Shaeli's time on the island.

"A sorry sight the two of you were," she said, the chair now rocking in a slow, steady beat. "The sea was dark, nothing much to be seen but a few dolphins in the bay, yet I suspect there were things we did not see." Here she looked at Ishaan, who took great interest in his cup. "We still wonder how that little boat found its way into our bay. Zeb carried you up – the little jevvi, Ebony you say? well, the blessed creature would not leave hold of you – so Zeb carried you both up and he fed the fire while I took off your wet things. Mumbling all the time you were, about what I couldn't say, we couldn't make it out, mostly. Only one thing was clear. 'The black wind knows', over and over, you said, all mixed up with the mumbles. We gave you a toddy and you slept properly for a solid day. The jevvi woke now and then to eat and go outside. A very clean creature, it is. Each time it would smell you and it seemed satisfied, but when you finally woke you made little sense. We fed you, I mixed another toddy, and you slept again. But there was still little sense to be had from you when you woke. When the wind favoured it, Ezebar bundled you into the boat and took you home."

"How did you know where to take me?" she asked.

"Skylights was a word that came through a few times," the old woman smiled. "And there was a boat late that second afternoon with news of the missing apprentice. 'Twas an easy connection." She looked at Shaeli. "Yet, this is not the reason for your visit. Last time, I knew you would return. Long have I waited for this day." She leant forward. "Tell me what the black wind knows."

"You know something of this, M'zena?" said Williver.

"Yes, though 'tis long since I have heard such a thing spoken of," she said. "It did not bode well then, and does not now, I fear." Her eyes went back to Shaeli. "Tell me of it."

So Shaeli told her of the dream brought by the black wind – of the one which had visited her mother many Winterings before – and of how it had rifled through her mind and sent her out to die on the sea.

"Yet the gods had other things in mind for you, lass, and you were brought to us," said M'zena, glancing again at Ishaan. "What did it seek in your mind, child, this wind? Why should *you* be so important?"

Shaeli answered honestly. It did not occur to her to lie to this tiny, stately woman. "One thing it sought, two things it found," she said. "I once found an old wand, a powerful thing, it seems, and it is the wand that it sought, but that does not matter. What matters is what it also found. What it found was that…" here she took a deep breath, "was that one of my sisters is King Tenelon's heir." Mahi drew a breath, and Ezebar's jaw dropped, but she went on. "Queen Irinesta feared for the child as King Tenelon lay dying, and she trusted my mother like no other. We are traders, and the child has lived as my sister, one of twins, hidden from the World for many Winterings. Yet now they have been taken, both of them, to Great Court. They were seen when the wind blew through my mind."

"This is a great loss and we are sorry for your dilemma," said Ezebar. He spoke not unkindly, yet his impatience was clear. "But what has that to do with us?"

Shaeli looked at him, but she turned back and spoke to M'zena. "Before Tenelon died, he spoke to those around him," she said. "Some called it a prophecy. He spoke of his child, of how it would rule; he said other things, but he also spoke of the old one who knows the way in. He said she would be found on Xyros." Shaeli looked at her, leaning forward, eyes ablaze. "Is it you? Do *you* know a way into Great Court? A secret way?"

Ezebar snorted. M'zena ignored him.

"Tell me why you think it might be me, child," she said.

"Because I remembered something," Shaeli said. "Something I heard when you found me. You said, 'this'll be the one who wants to know the way in,' or something like that, and 'the sea of Xyros'. Almarnoch told me where Xyros was. It is the old name for the Starisles. When I remembered what you said, the other parts of the prophecy seemed to make sense."

"I remember that," said Ezebar, looking at Shaeli with amazement. "I remember you saying that when we found her, M'zena."

"Your High Warlock knows his history. There are not many who remember the word Xyros," M'zena said, smiling at Almarnoch.

He nodded his thanks and spoke for the first time. "You also are familiar with it, I see," he said. "Have you lived here long?"

"A lifetime," she said, and then she laughed. "But I have lived many lifetimes. This shall be the last, I fear, but I cannot complain. 'Tis long since we landed on the shores of this land."

"Your people have lived many generations within the Four Lands," said Almarnoch.

"They have," she agreed. "Peaceful lives after the turmoil of our own place. Long I have walked your World, many things I have seen. One of them," her eyes glimmered at Shaeli. "One of them may be the path you seek."

"I knew it," she cried. "Thank the gods I ended up here."

"'Tis not the gods you need thank," said M'zena, now looking even more pointedly at Ishaan. "The Ammerr have known this as a safe haven these many Winterings."

Ishaan looked abashed. "How did you know me?" he asked.

"The eyes. The smell of the sea," she smiled, and shrugged. "The size of your feet. As I say, several times your people have brought ruined boats to our harbour. They are always discreet, but my eyes are still what they were. I suspected Ammerr the night Shaeli came, and though I did not see you, there are always... signs."

"Signs?" asked Ishaan.

"The dolphins," she said. "A peculiar set of bubbles, an odd swirl of water."

"She's showed me a few times," said Ezebar. "But I could not believe her." He shook his head and looked at Ishaan. "You're really Ammerr?"

"I am," Ishaan said. "But, M'zena, our time is short, and we must be gone before dawn. Will you tell us how to find the way into Great Court?"

M'zena thought for a moment, and then she looked up at them. "No," she said. "I cannot tell you the way in."

"Please, M'zena," said Shaeli. "You *must* tell us. You have to."

"I'll *not* tell you, child," she said. "'Twould break a promise and bring you nothing but peril." She smiled at Shaeli's crestfallen face. "Yet fear not. I cannot *tell* you, but I can show you."

It took a moment for what she had said to sink in. Then Shaeli knew.

"You'll come *with* us?" she said. "You'll *show* us the way in?"

"Yes," said M'zena. She held up a hand to Ezebar, who had opened his mouth to speak. "You're to say nothing, Zeb. My mind is made up. Come if you wish, I'd be pleased to have you near me, but I'll not be dissuaded."

He tried anyway. "But the house, the cow," he began.

"One of the boys from over the way will come," she said. "You can row over after supper."

"But..."

"No buts, lad, I told you," she said, then her tone softened. "I'll not turn away when the gods have one more task for me." She sighed. "I have often wondered why they have kept me here so long."

"You'll really come with us?" said Shaeli. "You'll come to Palveron to show us the way?"

"I'll come, child," M'zena said. "And I'll show you the way. But we do not go to Palveron."

* * *

# CHAPTER FIVE

By moonrise, Ezebar had rowed over to the neighbouring island and returned with the man who would look after their home. The man looked at them with a mixture of curiosity and suspicion as they packed whatever M'zena said she needed; the patchwork quilt; a carpet bag; a supply of tezz, though Captain Mahi said he had plenty. By sunrise they were gone, heading south against a cool wind, back towards Zirrus. But not to Palveron.

\* \* \*

She did not seem tired, though she had been up most of the night. She sat looking forward, laughing a laugh like the chiming of bells as the spray hit her face and the birds wheeled overhead.

Ezebar watched her, and though he had longed his whole life to go out into the World, to see the other Lands, he had never imagined it would be like this. He watched her laughing in the spring sunrise, waiting for her heart to give out. She had not been off their island in his lifetime, and he looked with increasing resentment at their new companions. That they should disrupt the end of her life for something they had no part in, something far beyond their quiet life, was almost cruel – and yet he would do as she asked of him, as he ever had.

\* \* \*

Shaeli watched Ezebar watching the old woman, and when she saw they were both chilled by the strangeness of the night and the coolness of the morning, she urged them downstairs to eat, for she had many questions still. She had watched the man, Ezebar, go from cheerful welcome to barely-hidden hostility as the night hours passed, but what intrigued her more was when she had seen him place a long flute in his pack. It reminded her of something, a night from her childhood. She watched him as he tended to the needs of the old woman, and when she tired, he took her to her room, the patchwork quilt over his arm.

Shaeli thought he would return, but he did not, and her questions went unanswered. When she went to her own bed later, the door was closed, and she hovered outside it for a moment, curiosity making her fist itch to knock upon it, but her good sense won, curiosity was disappointed and went off in a huff, and she went to her own bed. She lay down, tired but elated. The night had been long, but it had surpassed her desires. The sun was high overhead but sleep would be denied no longer. Kirrit already lay with her red curls tumbled on the pillow. Before Shaeli slept, she thought perhaps they might finally have some luck after all.

* * *

Ezebar heard the footfalls falter as they passed the door, but there was no knock and they were left to themselves. It suited him; he had no wish to talk to anyone.

They had been given a small cabin with two thin beds, and M'zena lay comfortably beneath the patchwork quilt on hers, yet he struggled to find comfort upon the other. His broad shoulders barely fit between the sides and his feet hung far off the end, and although he was tired, he could not sleep. Apart from the discomfort was the constant rocking of the ship, the thuds and calls from above, and the tumult in his mind. His whole life he had longed to go out into the World, to see the places he had heard spoken of so many times; Ashkanna, Nebillonia Straits, Xenel Island, Conroi, Palveron, Great Court, but now he was here, he could not be happy about it. He had imagined he would travel once M'zena died, and he had rarely begrudged her the time, but now here they were, both of them, sailing through the Starisles on their way to Zirrus, and his head hurt worrying about her. Why M'zena had agreed to accompany these strangers was far beyond him, but he would see to it that she was kept safe.

"I know you are worried, boy," came her voice from beneath the quilt, as always, knowing his thoughts as if he had spoken them aloud. "Yet if the gods give us this adventure, we must take it. There is more to this than our small lives, but we may yet play a great part."

"A great part in what?" he said, the worry colouring his voice with annoyance. "Who rules on Zirrus has nothing to do with us, nor most on the Starisles."

"Aye, lad," she answered. "So it would appear, yet all things are connected to all other things, whether we see the connection or no. In this you must trust me, Zeb, this is something I was meant to do. Now I am tired. If you cannot sleep, go out and see the World as you have always wished." She rolled over and mumbled something else. It sounded like, "or talk to that girl".

* * *

In the end, he did sleep, but fitfully, and not for long. When he woke, M'zena was still curled beneath her quilt, breathing heavily. He ran his fingers through his hair, splashed some water on his face, and went up on deck. Perhaps he would talk to "that girl" as M'zena suggested. He had a lot of questions he thought she'd be able to answer.

He did not find her on deck, but he found the Warlock, Almarnoch.

The old Warlock sat upon the raised roof of the cargo hold, looking south. The sun was halfway to the western sky, and they were far out to sea, the islands bobbing on the horizon off to their right. Ezebar realised he had slept longer than he'd thought. The captain was at the wheel above, the Ammerr and the elf standing with him, and as he watched, the thin man – Flin, he thought his name was – went up to join them, a rolled map in his hands. He wondered at their frowns, the heads poring over the map.

"They wonder if there would be more shelter within the isles or upon the open sea," said Almarnoch.

Ezebar groaned inwardly; here was another who read one's thoughts. "It depends on what one needs shelter from," he answered, hoping the groan had not surfaced on his features.

The Warlock appeared not to notice. "From that," he said, pointing behind them.

Ezebar looked back. In their wake, still a long way behind, were three ships, all bigger than the vessel they were on.

"Who are they?" he asked. "What do they want?"

"They are the queen's guard," said Almarnoch. "And what they want is us."

*  *  *

Shaeli woke with the thorn of impatience prickling her mind. She felt as if there was something she had forgotten. Some danger that lurked just out of sight around the corner.

Ebony followed her as she left Kirrit sleeping in her cot, and up on deck, she saw Flin and Ishaan up at the wheel with Mahi, and Ezebar standing with Almarnoch. All were looking behind them.

The sun was sinking into the islands to the west, and when her eyes followed their stares, she saw the ships in pursuit. She knew then that her instincts had been two steps ahead of her, that what had seemed so easy would never be so. She scurried up the steps to the wheel, eager to know what they planned.

It seemed they were all of a different mind. Ishaan favoured heading east; Flin into the Starisles; Mahi thought they should continue as they were – heading south as fast as they could.

She looked back and could see the ships were gaining; even in the short time she had been on deck their sails had become much clearer.

Mahi stood gripping the wheel, Almarnoch still stood with Ezebar below, staring back at the three ships in their wake. Williver was at the bow, and as she watched, Ezebar left Almarnoch and went to join him. She was aware that the ship had begun to buck beneath them since she had come on deck, and she looked around, expecting to see a storm clouding the horizon, but there was nothing, no clouds, no thunderheads studding the sky. Sunset was upon them, and the sea turned to iron, the waves like cast metal. Still, the ships gained on them, and as night fell, they could see the black and scarlet of Virrisian's flags flying from the masts.

It was darkness that saved them. They sailed into waters that Mahi knew, and as the sun set they turned west, into the islands. They crept ahead, two crew crouched in the bow and two in the masts, calling out as they approached islands. Kirrit had joined them on deck, watching for that which was impossible to see; the islands ahead, the ships behind. They huddled in blankets as the night passed, taking turns snatching sleep – after gathering belongings they might be forced to find quickly. Several times Ezebar checked on M'zena, but she slept on, oblivious to the tension growing overhead. He, too, gathered all they had brought with them, all except for the patchwork quilt covering M'zena.

As the sunrise hours approached, they looked anxiously to the east, but instead of seeing the bright colours of morning, all they saw was the milky whiteness of thick mist rising from the sea. Around them it grew, thicker and thicker from the warm northern currents, a mist thick enough to shroud a fleet. Yet the wind died as the mist rose, and they drifted sluggishly, all of them now lining the decks, squinting into the weak morning whiteness looking for shapes that meant something.

When the sun began to burn through the mists, the breeze rose with it and filled the sails. When they were able to look about them again, all they could see were green islands and small pleasure craft. The queen's ships had been lost – for now.

They wove through the last of the Starisles during the day. The sun was as warm as if it was full summer instead of early spring, and sweat stood on every brow, dripping into eyes that scanned the sea around them. Though they had lost the three ships, there was still the open water between the Starisles and

Zirrus to cross, and there was little hope they would make the distance unseen. They planned to sail through the night, if the wind held, and Mahi predicted they would reach Zirrus' shores mid-morning. They loaded their belongings into one of the small boats, ready to lower it as soon as they came near enough to land to row.

M'zena had come on deck after eating a hearty meal, and she asked Ezebar why everyone was so nervous. After he told her the reason, she went over and pulled Captain Mahi aside. She spoke to him, pulling on his collar and pointing to the west. He leant forward politely as she spoke, and then his shoulders rose, and he looked in the direction of her finger, nodding, slowly at first and then faster. He leant forward, kissed her cheek, and raced up the stairs to the wheel. M'zena watched him go, and then came back. She sat delicately, looking forward, pretending to ignore their looks. It was Ezebar who asked her.

"What did you say to him?" he said.

"I reminded our captain only of our weather," M'zena said mildly. "Always with the warm currents from the north we have a few mornings of thick mist. The wind is unpredictable. Following the warm currents and the mornings of mist come the northern winds."

"They blow true for half a Moon," nodded Ezebar slowly. "Strong winds, blowing hard from the north."

"Aye, lad," said M'zena. "And to the west, not far, is a small isle, steep and uninhabited. A sad little island, waterless and ugly. Its only grace is that it has a small harbour, hidden from the water around. A harbour where a small ship might shelter for a few days to wait for more favourable winds."

There was silence for a moment as they took in her words, and then, one by one, they smiled.

* * *

The island was, as M'zena said, small and steeply cliffed, the thin mouth of the harbour opening into an almost perfectly round bay. The cliffs hung high above, ferns and vines clinging to the face, shrubby bushes cluttered along the cliff top. There was barely room for Mahi to bring the ship about before he dropped the anchor, tucking the ship out of sight of the sea.

It was cool in the bay. The thin mouth opened to the south and the sun had dropped far into the western sky; there would be little sun to warm them except in the middle of the day. Mist began to rise from the waters before dusk darkened the sky, and soon there was nothing but white about them, no stars, no cliffs, not even the tops of the masts could be seen.

They went below, and after a meal they went to the little sitting room where Kirrit and Shaeli had sat with Illen during the storm on their last trip to the Starisles. Mahi brought a big pot of tezz with him, of which M'zena drank five cups, and they talked of anything other than the ships that pursued them.

Shaeli found a quiet moment to talk to Ezebar about the flute he'd packed. Curiosity had snuck back quietly from its huff, holding no grudges.

"Have you been playing for a long time?" she asked him.

He nodded. "My father gave me a flute when I was about ten Winters," he said. "He bought me better ones as I improved."

"Did you ever go to the skylights on Pa'laidiz?" she asked, trying to hide the smile tugging at her lips. "And did you practise the skylight melody under a Trader afterwards?"

His brows rose, lowered. "How did…?" He looked at her and the brows rose again. "You're the girl on the Trader. The one in the cape."

She smiled. "Yes," she said. "That was me. Isn't it funny that we should meet again? That it should be your island I landed on."

"I don't know that funny would be the word I'd choose," he said.

Shaeli blushed, just a little. "I'm sorry about this," she said. "Really I am, but you have no idea how important it is to me... to us."

"The choice is not mine," Ezebar said, his lips compressing to a thin line. "But neither is the concern for myself." He looked to where M'zena sat talking with Almarnoch. "She is old. I do not know how many Winters she has walked in the World."

"She is not your grandmother?" Shaeli asked. She cocked her head at him. "You don't look like you have much Irikai in you."

Ezebar shook his head. "I don't. A little, generations back, and no, she is not my grandmother. She is just M'zena. She has always been there. My mother died before I was ten, and it was just she and I when my father was away." He sighed, still looking at the old woman. "She has lived a long and remarkable life, but she cannot have much time left. I wished that her remaining years be happy and peaceful, as she deserves."

Shaeli looked at the old woman too. M'zena's eyes sparkled as she laughed at some joke of Almarnoch's. She looked back at Ezebar.

"She does not seem to begrudge it," she said, gently.

He looked at her, lips still pursed, and then he sighed again and his features softened. She saw a glimpse of the open face that had welcomed them to the little beach, but only a glimpse.

"No," he said, shaking his head. "She does not begrudge it. Not the slightest bit. She *enjoys* it."

"Perhaps, as she says, it is as the gods wish it," Shaeli said.

"I have no faith in the wishes of the gods," he said, the glimpse of softness in his face instantly erased. "I have faith in myself, and what I can see. The gods may have their *wishes*, but their *reasons* remain obscure."

"You're right," sighed Shaeli. "I often wish I knew what the gods had in mind. It might make it easier to bear."

Her eyes lost focus, staring at something Ezebar could not see, and he wondered at the weight which settled upon her face. She shook her head and the look was gone, but he was left with the wondering. She turned back to him, obviously trying to distract herself, yet her choice of subject was unlucky.

"You said your father brings you the flutes. Is he often away?"

"He *was*, yes," said Ezebar. "He spent most of the year delivering our kelp to Faunists, here and on Romynn. His heart stopped during the Wintering a few years ago."

"Oh, I'm so sorry," said Shaeli.

She spoke with such feeling that Ezebar was surprised. He could not know that she and Kirrit spoke most nights of Baroz, that Shaeli comforted her friend every time the happy reminiscing turned to tears; he could not know her thoughts turned to her own father a dozen times a day, wondering if Jarris had regained his strength. His senses.

"Do not be sorry," Ezebar said. "I am grateful he died at his own hearth. I was always afraid the sea would take him. It has been only M'zena and I since he died."

"What do you do with your kelp now?" she asked.

"I sell it in Pa'laidiz and let someone else worry about delivering it," he said. He began to say something else, but M'zena interrupted him.

"The pot is empty, lad," she said. "Will you see me to my bed?"

He hid his surprise well. It was not often M'zena required much help for anything, and certainly the day had not come when she needed help getting herself into bed, but he knew she would have her reasons for such a request. As the door closed behind them, her reasons became known.

"You've met this girl before, Zeb?" she said.

"A long time ago," Ezebar nodded. "It is nothing. Coincidence only."

"There is little of that in the World," M'zena said. She peered up at him. "You like her."

It was hardly a question, and not something he'd thought much about – at least he told himself he hadn't thought about it – but he nodded. "I don't *dis*like her," he said. "But I dislike them dragging *you* off into *their* dangers."

"Dragged or not, they're our dangers, too, now," she said. She was silent for a moment, her head bowed, and then she looked back up at him, her face grave, but her charcoal eyes gleaming. "I want you to watch that girl. Protect her if the need arises."

"Watch her? Why?" he said.

"Because she's special, Zeb. Can you not see it?"

He thought for a moment, of the way the others treated her, of the deep emotions that rippled across her face. "Perhaps," he conceded.

"Good," she said. "Remember all I have taught you, and keep your eyes open to all things." She waved a hand at him. "Now, go away and let me get ready for bed."

He smiled as he shut the door, but the smile was closed from his face as soon as the door closed off the light from the room. He could hear the others still talking down the passage, and he crept closer to listen to what they said. After a while, he left and went up on deck to sit, shutting himself within the white blanket surrounding the ship to think. He stayed there until his hair was damp with the mist. He had a lot to think about.

\* \* \*

Two days they stayed in the shelter of the little island. During the day they set a watch high in the cliff above, but only once were Queen Virrisian's ships seen, sailing through the sea to the south. On the third morning they woke again to the thick mist that had shrouded them every night, but mid-morning the bushes on the cliff above began first to tremble, and then lean with a wind that blew ever stronger from the north. Mahi readied the ship, and they waited for full tide before venturing back through the thin mouth to the sea.

A dozen islands could be seen, dozens of sails, but none belonged to Queen Virrisian's ships. The northerly winds filled their sails and they began to fly across the water. As night fell, the last of the Starisles loomed ahead, Irojadis lit by a thousand lights, and just before the last light died from the sky, Williver saw the ships. They were east of Irojadis, and so far away he was the only one to see them.

They turned their faces south, sailing into darkness.

\* \* \*

# CHAPTER SIX

They scurried across the sea with the northerly wind at their backs all through the night, spotting the lights of Zirrus' coastline as the sunrise hours approached. Mahi rowed them ashore and left straight away, bemoaning the fact he could not accompany them and wishing the luck of the gods upon them. He was sure *The Painted Lady* would be boarded before long, and declared he looked forward to the encounter.

"Be careful, my friend," said Flin. "They may not take too kindly to your lack of cooperation."

"I shall tell them nothing but the truth," Mahi smiled. "When we left Pa'laidiz, I took you to an island in the east. Can't remember which one. Had no idea you were fugitives. And as for Piet, the man ought to have come to me, if *he* knew. I am now returning to Palveron. All these things are very nearly true."

Flin laughed. "I hope it will be that easy."

"And do not forget, they will be watching when you reach Palveron," said Almarnoch.

"I'll not forget," said Mahi. "But your missives shall be delivered safely, that I promise."

"Good," Almarnoch nodded. "'Tis imperative that it be so."

They watched the silver splash of his oars as he rowed back, and when the ship had turned towards the Nebillonia Straits, they turned their faces inland.

He had left them near the town where Purple Leaf had dropped them the year before. They decided to find an inn on its outskirts and plan their next step. It was obvious they could not walk, nor ride. Even if Almarnoch had been capable, as he insisted he was, M'zena certainly wasn't.

They felt fairly secure as they reached the first buildings. While they had been on *The Painted Lady*, the danger of encountering one of the queen's ships had been ever-present, yet with the journey safely behind them, there should be no one who knew where they were, or who they were. Williver's ears were easily disguised with a low hat, and Shaeli kept Ebony hidden as the town began to grow around them.

They passed by the first inn, a squalid place with an odd smell pervading the air around it, but the next inn looked more promising. There was a neat garden before the open doors, a picture of a fish with a pipe in its mouth above it, and a stout woman sweeping the pathway leading up to it.

"A lovely morning," the woman smiled, as they approached.

"It is indeed," answered Flin. "Our party is in need of rooms, if you have any available."

"That I do," she said. "A nice suite that should fit you all, with a sitting room attached."

"That will do nicely," said Flin. "I am Fallyn of Marnissi. These people," he said, indicating Almarnoch and M'zena, "are my grandparents, the others my cousins. We are travelling to Marnissi so they can partake of the waters. Is there somewhere nearby where I can purchase a carriage and some horses?"

"I believe so," the woman said. "Won't you come in? I can show you to your rooms and you can speak to my husband."

"Thank you," Flin replied, and followed the woman down the path.

Shaeli raised a brow at Kirrit as they followed him, marvelling at how Flin had effortlessly lied to the nice woman who owned the inn. She looked back over her shoulder, and grinned at Almarnoch, who was escorting M'zena, wondering how he felt about suddenly becoming a grandfather.

They stopped inside the door as their eyes adjusted to the shadowed interior. There was a small sitting room just inside the doorway, its windows looking back out into the street. Further in was a bar, a little courtyard open to the sun on one side, the kitchens through an archway beyond. A wide staircase across from the bar led up into the shadows. Behind the bar was a tall man whose belly stood testament to years of partaking of his own product.

"Welcome to the Smoking Fish," he said, as they entered.

"My dear," said the woman, "these people are looking to buy a carriage and horses to journey to Marnissi. What was that you were saying last night about them up at the manor selling off a carriage?"

"Aye, love," her husband said. "The taxes have 'em scraping for money. Groomsman said they're selling the second carriage and the greys." He stroked his chin. "Should get 'em for a good price, I reckon."

"Give them whatever they ask," said Flin. "In these times of great taxes, the people must help each other whenever they are able. Can you see to this?"

"Aye, sir," said the man. "They'd be happy to have 'em sold so easy. I'll go up directly."

"Many thanks," said Flin. "And be sure you add a little something for your trouble."

"Very kind of you, to be sure," said the man.

"Will you be wanting a meal?" asked his wife, eager to please the gentleman who was so free with his coin.

"Most certainly," nodded Flin. "After we have washed the dust from our journey, I'm sure we'd all like something to eat."

"Would you like me to bring it up or would you prefer to eat down here in the courtyard?" she asked.

"The courtyard looks very pleasant," said Flin. "And our rooms?"

"This way," she said, leading them up the stairs.

As she had said, there was room enough for all of them in the suite upstairs. It was at the back of the house, overlooking a wide lawn where a few swings hung from the trees. A set of stairs ran directly from the sitting room attached to the suite down to the lawn, and the landlady told them this suite was used generally for groups with children who came from further inland to spend time by the sea in the summer. It was only a short distance to a pretty beach, she said, but these days not so many people had the inclination to holiday by the sea.

"They are wary of travelling," she said. "And their coin is kept for their bellies. 'Tis grateful we are for your custom."

"We are happy to provide it," said Flin.

"Things may change for the better, if the rumours of Tenelon's heir are true," the woman sighed.

"You may believe the rumours," said Flin.

The woman's brows rose. "Oh, it would give people such hope to know it's true."

"'Tis true indeed," said Almarnoch. "Removing Queen Virrisian from her throne will not be easy, yet I'm sure the People will prevail. You must try and encourage them to hope, for hope is a strong weapon."

She looked at him and nodded. "I believe you're right," she said, after a moment. "Now I shall leave you to get settled. Just come down when you're ready to eat."

She closed the door behind her, and Kirrit went around opening other doors, looking into bedrooms. Each room had three or four beds, some with bunks, all with round windows of coloured glass.

"I've found it, Flin," Kirrit said, opening one door.

"What, Kirrit?" he asked.

Kirrit giggled. "The bathroom."

Shaeli tried not to giggle with her, and Williver also kept his lips from twitching. The others looked blankly at the giggling redhead holding onto the door to steady herself. Flin shook his head, and sighed. He picked up his bag and walked straight through the door, pulling it away from the giggling Kirrit as he went and closing it behind him. This set Kirrit to giggling harder, and Almarnoch looked over at Shaeli questioningly.

"Flin appreciates a bathroom," Shaeli said, and then her own laugh rebelliously started to bubble up through her words. She looked at Almarnoch's unamused face. "Grandfather," she added, and she let the rebel laugh go. "Come on, Kirrit," she said, taking her friend's hand and dragging her across the room. "Let's find a bedroom."

Ezebar watched them go, mystified.

"An odd species, the young female," said Almarnoch, putting a hand on his shoulder. "One I always had trouble understanding."

M'zena made a noise that sounded suspiciously like a suppressed snort of laughter, picked up her quilt and went into the nearest bedroom.

After they'd all washed, they had a meal in the sunny courtyard adjoining the bar, and as they were finishing the meal, the landlord returned.

"I've been to the manor and they're bringing the carriage down for you to look at this afternoon," he said. "Happy to have found a buyer so soon, they were."

"My thanks," said Flin. "I'm sure it shall suit us, and if so, we shall leave in the morning."

The carriage, when viewed that afternoon, was imminently suitable. Flin paid the owner what he asked for it and the two dappled horses to pull it. The carriage had opposing seats inside and the front half of the roof could be folded back so the interior was open to the sky. Flin and Williver went over the harnessing of the horses with the groom, and the carriage and horses were put inside the Smoking Fish's large barn.

Next morning they were up with the sun and breakfasting in the courtyard when the landlord came in. He had been out readying their horses, and their baggage was stacked at the bottom of the stairs.

"I have news," he said, as he entered. "Old Pom next door says three of the queen's ships moored off the coast last night. Two have sailed on, headed for Nebillonia Straits. The other put ashore a large contingent. They are said to be searching the town for arrivals from the Starisles. 'Tis said a Warlock and an elf are among them." He looked at them. "I thought ye might have need of knowing this."

They were on their feet before he'd finished the words.

"Our thanks, again," said Almarnoch. "This contingent, they are on foot?"

The man nodded. "Aye," he said. "You should reach the other side of the town before they reach here. We will not tell them of your stay. The Smoking Fish will not help the queen's guard to arrest any more people needlessly."

"It is best you not try and hide the fact we were here," said Flin. "Though it is noble of you to offer, too many people have seen us, and we would not bring you trouble. Yet it would help to have more time. Tell them we headed west, towards the Drell Mountains."

The man nodded again. "Go through the kitchen, 'tis quicker," he said. "The carriage is ready. Behind the barn is a laneway that leads to a crossroad to the east. Take the way straight ahead, through the woods. It leads to the southern road, not as direct, but it passes through tiny villages only. No big towns where there might be guard."

"The Smoking Fish has been a fortuitous gift indeed," said Flin, pressing a small bag into the man's hand.

"There is no need," protested the man. "If the darkness the queen has brought to our Land is to be swept away, then the People must work together, as you said."

"Still, I wish you to have it," said Flin, gathering up his baggage. "Now we must go."

The others had gathered their bags and they headed down the passage and through the kitchen. Inside the barn waited the little carriage, the greys pawing the ground, and they threw their bundles in and climbed up behind them. Flin and Williver took the high driver's seat, and they drove out into the thin lane that ran behind the Smoking Fish between the backs of shops and houses, winding past lawns and sheds and washing flapping from sagging clothes lines. It crossed a couple of other thin lanes, heading south-east, before the space between buildings began to grow wider and the gardens broader, and they became more nervous as the space opened around them. Kirrit peered fearfully behind and Flin's hand moved to the pocket where he kept his throwing stone time and again.

At last the crossroads appeared ahead. Nothing could be seen on the road to the south, and only a tired old cart was on the road leading back into the town. They crossed the road and felt better when the trees of the little wood closed around them.

As the landlord of the Smoking Fish had said, the road was thin and took them on a circuitous route through tiny villages. For several days they edged south and east and south again, M'zena sleeping on the seat in the little carriage, the blue of the mountains ahead growing less hazy as they approached. When they knew their back road would soon join the main road, they found a tiny copse to rest the horses and plan their next step.

They had reached the low foothills that announced the beginning of the mountains, and in the valley below nestled a village with smoke curling into the air from its chimneys. The days were becoming warmer, spring flowers coloured the bush around them, and Shaeli was trying to concentrate on what the others were saying. She looked at the flowers and could barely believe that another year had begun and she was again far from home, travelling the Land with the constant fear of being caught, worrying about the twins, her father, Tarkoda, all mixed up with the needs of the moment. Again, she tried to make sense of the conversation flowing around her.

"We must tell them where we are," Williver was saying. "It is no use if they head to Palveron."

"But how do we do that?" asked Ishaan.

"I can reach Qiren, I'm sure," said Williver. "Or perhaps Koda. But what will I tell them? We still don't know where we're going." Here, he looked at M'zena.

"'Tis no use looking at me like that, young elf," said M'zena. "I'll tell you when the need arises, and not before. And your problem is easily solved."

"How?" Williver asked.

"They come from the mountains you say?"

Williver nodded.

"And there is a drell amongst them?"

"Two, yes."

"Then they will know of the sanctuary that lies in the foothills to the south, if your own people do not," said M'zena.

"Of course," said Williver. "The drell sanctuary lies between the lands of the people and elven lands."

"I remember Blenny talking about it," said Shaeli, at last catching hold of the thread of conversation. "Do you think they can reach it?"

"I'm sure they could," said Williver. "That is, if they have reached Lythnori in safety."

* * *

# CHAPTER SEVEN

To the south-east, Tarkoda was thanking the gods they had done just that.

They had left the Long Lea the day after Golden Eagle and Purple Leaf, but they had not followed the others over the Lea to the Valley of Stones. They had flown from Cave before the sun had begun to streak the World, and Tarkoda had turned the Zoi north, into the mountains.

He'd had to communicate the signal to the lead bird three times before it understood. Never had a Trader flown north from Cave, but the bird took the signal and with a last swoop over the Lea, he had sent his birds up, over the mouth of Cave, above the upraised arms of the old ones and those left without a Trader.

It had been easy, at first, the winds were not strong and Tarkoda followed one ridge after another over Zerrinius' feet, yet when they reached the mountain's knees, the gusts had begun, angry squalls that screamed at them, kicking up clouds of snow as they went, engulfing the ship in swirling whiteness. The air grew bitterly cold as they flew higher and higher, the birds straining at their ropes, the Trader buffeted by strange currents and sudden updraughts. Deep crevices, banked snow and black rocky outcrops sailed beneath them, but Tarkoda kept his eyes on the hip of mountain above.

Lesser mountains crowded so closely to Zerrinius that to fly between their peaks would be to invite disaster. Going over Zerrinius' hip had been deemed the safest of all routes considered, but many of the Fleet thought the idea madness, and as Tarkoda zig-zagged his way up the mountainside, he was inclined to agree with them.

The day was passing and still the hip seemed no closer. Twice the ship was pushed down towards the mountain by a savage gust, towards disaster, and twice the Zoi pulled it back above the black cliffs that grew like teeth from the mountain. The view that seemed so picturesque from the Lea seemed a nightmare close up, and each of those on board knew that if the Trader fell, they could never make it back down.

And then they were there, flying over the last ridge. It had been a long pull, and before they flew over, Tarkoda looked back down. The mouth of Cave was invisible below, but the Lea and the Valley of Stones were laid out like tiny models of themselves sitting in the golden light of the afternoon sunshine. The image disappeared for a moment, and he started, then realised a cloud had drifted between them and the picture so far below. He took a last look at his home and turned forward, grimly focussing on the task ahead.

As they flew over the last rise, a great gust slammed into them from behind, blowing the Trader against a craggy bluff. The mountain beneath them was thick with snow, great drifts broken only by hard black rock, and those on deck cried out as the side of the Trader hit the bluff. There was a terrible thud, clumps of snow fell onto the deck, and there was a long grating sound as Trader scraped against rock. Tarkoda signalled to the Zoi and they pulled away from the rocks. He looked up and saw the balloon was well clear, and he sighed. He wished Andos was with him.

Tarkoda looked down at those on the deck. *Not a trader amongst them*, he thought, *and me responsible for their lives*. Yet they looked to him as the bluff scraped past and he tried to sound reassuring as he spoke.

He turned forward again and guided the Trader across the wide hip, wondering if they could really fly to Lythnori or if they would be blown into a bluff that would splinter the ship or give the balloon a rip from which they could not recover. And where would they find somewhere to land? The Zoi were well rested and there was ample food for them, but they could not fly endlessly. Still, he would almost rather this than going back beneath the mountains as they had talked about.

It had been a long Wintering, the longest in his memory, and he had yearned for the year to begin. He had worked hard during the days, and talked plans and strategies through the night, listening to every point of view, every far-fetched supposition, every plan as it was discussed, discarded, a new one proposed. He had heard so many "what-ifs" during the frozen Moons that he didn't care if he never heard the expression again. Finally they had decided what to do, the Fleet had been consulted, their plans made. All this had been coupled with the worry for his sisters, his father, the whole Fleet. His heart had ached for Kirrit, too, for the loss of Baroz had been a blow to them all and he had spent many hours comforting her.

And Shaeli was never far from his thoughts either. He wondered if they would even reach Meoro Pass in safety let alone find Flin's friend and reach the Starisles. The chances of them finding who they sought he thought slim, but, more than this, he worried about the weariness that had etched his sister's face these last Moons. Her burden was great, and he would do his part in helping her bear it. He looked ahead, eyes peering across the huge expanse ahead as if he could see the gusts that might spell their doom.

An odd colour caught his eye. Around there was nothing but the whiteness of the snow and the dark sides of rocky outcrops, but ahead he could see blue, a shade of blue he had never seen before, a blue bright, yet deep; light and pale, but incredibly vivid. He lost sight of it for a moment, and then it appeared again, a little closer. The blue speck grew rounder and brighter ahead of the wings of the Zoi, and Tarkoda called down to the others watching on deck.

Each of his companions were wrapped in thick coats, hoods, and gloves, and although they could have been below, none had wanted to miss the flight over the mountain. They had stood, shivering despite the heavy clothes, marvelling at the sights around them as Tarkoda guided the Trader up and over the vast hip. They came up at his call; two drell, Blenny and Wendll; two elves, Llianas and Qiren – Illen had stayed with the old ones in the safety of Cave; two Ammerr, Cheval and Olando; and one man, Spotjaw, all crowding onto the little triangle of deck to gaze at the uncannily blue patch growing ever closer.

"It looks like a lake," said Olando, after a while. "Yet a lake of no colour I have ever seen before."

"I think you're right," said Qiren. "Incredible, a lake this high. It must be frozen, and that's why it's the colour that it is."

Yet, Qiren was wrong. The lake, for lake it was, was not frozen. When they came closer they saw its surface was clear, reflecting the heights of Zerrinius upon its liquid face, its clarity broken only by surly gusts. On one side, the mountain had pushed out an arm to cradle the tiny lake, and on the other side a pristine meadow of white snow sparkled in the afternoon sun. Tarkoda signalled to the birds to circle the lake, and when the Trader flew above it they looked down into that incredible blue.

It was impossible to tell how deep it was, yet it seemed endless, as if it went on down into the very centre of the World. Every now and then the water shivered, not with the wind but with something that stirred within its depths, and at these moments a curtain of fine mist breathed from the surface and dissipated into the cold air.

Tarkoda grinned at Llianas beside him. Yes, he decided, he would much rather be here than somewhere far below in the belly of the mountain.

One of the surly gusts must have taken offence at his wide grin in this solemnly beautiful place, and it pushed the Trader precariously close to the arm that hugged the lake. He tugged on the lead line and the Zoi pulled them back over the water.

Tarkoda, the sacrilegious grin gone, turned the birds to the north.

They continued across the wide hip of the mountain, watching the blue lake recede. Soon it was lost back into the black-and-white expanse, and the only thing that was blue was the high, pale sky above them.

*  *  *

Tarkoda began to be nervous when they began to lose the sun.

The shadows of afternoon were long and the wings of the Zoi beat ever slower. He must find somewhere to land the Trader before night fell; it was one thing to fly across open water in the dark, but here, surrounded by peaks and crevices, there was no such luxury. If darkness fell, it would be all too easy to fly the Trader into the mountainside.

The broad hip of Mount Zerrinius had taken long hours to cross. When he'd seen the last ridge, he had been relieved – they had crossed the highest point – but when he saw what lay on the far side his heart lurched.

The other side of Zerrinius was a windswept, jagged place, the ground invisible beneath thickly banked clouds. It seemed strange to be flying above cloud, and his eye followed the sharp ridges and ugly crevices that tumbled down to the layer of cloud.

The lesser mountains crowded around Zerrinius as if for protection, their peaks poking through the cloud, and far ahead, the lesser peak that was the Mountain of the Dragons pushed its gnarled white head into the sky.

Down they went, buffeted by winds swept up from the valleys below and down from the peaks above, and Tarkoda saw fear rise in the eyes of his companions – Llianas and Cheval looked particularly nervous – and he hoped they did not see the fear mirrored in his own.

As the afternoon shadows grew long, as the first colour of sunset turned the snow to drifts of pale apricot – as he'd begun to despair – he saw it, a thin valley between steep slopes, a pile of tumbled rocks in its centre. He turned the Trader into the valley and circled the rock pile, assessing it, then he spoke to Olando and Qiren. Both had spent a few days practising lifts and landings down on the Long Lea, circling the tiny Landing behind the sheds, but the Lea had soft steady winds and a firm landing post and it was very different up here on the mountainside, yet they listened closely to his words, nodded at his plan and assumed their positions. All he could do as they went in to land was hope they had learned their roles well.

They missed on the first pass. As the pile of boulders passed, Tarkoda yelled, "*now*" and Olando threw the landing hook into the rocks. Qiren stood ready with a rope beside the open landing gate, but Olando's hook failed to find purchase and fell down into the snow drifts beneath them.

"Pull it up," Tarkoda called to him. "We'll go round again."

What the Zoi thought of landing in this desolate place he could not know, but they performed their part, as always, with the utmost precision.

Olando's second throw worked better. The hook held tight and the long rope uncoiled steadily as Tarkoda signalled to the Zoi to land. Qiren threw the second hook. There was a tense moment when it scraped across bald rock, and then it fell into a crevice and held tight. Koda flew down the stairs and ran to the landing gate. There was no Landing here, no stairs to rush down to secure the Trader forward and aft, but the rocks were close and he judged his moment and leapt across. He jumped cleanly onto a bare rock face, but the rock was slippery and his feet slid from under him. He fell heavily, but was up and finding solid purchase straight away. He caught the rope Qiren threw as the Zoi began the backdraft that would bring the Trader to a halt, and Tarkoda wrapped the rope around an outcrop and pulled at it as the other ropes pulled tight and the Zoi put down their feet. The snow was deep, but not deeper than the long legs of the birds and the ship floated to a halt.

They heaved on the three ropes and brought the ship close to the rocks, and then Qiren and Olando leapt over to join Tarkoda and they clambered down and Koda and Qiren unharnessed the birds while Olando unlashed a ladder and opened the doors to the nesting space. The birds flew in and Koda climbed up to feed them, then they shut the doors, trusting that the thick straw padding and their bulk would keep the birds warm overnight. They secured more ropes to the rocks, lashing the ship tightly, and then they climbed back up and crossed to the Trader.

Tarkoda looked up. The balloon was well above the long pile of rocks, and in this thin valley they were sheltered from the worst of the gusts. He trusted that the gods and the Warlocks' protection spells would keep them safe, and he smiled up at the balloon; yet it was a cheerless smile, born of many emotions, just as this Trader had been born of many other Traders.

The ship was the one intended for Kirrit's brothers. It had been worked on steadily for many Winterings, and would have been completed by the next, but the Fleet had given it over to Tarkoda for use. There had been some voices of dissent in this plan, but in the end the Council of Traders and the old ones had given their permission, and the ship had been made ready to fly, yet there was much unfinished. Below decks there were no rooms, just an open expanse with a sink and an oven in a far corner. They had bedrolls in another corner, a couple of old couches circled a low table, and that was it; no inner walls, no storerooms, just the stairs leading up to the deck. The wood to complete it even this far had come from other Traders, those too damaged by the black ship to ever fly again.

So, too, had the material for the balloon come from fallen Traders. The balloon intended for this ship had not yet been woven, and so the tailors had cut pieces from ripped and burnt balloons and sewed them together. There were pieces of Blue Snake, Little Moon, Sky Lark, and others in the balloon that fluttered above the ship, each a reminder of the Traders that had been destroyed by the black ship.

The Zoi had been confused when they'd flown from their cave at the end of the Wintering. Those of the Fleet who'd had a Trader to fly had gathered before their ships as they had at every first thaw since time immemorial. Those who would be staying at Cave had gathered before the fire pits.

The birds had flown from their tunnel, circled the expanse, and then the flock had landed in the space between the Traders and the fire pits, but their confusion had not lasted long. They had sorted themselves into groups and gone to stand before the ships brightly bobbing with the just-performed Lift spell. Many birds were left with no whole ship to stand before, yet these seemed content to remain a flock separate from those who would be leaving. Tarkoda had been amazed and gratified when the lead birds of Purple Leaf had come to stand before him. He had looked at his father, seen only blank incomprehension, and turned to Jeth for reassurance. His uncle had smiled, and nodded.

"'Tis as they wish it, lad," he'd said. "And I think they know you'll be having more need of them."

And so, with an unfamiliar ship, an inexperienced crew, and the memory of fallen Traders above, Tarkoda took great heart from the familiarity of the birds. Though he worried about them all that night, it was needlessly, for when he went down to release them into the sunrise hours, the snow blushed pink with the dawn, their cries had been joyful, the air inside the nest warm. They circled the sky above the Trader, stretching their wings, and then they flew back down to be fed and harnessed. When he clambered back up to the rock landing, Spotjaw had a fine breakfast ready and he ate hastily, going again over the procedure for the lift with Olando and Qiren, yet he was not really worried: lifts were always easier than landings.

The sun was a white triangle between the mountains to the east when they went back down the rocky Landing to release the ropes and Tarkoda went over the Zoi's harnesses again, giving each bird a final scratch and a word of encouragement. He reached the lead bird, giving him a good rub before the long flight, then he stepped back to look up at the tracings covering the balloon. The ground disappeared beneath his feet.

There was a thunderous cracking sound, the snow beneath him dropped away and he was falling. Suddenly he was looking between dangling legs at a deep crevasse, sheer sided, with sharp rocks far beneath, great drifts of snow dislodged by his feet smashing down onto them. The crack kept opening with a thunderous rumble, all the way to the edge of the mountain, thick clumps of snow plummeting downwards and crashing apart far beneath.

It was only by luck that he had one hand still on the lead bird's harness line. The bird was pulled forward with the sudden wrenching heaviness of Tarkoda's weight, its neck bowing, its talons gripping the edge of the crevasse.

Koda looked up, his arm straining to pull itself from the socket. He gripped the thick leather of the harness line tighter, and looked into the eyes of the great bird.

The Zoi squawked, Tarkoda saw the traces behind him tighten, and he understood the other birds had taken the strain of his weight amongst them. The lead bird lifted a leg, took a step back, lifted the other leg, took another step. Koda was pulled higher. He could hear the others yelling, Olando calling for a rope, but he ignored them, and kept his eyes on the eyes of the Zoi. Again the bird lifted a leg and took a step back, again he was drawn closer, close enough to touch the rock at the edge of the hidden crevasse. He glanced again between dangling feet at the sight of the far-off rocks, and then he looked there no more. With another step from the bird he was able to bring up his free arm, and grab at the rock. Qiren's face loomed beside the Zoi, pale in the dawn light, a loop of rope over his shoulder, yet it was not needed. With another step back, the Zoi brought Tarkoda's head level with the hole, and then the bird straightened his neck, and he was pulled up and over the edge. His legs were still dangling over nothing when Qiren grabbed his shoulder and pulled him the rest of the way.

He lay panting in the snow for a moment, then stood on legs that trembled, dragging deep breaths of cold air into his chest, nodding at Qiren's questions. He turned to the lead bird, his fingers relaxing on the harness line as he leant against the bird's chest. It was the third time these birds had saved his life and he could only hope they knew the extent of his gratitude. He went through the lines, touching each bird with hands that trembled still, yet he called orders with a voice that held none of the trembling of his hands.

The hooks were released and their ropes coiled again on the deck. Tarkoda signalled to the birds as Qiren unhooked the last rope and closed the landing gate, and the birds lifted them cleanly away from the rocks.

Tarkoda's step had shattered a huge chunk from the middle of the valley, and when they flew over the crevasse he shuddered. He would have to be more careful. It was not only his own life for which he was responsible.

He looked north, and signalled the Zoi to take them down the other side of the mountain.

\* \* \*

That day he flew the Trader down, current by current, cliff by cliff, lower and lower over the northern slopes of the mountain. The clouds that had been below them at dawn were blown away by the morning's winds and they could see what lay ahead. Lesser mountains crowded the landscape between Zerrinius and the mountain where the dragons once lived, and Tarkoda tried to plot a way through them while he had the advantage of height. By afternoon, clumps of low bushes and then trees and patches of green appeared on the ground, and he breathed a little easier. They began to see signs of life in the drift-thick mountainside; herds of huni deer and lone mountain goats grazing on spring shoots, their coats still thick with Winter fur; eagles circling for prey, and high up on a ridge, Llianas spotted a pack of jenka stalking over rocks on the mountain. Tarkoda, feeling further relief because he thought he had seen a way through the valleys ahead, started to look for somewhere to land the Trader for the night.

Down into another valley they flew, this one with a tiny creek already thickening with the snow melting at its edges. Tarkoda scanned the ground ahead, looking for the right trees or a sturdy rock pile on which to moor for the night, for he knew the Ammerr would be anxious for the waters of the little creek. When he finally saw somewhere he could land safely, he could barely believe it was there.

As they rounded a bend, the high mountain valley opened out, snow-capped mountains cradling it in silent majesty. A small forest grew up around the gurgling creek, here and there a tiny spot of colour heralding that soon there would be spring flowers in abundance, yet what lay between the forest and the side of Zerrinius took their eyes from the view and the breath from their bodies.

In the centre of the valley was a small fortress, almost tumbled into ruin, but still grand and somehow full of fierce pride as it stood forgotten and desolate in this beautiful place. One of its turrets remained standing, the crenellations almost intact, but most of the main section of the fortress had fallen and lay in moss-covered mounds between the remains of the walls.

Opposite the fortress, on the mountainside, were the ruins of another great edifice. Little of it remained, most of this second ruin lay in an unrecognisable lump that had fallen down to the floor of the valley, but clinging to the mountain remained the edge of a great column. Standing atop the column was the unmistakable form of a Zoi. Only one leg, a portion of body and a piece of wing were left, these ten times the size of the birds themselves, but still it was impossible to not know that here had once stood an enormous statue of a Zoi, carved from the side of Zerrinius.

Tarkoda directed the Zoi to fly them around the fortress. As they circled it, what lay in what had once been its forecourt surprised him almost more than anything else in this place.

Before the proud, ruined fortress were tall posts still pointing strongly into the sky, between them in tumbled ruins the remains of a several Landings. The shock must have been plain on his face, because when he looked at Qiren, the elf offered a grim smile.

"Shall we look more closely at what remains of the old tunnel?" he asked.

Tarkoda started.

A tunnel. Of course that's what it was. He had not seen it until Qiren had said it, but surely that was what the ruins on the mountain had once been. The remains of the column had been one of a pair, flanking a tunnel that had long since fallen back into the mountainside. Tarkoda wondered what had sat on top of the second long-gone column.

He flew the birds towards the broken statue of their ancestor, flying the Trader born of many others over the ruins of the tunnel. As they flew closer, they could see bits of the fallen edifice lying on the side of the mountain, and here and there they could make out pieces of the broken puzzle – the beak of the Zoi, a length of shattered column – but determining the shape of the twin column proved impossible. They circled it three times, scanning it for clues of its origin, but nothing could be seen apart from its fallen majesty; no history was to be found in its ancient bones.

On their last pass, Llianas thought she saw a crevice in the tumbled rocks – a place where the tunnel still opened into the mountain – but it was small and she was unsure. Tarkoda directed them back to the other ruins, to the ancient landing posts that stood as proudly as the lost fortress before the remnants of forgotten Landings.

Qiren and Olando sank their hooks in on the first pass. The Zoi, familiar with the shape of the posts, made a faultless landing. There was no Landing to leap onto, no stairs to run down, but the wind was nonexistent in this sheltered valley, and they were able to secure the final ropes at their leisure. Tarkoda swung out the arm of the boom usually used for cargo and lowered himself down to the ground. He secured the ropes, caught the hemp-rope ladder thrown down from the landing-gate and tied it firmly to a thick log, and then one by one, the others followed him down.

Qiren and Olando came first, then Llianas and Cheval. Blenny and Wendll followed them, Spotjaw easing his long frame down the ladder behind them. They were all silent in their descent, fearful and wondrous of the treasure they had found. As Tarkoda waited for the others, he wished that his sister was here to share in the wonder.

Without speech they went to worship at the feet of the remaining turret. Olando circled the perimeter, found a sunken doorway and stairs still clutching the inside of the turret, tested them step by step, and step by step they followed him to the top.

They came out above the ruins, above the top of the Trader, looking towards the fallen tunnel, the half-column, and the remains of the carved flying Zoi. They could see down the valley to a clear path between crooked mountains, and they wondered; wondered why this place was here, why it was so forgotten, so forlorn, and again without the need for mere words, they went back to the Trader to release the Zoi and ready for the night.

*  *  *

Later, Tarkoda was most grateful that the Zoi were safe. When the sun was setting and they were sipping tezz beneath pale lamp-light, Llianas heard them.

They came from the crack in the fallen tunnel, hundreds of them. They circled the tunnel mouth and then headed for the Trader, swarming it, seeking a crevice to creep through to the warm-blooded creatures inside.

They waited until the last moment to close the shutters. The Trader had no glass at its windows, but they watched them coming and recognised their stench.

The tiny bats thudded their bodies against the side of the ship, sensing the warmth within, but they could not penetrate the skin, either above or below decks, and soon they moved on into the valleys and hills, seeking huni deer, goat, jenka, and other creatures to feed off. Tarkoda and Spotjaw went down to check the birds after the bats had gone, and found them unharmed.

They remembered the far-off crease of light they had seen on their journey beneath the mountain before they had disturbed the coven of bats that had chased them deeper into the tunnels; the bats who sought blood. They knew these were the same creatures who had found them deep beneath the mountain, and the fallen tunnel was the source of the light they had seen.

There must have once been an oft-used way beneath Zerrinius, a way to Cave. Why else would there be a Zoi above the column, landing posts outside the forgotten fortress? They talked long into the night about how ancient a pathway this must be, wondering if Traders had been able to fly beneath the mountain, but arguing it was not possible, the tunnels had not been that big. Yet why else were there posts here, they said; why else was the tunnel mouth flanked with the giant bird? On they went, round in circles, one of them wondering occasionally where Shaeli and the others were, but in the end exhaustion drove them to their beds, such as they were.

\* \* \*

When morning came, the valley of the proud fortress was an even more beautiful place, the view even more glorious. The mountains pushed snow-capped tops into clear, pale sky, but here, though drifts still lay banked in shadows, the spring warmed their faces, and they heard the calls of birds in the trees of the little forest. It was a peaceful place, bereft of anything but its graceful beauty.

They released the Zoi to stretch their wings in the sheltered valley, and then they climbed the rocks that had once been the entrance to the tunnel and found the place Llianas had seen the day before, the crevice where the bats had emerged. They looked into complete darkness; the light that had been thin gloom on their way beneath the mountain did not give them a view from this place into that one.

Tarkoda dropped a pebble into the hole – just a tiny one, for they had no wish to disturb the awful creatures again – and they listened as it bounced down into the darkness. There was a moment of distant squeaking and then it grew silent once more.

They clambered back down to the floor of the valley, examining the fallen columns, the pieces of ancient statue as they went, and when they reached the Trader they harnessed the birds.

Tarkoda took them on one final circuit around the proud old fortress before they flew down the valley. He felt the need to salute it somehow, and it seemed the Zoi felt the same, for one by one they called out as they passed the remaining turret, their cries echoing through the quiet valley. Tarkoda turned their heads north, but his eyes stayed on the fortress until it was gone from sight. He was somehow loathe to leave it.

\* \* \*

They followed the valley around Zerrinius' feet at the same time Shaeli was boarding Captain Mahi's ship at Meoro Village. Beneath the Trader, patches of grass dotted the valley and spring flowers snuggled in sunny corners, most of their buds still tightly furled. The tiny creek they followed gathered others to it as it ran through the valley, but Tarkoda gave little heed to its merry gurgle, scanning the sky ahead for the easiest way. He did not want to take the Trader over the shoulder of another mountain, but from what he could see, they may well have to.

The valley of the happy creeks seemed to end in a steep-sided, dead-end canyon, the arms of two lesser mountains stretching out to shake hands across their path. The shoulders of these two smaller mountains were thick with snow, high enough to give the Zoi some trouble, but the closer they came, the less there seemed to be any alternative. As the walls of the canyon began to rise around them, he wondered if the creek disappeared below the ground ahead.

He signalled the Zoi to take the Trader higher, accepting the fact he would have to take them over snow-covered cliffs again, and then he saw it. The canyon narrowed ahead, but it did not end, the reaching arms of the mountains had just missed each other, creating a thin crooked path that wound beneath the snow-covered heights, and he judged the width of the twisted valley and knew it was wide enough to accommodate them. He twitched at the lead lines and turned the Zoi into the thinning canyon.

The canyon walls grew higher around them. Below, the creek lost its happy voice and the trees disappeared, replaced with rocks the colour of dried blood and snow-drifts untouched by sunlight. The cliffs around them grew redder also, the snow banked above cutting clear lines against the dark red rock. There was an eerie quiet in the twisted valley, no birds flew here, no trees or bushes swapped stories between rustling branches, the creek's cheerful voice slowed and softened to a whisper of trepidation.

Around the first tight corner they stood silently behind Tarkoda as he gave the birds almost imperceptible signals. Qiren tapped Tarkoda's shoulder and pointed above the Trader, and Koda leant over so he could see above the balloon.

The cliffs either side had continued to grow, and far above, the dark red of the cliffs were replaced by even more towering cliffs of thick white. Tarkoda's shoulders rose and fell at the sight of the massive snow cliffs, but he kept his face still, merely putting a finger to his lips so they all understood the need for silence. He did not need to tell them what would happen if the cliffs of snow above were dislodged.

Around the second crooked bend they went, their eyes drawn again and again to the thick cliffs of snow above, understanding why the water below moved with such trepidation through this place. At last they began to see the opening of the canyon, the lowering of the cliffs ahead, and Tarkoda signalled the birds and they pulled harder, eager also to move the Trader from this twisted valley.

A sudden crash turned their eyes back. At the last bend, a small rock had fallen onto the floor of the canyon, and as they turned, a few more followed it, red dust floating into the dimness. Another rock tumbled into the canyon. A crack opened in the cliff of icy snow above. The crack grew, groaning as it widened. One small lump of snow dislodged from the bank.

Tarkoda watched no more. He turned forward, signalled the Zoi again, and prayed they would reach the edge of the cliffs before they were covered. He was the only one who did not see the cliffs of snow begin to fall into their wake.

As the Zoi strained at their harnesses, the canyon behind them disappeared. Slowly at first, and then with frightening speed, the cliffs of snow began to fall. The sound that accompanied it gave them all nightmares for a Moon afterwards, a roaring thunderous sound that almost swept their brains of coherent thought.

Behind them the twisted valley had become a falling, churning mass of white, the massive amounts of snow slamming down onto the poor little creek. Faster and faster the surrounding snow was dislodged; bigger, wider chunks fell from the blood-red cliffs; faster Tarkoda urged the birds as the avalanche of white began to chase them up the canyon.

The Trader had picked up speed, but the avalanche came at them with the speed and strength of a maddened herd of bulls. Tarkoda glanced over his shoulder and then urged the birds to further speed, but the Zoi did not have need of his urging, for they, too, could hear the roar behind them and knew it chased them as well as any of those on deck.

Tarkoda saw the canyon widen, the cliffs lower ahead, but still he did not know if they would make it. He gave one last signal to the birds, and then the Trader was flying up, up and forward so swiftly that the others almost lost their footing. Suddenly the avalanche was behind them, but also beneath them, and instead of engulfing the ship, they were covered only in a fine white powder, a cool breath blown at them from the body of the beast.

Out they flew from the cloud of snow, out into bright sunlight, and Tarkoda brought the birds back down and slowed their pace. His own heart was beating loudly, and he could imagine the birds' hearts beat in time with it.

He looked back at the twisted valley. The canyon was gone, filled with the snow that had been towering cliffs only moments before. White snow-clouds still billowed from the settling avalanche, the little creek had thinned to a mere trickle, its water dammed with the thick snow, but soon it would work with the spring to remove the snow, and there would be nothing but the blood-red rocks left in the thin canyon.

Qiren, his eyes starkly bright in his pale face, looked at Tarkoda.

"'Twould have been better if the snow-cliffs fell *before* we passed through," he said, attempting to pull his mouth into a smile.

Tarkoda did the same with his own mouth, and it felt just as unnatural as Qiren's looked. He turned his head forward, not sorry to leave this place, and saw the valley opened out again – not much, but enough to allow them to feel the sun on their faces and give thanks for some space about them. Though it was only mid-afternoon, he began to look for somewhere to land. He knew the birds would be tired after the hard pull and he wasn't ashamed to admit the experience had drained him also, but it was some time before he saw a place to stop. When he saw the ancient landing posts in the ground in a natural clearing, he almost wasn't surprised.

\* \* \*

Days passed as they followed the winding paths between the mountains, down valleys and up over the boots of lesser mountains they flew, Zerrinius receding to the south and the Mountain of the Dragons growing in the northern sky. They came across the landing posts with such regularity that none of them were surprised anymore, they just looked for them as the afternoons passed. Between the landing posts were old Landings, most rotted long ago into weed-choked piles; one that had seemed promising had splintered and fallen into a dusty heap as soon as Olando had placed a foot upon it, so they trusted none of the others. All but two of the landing posts still stood steadfastly straight; the two that weren't were merely crooked, and then only a little.

When the Dragon Mountain grew closer, the ground became rockier, the creeks muddier, the trees shorter, and soon they were winding their way over the mountain's roots. Surprised yet again on this journey, they saw two tunnels – only a day's flight apart – and they knew these were the ways that Williver and Ishaan had explored, both dark tunnels leading down into the vast labyrinth beneath. Both tunnels were at the end of a day's flight, there were landing posts nearby, and they were able to explore them, though they did not venture far, all of them save Qiren had memories of that place they did not relish revisiting, but they studied the tunnels for a short distance and stood silently before the symbol carved inside each tunnel mouth. They were similar to the one they had followed through to Cave, but the starburst in the centres had subtle differences, and the writings circling the starbursts were very different. Cheval transcribed each carving to paper, described their place in the mountains and the day of the journey on which each was found.

The Zoi seemed to be enjoying themselves immensely, sweeping off into the mountains each afternoon when they were unharnessed, calling in loud choral voices to each other, staying away until sunset each evening. Tarkoda knew they foraged for themselves at these times, for when they returned they were not hungry, just content to drink deeply at whatever stream ran nearby – and there was always one – and then go to their nests to sleep until sunrise. When they woke they would circle the Trader, calling to each other before Tarkoda fed and harnessed them. More and more as the days passed, he wondered if they had some memory of this path through the mountains; some inherent knowledge of journeys undertaken by their ancestors in centuries long past.

One afternoon as they looked for the pattern of a fallen Landing, Tarkoda found something about the configuration of the mountains familiar. He was just pointing it out to Spotjaw when Llianas came leaping up the stairs.

"This is the northern side of the Dragon Mountain," she cried. "We must be nearly there." Her brown eyes shone in the afternoon light. She leant over the front of the Trader, her braid swinging out and hanging over the rail. "Look, there's the wood pile above the the little cave you sheltered in the night before I joined you." She grinned over her shoulder. "It looked so warm and I had to sit there freezing all night."

"And happy we were that you did join us," said Spotjaw with a grin of his own. "We were just saying that we must be close to the other side."

"I think we're very close," said Tarkoda, "and I think that round the next bend will be something we have seen before."

"What?" Llianas asked.

"That," said Tarkoda, pointing up on the side of the mountain.

Coming into sight around a bluff was the opening of the tunnel to the dragon's lair. Llianas called to the others as Koda signalled to the birds to fly them up. The Zoi responded more slowly than usual, but they pulled the Trader up so they could see the place where the tunnel began. They looked down at the empty pool, the dragon bones at the entrance and the path they had followed up to it, then Tarkoda took the Trader down over the sliding rock hill that had given them such trouble, and there, right where he'd left it, was the rope he had tied to a stout boulder. Llianas grinned again.

"Lucky for me you left that there," she said.

"We're lucky you came," he grinned back, and she blushed and looked forward again.

The afternoon waned and still there was no sign of landing posts, but Tarkoda knew there would be none. It made sense that the small squat garrison on the edge of the elven lands was their destination, and as the light was just beginning to drain from the sky, it was before them.

Qiren hailed the surprised elves who stood with their bows drawn as they flew near, and Tarkoda scanned the place for somewhere to land. Behind the garrison, unseen on their first journey, was a wide courtyard with the tall standing posts that proclaimed that Traders had been here before. Before the elves of the garrison could protest, Tarkoda had brought the ship down to a smooth landing in the windless courtyard.

Qiren and Olando had become adept at lifts and landings on the journey, Spotjaw and Cheval had both been helping and were learning a great deal. If something needed doing in the rigging, some tangle or tear, then it was Llianas who climbed fearlessly above and repaired the problem almost as easily as Andos could have. Wendll and Blenny had fed them throughout the journey, good-naturedly arguing with Cheval and Spotjaw over the nuances of each culinary delight, and Wendll had begun to practise juggling, spending long hours with Spotjaw tossing things back and forth. As they descended down the ladder held by the wide-eyed elves, Tarkoda gave thanks to the gods for such people as these; for amateurs, he could not have asked for a better crew.

* * *

The elves had only arrived at the garrison a few days before. They told the travellers at dinner they had to come before the spring run-offs began in earnest, for many of the waterways were impassable during spring. It had been many Winterings since outsiders had tried to breach the security of the dragon's lair, and while the elves had grown somewhat complacent, they still took their duties seriously. They had questioned Qiren and Llianas closely when they'd arrived, and the looks they cast at the others were decidedly suspicious, yet they had seen the drell and the others as they'd travelled through Lythnori last year, and once they'd had their questions answered satisfactorily, they welcomed the unexpected respite from the loneliness of the garrison.

The elves could barely believe the Trader had flown over Zerrinius and through the unknown valleys of the south. They goggled when Blenny, ever the showman, described the blue lake, the hidden crevasse which had opened beneath Tarkoda's feet, and the avalanche in the twisted valley. When the Trader flew from the garrison the next morning the elves waved them off with drawn smiles instead of drawn bows.

They would reach Lythnori that day. The land that had taken them days to traverse on foot before the Wintering was easily covered by the strong wings of the Zoi; the swelling streams and rivers no match for the Trader.

It was a lovely day. The breeze drifted gently over the Land, making the heads of the flowers bow in greeting to it, and the flowers were blossoming in their thousands. On the trees and in the grasses beneath, bright colours dotted the green, the new, blush-red leaves on the trees adding their vibrancy to the scene, and clumps of vividly yellow trees dotted the forest edges, the flowers the colour and texture of new chicks, the sunshine captured in their showy blossoms. They flew low over the vibrant land with the mingled scents of the spring flowers wafting up to them.

They must have seen three dozen varieties of birds throughout the day; tiny darting birds, beaks trailing twigs or soft grasses; courting birds, the males showing their colours to the duller-toned females who appeared unconcerned with the manly attentions; whole flocks swirling in the sky like windswept leaves. Butterflies followed their own intricate dance pattern, the steps of which reminded Tarkoda of the courtship patterns of the giant moths at Cave, and dragonflies flitted over waterways, darting from the hungry mouths of frogs and fish. The Land was coming alive around them, and while those on the Trader enjoyed the scenery, they looked forward to arriving at Lythnori with varying degrees of emotion.

Spotjaw, Wendll and Blenny were enjoying their time on the Trader. Blenny was occasionally seen buried so deeply in his thoughts that he had to be called several times before he heard them, but he was mostly his genial self, ever ready with a story or a joke. Whatever path they took seemed to suit him also, and Spotjaw and Wendll were content to follow Blenny.

The Ammerr, too, seemed happy to follow wherever the journey led. Cheval had taken Motin's death at the black lake beneath Zerrinius badly, but she talked of him often with Olando, and Olando, while also mourning his friend, was an optimistic person and kept smiles on many faces with his own unfailing grin.

Tarkoda was worried about their return to Lythnori, but not unduly. He was unsure why it was so imperative they return there, but he had Qiren with him, and Lythnori, while not Qiren's home, was well known to the elf. His concern had revolved around reaching elven lands safely, and it been accomplished much more easily than he'd dared hope. He wondered again about the buried tunnel, the ruined fortress, the landings posts placed so strategically along the way. Even the twisted valley would not have been a problem if the snow had fallen *before* the Trader had gone through, as Qiren had said. These things kept his mind busy as Lythnori grew closer. He smiled at the two elves who stood beside him on the deck, wondering how they felt about reaching their own lands.

Qiren seemed to show no sign of nerves, yet he was worried. Worried about what they would say when they knew, worried how those at Lythnori would react when he told them what he wanted them to do. He had worried throughout the Wintering, and though he had thought their plan the only course of action, he was still pensive about how those at Lythnori would react, his father not the least. He knew of his father's presence there, and though he would be pleased to see him, he did not relish what he would say.

Llianas, standing beside Qiren, was leaning forward as if eager to arrive, yet everyone knew she was far from eager. She had been forbidden to accompany Williver, and yet go with him she had. She knew she would be called to account for herself, and she dreaded it. Still, when the hill that had Lythnori as its crown came in to sight, she felt some excitement too.

Over the rivers they flew, the female Zoi calling out a note that rolled over the forested hill. High up on the crown they heard an answer; a herald blowing greetings from the towers in the treetops.

Tarkoda circled the hill, looking for a place to land. He knew the clearing at the top was too closely surrounded by trees to provide them a safe landing, but on the far side of the hill he saw two trees, long-dead giants, just the right distance apart to provide solid anchorage. He brought the Trader down, circled the trees and judged them adequate, and called to the others instructions to land on the next pass.

They worked well and the landing was made with ease. As usual, he lowered himself down with the boom, and Olando followed him, helping to secure more ropes and the hemp ladder Qiren threw down from the landing gate. They were unharnessing the Zoi when the procession came from the trees. It could only have been called that. It seemed half the elves of Lythnori had come down to greet them; Qiren's father, Williver's parents and his friends Ky and Jocovar, many other faces he remembered from his time here before the Wintering, and in their midst, the figures of the Lord and Lady of Lythnori.

Xyrrol and Mithrina walked sedately down the slope, unaffected by the gaiety of the elves around them. Neither of them took their eyes from the group gathered beneath the Trader, neither watched the majestic sight of the Zoi taking flight. They came to stand before the travellers, and the chattering crowd fell instantly silent. Mithrina spoke.

"Where are the throwers?" she asked. "The other Ammerr? Where is Williver?" They could tell she was not pleased. "And where is the wand?"

\* \* \*

Qiren moved first. He went to stand before the Lord and Lady of Lythnori, and bowed his head in greeting.

"You do not answer me, Qiren," Mithrina said. "Where is the wand? Where are the others?"

"I bring their greetings, Mithrina," he answered. "But they were not able to return here. Many things happened on their journey beneath the mountain. One of the Ammerr was lost, yet something else was found." He shifted. "Yet the tale cannot be told here. We must speak in private."

"You shall not tell us where we may or may not speak, Qiren," said Xyrrol, the sternness in his voice apparent also on his furrowed forehead.

"Forgive me, my lord," said Qiren, bowing his head again. "Yet I must insist. Will you come onto the Trader, or shall we be given the hospitality of Lythnori?"

Xyrrol was furious, and opened his mouth to reply, but Mithrina spoke first.

"You shall be at our door within the hour," she said. "Do not keep us waiting."

She did not wait for a reply, but placed a hand upon Xyrrol's arm and they turned and went back up the hill.

This time they were not ignored by the other elves; this time there were many greetings, many questions, and their weapons were not asked for. Llianas took much good-natured ribbing on her absence, alternately grinning and blushing. Qiren went straight to his father and was embraced and greeted warmly, yet the older elf's face was grave.

"You are worried, my son," Tyllerin said, and Qiren nodded.

"I wish you to come and hear the tale also, Father," was his only reply, and Tyllerin nodded.

They left the Zoi to fly and forage, and went up the slope beneath Lythnori's forest. Spring was pushing bright colour through the ground here, too. Tiny bells of white ringed the trees, and here and there colourful sprays fell from the trees, flowering parasites living off the richness of the thick trunks. The air was filled with their perfume, and the cool breeze and thick shade made memories of the brightness of the day outside. The days grew ever warmer, the snow was now almost gone from the lower lands, and was shrinking in the mountains surrounding them. Spring would dance its short, giddy frolic, and soon the World would turn its thoughts to summer; to long, hot days and too-warm nights. Tarkoda wondered where he'd be by then.

They had reached the top of the hill, and the amazing sight of Lythnori opened before them; the houses built in and around the living trees, the coloured windows catching the sun's rays, the wide pool in the centre with its creeks like wheel spokes, the towers standing high above the canopy, yet they did not linger over the sights, they merely drank deeply of the waters of the pool and went over to stand before the door of Xyrrol and Mithrina.

Xyrrol was waiting for them, lips pursed, clearly displeased, yet his tone as he ushered them inside did not show anything but politeness. They were shown to the courtyard room where the vines still blossomed and Mithrina still fed the fire-beaked birds, yet she did not look at them as they entered, but continued to murmur to the birds scurrying at her feet. Finally she scattered the last of the seed and turned to face them.

"Who is to tell the tale?" she asked, sitting on a fan-backed chair and lacing her elegant fingers together. She looked expectantly at them, her lips as thin as Xyrrol's.

Blenny stepped forward and the rest tried not to look relieved; each had dreaded reciting the story, yet Blenny seemed to relish it. His regal air was intact by the time he'd finished the first step, his voice took on the prophetic quality that he used in his shows.

Xyrrol took a seat beside Mithrina, and after a moment he gestured to the others to take a seat also. They sat down on the benches that ranged the garden.

"I am honoured to recite the tale of such a journey, so I am," Blenny began. "The way was filled with peril, one of our company was lost beneath the mountains, but we succeeded in our task. Our journey back to your lands was also perilous, but the way was filled with wonders, and this I will tell of also."

"Proceed, then," said Mithrina, her lips more relaxed with Blenny's eloquent beginning.

"The journey was long, we know not how many days we wandered beneath the mountains," said Blenny. "But I shall begin at the entrance to the lair. A great sight it was, the pool shadowed by the massive bones, but the air there was filled with regret, and so that night we camped as far from it as we could. During the night, we were joined by an unexpected companion."

Here, Llianas shifted uncomfortably, and Mithrina threw her a cold glance, yet Blenny went on and Mithrina turned her eyes back to the drell.

"The gods were smiling on us when they sent us this companion," he said. "For it is likely none of us would ever have been seen in the World again, if not for her."

Mithrina looked again at Llianas, this time with interest, but Llianas was avoiding Mithrina's eyes and kept her own on her hands.

"The next morning we took one final look at the sky, and went into the lair," continued Blenny. "Such a sight is almost impossible to describe, but we did not linger long there; 'twas a sad and lonely place, and so we ventured deeper into the dragon's tunnels. In their mines we saw another skeleton like the ones we had seen in the lair and beside the pool."

"This we know," said Xyrrol. "The mines have been searched many times."

"Yes, my lord Xyrrol," said Blenny. "But Shaeli was given a vision, a vision which showed her that something lay *beneath* the bones of the dragon, something that had lain hidden these long Winterings, hidden in the rotting remains of the dragon's stomach."

Blenny was the recipient of the very reaction he'd intended, and paused so he could appreciate it.

"*Beneath* the bones?" said Xyrrol. "*What* lay there?"

"It shall be told," said Blenny. "But not yet."

He told them of the journey beneath the mountain, of the tunnels that led back to the surface, of the cave of bats, of how Llianas had saved them from the suckling, poisonous creatures. Here, both Mithrina and Xyrrol looked at Llianas with new eyes, their tight mouths now turned to the softness of awe. Then Blenny told them of the narrowing of the passage, of the path across nothingness, of the distant pockets of crystal and far-off caverns, and he told of the final emergence to the black lake and the loss of Motin to the stinging, hook-toothed eels. Here, Cheval accompanied the story with soft weeping – the death of Motin still rode starkly in her mind – but Blenny moved on to the fishing of the great eels by the Zoi and the coming of the ancient punt. The fight against the giant was relived, for the elves and within their minds, and each shuddered with the remembering. The walk through the cave of the Zoi was told quickly, and with the gratitude it deserved, but the walk into Cave and the devastation they'd found there took longer. Tarkoda found himself adding details; embellishing Blenny's tale with what he'd heard from Andos, Eenis, others who had lived through the coming of the black ship. Xyrrol and Mithrina sat silently through the telling, their faces neutral, but the air within the living house trembled, as if the very trees felt the devastation of the far-off Cave. As the tension rippled through the air, Blenny spoke briefly of the Wintering among the traders, of repairing the Fleet, of the injured and the dead, and then he stopped. It was clear Xyrrol and Mithrina thought him about to continue, for they both leant forward, intent on the tale, but Blenny turned, and looked at Qiren. Qiren looked first at his father, and then he stood, sighed, and stepped forward.

"With the devastation of the Fleet and the taking of Tenelon's heir, there were many decisions to be made," he began. "By day we aided the traders as best we could, repairing their ships, clearing the rock-falls, but by night we talked, over and over we discussed what was best, what course would be wisest. Finally we decided, and we began." Here he looked again at his father before his eyes turned to the Lord and Lady of Lythnori. "We had the means, and the tools, but not your permission," he said. He picked up the pack at his feet, and pulled out a thickly wrapped bundle. "It is not complete," he said, his voice apologetic. "But she found it, and so we knew we had no choice."

He had unravelled the bundle as he spoke, and what he pulled from the wrapping made both Xyrrol and Mithrina gasp. Tyllerin looked at what his son held and raised his eyes to the sky.

Within the faded wine-velevet cape lay the wand. Shahlita's wand. Shaeli's wand. They had become one. Ishaan had spent long hours repairing the rose-blushed gold, rebraiding the intricate web that covered the haft. Where holes had once showed the loss of stones, now there glittered new gems; one the blue stone given to Shaeli by Ishaan during her Cave year, for the shape of it was exactly the shape of one of the empty spaces in the haft of the wand, and at the tip was the thing that drew every eye, every breath. The stone was now in the place for which it had been destined, and none could deny its right to be there.

"Ishaan has done it justice," said Mithrina, at last. "And paid great homage to his grandfather."

"So *this* is what was found by the child beneath the dragon's bones?" said Xyrrol.

"Yes," said Qiren. "But she does not want it. She wished it returned to elven hands. To you."

Xyrrol took the wand from Qiren, the reverence plain upon his face. He squared his shoulders and looked at them.

"The gods have chosen her wisely," he said. "And the wishes of the gods are not to be denied."

*　*　*

When the dream from Williver came, it was not Qiren who received it, but Llianas.

They had spent the lengthening days at Lythnori readying the Trader for the trip to Palveron. They had been welcomed for meals in many homes, and spent much time talking with Xyrrol and Mithrina. They slept mostly on the Trader, for Tarkoda would not leave the Zoi alone, and the others did not like to leave Koda alone, for he grew increasingly impatient to be gone to Great Court, to see his parents and find out what was happening in the World. He went over the planned route with Spotjaw and Qiren, and both were confident of finding an easy path through the mountains to the south-west. The drell and the Ammerr became very popular among the elves, particularly Williver's friends, Ky and Jocovar, who both spent long hours on the Trader swapping stories and wine-skins. The two were told the story of the journey beneath the mountain, shaking their heads in some places and whistling, amazed, at others. They longed to go beneath the mountains and explore, to map all the tunnels beneath the range, and they vowed to make a journey south to explore the old garrison the Trader had found on the northern side of Zerrinius.

Llianas, having survived the lecture Mithrina felt obliged to give her, had then been praised for her efforts beneath the mountain, and most surprisingly, been given permission to continue on with the travellers when the Trader left Lythnori. Ky and Jocovar begged for permission to go also, but were denied; Xyrrol said he had other things in mind for them, and then they begged to know what those things were.

Llianas came running from the trees one morning, so early there were few birds awake enough to see her. She had stayed at Lythnori the night, and by the time she'd scurried up the ladder to the deck, Tarkoda and Olando were coming up the stairs from below, pulling on their shirts and running fingers through tousled hair.

"It's alright," she said, as she pulled herself up onto the deck. "It's just me." She looked back over her shoulder. "Here comes Qiren. I woke him before I came. Wake the others," she said, her brown eyes unreadable in the pre-dawn light. "I have news. News from Williver."

* * *

In the dream, she had been running, running through the tunnels below the dragon's lair. She was looking for something, a way out, a way up, and she could not find it; every time she turned a corner there were only more tunnels and they all led down and she didn't want to go down, she wanted to go back out into the sunshine where everything was easy to see. Down here there were things she didn't want to face. She came across a room, but it wasn't an empty rocky room like the ones they had stayed in beneath the mountain, this room was full of clothes, racks and racks of bright costumes, feathers on some, jewels on others, each gown more elaborate, more intricate than the last.

*That's funny,* she thought. *I didn't know I had these.*

And then she wasn't in the room anymore, she was wandering aimlessly in the tunnels again, and she wasn't sure how she'd come to be there, and again she began to run, knowing there was a way up, a way out, but she could not find it. She turned another corner, and there, standing in the middle of the tunnel, was Williver. She slid to a halt before him.

*Oh, thank goodness,* she said. *Do you know the way out?*

He smiled. *Of course,* he said, taking her hand. *Come, I'll show you. I have something to tell you.*

*What?* she asked.

*It can wait a while,* he said. *Let's go this way.*

He led her through an arch, and they were in the lair. Oddly they could see across the empty expanse and she looked about as they crossed the floor. Their feet sounded strange in the vast cave, and when they reached the other side, they looked back. Llianas turned to go on, but a gasp from Williver turned her back.

*What is it?* she asked.

*I thought I saw a light flicker,* he said. *Up in one of the nests.*

He peered into the cave for a moment, but then he shook his head and they went on. Ahead she could see a triangle of light, and when Williver took her hand again, they were no longer walking, but gliding along the tunnel and the triangle of light grew and grew.

Suddenly they were standing in bright sunlight on the ledge before the entrance to the lair. Below them spread the foothills, and in the distance the mound that was Lythnori. Williver pointed across to it.

*'Tis time to return, Llianas,* he said.

*Return?*

*Yes,* he said. *Did you not know we walk in the dreamworld?*

She frowned. *Yes, I guess so.*

He smiled. *Where do you sleep tonight? Have you reached Lythnori?*

*Lythnori?* she said, confused for a moment. *Oh, yes. I suppose that's where I really am.*

*I'm glad. Tell them, when you wake, that we shall be waiting for them in the drell sanctuary to the west. Tell them to come with all haste.* He smiled at her. *You will remember?*

*Of course,* she said. *But...*

As she said the word Williver's image began to shimmer, to fade, and before she could say anything else, he was gone. She sighed and shivered. She would have to walk home by herself. Her feet started on the path that led back to the pool with its skeleton sentinels, but she never reached it.

* * *

Lianas told them what Williver had said, and they began to ready the Trader. The Zoi were well rested and came eagerly to the harness, and before the sun was halfway up the sky they were gone. Most of Lythnori came to bid them farewell, Xyrrol and Mithrina at their head. They had not been surprised when told the Trader was leaving, and while still displeased at Williver keeping the secret of his dreamworld journeys, this time they accepted its necessity. They had said and done all that had been needed during the past days, and they could only ask that the gods smile on them now.

Xyrrol and Mithrina waved with the rest of the elves as the Trader lifted into a bright spring morning. The air was full of the scent of blossoms, the calls of courting birds, and the voices of the elves. Those on the Trader waved to those on the ground, eager now they were leaving.

As they circled the hill, the heralds sent a merry call to them from the platforms high above the trees, and the Zoi returned the farewell, their voices chiming across the valley.

They crossed the two mighty rivers thick with run-off, flew over the pockets of forest and the chick-yellow trees, the courting butterflies dancing among new blossoms, then Tarkoda took them higher, above the cliffs that edged the valley to the west. They took a final look at the valley of Lythnori, and flew inland.

There were mountains ahead, and their way was uncharted for they had talked only of the route to the south-west, but now they needed to travel much further north than they'd thought. Still, the snows and unpredictable winds of early spring had gone, the skies were mild, the land beneath showing all its finery. The breezes were constant, the thick streams and spring floods easily managed, and the mountains grew less wild the further inland they flew. Landings were completed mostly without worry, but once, amid gusty rain in a thin valley, they had taken three tries to land.

No further word was heard from Williver, and they kept to their course, trusting to Blenny's memory to guide them to the sanctuary. Spotjaw told of the one time they had sheltered there with their wagon, almost a decade before, he reckoned, but then they had come to it from the east, and he did not recognise the mountains on this side. Yet, as the days passed, the distance was traversed, each problem surmounted, and as Williver had bidden them, they made all haste to the sanctuary of the drell. Yet when they came to it, there was no one there.

* * *

# CHAPTER EIGHT

At the Landing in Palveron, Mareesha was pacing the deck of Purple Leaf, her eyes turning again and again to Great Court. It sat as serenely as ever, its turrets and glass shining in the midday sun.

The gates to Great Court had been closed to the People since before the Wintering. Few but the guard had passed through them since then, and the mood in Palveron matched Mareesha's own; worried and unsure, the knot of fear curled in its stomach.

The Trader had been met at Serrat, as Almarnoch had predicted, and "escorted" to the city. They had been there more than a Moon, and every day she had gone to the gates with Taffka to seek an audience with the queen, and every day they had been sent away. Every day but today. Today only Taffka was allowed through the gate, weaponless and alone. Mareesha was refused. She had come back to the Trader to wait. Again.

Since first thaw she had been waiting. Waiting and worrying; fearing for the lives of all of her children, the fates of each of them unknowable. She felt sick most of the time, the tight knot in her stomach robbing her of the ability to taste food or sleep through the night. She woke each night with cold sweat crawling over her and a scream in her throat, and she would roll over and cling to Jarris' comforting back, drawing the strength from his sleeping body that she could not draw from his mind during the day. Worry for him, too, creased her brow.

He sat beside her in the sunshine, and daily he was becoming more himself. His right hand showed some weakness, but he slept and ate well, and he had regained most of his strength, yet his mind had not returned to what it had been, it was stuck somewhere in the past and he continually asked after the children. When they would tell him again that the children were not aboard, he would look confused, and then nod and go back to what he had been doing. They did not bother telling him where the children were. It was not that they had not tried. When they'd flown from Serrat after first thaw they had explained it to him again and again, but he never remembered, and had become distressed when they'd tried too hard. Now, they'd give only simple explanations, and he seemed more satisfied with that. In other ways he was his old self, but a bewildered, vaguer version, and his hair had almost covered the scar left by the rock when the bolt tunnel had been blasted by the black ship – but of course, he remembered none of that either. His fingers would probe the scar at times, that confused look on his face, but it was the one thing he never questioned, the scar, the one thing he did not ask about. He was content to sit in the sun, carving shapes into pieces of wood, sleeping often, and he spent long hours just staring up at the balloon. He smiled at Mareesha as she paced the deck, wood shavings in twisted ribbons at his feet like curls cut from hair.

"Worry not, my dearest," he said, smiling the vacant smile that had replaced his wide grin. "It will all unfold as it should."

He turned back to his wood, the foolish smile still on his lips, and it was on Mareesha's tongue to scream at him, to wipe the foolish grin from his face, to yell and scream until he came back from wherever he was hiding – until he came back so she could *lean* on him again – but she bit down on the tirade and pushed it back inside. It gathered with the knot of fear in her stomach, making a harder, redder, *tighter* knot.

She did not have to pace much longer. Taffka was dropped off in the square by the guard. Mareesha was now used to the sight of them, for they had been surrounded by Virrisian's soldiers since they'd left Serrat. They had been on the Trader, and even here they watched the Landing day and night, taking note of their comings and goings, watching everyone they spoke to, watching who visited the Landing, yet visitors were few. Few people wished to be seen speaking to the traders this year. All knew the rumours of treason that abounded about them, and that they were watched by the guard. The citizens of Palveron watched also and waited to see what would happen at Great Court.

The other Lands also seemed content to wait. Many had been sent from Ashkanna, Wokk and Romynn to enquire about the rumours of an heir and of Virrisian's intentions, even a dignitary from the Starisles had asked to be granted a hearing, yet few had been seen. The ambassador from Wokk had been granted a lengthy interview, but none of the many vines of rumour and innuendo had fruit bearing news of what had transpired there. The city waited with drawn breath to see what would happen next.

The Head Trader knew what was to happen before them all, and he knew they would not be happy with the news; not the people of Zirrus, nor those on other Lands.

Taffka's face said that the news was not good as Mareesha met him at the end of the Landing, but he said nothing, only took her hand, and led her back to Purple Leaf. They were all waiting, Renn, Rafi, and Rhubic – who had never returned to his own Trader after Taffka's injury – came from Golden Eagle. Jeth, Eenis and Andos stood on Purple Leaf's deck, and even Jarris looked up expectantly as they came through the landing gate.

"It is bad," said Taffka. "Very bad." He did not make them suffer by procrastinating. "I have talked long with the queen. It does not bode well."

"You told her of the black ship?" asked Jeth.

"I did," he said. "She made noises of concern, yet she appeared largely... *un*concerned. She hurried on to those things which concerned *her*. The only thing that lessens her terrible edicts is she gives assurances the twins are at Great Court, and safe. That she does not know of the black ship's destruction at Cave is impossible, for it must have brought the girls here. She made veiled references that their continued safety depends on how we next proceed."

"She let you see them?" asked Mareesha.

"No, Mareesha," Taffka said. "I did not see them, but I believe they are there, as she said. There is little reason for her to lie." He drew a deep breath before he went on. "What the queen wants is this." He stopped again, and his face tightened. "If the heir renounces the throne at Autumn's Eve, both girls will be released. So she says."

"But you do not trust her?" said Renn, reading her husband's face as unerringly as ever.

"No. I don't trust her," Taffka answered. "For she puts other conditions upon their release." He stopped, drew another deep breath and puffed it out. "The queen questions the loyalty of the Fleet. She thinks they have been instrumental in aiding the rebels. She thinks we side with those who have been worrying her guard and the Land."

"That's ridiculous," said Jeth. "Many may have felt like it, some have given food without trade, but we have shown more than our share of loyalty."

"This I told her, and more," said Taffka. "I spoke of the landingholders, the higher tariffs, but these things matter not. She has heard *rumours.*" Taffka spat the word. "Rumours. She knows as well as I that if there *are* such rumours they are untrue, but she asks for proof." He shook his head.

"Proof?" said Renn. "What kind of proof?"

"The Traders are to return to Cave," said Taffka. His voice seemed forced, as if his throat could hardly speak the words. "All of them, but for these two. We are to remain in Palveron."

"What?" said Mareesha, appalled. "Send the Traders back to Cave? Why? This provides Virrisian with no *proof.* It punishes the Lands, the people."

"*She* thinks it will provide the proof that she seeks," said Taffka. "She says she believes the rebels move about on

Traders. If there are no Traders then their raids will lessen, and they'll be more vulnerable to capture. And punishing the Lands or their people I believe is yet another motive. She did not say so, but..."

"But she seemed pleased with the thought," Mareesha finished for him. She shook her head. "She has not changed from the spiteful child she was."

"What about the ships trading on other Lands?" asked Rafi.

"When they return, each will be escorted to Serrat," replied his father. "She has sent messengers to every landingholder. Each will have soldiers waiting to escort every Trader back to Serrat. Those now on other Lands will be met as they arrive."

"I always knew the landingholders were going to be trouble," said Rhubic.

"Aye, lad," said Jeth. "None of us liked them."

"And there is no dissuading her?" asked Renn. "Perhaps if she'll only delay."

"She has already *done* it, Renn. The messengers have been sent," said Taffka. "I believe soon after our arrival. Already the Traders are being returned to Serrat. Some may be at Cave even now."

There was silence for a long, horrified moment.

"This is why we've seen no other Trader," said Jeth, at last. Taffka nodded.

"And why she kept us waiting for so long," said Mareesha. "This was her plan, for us to come to Palveron and then leave no other Trader in the skies."

It was not a question, but again, Taffka nodded. "I believe it was," he said.

"And so we are bound to do as she says?" said Mareesha, yet she did not wait for Taffka to nod, she went on, her voice rising. "We are to wait here, under *her* eye, until Autumn's Eve, and she'll make one of my girls stand before the people and renounce the throne."

Taffka met her gaze steadily, and nodded once more.

"Will the People believe it?" asked Eenis.

"I think if the throne is renounced, publicly, people *will* believe it, and it is on this she relies," said Taffka. "They believe there is an heir, Irinesta made sure of that, and the queen's denying it, speaking of the madness of old E'Nith, is not really believed, no matter how many edicts she sends out. I believe she will admit there may be some truth to the rumours, although there is no proof of such a thing, but if the throne is renounced," Taffka shrugged. "The people are cowed. Apart from the rebels, they are pessimistic, dependent on the queen's good will."

"You think they want answers," said Jeth, "yet they'll not fight for change?"

"I think their hope has been covered by fear and hunger," said Taffka. "As she intended."

"And the people will suffer the year without Traders," said Eenis. "Crops will go undelivered, goods will sit in warehouses, there will be no Faunists travelling to the tiny villages. Surely they will protest."

"I said this to her, and more," said Taffka. "But she swears it is for this year only, and she is unconcerned with... well, she called them 'minor discomforts'. And she gives her word, whatever that may be worth, that next year we may fly again." Taffka shifted uncomfortably. "Under certain conditions."

"What *conditions*?" asked Jeth. "Since when do Traders fly with 'conditions'?"

"If the queen has her way, next year we will fly into the World with four of her guard on each ship, to be accommodated by the Trader in return for their 'protection'." Taffka said the words with undisguised disgust.

Jeth began to sputter, but Taffka held up a hand.

"There is more," he said.

"*More?*" cried Jeth.

"More and far worse," answered Taffka. "The queen is to tell us where to fly, what to carry and where to land. Even who we may carry *for*." Every eye was upon him, each one of them incredulous at his words. "And the other Lands are to *pay* our good queen. Pay for the privilege of using her Fleet. '*My* Fleet', that's what she called it," he said.

The words were too much for even Taffka to bear. His head dropped into his hand.

"The Fleet will never agree," said Jeth.

"They will have no *choice*," said Taffka, far too forcefully, his head snapping back up, eyes blazing. He passed a hand across his eyes and Renn moved closer to him. When they saw his eyes again, they were calmer, but filled with anguish. "I'm sorry, my friend," he said. "But these things are not for negotiation. The Fleet must have the protection of Cave during the Wintering, and Cave lies on Zirrus land. These things she made painfully clear to me. While the queen rules, we must not falter in doing as she says, not if we want the twins returned, not if we want the Fleet to survive. *And* we are not to speak of this in the World. This matter is to remain between the Fleet and Great Court." He sighed. "This last is almost the worst. We are to let the World believe we agree with this, even that we *seek* her protection. If all these things are agreed to, then our girls will be returned."

"What is to stop us from defying her *after* the girls are returned?" asked Rhubic. "She would have nothing to bargain with then."

"I am to return to Great Court on the Full," said Taffka. "I am to swear this before her and sign an agreement. While she is queen, the agreement will stand."

No one spoke. They all knew the word of Taffka was unbreakable. If the Fleet Leader agreed to this, it would be so, and they knew it.

The next words were unexpected. They were faltering and hesitant at first, but sensible, comforting words, as Jarris' had always been.

"Sign without fear, old friend," he said.

They turned to stare at him. They had almost forgotten he had been sitting there, listening.

"Let her think us beaten, for now," Jarris said slowly, quietly. "Let her see what the World would be like without the Fleet. Let them *all* see. Let her answer the questions from the other Lands, for I think they'll not be happy. Let her have her moment. Let her think she has all as she wishes it."

Jarris smiled. It was not the confused smile he had worn of late, but a more familiar smile, an old smile. *His* old smile. Mareesha began to cry.

"She has not met my children yet," Jarris said, and his eyes were no longer confused either. "And when she does meet them, all agreements will be made void."

\* \* \*

# CHAPTER NINE

Days later, far to the north of the city, Fezzik of Boccra, blacksmith turned rebel, watched as a Trader disappeared into the eastern sky. He had come to a tiny village on the banks of the River Zerrin to speak with the people who directed the rebels in this part of the country. A leader had taken over the rebellion in all the lands to the south, a leader he was proud to follow, and their concerted efforts had proved successful, for the most part. Those who lived along the banks of the mighty river were being persuaded to join their group, and Fezzik had had little trouble in the persuading, both here and on the other side of the Clahren. The plan he had come up with before the Wintering had been wholly endorsed by the new leader, one who had proved both wily and devious.

The plan was to disrupt as many deliveries to Palveron as possible in the hope that the people of the city and those closest to the queen would begin to feel a little of the discomfort being felt in the country, as some kind of protest. The hope was slight; ships and Traders kept the city from being wholly cut off, but any supplies brought from the country were harried mercilessly. Increasingly, the guard had to turn their attention from the towns and villages to escort the wagons to the city – and to protect themselves, for keeping the guard hungry and distracted was also one of the rebels' main concerns, and another facet of Fezzik's plan. The tactic used so long on the people was being used now against the guard, who never knew where the rebels would next strike. Horses were stolen in the night, flaming arrows flew over garrison walls, stores were mysteriously poisoned or ransacked before delivery; those of the guard who had committed the worst offences began to disappear, sometimes their bodies were found, but mostly they were just never seen again. The guard began to move about in larger groups.

Today, as Fezzik had been preparing to leave, a contingent of guard had ridden into the town, and he had watched them from the barn where he'd been saddling his horse. He was close to the edge of the village and could see the small Landing just outside the last buildings. The guard rode directly to the landingholder's hut and dismounted. The landingholder came out, nodded to the head of the guard, and looked expectantly into the sky to the north. Fezzik, his view blocked by the barn, had slunk from the building and edged his way closer.

In the last house in the village, the garden was overgrown and a thickly gnarled tree grew in one corner. He crouched and ran to the shadow behind the trunk, then shimmied up into the branches. Still he could not see the sky to the north, but he had a leaf-framed view of the Landing, and he knew the guard were waiting for a Trader, though for what reason he could not guess. When the Trader landed, its balloon showed a dark patch like a stain on the lightly coloured butterfly pattern, a dark patch sewed obviously over a large hole, and Fezzik wondered at that, too; this was the second Trader he had seen this year with a patchwork balloon.

The traders went about the business of securing their ship, eyeing the guard as they did, and when they were done, the guard circled the Landing. Fezzik could hear nothing of the exchange but he saw the traders listen as the head guard spoke, then begin to gesticulate wildly.

People began to come from the village, one of them the lady of the house where he had been staying, and they walked across the field towards the Landing. Some of the guard went to meet them, and the people milled about for a moment, but when the guard lowered weapons, they turned as one and came back. Fezzik heard some of their words as they went past the garden where he watched from the tree and he understood that there would be no trading that day.

The guard returned to the ship, and half a dozen of them boarded and ranged themselves around the edge of the deck. The traders watered their birds, and with their shoulders set sullenly they untied their ropes and lifted into the sky. The rest of the guard mounted, the head guard stopped to speak with the landingholder and then they rode away.

Fezzik watched them go, watched the Trader dwindle into the eastern sky, and then slid from his tree and went back to the village. It was the lady of the house who told him, tears standing in her eyes, that the Traders were being sent back to their Cave. She said that it had been ordered by the queen and the Head Trader. Fezzik wondered how the queen had persuaded the trader to agree to such a thing.

He rode away soon after, and on his journey south he learnt also of the reason the Trader's balloons showed such visible scars; a woman who had grown up a trader had spoken to those on a ship before the guard arrived to escort them back to Serrat, and was told of the thing that had attacked the Trader's Cave; the black ship which had destroyed balloons, ships and killed dozens. He rode south with all haste to inform his leader of what he knew, and as he rode, he began to pass people, in wagons and on foot, who were on their way to Palveron. There was a feeling among them that if the queen would see them, she would understand more fully their plight; a feeling that she was unaware of their suffering, and if they went together to stand before her that she would help them; a feeling that with the loss of the Traders there was no other hope than that. Fezzik tried to dissuade several families, telling them to return to their homes, but they would not listen, they merely turned their faces away and rode staunchly on; their faith in being heard by their monarch unwavering.

He also saw large groups of guard, each formation heading south towards Palveron.

He saw one more Trader in the sky before he reached the rocky stronghold where the rebels hid, flying east across the

Bay of Islands. It would be the last of the great ships that he would see in a very long time.

He reached their little stronghold at dusk, a place secured by a thin gorge and two score of archers protecting its approach. Fezzik was hailed as he rode up, and though he wanted badly to see Verlie, ensconced here in safety with Pemba and the children, he went first to find his leader to tell all he knew.

Afterwards, he rode deeper into the compound. There were a few buildings scattered along the edges of the ravine, but not many for the hundreds of people who lived here. They lived higher, in one of the many caves that were scattered along the high cliffs, but there were still people gathered in a few of the buildings, used as communal buildings, to prepare food, to talk strategy, to make weapons, and Fezzik was hailed as he passed, but he kept going until he came to a ramp. There were many of the ramps zig-zagging their way up the sides of the canyon, each designed to be pulled up if the need arose. Often they discussed what they would do if their compound was discovered and attacked, for the threat was a very real one; several rebel strongholds had already been found, and one of them, near Conroi on the northern tip of the Land, had every person killed, no matter how old, from the tiniest of babes to the bed-ridden. Yet they felt secure here, the rocky ravine was one of dozens surrounded by dry dusty land, and they kept lookouts at every approach.

There was only one water source in the canyon, a small spring that seeped from the rock at waist height at the end of the ravine, and there was always someone there filling water bottles. Fezzik was hailed by the Warlock, Bekerra, as he passed, and then she went back to pulling small water spouts from the spring with which to water the old tree that stood nearby. The patch of grass that had grown beneath the spring was browning, but the tree that grew beside it was given its due, for it was the one cool, green thing in this rocky place. The birds and other creatures were given time at sunrise and sunset to drink there too, and the children would often gather in the cave closest to watch them, whispering to each other at the bright plumage of that bird over there, or the length of that lizard down there. A few adults always accompanied them, for once or twice, a small band of jenka had come slinking down a steep crack in the canyon to drink at the spring's cool water. The children of Pelazarus and Pemba were usually there watching and whispering with the rest; they had rebounded from the loss of their father, brother, sister, and their home, much better than Fezzik could have hoped. They spoke often and happily of their loved ones, recalling funny moments and creating family legends with which to remember them, the eldest children prompting the memories of the younger. His brother Fozar, a frequent visitor to the compound, unfailingly brought them small gifts, a game or a bag of lollies, and he would sit with the baby dandled on his knee coaxing gurgles of laughter from her. The child, born early and sickly that terrible Wintering when Pelazarus and Pemba and the children had been thrown out of their home into the snow, was now a thriving, bonny girl, her smile just like her father's. Like her children, their mother, too, was given less and less to deep depression as time passed; Pemba, like Verlie, still spent long hours in the forge that had been built here, providing what weapons they could to the rebellion.

    Fezzik's son, Arral, was often with the children who went to the spring each afternoon. Though he was much quieter than he had been before the loss of his sister, much more inclined to long moments of silence, he seemed to be coping. When Fezzik was in the compound, Arral shadowed him everywhere, offering to help a dozen times a day, ever ready to lend a hand. Fezzik disliked the tired look that was often on his son's face, the look of a worn-out old man exhausted with the World, but more than that he disliked the change in his Florry since Zeffy and Pim had died. She rarely smiled and he had not heard her laugh since the morning the guard had come and taken her mother, killing Zeffy and Pim in the process. She was clingy and tearful, would go nowhere without her mother or father, and when Fezzik was away, she was even worse. Verlie had to take her everywhere, and was exhausted with worry for the child; Fezzik was at a loss as to how to restore some peace into the heart of the formerly happy child.

As he climbed the ramps to the cave where his family stayed with Pemba and another widow, other greetings came from the caves he passed. The caves here were not lofty – Fezzik was continually bumping his head – but they went deeply into the rock, and the one containing his family was about halfway up the side. The ramp led up to a little platform at the entrance of the cave, and he ducked as he went inside. There was soft light coming from the back where the bedrolls were, and he waited a moment until his eyes adjusted to the change. He stepped over a knee-high fence he had erected just inside to keep the crawling baby from the long drop to the canyon floor, and then Arral yelled from the back of the cave and in moments they were all throwing themselves at him. Zeffy stood unspeaking, clutching her mother's skirt as Fezzik gave Verlie a tight hug, but when he scooped her up and nuzzled her, she gave him a brief smile and put her arms around his neck, and she did not let him go until she fell asleep in his arms. After he had carried her to her bedroll, he stood looking down at her for a long time. Even in sleep her face looked troubled, and, like Arral, she looked far too old, a wizened version of her former self.

He sighed, tucked the blanket around her shoulders, and went to tell Verlie and Pemba that the Traders were to be banished from the skies. His plan to deprive the city of some of their luxuries would now be so much easier, and yet he did not relish what the loss of the Traders would mean to the World.

\* \* \*

He did not stay long in the compound where the rebels hid. A few days after his arrival, the leader called for him and sent him to meet a contingent of guard escorting wagons loaded with grain. How the information was gathered, Fezzik did not know, but he never questioned it. Now that the rebels were all working together, the task of the food wagons was made much easier and he did not concern himself with the spies that garnered the information, he just went where he was told and did his best to follow orders.

This task would not be easy, however. The wagons were many, the guard said to be almost a hundred, but he gathered all the rebels to him and they set out at sunrise. More rebels would join them on their way, but he looked at the two score accompanying him and hoped it would be enough. Capturing these wagons would mean much food in the bellies of the rebels, his own family included, and he was determined they would not fail.

Bekerra rode beside him on her huge horse, the former guard, Bithani, beside her. The two had become inseparable, and shared a shallow cave beside the one occupied by Fezzik, Verlie, Pemba and the children. Fozar rode just behind the two women, and he thought of the long look Fozar had given Pemba as he'd mounted. Fezzik did not ask about it, merely filed it away for future speculation, turning his thoughts to the task ahead.

Mid-afternoon found them hidden behind a hill overlooking the road leading south, the dust of the wagons hanging over the road to the north. His party had been joined by many others, but when the wagons came closer his eyebrows contracted; the force with the laden wagons was bigger than he'd been told, at least double what he'd expected. Still, he did not baulk at the task, the element of surprise was as good as he would get, and he waited for the signal from below.

Bekerra came from a side road as the wagons approached, then dismounted and stooped down, seemingly inspecting her horse's hoof. He heard a shout from one of the soldiers, and he raised a hand. Arrows were notched, swords were drawn, but still they waited for the signal. Below them Bekerra looked up at the approaching guard, seemingly surprised to find them before her. She stood straighter, lowered her head in deference to the soldiers, and put a hand up on her saddle. When the hand came away it held a staff which spewed fire at the forward soldiers, and Fezzik stood up with a cry and led the charge down the hill. Arrows flew through the air as he leapt onto the road and then his only thought was to fight the soldiers who turned towards them. Many were killed before they had time to draw weapons, yet the fighting was fierce for a long time. Arrows crashed into the soldiers from both sides of the road, Bekerra's fire took out dozens more, and by the time the last few dozen surrendered, over a hundred soldiers lay dead or wounded in the dust, among them rebels, some dead, some wounded, and their dead and wounded alike were carried to the waiting wagons. The surrendering soldiers were tied in a long line, their weapons were thrown onto the wagons, and then Fezzik led the band back to the north, leaving the queen's guard tied to each other in the road.

It was after dark when they separated from their fellow rebels, dividing the wagons and the wounded amongst them, and then they took a circuitous route back to the rocky valley where they were greeted with enthusiasm. The stores were taken by willing hands to the caves, and then Fezzik went with Bekerra to report to their leader on the success of another mission.

\* \* \*

# CHAPTER TEN

Jarris had been right. Taffka had begrudgingly signed the queen's agreement, yet almost before her seal was dry, the protests had begun.

Perhaps she had underestimated the loyalty afforded the Fleet by her own people, but the reaction from the other Lands was immediate and forceful. Ships began to arrive in the harbour, bringing delegates, ambassadors, knights from every one of the Lands. The Wokkii were smallest in numbers, but the other Lands more than made up for them.

From Romynn there came ten ships bearing knights, officials from each province, and a large number of archers and footmen.

Ashkanna sent only five ships – at first. As each delegate was sent away from the gates without audience, Ashkanna sent another ship, an ambassador of higher rank, until by spring's end there were six lords and three of Ashkanna's royalty asking for audience. Each ship had its own contingent of soldiers.

The Starisles sent few ships, yet they were full of dignitaries who were at the gates of Great Court at sunrise and would not leave until the sun had set each night.

They were joined by many of the people of Zirrus. Each day saw more and more people fill the city, people from all over the Land. Some came in carriages, some on horseback, some came into the harbour in small boats, but many more came on foot. Farmers, merchants, entire families walked into Palveron and up the road to stand before the closed gates.

In front of the gates stood stony-faced soldiers, answering no questions, meeting no eye. The guard also paced the parapet above, looking down on the ever-increasing crowd and the houses beyond.

Opposite the gates, across a wide avenue, began the plush houses of Palveron's elite, and their fences became perches for people wanting somewhere to sit, their steps became seats for children to rest, mothers to feed their babies. Any garden exposed to the melee was soon trampled, gardeners chased young men seeking a better view from trees in their gardens. Several householders took offence at the intrusion and did their best to keep the crowd from their properties, many more simply hid behind closed doors and watched from high, curtained windows. Some opened their doors and fed as many of the poor as they could, and the poor were many. If the people of Palveron had not known the state in the country before, the loss of the Traders brought the extent of this home to them. Day after day they came, tired, hungry, and all looking to Great Court for answers, and at first they were quiet, weary enough to stand staring at the soldiers, but as each day passed and the crowd rubbed against itself, the mood began to change. Here and there, someone with a passion and a voice to go with it would stand above the crowd, shouting of the things the queen must do. More and more often they talked of the heir, and hope began to shine more brightly in many faces, but the more wary looked at the soldiers, at the closed gates, and wondered how long this would be allowed to go on.

Those on the Landing in the square watched the travellers wash about beneath them. Many of those entering Palveron came through the square, a tidal flow that continued to wash in, but never recede. At first the flow was a trickle, but as the trickle became a wave their hopes began to rise; many of those who were turned away from the gates of Great Court came up the stairs of the Landing to seek words with the Head Trader. Taffka saw them all in a room on the Landing, and told each the same thing: the Fleet had left the World at the queen's request, and would return to it as soon as she allowed them to, with soldiers for protection. As loyal subjects they must defer to their queen. More he could not say.

Yet on the subject of the black ship he was very vocal. Speaking of it had not been forbidden by Queen Virrisian. She had said they must not speak of the twins, yet to Taffka she'd made little of the ship, and he used this to his best advantage. That she knew nothing of the black ship, as Taffka had said, was impossible – yet he liked to let her believe he knew nothing of a connection. It made it easier to speak of it to the delegates from other Lands.

Of the ambassadors from Wokk, he saw nothing, yet each of the other Lands sent several different representatives; three members of the contingent from the Starisles came every few days. When told of the black ship, no one from any of the Lands showed great surprise; dismay and horror at the damage done to the Fleet, yes, but the existence of the ship that flew so high was not a surprise to those in the upper echelons of each of the Lands. Each knew of the rumours of such a thing, each had looked for information on it and found none, but each gave Taffka another piece of the black ship's puzzle. It had been more than fifteen Winters since the thing had first been sighted, mostly across a great distance, most often near the Nebillonia Straits and the southern end of Ashkanna, occasionally at the Starisles and more rarely near Romynn. All the Lands had stories of ships lost and strange lights in the sky. No one knew if the Wokkii had knowledge of such a thing, for they spoke to no one from the other Lands and never visited the Head Trader.

In these meetings between Taffka and the other Lands, Jarris sat in a corner of the room, carving a piece of wood, saying nothing, looking at no one. They all knew of the injury he had suffered – his addled senses had been the subject of rumour since they'd flown into the city – and Taffka made sure the connection between Jarris' injury and the black ship was made. He ignored Jarris at the meetings, and none of the delegates spoke to him.

At one of these early meetings, Taffka was speaking to several people from Orrellis. This contingent had come to represent the Lakes' country almost as soon as the Traders had started being escorted back to Serrat, and Taffka had met with them several times. They were leaving when Andos came bounding up the steps, a few pieces of wood under his arm. He stopped, breathless, as the contingent went down the stairs, and then he came across to Taffka, looking like he wanted to run, but not daring to.

"I have news," he said in a low voice.

"Come inside," said Taffka.

Jarris stood as they entered, brushing the wood shavings from his trousers slowly and deliberately. He looked up as they came in and Taffka closed the door behind him. Jarris grinned.

"I'm rather enjoying being an imbecile," he said. "It's very interesting, the looks people give you."

Since the day on the deck when Taffka had told them of his meeting with the queen, Jarris had regained himself. It was as if something had been switched back on inside his mind; some light had been turned on in a room which had been left in darkness.

Mareesha had sobbed against his chest for a long time when she realised he had become himself again, and her eyes had since lost some of their haunted look.

Jarris had had bad moments as he remembered the coming of the black ship, and was told what had transpired after he'd been hit by the rock, but he squared his shoulders and listened as they told him the rest. He knew that Shaeli was headed for the Starisles, Tarkoda was trying to fly a Trader over the mountains, and the twins were in the castle. These things registered not at all on his face, nor in his heart; it seemed he had known them all along, somewhere inside. He decided he would keep his recovery secret from the outside; he did not know why, it just seemed to him that it may be useful sometime.

"Andos has news, Jarris," said Taffka.

"What news?" Jarris asked, instantly serious.

"I've been down at the bay," Andos said, laying the half dozen pieces of wood on the table. "I was looking for driftwood for you, Jarris."

Jarris picked up one pale, twisted piece. "Thank you, boy," he said. "They will be useful. Go on."

"As I was leaving," Andos said, "I was passing that camp, you know, the one beside the bay?"

Taffka and Jarris both nodded. Many of the people that had begun to fill the city were very poor, yet they had brought tents and wagons with them, and they had drawn them together in a large park beside the bay. The camp was growing every day, and had had an almost carnival atmosphere about it, at first. Then they had begun to run out of supplies, the thick grass was worn down by the many feet and tents covering it, and the people there had started to seem a little dirty, a little desperate. The people of Palveron skirted the camp and the others like it that were springing up throughout the city.

"As I was going past the camp," said Andos. "A man came out of the crowd. He pushed this at me," he said, pulling a small leather pouch from his vest.

Taffka took it. "Did he say anything?" he asked.

"He said," Andos swallowed. "He said, 'They are safely back on Zirrus. I left them less than a Moon ago', and then he was gone."

"Shaeli," said Jarris. "He means Shaeli." He turned to Taffka. "It must have been that friend of Flin's, Captain Mahi."

"Let's see what we have, then," said Taffka, unrolling the pouch.

It smelled of spices as he opened it, and a fine dust fell from the papers he pulled out. Andos sneezed.

"He must have had it hidden in a barrel of spice," Taffka said. "It is from Almarnoch," he added, as he unfolded the papers. "And a note from Shaeli." He folded them again, put them back into the pouch, and pushed the pouch inside his shirt. "The others will want to hear."

Jarris stood, his face alight, and he crossed eagerly to the door. "Mareesha will be so relieved," he said, his hand on the door knob.

"Do not go hastily, my friend," said Taffka.

Jarris stopped and looked back at him. "Ah, yes," he said. "I forgot I was unwell." He grinned, walked back, and gathered up the driftwood. He held out an arm to Andos. "If you would be so kind as to help your poor uncle back to the Trader?" he said.

Andos took the arm, suppressing his smile as he opened the door. The three of them went over to tell the others they had news of Shaeli.

\* \* \*

# CHAPTER ELEVEN

Williver woke Shaeli with a hand on her shoulder. She rolled over and looked up at him. The light was thin, but she could see the shapes of the leaves up behind his head and the deep blue of the morning sky. His face was in shadow, but she could see the gleam of his smile.

"What's happened?" she asked, and sat up.

Ebony stirred and stretched on the pack beside her.

They were in a small copse in the foothills. The journey south had been uneventful; they had kept to the lesser roads and back trails, sleeping in the trees far off the road as the nights warmed around them. Shaeli could smell the spring flowers on the dawn light, and she looked around, pulling a few stray leaves from her hair. The others were still softly breathing mounds of shadow. One of the horses blew and stamped its foot, and she looked over at the little carriage. Ezebar was huddled asleep at the foot of the steps, and the horses were tethered nearby. M'zena slept in the carriage, swaddled in her patchwork quilt, and Shaeli smiled through the darkness. She had grown very fond of the old woman as the days had passed. She looked expectantly at Williver.

"Well?"

"I have seen Llianas," he said.

"Llianas?" asked Shaeli. "But I thought you were going to try to contact Qiren tonight, with the fire, like you did before with Ellirra."

"I was," he said. "But tonight I met Llianas in a dream."

"By accident?"

He nodded. "Almost. I saw a strange spiral as I wandered over the hills of Lythnori in the dreamworld, and when I followed it, I found myself wandering the tunnels beneath the lair. 'Twas there I found Llianas."

"Was she having a nightmare?" asked Shaeli.

"No," he said. "Not quite a nightmare, but she was on the edge of that plane, I think. I led her back to a gentler place and told her to tell them we will meet them at the sanctuary."

"Do you think she'll remember?"

"I'm sure she will. But I wanted you to know, before I woke the others, that they are safe. They have reached Lythnori."

The knowledge sunk into her still-sleepy mind. "Oh, Williver," she said. "That means they found a way over the mountains." She scrambled up. "I have to tell Kirrit. Almarnoch. We have to tell them all."

"Most of us are awake already with your chattering voice, miss," said Almarnoch, sitting up. "Not that slumber was a particularly comfortable place." He put a hand to his back and groaned as he endeavoured to straighten it. "What is it you have to tell us?"

"Tarkoda made it to Lythnori," she said. "They made it safely."

"Thank the gods," said Kirrit, also sitting up, all tousled red hair, freckles, and yawns. "That's one less thing to worry about. Your brother must be cleverer than he seems." She yawned around her grin, and Shaeli smiled, knowing Kirrit had been fretting over Koda and the others, and that she would much prefer Tarkoda were here so she could tease him in person. "What's for breakfast?" she asked, scratching her head.

"A fine question, lass," said M'zena, opening the door of the carriage and coming down the steps. "I was just going to be asking it myself. If we're to be up with the birds we'd best have some tezz, eh?"

She looked at Ezebar, who sat leaning against the wheel of the carriage, wrapped in his cloak. He sighed, but they could all see that he was smiling.

"I'll stir up the fire," he said. "There's some tezz left, and some dried fruits and bread, a few honey cakes, but not much else. Our supplies are getting low."

"We'll have to venture into a town soon, then," said Williver. "We need only enough to see us to the sanctuary. We are almost at the place where we need to turn east aren't we, M'zena?"

She nodded. "We are. It would be wise if supplies are gathered soon. The towns and villages do not venture far into the foothills and soon we shall leave them behind. People around here know the mountains are the province of the elves."

"That's true," said Williver. "They hunt only along the foothills, and leave the mountains to us. The drell sanctuary is not far in, yet we may have to wait for Blenny before we enter, for though I know approximately where it is, I do not know *exactly* where it is to be found."

"Don't worry about that," said M'zena. "I know where it is, *exactly*."

"May I ask how you know of the drell sanctuary?" said Almarnoch.

"You may," she said, settling herself on the grass beside where Ezebar stoked their small fire. "I travelled there long ago with a friend."

"There are not many in the World who even know such things exist," said Almarnoch. "I myself had only heard rumours until Shaeli told me of them, and *you* once stayed in one?"

"Oh, more than once," said M'zena, with an airy wave. "Several times. At *this* one. There are others I have visited."

Almarnoch's eyebrows quivered. "Several times?" he asked, obviously eager to know more.

"Yes," said M'zena, plucking grass from her skirt. "Several times," she said, obviously not willing to tell more.

"And you'll really be able to find it again?" asked Shaeli, her curiosity matching the Warlock's. "I know the drell use protection spells to hide them from the outside."

"They do," agreed M'zena. "Yet the way is clear in my mind, and the signs of magic are always there, if one knows how to look for them."

She smiled, and plucked at a few more grass seeds as the others continued talking of the supplies they needed, the journey ahead, of the Trader safe at Lythnori, or perhaps even now on its way to meet them. No one noticed Almarnoch looking at M'zena, his eyes thoughtful. No one but perhaps M'zena herself.

They were high in the hills, and after they'd breakfasted, they harnessed the horses and followed the road around the side of a steep hill. They came out through the trees, and the lower hills and plains spread out before them.

It was still early, and mist lay secretively in pockets, hiding from the sun's rays. The flowers of spring were drifting their scent out on the breeze, but the once-light perfume was becoming mustier as the flowers began to fade. Below, the hills bumped their way across to the plains, their mounds growing lower and lower as the cloth of the grasslands covered them. Far across the plains, in the distance, there grew a dark blue-green mound, a smudge against the pale horizon.

"What's that?" asked Shaeli, pointing at the dark smudge. "Is it the forest?"

"Aye. 'Tis M'Zen'sclahr, lass," said M'zena.

Shaeli nodded and turned her eyes to the hills below. "Williver," she called. "Is that smoke or mist down there behind that hill?"

Williver sat up beside Ezebar, who was driving the little carriage, and they had the roof pulled back so those inside the carriage could see them and the sky above. Williver followed her finger with his eyes.

"Smoke," he said, after a moment. "And enough of it to be a village, not just a farm. Perhaps a good-sized one."

"Good," said Shaeli. "Maybe there'll even be a Trader there, and we can ask them for news."

They had not ventured into many towns or villages, but each time they had, they had looked for a Trader. News of happenings in the outside World was anticipated, and each time they went near people they listened to the conversations around them, but they asked few questions. Seeing a Trader was to see those who they could question without fear, or pass on information for them to carry to Palveron, yet many days had passed and they had yet to see a Trader even flying in the skies, let alone see one they could speak with.

They did not reach the village where they'd seen the smoke that day, but Ishaan caught some fish in a lake they found cupped in the hills, and they camped beside its mirrored waters that night and made their way to the village the next day.

The sun was high when they reached it, and they looked forward to a decent meal. They decided to leave the carriage out of sight in a secluded glen on the hillside above the village and walk down. M'zena declared she needed a nap, and reminded them to buy plenty of tezz. Ezebar said he would stay with her, and Almarnoch decided he, too, could do without the walk. He was sitting on a fallen log when they left him, stuffing his pipe.

\* \* \*

They walked into the village and disaster smiling and talking. They were sure they had evaded the queen's guard far back to the north, and they did not notice what a quiet place they were entering; at least, not at first.

It was a pretty place, nestled within the hills, a thick creek running on the far side of it. The houses were almost all the same, with high roofs and brightly painted gables and shutters, each with a patch of garden filled with well-ordered flower beds and strictly pruned trees, with white gravel paths leading up to many-hued doors. The village was huddled together, the streets thin and winding, but the houses and gardens were picturesque in the sunshine, framed by the rich patterns of the hills.

Williver noticed it first, the quiet. He looked about, saw few people, and those he did see avoided his eye. He began to look more carefully at the houses lining the streets.

Ishaan picked up on it next, and as they rounded a corner, he thought he saw someone duck out of sight just as they turned in. His hand moved to his sword.

They came to the square where a long Wintering Hall squatted beside a large well. The roof of the hall was peaked and thick shutters were closed over the windows. Near the Wintering Hall at the edge of the village was a Landing, empty. Shaeli sighed, and pointed to the other side of the square.

"There," she said, pointing to a shop showing its wares in the front window.

She and Kirrit headed towards it, Williver, Ishaan and Flin following. Flin had noticed it too now, the silence, the tension in the air. He hurried to catch up with the girls.

They were fluttering about the shop, laying things on the counter when he entered. Behind the counter stood a tower of a woman, her hands folded across her mountainous bosom, watching the girls lay things before her.

"A slab of bacon, if you please," Kirrit was saying as they entered. "And a few dozen eggs."

"Yes, miss," the woman said, bobbing. Her bosom wobbled. She pulled the meat from beneath the counter, wrapped it, and counted the eggs into a basket.

"Have you seen a Trader lately?" asked Shaeli.

The woman looked at her strangely. "No, miss," she said. "No one's seen a Trader." She looked out the window. "Will that be all?" She licked her thick lips.

"I think so," said Kirrit, laying a jar of preserves on the table.

"Hurry, please, my good woman," said Flin. "We have a long way to go today."

There were no questions from the woman, no pleasantries, and this made Flin all the more nervous. Williver and Ishaan stood near the doorway, looking out at the square.

The woman stated a price far too quickly, and Flin knew she had guessed it. She wanted them gone and Flin agreed with her; he wanted to be gone, too. They put the supplies in their packs, and walked back out into the sun, the girls now wondering at the solemn looks on the faces of the others. They were halfway across the square, and Shaeli had opened her mouth to ask what was the matter when it happened.

\* \* \*

Kirrit was hitching up her pack, the little basket of eggs in one hand. She turned around to say something to Shaeli, saw her friend frown and open her mouth, then an arrow thunked into the ground beside her foot, bouncing off the cobblestones. Kirrit jumped, dropped the basket of eggs, and a tiny scream left her throat. Shaeli's hand moved to her amulet and she tucked Ebony beneath her hair.

"Stop where you stand," cried a woman's voice. "Stop or die."

The door of the Wintering hall opened, and the queen's guard began to pour out. From the buildings around the square there rose archers, and across the square more soldiers came from behind the landingholder's squat hut.

"Run," cried Williver, pulling the short wand from his belt.

Flin had his stone out before the word left Williver's mouth. He began firing at the archers in the buildings ahead with one hand, grabbing Shaeli's arm with the other, and pulling her across the square. Behind them, Williver was firing at the guard running from the hall and Ishaan had drawn his sword.

Kirrit ran before them all, looking back at the square which moments before had been empty. Now it boiled with guard, all of them pelting across the stones towards them. She turned and kept running.

Just ahead was the street where they had entered the square, and Kirrit ran towards it, but more of the guard stepped from between the buildings and she hesitated. A blast from Flin's beam flew past her head and slammed into the soldiers. Three went down, and a beam from Shaeli leapt past Kirrit's head on the other side and took out another, but more took their place and Kirrit swerved and ran in front of the buildings towards a smaller street nearby. Guard appeared barring the way down this thinner street, too, but there were only four, and Flin took care of them easily, the bolts flying past her head in rapid succession. Kirrit looked back over her shoulder, thankful for Flin's good aim, and saw he and Shaeli were close behind her, Williver and Ishaan not far behind them.

Flin still had his hand on Shaeli's arm, and she was firing behind her with her smoky quartz at the guard who had come from the Wintering Hall. Rich grey fire hit two who were gaining on Williver and Ishaan.

Kirrit saw that Ishaan was struggling to keep up and Williver was dragging at him with his free arm. Williver fired up at the archers surrounding them, but as each fell, more replaced them. Kirrit ran into the street, dodging the fallen soldiers, and her vision was blurred by the sudden transition into shadow. She almost tripped before her eyes adjusted to the shade, then she saw the street narrowed ahead and she ran on, glancing over her shoulder to make sure the others had all reached the little street, pacing herself so they could keep up.

The guard reached the street's entrance and began to pour in behind them. The street was thinning into a lane, the backs of the houses turning blind eyes to the chase. Ahead was a corner and Kirrit thought that if they could just stay in front of the guard they might be alright. She dashed towards the corner, hearing Flin and Shaeli panting now behind her.

Around the corner she ran, seeing nothing but the backs of houses before her, and her heart leapt in her chest. They might make it. A scream from behind skidded her to a halt.

She had turned the corner, but the others hadn't.

She went back, and looked around the edge of the building. The others were covered by a thick net, on their knees, struggling. Kirrit looked up, saw soldiers grinning above, looked back and saw the others from the guard were closing on her friends. Flin and Shaeli were firing furiously at the thick ropes that covered them, Ishaan and Williver were hacking at the net. Kirrit ran forward and began pulling at the ropes.

"No, Kirrit," cried Shaeli. "Run. *Run.*"

Kirrit hesitated, looking down at her friend. She took Shaeli's hand through the ropes, squeezed it, and then she turned and ran, back around the corner and down the lane. She looked back only once. Six of the guard had rounded the corner and were racing after her, so she turned forward again and just ran, down the lane, around another corner and then another, and then she saw the end of the streets, the last small houses that had seemed so picturesque on their way into the village. Kirrit kept running.

She looked back again as she left the last houses behind, and saw only two soldiers still following. One, a woman, was flagging, slowing down at the last of the houses, but the other, a man, was closer, and he did not look tired. Kirrit turned her head forward again and ran into the hills.

She followed the road for a while, and then she turned to the right and leapt into the bush. She jumped over tufty grass, dodged trees and pushed through scruffy bushes, running uphill, dragging air into her lungs, pulling herself over rocks and tumbling across thin creeks. She did not know how long she ran, she only knew that she had never run so far, or so fast. For a long time, the soldier behind her kept pace, she could hear his footfalls thudding over the ground, but he did not gain, and at some moment she began to draw ahead and the footfalls began to recede. She dashed around trees, over fallen logs, trying somehow to go in the same direction as the road as the sounds of the soldier following became erratic, and after a while, stopped altogether. Kirrit ran on and still on, and then, finally, she allowed herself to stop.

She leant against a tree, trying to listen to the bush around her above the heaving of her breath. She drew in gulps of air and listened until her heart had returned to something like its normal rhythm. She could hear nothing but a few birds, and she turned to her left and began to trot through the bush, hoping she would come across the road. It took a long time to find it, and when she did, she found that she was high in the hills, for she recognised their own tracks from when they had passed this way that morning and she ran back down the hill, following the tracks made by the carriage. She looked at the sun, and was shocked to see it was low in the sky and ran faster. It seemed to her that she had been running forever when she saw the tracks turn off the road. She pelted around the corner and almost ran straight into Almarnoch.

He was standing at the entrance of the glen and had obviously been looking down the road towards the village. Ezebar was on the far side.

"I knew it," Almarnoch said, as Kirrit pulled up before him, breathing hard. "What's happened?"

"There were guard," she panted. She was a mess, her hair a flaming tangle, dirt and scratches covering her arms and face, her eyes wide and wild. "Scores. They caught the others in a net." Her face crumpled. "Shaeli told me to run, Almarnoch, so I ran, and..." Her voice began to hitch. "And they chased me for the longest time, and then I was right up the hill, and... and... oh, Almarnoch, what are we going to *do*?" She began to cry properly.

"There, lass," he said, putting his arm around her. "Why, we'll go and get them, of course."

"But *how*, Almarnoch?" said Kirrit. "There are so many. I don't know how they knew where we were, but they did. They were *waiting* for us. How did they *find* us?"

"I know not lass," he said. "We shall only deal with things as they are. Releasing Shaeli is paramount." He looked over to where Ezebar was standing beneath the trees. "I shall go down. Stay here with the carriage."

Ezebar looked over his shoulder at the carriage, and then back at Almarnoch.

"I think I best come with you," he said.

"Your place is here, lad," Almarnoch said. He took his staff from where it leant on the log, the same log where they'd left him sitting so peacefully with his pipe.

"Still," Ezebar shrugged. "I'll come just the same. She would want it that way." He looked again at the carriage. "She still sleeps," he said to Kirrit. "Tell her all when she wakes." He walked to the carriage and returned buckling on a short sword. Williver's bow and quiver were over his shoulder. "I'll guess Williver will not mind me borrowing these," he said. "Shall we?"

"Should I come too?" asked Kirrit. "I have my cross-bow."

"No, lass, stay here," said Almarnoch. "But light no fire, and if we are not back by morning, go to meet Tarkoda as planned. You can harness the horses if need be?"

"I think so," she began. "But…"

"There is no time," Almarnoch said. "You will do what is needed, Kirrit. I have the utmost faith in you."

He turned, and he and Ezebar were gone, down the road the others had followed to disaster hours before.

Kirrit turned her face to the dying sun. She sat upon the log recently vacated by Almarnoch, and wrapped her arms around her stomach. Fresh tears began rolling down her cheeks as she rocked herself back and forth.

\* \* \*

The sun set as Almarnoch and Ezebar made their way down to the village. They did not go directly in, but skirted the perimeter, seeing what they could before they ventured further. They crept around until the creek on the far side stopped them, and then they followed its course around the other side.

The village seemed quiet, lights on in only a few of the houses, but as they neared the square, they began to hear the sounds of revelry and see red-tinged light. They crept past a few low warehouses, and then they came to a bridge that crossed the creek. They went beneath it, into dark shadows.

The low bridge over the creek was behind the hut of the landingholder, and they could see the Landing and the square beyond it. The Landing was empty, but the square was full, full of the guard standing around fires that had been set upon the cobblestones. There were tankards in every hand, barrels open and spewing grog beside every fire, and the carcasses of several pigs turned over one of the flames.

It seemed the guard were celebrating and they did not have to ask what they were celebrating. They looked at the roaring fires, the guffawing soldiers, searching for some clue as to where the others were being kept. They stayed in the safety of the shadows beneath the bridge where they could see across the square.

They were about to venture out when footfalls on the bridge made them shrink back under cover. The footsteps were slow, winding across the wooden bridge, and as they crouched in the shadows, the owners of the footsteps began to speak.

There were two of them, a man and a woman. The words they spoke were slurred, but as they came closer, they could tell they were walking close together, and they had been over the bridge in the pursuit of amorous entertainment. They stopped directly above where Almarnoch and Ezebar crouched beneath the bridge. Ezebar could see them through a crack in the palings as they embraced; they were soldiers, and after the embrace they did not go on over the bridge, but stopped to talk.

"I hope we don't have to go back to Palveron," said the woman. "Now that we've caught the fugitives, they're all saying we're going to be sent back."

"You've enjoyed your time here?" said the man.

"You know I have," she answered. There was no talking for a few moments, and then they continued their conversation.

"There *will* be many returned to Palveron," said the man. "But many more will stay in the country to keep the rabble in check." There was a spitting sound. "Murderous scum. Twelve killed today, dozens wounded. The sooner we deal with these rebels, the better."

"What is to be done with them? The ones in the hall."

"Dealt with quickly, is my guess. The one they really wanted is gone."

"The one they took in the carriage this afternoon?"

"Yes," said the man. "The others are of no consequence."

"And the one that escaped? The other girl?"

"She is of even less consequence. As are their other companions, the ones who remained with the carriage they were using."

"But won't they try to rescue the other?"

"They have little chance of that. Once the carriage reaches Mesbottee there will be two companies to escort them to Great Court. We have the others here, and they're not likely to escape, not with that stone and the elf's wand locked in the shopkeeper's safe."

"And how long are we to keep them in the hall?"

"Until the girl has reached Mesbottee. She is the one Queen Virrisian wants, and you know the queen always gets what she wants."

"And then?"

"Then we may do with the others as we wish. The soldiers are unhappy at the loss of their comrades today. I fear what they will do to them will not be pretty."

"Well, these traitors should have thought of that before they joined the rebels," spat the woman.

"Come, let's go find an open barrel," said the man. "My tongue is dry from the work it's done on you this evening."

The woman giggled and the pair stepped off the bridge and went back to the square.

Ezebar stuck out his head and watched them wobble their way around the landingholder's hut and on into the square. He came and squatted before the old Warlock, yet he could see little of him in the deep shadow.

"They are in the Wintering Hall," he whispered.

Almarnoch nodded.

"It will not be easy to release them," Ezebar said.

"We must find their weapons," said Almarnoch. "But more importantly, Shaeli has been taken. Our first thought should be to follow her." His eyebrows folded in upon themselves. "Yet we must free the others." He went and peered out into the night. "There are horses," he said. "They are tied beneath the Landing. One could follow Shaeli more quickly if one had a horse." He peered at Ezebar. "Do you know how to ride, lad?"

Ezebar nodded, but Almarnoch said no more. He merely stood staring across at the square.

"I shall retrieve Flin's stone and Williver's wand," he said, at last. "Then there shall be a diversion. Take this opportunity to take one of the horses from beneath the Landing. Go over this bridge and follow the road to the west. You will come to another road, a wide, well-travelled road from the north, with a large town at the crossroad, Mesbottee. The western road leads inland, between the great forest and Lake Marnis to the city of Marnissi. This is the path they will take."

"You want *me* to follow them?" said Ezebar. "The ones who have taken Shaeli?"

"I do," Almarnoch nodded.

"Alone?"

"Aye, lad," said the Warlock.

"And you'll free the others alone?"

"Yes."

"How?"

"Do not worry about it. It shall be done and we shall follow as quickly as we can. But you heard what they said. Once they reach Mesbottee, they will have more soldiers taking Shaeli to Great Court."

"You think I can free her alone?"

"If the opportunity presents itself, I think you will," Almarnoch said. "But if you cannot, then we cannot free her if we do not know where she is. Look for us at the Landing in Marnissi."

"There will be no meeting at the Landing in Marnissi," said a voice, and a dark figure ducked beneath the bridge.

Ezebar drew his knife, but the figure held out a hand.

"You have no need of weapons, my friend," said the man. "I come to help."

"Who are you?" asked Almarnoch.

"My name is Llok. I am head of the village," the man said. They could see his teeth as he smiled. "I am also the shopkeeper. I'd have come sooner but for those two who stopped to chat on the bridge. Thought they'd never leave." He pulled out a bundle from his jacket. "I believe these belong to your friends," he said, unravelling the bundle. Inside were Williver's wand and Flin's stone. He passed them to Almarnoch.

Almarnoch took the bundle, stared at it, and then rewrapped it. "Why do you do this?" he asked.

"Because they have been in our village for a nigh on a Moon, searching for you. Because they have wreaked havoc upon us, eaten half our livestock, and made our children scared to leave their homes."

"How did they know we would be coming this way?" said Almarnoch.

"They were merely lucky, though their captain planned your capture, should you arrive," said Llok. "Every village along the foothills has soldiers waiting for you. Hundreds wander the hills and the plains in search of you."

"Yet, painful as it may be, having the soldiers here does not *threaten* your village," said Almarnoch. "Yet aiding us will. Why do you take this risk?"

"My wife served your friends today," he said, his voice low. "She wanted to warn them, she feels terrible, but we, the children and I, were upstairs with the queen's soldiers. Two watched her from the shadows. The threat was made perfectly clear to us, to the whole village. We decided that we were going to release your friends ourselves, but then one of my sons saw you down beside the creek, and watched you go beneath the bridge. I knew I should come and tell you of our plan."

"But why?" prodded Almarnoch. "*Why* should you do this?"

"Because *this* time the queen has gone too far," said Llok. "This time she wounds the People too deeply, and this time we will not suffer it."

"What do you mean, *this* time?" said Almarnoch. "What has she done?"

"I told you there would be no meeting at the Landing in Marnissi," he said. "No one meets at Landings this year. There are no Traders. She has sent them all back to their Cave."

Almarnoch said nothing. Ezebar asked the next question.

"When did this happen?" he said, clearly appalled.

"Almost as soon as they appeared," he said. "Why she allowed them to fly into the World at all, I don't know, but within the first Moon, word came to all landingholders that soldiers would arrive to escort the Traders back to Serrat. Oh, it is said the Head Trader agrees with her, but few believe that. We did not see even one Trader and our produce rots in our warehouses."

"And *this* makes you take the risk of freeing our friends?" said Ezebar.

Llok nodded. "We must all do what we can to return our Land to what it was, especially if the rumours of Tenelon's heir are true."

"The rumours are true," said Almarnoch. "This you can believe."

"Then it is worth trying to free your friends," said Llok. "And if our plan works, the risk to the village will not be great." Again they saw his teeth gleam. "Because they'll be blaming you."

"A fair enough exchange," said Ezebar, with a gruff laugh.

"Tell us your plan," said Almarnoch.

Llok told them. They whispered for a long time in the shadows beneath the bridge, and then Llok slipped back out into the night.

"Remember," he whispered as he left. "Wait for a while after we start. They'll be more distracted then."

Ezebar and Almarnoch watched him disappear into the shadows, and then they sat down to wait for something to happen.

* * *

It did not take long. They sat for only a short while, watching the soldiers grow increasingly drunker, before a scream shattered their revelry.

From a building on the left of the square, a woman came running, a huge woman, and behind her enormous bosom there must have been enormous lungs, for her screams rolled easily over the drunken voices of the soldiers. She ran at a surprising speed for all her bulk, shepherding half a dozen small children before her, never stopping the screaming as she ran.

"*Fire*," she was screaming. "*Help*. Fire in the warehouse. Help. *Fire*."

She ran to the well and began pulling the rope of a bell. The bell tolled loudly but its sound was still overshadowed by the woman's screams.

Heads began to turn, shouting ceased, and before the soldiers could react, the villagers began to converge on the square, buckets in hand.

The woman was pointing now, pointing behind the square, still screaming about the fire in the warehouse, and the villagers began to run with their buckets in the direction she was pointing, urging the soldiers to help them. Behind the shops and houses edging the square a red light was growing, and white smoke began to drift into the dark night. The soldiers began to run with the villagers, taking up buckets and empty barrels as they went, stumbling and laughing as they followed the villagers from the square. The landingholder came from his hut, grabbed a bucket from beside his door, and followed the rest.

Few soldiers were left in the square and these moved across to the far side, peering down the street to where the others fought the fire, looking back over their shoulders at the Wintering Hall occasionally.

Down at the edge of the creek, a line of people formed to pass the buckets from the water up the slope, but the edge of the burning warehouse was all Almarnoch and Ezebar could see from their place beneath the bridge.

"Now is our chance, lad," said Almarnoch.

"You're certain this is the best course?" said Ezebar, his face showing his doubt even through the shadows. "If I help you release them, they could also follow Shaeli, and together we could release her."

"But then the guard here will *also* follow. They will see us cross the bridge," said Almarnoch. "One rider I think they'll not worry about. Seeing the others will only bring pursuit." He looked at Ezebar. "And that course would also leave Kirrit and M'zena without protection. 'Tis best we all go to sanctuary and then follow on the Trader."

"You're not concerned the Trader will be stopped?"

"My concern is to reach Shaeli as quickly as possible, beyond that, I know not, but you must go now. If you find no opportunity to release her, do what you can to slow them down. If they reach Marnissi, remember the Proud Pig." Almarnoch grasped his shoulder. "Now, go, and the gods go with you."

Ezebar nodded, and ran crouching from beneath the bridge to the landingholder's hut where a dozen horses stood saddled. He went among them, selected one, and before he left he looked around the edge of the hut at the few soldiers not helping with the fire. Their backs were turned and he went back to the bridge, leading a horse that was as black as the sky. One star blazed on its forehead, and it nickered as he led it down beside the bridge. He thought the creek shallow enough upstream to lead the horse through it, rather than going over the bridge where he would be more easily seen. He looked beneath the bridge, thinking to tell Almarnoch his intentions, but the Warlock was gone.

The creek was as shallow above the bridge as he'd thought, the water not even reaching the tops of his thighs, and when he reached the other side he led the horse into the trees and mounted it out of sight of the village. He patted it and spoke a few quiet words in its ear, and then he dug his heels in and rode into the west.

\* \* \*

# CHAPTER TWELVE

Almarnoch crept around the edge of the Wintering hall. In the distance he could hear the shouts from those who fought the fire, and above the housetops rose its glow, sparks and smoke flying up into the night sky. The shopkeeper had told them that he would rather burn the produce than have it rot in the warehouses, and Almarnoch hoped that they managed to keep it contained to the warehouse.

He went to the back of the Wintering Hall, running his hand along the wood. Three times he walked along the back of the hall, his hand caressing the timber, then he stopped at last near a corner of the building, put one hand against the wood, and closed his eyes. His lips began to move soundlessly, and the end of his staff began to glow.

The timber on which his hand rested began to glow like the fire on the horizon, yet it did not burn. Slowly it began to peel itself away from the timbers around it, its nails making popping sounds as they came free. The timber was wide, and when it had finished peeling itself up and away from his hand, there was a hole large enough for Almarnoch to crawl through.

He stuck his head through the opening and was looking at the three captives, all with eyes wide and turned to him, each tied at hand and foot, each showing some cut or bruise from the struggle that afternoon. Ishaan's eyes were rimmed with grey circles, a clot of blood drying in his hair. Flin sported an eye just beginning to turn black, and Williver had a lump on his forehead, yet each looked at Almarnoch with hope in their eyes. They had spent the afternoon with fear in their hearts and fists upon their bodies, and each now strained at his bonds as Almarnoch crawled through the hole. The old Warlock pulled a knife from his belt and had them free in moments, and then he told them briefly what had happened during their captivity.

"We must follow Ezebar," said Flin.

"No, Flin," said Almarnoch. "They must think they have her safely away. They must think we have gone back into the mountains. We must make it to the sanctuary."

"How do we do that?" asked Ishaan. "Make them think we do *not* follow Shaeli?"

"We let them see us go," said Almarnoch. "We may relieve them of a few of their horses in the process, but we will have them search for us here, in the hills."

He told them his plan and they agreed, though Flin not happily. He wanted to follow Shaeli immediately, but Williver could see the sense in Almarnoch's proposal; sanctuary was not far, they would be much faster in a Trader, and if those who held Shaeli prisoner thought that they were no further threat, then so much the better. They slipped out the hole Almarnoch had made, and crept back around the side of the building.

The redness in the sky had lessened, and they knew the fire was being brought under control. Almarnoch pointed to where the horses where standing, and Williver dashed through the shadows to them. He went among the horses, and for a while they could see nothing of him, and then he came back, leading four horses behind him. They helped Almarnoch into the saddle and then they mounted.

"Ready?" asked Almarnoch. When the others nodded, he held his staff before him and uttered a cry. He dug his heels in and the horse leapt forward.

The others rode behind him, and they did not leave quietly; they thundered across the square and watched with satisfaction as the surprised heads of the soldiers turned to them and shouts went up. When they rode out of the square the rest of the soldiers were running back into it.

The guard shouted amongst themselves, horsemen dashed to their horses. They saw some were missing, and leapt onto the others, and each one fell into a heap as they tried to ride off, courtesy of the severed girths and reins left by Williver.

As the captain of the guard rallied his men to follow the fugitives on foot, the shopkeeper, Llok, came and told him that his safe had been opened and the weapons were gone.

* * *

The four horses galloped up the slope. Almarnoch was sure they would be followed, but he also knew that Williver's handiwork had given them time.

Up the slope and into the hills they pushed the horses, into the copse where they'd left the carriage, to be met by Kirrit's crossbow.

"Stop where you are," she cried, the bow quivering, but aimed squarely at them as they barrelled into the glen, a fierce frown on her face. "Oh, thank goodness," she said, when she saw it was them. She lowered the crossbow, but not the frown. "Where is she?" she demanded. "Where's Shaeli?"

"They have taken her, Kirrit," said Almarnoch. "They have taken her to Mesbottee."

"Well, why are you *here*?" she cried. "Why haven't you gone to save her?"

"All in good time, miss," he said. "For now, we must harness the horses. They will be coming."

"They're already harnessed," Kirrit said. "I saw a fire, a big fire, at the village, and we knew you'd done something. We figured we'd have to leave quickly, so M'zena and I harnessed them."

"Well done," said Almarnoch. "We must go with all speed, then. Where is M'zena?"

"I am here, sir," said M'zena, coming through the gloom, leading the horses and the little carriage. "You've sent my boy into the west," she said, her voice as thick with shadows as dusk.

Almarnoch peered at her. It had not been a question and he knew it, but he gave a nod. "I will tell you everything when we reach sanctuary, but for now we must go," he said. "Williver, take the carriage. Flin, tie his horse to the back. Let's go."

They had to head back down the slope a short distance before they reached the track that would take them into the mountains. They could hear the guard coming up the hill as they turned off into the track. Almarnoch stopped his horse, and waved his staff behind them. Signs of their passage into the thin lane were erased, only the tracks leading back up the mountain marked their passage. They rode into the darkness of the mountains, leaving Ezebar and Shaeli both alone, somewhere to the west.

* * *

There was little moon to guide them along the thin track, and soon they had to slow their pace, trusting the guard would be confused enough by Almarnoch's magic not to find their trail until morning. They planned on being far into the mountains by then.

They stopped only once, just before moonset. Their path went through an avenue of tall trees, the trunks crinkled and silver in the pale moonlight, their tops thick with scented blossoms. At the end of the avenue the track ran through a small creek, and they stopped here to fill their containers. Of the supplies they had bought at the village, only Kirrit's had survived, yet she had bread and fruit, and happily for M'zena, the tezz, and so they had breakfast to look forward to. M'zena insisted on inspecting the wounds of the three captives before they continued, and by the light of a small orb, she looked them over, bathed and dressed their wounds, and peered suspiciously at the grey circles beneath Ishaan's eyes.

"You look unwell, lad," she said.

"I need only a good long swim, that is all," he smiled. "But I thank you for your concern."

"Then we best keep going," M'zena said. "For I think you'll find something to suit you when we reach sanctuary."

They had let the horses drink deeply, and they gathered them from where they cropped at the grass and went on.

Between moonset and sunrise the air grew cold, and Kirrit shared the patchwork quilt with M'zena in the carriage. The going was slow, for it was very dark, but as the sky turned from black to deep blue they began to see something besides the track unrolling before them.

They were in a thick forest, the branches meeting over the top of the track. Here and there they passed one of the trees they had seen in the avenue the night before, the delicate lilac and silver blossoms wafting a light perfume into the sunrise hours. As the day lightened, they could see through the treetops to the mountains around them, and the sounds of the day began to fill the air, soft bird calls and the rustle of small animals in the scrub beside the track. The thick shadows on the tree-filled slopes created sleeping bodies from the hillsides; a bent knee, a curved shoulder, the roundness of a hip and thigh.

They were in a wide valley, and as the sun gave them light, M'zena looked at the landscape around her and seemed content. She had dozed against Kirrit's shoulder through the night, but with the brightness of the sun she seemed alert again. They stopped to rest the horses, ate the bread and fruit, and Flin heated some water so they could have tezz, yet they were all impatient, and soon they went on, following the thin track further into the valley.

As the morning passed, the valley thinned, and the track they had been following became an animal track beside a wide stream. M'zena sat up beside Williver, peering at the way ahead, holding on to the side as the little carriage bounced over the grassy track. Closer and closer drew the hills on either side, wider grew the stream beside them.

As the end of the valley came into sight, M'zena began to smile. The stream they had been following fell from a small waterfall at the valley's end, and on either side, the hills were steep and crowded closely together. The grassy track ended, but M'zena told Williver to drive as close as he could to the waterfall. As they came near, the spray from the little fall blew at their faces, and Ishaan looked at it longingly.

M'zena stood, and raised a hand before her. She was only slightly taller standing than the elf sitting beside her, yet the power that began to emanate from her as she began to chant took everyone but Almarnoch by surprise. He had ridden in the carriage through the morning, giving his horse over to Kirrit, and he looked up at the tiny, chanting woman, his eyes following her every move.

The words she spoke were unrecognisable, yet the magic they created was instantly obvious. The waterfall ahead grew silver, and in front of the carriage the water began to part, the curtain of silver drawn aside by M'zena's magic. Instead of waterfall and stream, the grassy track continued on, beneath, and yet beside the waterfall. Williver clicked to the horses, urging them through the parted water curtain, and the others followed.

Under, yet beside the falls they went, and ahead the grassy track began to wind up, out of sight. Kirrit looked back over her shoulder, expecting to see back down into the valley they had left, but she could see nothing but trees and bushes, she could not even hear the waterfall anymore.

Up the slight rise they went, the track curving to the right around the hillside, and then they came out of the trees onto a wide flat meadow. Far across the meadow there was another waterfall that fell into a willow-lined pool. The water meandered from the pool across the meadow towards them, and disappeared on their left, creating the curtain of falls below.

To the right, across the grassy expanse, rose a cliff of golden stone. At its base, carved into the cliff side, tall columns flanked an arched entrance. They could see other doorways and windows cut into the stone along the base of the cliff, and higher in the golden rock were more windows and jutting balconies. Those who had been to the Drell Mountains recognised the mastery of the rock carvings, yet it was not the carved cliff which set their hearts to racing, but the Trader that was moored before it.

It was moored to a set of posts standing in the ground to one side of the main entrance of the cliff-face castle; posts that looked suspiciously like landing posts. The balloon that had been made from a dozen ruined balloons glittered with a score of colours in the bright sunshine, the doors of the nest were open, and the birds were resting in the shade beneath the Trader. Up on the deck, a few figures stared back at them.

Kirrit whooped, and kicked her horse to one final effort, galloping across the meadow, yahooing and waving. Those on the Trader were scrambling down the ladder, others came from the castle in the cliff, and by the time she'd crossed the meadow they were all gathered to greet her. She threw herself at Cheval and Llianas, hugged Wendll and Blenny, grinned at Spotjaw, Olando and Qiren, and then she found herself in front of Tarkoda.

"Never thought I'd be this happy to see you," she said, as dry as elven toast.

"I'm inclined to agree with you," said Tarkoda, his tone equally crusty. "For once."

They looked at each other for a moment, and then he pulled her into his arms and kissed the top of her head. When he let her go, Kirrit's eyes were overly bright with held tears and she was blinking hard.

The others had come more slowly across the meadow, and as they reached the Trader, Spotjaw and Olando moved to take the horse's heads.

There was a flurry of greetings. There was much hugging and kissing, and Llianas leapt at Williver as he climbed from the carriage.

"They let me *come*," she cried. "They let me come."

"So I see," Williver smiled.

He hugged her, greeted the others, and then turned to help M'zena down from her perch on the driver's seat. Almarnoch had been the only one to come from inside the carriage. Tarkoda frowned.

"Where's Shaeli?" he asked.

"We have bad tidings," said Almarnoch. "We have much to tell and much to hear, yet we have introductions to be made, horses to be unharnessed, and bellies to fill. I trust you have supplies?"

"Yes, we were well stocked by the elves at Lythnori," said Koda. "We were just going to eat in the drell castle."

"A wondrous place it is," said Olando. "You had no trouble finding it?" he asked Williver. "Even from the air, Blenny had to guide us in. It was unseen until we were within it."

"It was not I who showed us the way in," said Williver. "The valley below I knew held the way to a sanctuary, but it was M'zena who brought us here."

He looked down at the old woman, smiling, and she took the smile from his face and gave it to Blenny.

"Long Moons have passed since I was here," she said. "Yet my friends made sure I would not forget the way, if I should ever have need of sanctuary."

"My mother sends her greetings, M'zena," said Blenny, coming forward to take the old woman's hands. "She saw in the smoke that we would meet here."

They all blinked at the familiar greeting. Almarnoch frowned.

"It seems we have much to discuss, indeed," he said. "Let us release the horses, and go into the castle."

The horses were quickly unsaddled, and they left them to crop the grass. Blenny assured them they would not stray from the meadow, and then he led the way to the golden cliff. The Zoi watched lazily from the shade beneath the Trader as the group disappeared inside the shadows.

Inside, the carved cliff was even more magnificent than outside. It was cool, and dim, but as their eyes adjusted, the true wonder of the place was revealed. They were in a wide hall, arched doorways leading from it in several places. Grand statues circled the room, and the ceiling was covered with stone leaves and vines. Broad stairs led up on either side of the hall.

They followed Tarkoda up the stairs on their left, windows carved into the outside wall lighting the way. They came out in a room with a balcony cut through the cliff, letting in the brightness of the day. It was not a large room, but in the centre a magnificent table grew from the rock floor in curved vine-like tendrils, mimicking the carvings on the ceiling of the hall below, and on the table was laid a cloth and platters of food. Benches studded the walls and low stools grew around the table, carved faces smiled from depressions in every wall. The railings of the balcony were thick and round, and from its lofty heights they looked down over the Trader and the meadow. Blenny showed them where water came from a tap which filled a bowl against the wall, and when they had washed, he jiggled something near the floor and the water drained away.

Ishaan looked down at the willow-lined pool below the falls across the meadow, and Cheval promised to take him down as soon as they'd eaten. He turned reluctantly from the balcony and joined the others at the table.

Tarkoda told them briefly of the Trader's journey across the mountains – leaving out the times they'd come so close to disaster – and their eventual arrival at Lythnori. Almarnoch was most interested in the fallen tunnel with the broken statue of the Zoi flanking it that they had seen on the north side of Mount Zerrinius. He heard what had transpired at Lythnori, and nodded his approval, and then he asked how long they had been at the sanctuary.

"We arrived only yesterday," Tarkoda said. "We were worried that something had happened when you weren't here."

"So it had," said Almarnoch, and he told them of what had transpired in the village.

Flin, his eyes on the Warlock, but his mind on Shaeli, did not think to mention who had been leading the guard that had captured them.

"We must fly, then," said Tarkoda. "I can have the Zoi ready as soon as we've eaten and Ishaan has immersed himself."

"We cannot be hasty," said Almarnoch. "For there is more." He looked steadily at Tarkoda. "Traders do not fly the skies of Zirrus this year."

He told them then what he'd learnt from the shopkeeper in the village, and the more he spoke the angrier Tarkoda became. After he'd vented his anger at the queen, he began to review ways and routes and villages, to plan how they could avoid the guard.

Almarnoch turned to M'zena. "Now comes the time for you to tell us how you know this place," he said. "'Tis clear you have met Blenny before."

"That is so," she said. "His mother and I met when I was a younger woman." She smiled. "A much younger woman. I was travelling near the Drell Mountains, and we chanced upon each other. We have been friends ever since."

Blenny looked at her and smiled. "What she does not tell you is that she saved my mother's life," he said. "My mother had journeyed into the mountains to find an obscure herb and she was attacked by three hunters who thought to add a drell to their catch. M'zena fought them off. Killed one, my mother said, and wounded the others, then she put my mother, who was also wounded, onto her horse and took her home."

They all looked at the tiny old woman and tried to imagine her fighting off three hunters.

"The dragon gates are a glorious sight," said M'zena, studiously ignoring their amazed looks. "The city is a place I shall never forget." She picked up a cup. "Is there any tezz?" she asked.

Llianas stood, her brown eyes filled with wonder. "I'll make you some," she said. "Qiren will you light the brazier for me?"

Qiren lit a small brazier filled with fire-rocks and Llianas set the water to boil. She came back to the table, the wonder still plain on her face.

"Why were you there?" she asked M'zena. "In the mountains. Were you all alone?"

"Yes, lass," said M'zena. "I just thought I'd go for a ride, you know, to have a look."

"And you could ride a horse?"

M'zena laugh tinkled through the room. "Yes, child. As I said, I was much younger then," she laughed. "It was more Winterings ago than I care to think about, but yes, back then I loved to ride. I spent many Winterings exploring the Lands with my horse. Shadow and I went everywhere, and on one journey, Blenny's dear mother brought me here. There were still drell living here then, but few, and it was not long afterwards we escorted them back to the mountains."

"We hoped one day to be able to journey here once more," said Blenny. "Perhaps even live here again."

"It has been long Winterings since drell lived here," said Williver. He looked at M'zena. "Many Winterings."

"So it has," said Blenny.

They all looked at M'zena. M'zena looked at Llianas.

"Is that tezz ready yet?" she said.

Llianas jumped up and hurried to mix the tezz. She brought the pot back to the table, so she did not miss anything.

"May I ask, where did you go after you had visited the city of the drell?" asked Almarnoch.

M'zena looked at him. It was a sly look. "Why do you ask?" she said.

"Because Blenny may not be the only one to have met you before," said the High Warlock.

M'zena clapped her hands like a girl. She sounded like one when she spoke. "You remember," she cried.

"Yes," said Almarnoch. "Yes, I think I do."

There was silence in the room. They all looked from Almarnoch's amazed face to M'zena's triumphant one.

"You were such an eager young lad," she said.

Kirrit and Tarkoda looked at each other, both unable to imagine the High Warlock as either eager *or* a young lad.

"I *cannot* believe it is you," said Almarnoch. "It is fifty, *two* and fifty, years since my first year in Palveron."

"Your memory for the year is probably better than mine," grinned M'zena. "'Twas a few lifetimes ago."

"But she was..." Almarnoch corrected himself. "If it *was* you, then you were already..." He stopped. "I'm sorry, I don't want to appear ill-mannered, but..."

M'zena cackled. "But even then I had seen many Winterings?" she asked.

Almarnoch nodded. "Forgive me, but yes. The woman I met at Great Court had seen at least fifty Winters, her hair was white at the temples and her face was lined. And yet..." Almarnoch looked at her. "And yet, your voice has the same quality. I have never heard another like it. *And* she was also of the Irikai. Other things, too, that you have done on our journey, a gesture, a saying; these things have had me in mind of her *before* I heard what you had done for Blenny's mother."

The others were all leaning forward. Kirrit was thinking that the two people who would be the most curious to hear this conversation were not here, and her mind wandered for a moment, wondering about them, worrying about them, and then she turned her mind back so she could tell Shaeli everything later.

"I was more passionate, then," M'zena was saying. "And I had more energy." She laughed again. "I was taller, too."

"Yet if it *was* you," said Almarnoch. "And you had *then* seen more than fifty Winters, then now, *now* you must have seen a hundred Winterings."

The amazed eyes turned again to M'zena did not seem to bother her. She shrugged and smiled that sly little smile.

"Something like that," she said. "I pay little attention."

Kirrit asked the question that Shaeli would have. "How did you meet?" she asked. "Tell us."

"I was, as M'zena said, a young lad," said Almarnoch. "I had just arrived from Cave. Taffka's grandfather brought me on Golden Eagle."

Tarkoda and Kirrit looked at each other again, unable to imagine a time so far removed from their own.

"I had just had my Cave year," Almarnoch continued. "The Cave Warlocks had determined I had some ability, and they had sent me to be trained in Palveron. They thought I should be apprenticed on the Warlock Island, instead of staying at Cave with them. Teff, Taffka's grandfather, took me to Great Court to ask I be considered."

"I thought Warlocks spent only their final year at the Island of Warlocks?" said Flin.

"Most do," replied Almarnoch. "But every year, six are taken as apprentices to the Warlocks on the Island itself. Many apply, and I was fortunate enough to be successful. I spent the next thirty Winterings on the Island." Almarnoch paused a moment, his eyes back in that far-off time. "Yet it was on that first day at Great Court that I happened to meet M'zena," he continued. "Teff had seen the king, old King Tenelon's father, King Tarkon, and introduced me. I was so nervous I could barely utter a word, but I remember the king was very kind, and he allowed me to apply to the Warlocks. In those days, one had to seek permission for every Warlock apprenticeship, because some years before there had been trouble with a few rogue Warlocks thinking they knew more than the king. There was some kind of uprising, here and on Wokk, and the law had been enacted to ensure against such a thing happening again. That was in Tarkon's father's time, and of course, that is no longer the case, the law was repealed when Tenelon took the throne." He cleared his throat. "Anyway, we had just been dismissed from Court, and were about to leave the hall, when a small woman, one of the Irikai, stormed into the king's presence. She stalked straight past Teff and I, two courtiers trailing her saying she would have to wait her turn. The woman replied that what she had to say could *not* wait, and the king must hear her at once."

Almarnoch looked at M'zena. She seemed to be enjoying the retelling.

"I told you I had more energy then," she said. She grinned and Almarnoch shook his head at her. She cackled and waved a hand at him. "Go on," she said.

"The king smiled, and bid her speak," continued Almarnoch. "We did not leave the hall. Teff was as interested as I in who she was and what was so important she would enter the court in such a manner. 'I come to speak for the drell,' the woman cried. She told of coming across three hunters after a single female drell. Those she had taught a lesson, she said, but she wanted…" Here Almarnoch chuckled. "She practically *demanded* that King Tarkon outlaw the hunting of drell, then and there, on pain of death. It had been frowned upon by most for many Winterings, yet there are always those whose hearts hold little compassion, who hunt for the meanness of sport instead of the need to eat. The king agreed with the woman's… let us call it a request, and it was so. The hunting of drell has been outlawed since that day."

"Not quickly enough to save this place from being abandoned," said M'zena. "But a step forward."

"When she left the court, as swiftly as she had entered it, Teff followed her," Almarnoch said. "Outside the castle we spoke to her, and Teff offered her lodgings on the Trader, for he had a great interest in drell."

"A fine man," nodded M'zena. "Many a talk did we have, and many I had with the young apprentice also, in the few days I spent with them on the Trader in Palveron." She smiled that sly little smile.

Almarnoch shook his head. "I still barely believe it is you, yet now, I do not know how I did not see it at once."

M'zena cackled again. "We are both much changed, young Warlock," she said. "Now I have finished the tezz and we have told enough tales. 'Tis time to take our friend for a swim."

Ishaan looked at her gratefully. He had not wanted to miss anything, yet his eyes were rimmed with dark circles and his movements were slow.

They gathered the remaining food and put it away. Spotjaw shook the cloth and they took everything back down the stairs. They realised how hot it was when they came from the cool shadows of the cliff castle. The meadow faced the north, the sun was not even halfway down the sky, and the afternoon was very warm. Spring was passing, and soon would begin the long hot days of the summer.

"When shall I ready the Trader?" Tarkoda asked Almarnoch, as they walked out into the bright afternoon.

"The day will be gone before long," said Almarnoch. "And there are too many mountains to traverse before we reach the safety of the plains. We cannot fly the Trader through them at night. The sunrise hours will be best, I believe. It will give the birds more time to rest, for once we lift, we don't know when we'll be able to land again. How have you found your new Fleet members?"

"The others have done well," said Koda. "Most lifts and landings were made without too much trouble, but it will be good to have two born traders on the ship with me. You and Kirrit." He looked across to where Kirrit walked with Llianas.

"Kirrit's experience with a Trader is not the only reason you are happy to have her on board," Almarnoch smiled.

Tarkoda looked back at him, alarm etched plainly on his face. "Well, no," he said, far too quickly. "I mean I *like* Kirrit, but she... I mean she's... I think that I..."

"Don't worry, lad," said Almarnoch. "I'll not tell a soul. But just so you know, she feels the same. Kirrit has ever blustered at those she loves best."

Tarkoda opened his mouth, but nothing came out, so he closed it again. The tips of his ears had gone pink, and he sought for something else to talk of.

They had almost reached the falls and the pool that had formed not far from it. The willow trees surrounding the pool were thick with new leaves, and dragonflies buzzed across the surface, and the water was incredibly clear, a few fish swimming lazily against the current.

Tarkoda was saved from thinking of something to say as they reached the pool, and they all began to remove their outer clothes. Ishaan had his off before they were halfway across the meadow, and he had disappeared beneath the water before most of them had even reached the pool. They could see him moving slowly through the crystal water beside the startled fish. Even Almarnoch was removing his robe in order to wash, and Tarkoda took off his shirt and dived into the water. He didn't notice Kirrit watching him as he did, though of course Almarnoch did. When Almarnoch looked away, M'zena caught his eye and winked, and he knew that she also saw the current moving under the surface between the two young traders.

Tarkoda swam across the pool, and then rolled over on his back and swam lazily across to where Flin sat on a rock, inspecting a large bruise on his ribs.

"The one on your eye is a better colour," said Tarkoda as he swam up.

Flin smiled. "We gave as much as we received," he said.

"You have always been generous," Koda smiled back, and then his face grew serious. "Shaeli was not harmed in the scuffle?"

"I think not," said Flin. "They were careful with *her*. She managed a few good kicks after she'd..." He stopped, and his face paled behind the purple bruise.

"What is it, Flin?" said Tarkoda. "What's the matter?"

But Flin was scanning the pool. He saw Kirrit and called to her, ignoring Tarkoda's questions. Kirrit swam over, her stroke long and clean, and she was smiling until she saw the look on Flin's face.

"What's the matter?" she said, echoing Tarkoda's question.

"When we were caught in the net, Shaeli told you to run," Flin said, taking her hand.

Kirrit nodded. "Yes. I ran. I couldn't help."

Flin nodded.

Almarnoch moved closer to them.

"I know," said Flin. "But, did anyone follow you?"

Kirrit nodded again. "A few of the guard, yes, but I lost them."

Flin looked for Williver and called him over, too, and then he turned back to Kirrit.

"And nothing, no one else followed you?"

"No, Flin. Why?" Kirrit said.

The others were all looking at them now, listening.

Flin looked at Williver, and then took a deep breath. "When they came, when they were taking the net off, Shaeli did one thing before they grabbed her arms," Flin said. The bruise around his eye cut stark lines against his pale face. "She threw Ebony towards the lane where Kirrit had gone. She threw her and she told her to run, to run and find Kirrit."

Williver stared back at Flin and then he slowly nodded. They both looked at Kirrit.

Her face grew as pale as Flin's. "She never came," Kirrit whispered. "Ebony never came."

\* \* \*

# CHAPTER THIRTEEN

At first, Shaeli didn't know what had hit her. One moment they were running along the thin lane, the guard almost on their heels, the next she was falling, thick ropes thudding against her head, her shoulders, pinning her limbs so she could not even put out her arms to save herself. They fell in a heap, thudding into the cobblestones, Flin still clutching one of her arms, Williver and Ishaan on top of them, all of them struggling against the thick rope. She began firing at the bonds that held her arms, at the soldiers now almost upon them. She saw Kirrit hesitating at the corner of the lane, then she ran back and began tugging at the net.

"No," Shaeli said. "Run, Kirrit. *Run.*"

Kirrit had looked at her, anguish bare on her face, but she stopped pulling at the ropes, squeezed Shaeli's hand, and she ran.

Shaeli watched her bolt around the corner, and then she turned her attention to the tangle of net around her and the soldiers who had reached them. Some of the soldiers thudded past and continued on up the lane and around the corner in pursuit of Kirrit, and here was the only glimmer of light in the darkly disastrous day. Shaeli knew Kirrit would outrun them.

She managed to wound two before they overcame her by sheer numbers. A squat, lumpy man held her wrist while another wrenched the stone from her hand, even as she fired a final bolt. One of the grinning soldiers above fell onto the cobblestones, grinning no longer. Before she had time to think, another soldier had pulled her amulet through the net, cut her belt, and pulled the pouch free. She was immediately struck with a sense of loss, for the amulet Eenis had made for her, and the stones within it.

Flin, Williver and Ishaan had the same experience, yet the soldiers who took their weapons were not as gentle as those who took Shaeli's stones.

The soldiers began to untangle the net that bound them. Williver came first, his arms pinned by two soldiers, another holding a sword to his throat. Ishaan was pulled out next, a struggling Flin behind him, but he was quickly subdued with a blow to the head. As the last of the net was pulled off Shaeli, she managed to free a hand. Ebony had lain curled in her shirt during the chase, but now she pulled her out and flung her towards the corner where Kirrit had gone.

The jevvi sailed between the soldiers, arms and legs splayed wide.

"Find Kirrit, Eb," she yelled. "Run to Kirrit."

A few of the soldiers grabbed at her, but Ebony easily evaded them. She scurried around the corner, looking back once at her mistress, and then she was gone.

"Leave it," yelled one of the soldiers. "It matters not."

Shaeli managed a few well-placed kicks as they pulled her up. One kick she aimed at the soldier who held her amulet, and the place in which she kicked him caused him to double over. He dropped the amulet and clutched his belly, his face going satisfactorily crimson. Some of her stones rolled out onto the cobbles.

Another soldier, the one who had yelled at the others to leave Ebony, picked up the stones and put them back in the pouch. He came to stand before Shaeli, and her eyes widened when she realised she had seen this man before. It was the ginger-haired man with the secretive eyes who had smiled at her so sickeningly in the tavern of Borsal and Dorkit; the one who had later used a child as leverage and killed Borsal.

His face was pale and showed the scars of old pock-marks. His ginger hair was thin and greasy, his lips almost non-existent. He grabbed Shaeli's face, the fingers and thumb digging into her cheeks, and he leant in so close that his nose almost touched hers. His eyes held little colour and less feeling.

"I would not do that again, if I were you," he said. His breath smelt of old ale and dead smoke. He pushed at her face and released her, and she did not need to see her face to know his fingers had left red marks behind. Her cheeks burned where he had touched them. "Take them to the hall," he yelled. "The captain will be pleased with your efforts this day. You have earned your reward, and there shall be barrels to thank you later."

There was a rousing cry, and the four of them were pushed back down the lane. The backs of the houses were still blind to them. Or so it seemed.

Back into the square they went, surrounded by soldiers who shoved them at every step. The basket of eggs Kirrit had dropped lay on its side, the eggs broken and trampled into the stones. As they were led into the Wintering Hall, Shaeli saw the woman from the shop standing in the shadows of the doorway across the square, her hands clutched together. Shaeli smiled grimly at her as she was thrust up the steps into the hall.

It was dim inside, and as their eyes adjusted they could see a Wintering Hall much like other halls across Zirrus; several wide fireplaces, the centre of the hall open, the edges containing smaller rooms. The fireplaces were empty, all but one swept clean, bedrolls were stacked through the open doorway of one room, but in others there were the packs and possessions of the queen's guard. The one fireplace not empty was surrounded by the soldiers' cooking equipment and the rubble they'd left scattered around it. It appeared they had been there for some time, for there was a large pile of rubbish in one corner and the walls were marked with the slashes of swords and the puncture marks left by arrows, as if they had used the hall for training and games of marksmanship.

Past the soldier's dishevelled camp they were taken to a room at the back. Inside was the last person Shaeli expected to see, but it was Flin who reacted first. As they entered, the captain of the guard turned around.

"*Pizar?*" sputtered Flin. "*You?*" He squirmed in the grip of the soldiers who held him. "Tell them to release us. You know we have done no wrong."

The young man who had befriended Shaeli during the last Winterings, the pleasant young guardsman who had smiled so charmingly at Arinola's ball, now smiled in a completely different way.

"I know nothing of the sort," Pizar said, the not-at-all-charming smile planted firmly on his face. "I have my orders, and I am pleased to be able to fulfil them." He looked at his men. "Take these three into the next room and bind them well. Bring me their packs. In a few days you may do with them as you please. Your queen has no use for them. And ready the carriage, I want to be out of this pitiful village before the midday hours pass."

Flin, Williver and Ishaan were pulled from the room, all three struggling and shouting. Shaeli struggled too, realising she was to be separated from them. If she was not frightened before, she was now. She was instantly and horribly aware of just what had happened. She looked at Pizar, tears standing in her eyes.

"Please," she said. "*Please*, Pizar. I thought we were friends. I thought you knew…"

Pizar looked back at her with no trace of sympathy. "Knew what?" he said, a sneer curdling the charmless smile. "Knew that you were conspiring against the queen? Plotting to overthrow the throne? Aiding rebels? Oh, yes, Shaeli, I knew all this and more."

"But those things aren't *true*," she cried. "Pizar, you *know* me. We spent so much time together."

"I would not have attended that old woman's parties by choice, Shaeli," he said, the awful smile finally gone. "I was there for a reason."

She looked at him, and in his cold stare she saw the truth. "You were... *spying* on us? Pretending?"

"I was doing what I was ordered to do," he shrugged. "What I had to do. None of it actually *meant* anything to me. Becoming your new and charming friend was my duty. Nothing more." He barked a laugh at the look on her face. "My cousin is master-at-arms to the queen. Sir Azeron of Maxx. 'Twas his idea. Our good queen does not trust the Traders, your family in particular, and it seems with good reason. There were several things of interest to her and my cousin, and the things I discovered have been put to good use. You and your friends, others too, spoke far too freely. I merely had to listen. Even when the inn was attacked, when that man was killed, it was all under my orders, yet it was too easy to make you think it wasn't my fault."

She closed her eyes against his betrayal, holding back the tears which burned her eyelids. The knowledge that he had duped them all, that Borsal had been killed and Dorkit driven mad by her husband's death was due to him, was a devastating blow and added to the burden of guilt she felt for so many things.

Others came back into the room, and she opened her eyes to see them dumping the familiar packs on the floor. Pizar came and took her pack too, and then one by one he upended them on the floor and inspected the contents. The supplies they had purchased at the little shop were thrown to the soldiers, their other meagre possessions kicked aside.

"Where are the others?" Pizar asked.

"Others?" Shaeli said, trying to look surprised at his question. "What others?"

"You travel with an old couple in a carriage," said Pizar. At the look on Shaeli's face, he gave another short laugh. It was nothing like the light, pleasant laugh he'd used at Arinola's. "You were seen when you reached Zirrus. The owner of the Smoking Fish was unwilling, at first, to tell us what we wished to know. But after some... shall we say, persuasion, his wife was more than willing to speak for him. She told us there were three men, two young ladies, and an old couple in a carriage, and which direction you went. She was *most* helpful. The foothills are filled with soldiers who have waited for you to poke your noses back out of the forest. I am fortunate indeed that I was the one to capture you. Now, do not make me ask you again. Where are the others?"

"There *are* no others," Shaeli said, thinking as quickly as her terrified mind would allow. "There's only the five of us. The old couple stopped a few days ago, at their farm. You have the three men, and Kirrit ran. The old people, they were only helping us, giving us a lift in their carriage. We've been walking for two days."

It was all she could think of to say. Though there were four men with her, if the poor landlady at the Smoking Fish had told Pizar three, she would not correct the assumption.

"If this is the truth, it matters not," sneered Pizar. "My soldiers will search the hills tomorrow. If the carriage is found, the old ones will be thankful they have already lived their lives. Kirrit will be found too, though she may live longer than the others." He chuckled humourlessly. "I think she will make fine sport for the men."

Shaeli's face grew even paler, and Pizar laughed that short, ugly laugh again.

"Be thankful that *you* are wanted by the queen," he said, putting his face close to hers. "Or you'd find *yourself* as entertainment."

Shaeli recoiled and the soldiers in the room guffawed at her. Pizar laughed with them.

"Tie her to the chair and ready the carriage," he said. "Deal with the other three in a few days. You may reward the soldiers for their work this day, and at first light search the hills for the carriage. Two old people and a frightened girl will not go far."

He stalked out of the room and Shaeli was pushed into a chair and bound to it hand and foot. As the still-laughing soldiers left the room, she could see the others out in the hall going through packs, fighting over the contents that were being pulled out. Shaeli realised it was the packs of their dead companions that the soldiers were fighting over, and she turned her head from the sight, disgusted.

She looked at their own belongings strewn across the floor, and this time she could not stop the tears from coming. They rolled down her face and she could not even wipe them from her cheeks, yet she did not let herself cry for long. She lifted her chin and looked back out at the guard.

Two women were fighting over a pair of boots. A few men watched, amused as the women tussled. Others were eating the supplies that had been pulled from the packs, and still more were rolling barrels from one of the rooms. The barrels were rolled out the door and carried down into the square where others of the guard were piling branches in several spots on the cobblestones.

As she watched, Pizar came back up the steps, followed by a small man with thinning hair and a meek, nervous manner. Pizar walked through the hall, and Shaeli averted her eyes from him as he reached the door, yet he did not come into the room. He went past, and stopped just outside the door where she could not see him.

The nervous man stopped behind him, in the open doorway. Shaeli kept her head down, but she looked sideways at the man. He glanced at her as she peered through the curtain of her hair, and she was instantly puzzled. His manner seemed nervous, his voice trembling as he spoke to Pizar, yet the eyes he turned to Shaeli were neither nervous nor meek. They were filled with a steely determination.

"The weapons shall be in my safe for *how* long?" the little man was saying as he looked at Shaeli with those determined eyes.

"Until my soldiers have finished their business," Pizar said from somewhere out of sight. "A few days, and they will follow me to Palveron. I know you'll be sorry they leave so soon."

"Oh, in*deed*," said the little man. "It has been an *honour* to serve the queen."

"I'm sure," replied Pizar's voice. It was riddled with sarcasm.

"It is only that those strange weapons make me so nervous," said the man. "The elven one in particular." *Elven* came out with a little squeak.

"A few days only, Llok, as I said." Pizar's voice held less than a shred of patience.

"Of course, of course," was the creeping reply from the man, Llok. "One more thing only, my good captain."

"What?"

"It seems your people, well, they appear to be stacking wood for a few fires in the square," said Llok.

"I have given my permission for them to reward themselves," said Pizar. "You will accommodate them in all they ask, as the queen requires."

"Yes, yes, of course," said Llok. "But, I'm sorry, the fires. They could be of concern. To the village."

"They will be fine," answered Pizar, clearly impatient. "I do not wish to be bothered with such things. You have done as I wished thus far, do not risk my ire now."

"No. No, of course. My apologies," said Llok, his voice a squeak again. He gave a little bow, and apologised again.

"Enough of your whimpering, Llok," said Pizar. "Leave me."

"Yes, captain, I'm sorry," said the man.

He bobbed in that funny way again, and before he turned and left, he glanced at Shaeli. This time she was sure of the steel in his eye, and she watched as he went back down the hall, wincing at the calls and missiles hurled by the soldiers. He did not look back before he fled the hall.

The fight over the boots was finished now, the winner trying the boots on for size, the loser sporting a bruise on her cheekbone for her efforts. The others were starting to move out into the square, and through the door she could see some of the barrels were already being opened. Her view was blocked as someone came through the door, a tall man, a soldier who came straight to Pizar. He dropped his head to Pizar, who still stood out of Shaeli's sight somewhere to the left.

"I lost her," said the tall soldier. His hair was damp with sweat, and there was a long scratch down one cheek. He had a whip coiled at his belt and he ran his fingers over it. He had once used that whip on the husband of a young woman named Kora, as an inducement for Kora to remove her clothing as her home burned and her mother ran screaming into the trees. His sport had been stopped by two burly men who'd protested at the treatment of the family whose land was wanted for a new outpost. His captain, Pizar, had let the men take the family and ended the fun. He looked forward to trying his skills with the whip on the redhead who had escaped him this day. "She took to the trees."

"Very well," said Pizar. "Make sure you look thoroughly tomorrow."

"Oh, I will," replied the soldier. "I most *surely* will. I dislike losing such a prize."

"See that you find her then," said Pizar, and the man bowed again and went back out into the square, his fingers still caressing the whip.

Shaeli's heart did a little jig. Kirrit had escaped. That, at least, was something, yet she had little time to rejoice. Pizar came back into the room, dropping a pack at the doorway. He untied her, and pulled her roughly to her feet. Her wrists and ankles were numb from the thick rope and she stumbled as he picked up his pack and pulled her through the hall. The few soldiers still inside laughed at her as she was pulled through the room. One, the woman with bruise on her face from the fight over the boots, put out a foot to try and trip her as she passed. Shaeli looked back over her shoulder, hoping to see something of Flin or Ishaan or Williver, but only the woman with the bruised face followed her out the door. Whatever room the others were in had its door closed to her, and she walked out into the square without the sight of a friendly face to accompany her.

Across the square to the Landing she was led, and behind the landingholder's hut. Here waited a squat, ugly carriage and at least a dozen horsemen, already mounted and obviously ready to ride, one of them the ginger-haired man with the pock-scarred face. Shaeli began to tremble as she came closer, began to pull at the tight grip around her wrist, but Pizar pulled her on. There were other horses tethered near the carriage, but it seemed only those already mounted were to accompany them. Pizar led her to the carriage, Shaeli pulling and struggling as she went, but it was useless. Before he pushed her up into the carriage she took one last look at the village that had been their undoing. The square was now filled with the guard, each of them with their hand filled with a mug of the village's ale. They were rowdily cheering her departure.

There was only one of the villagers who she could see. It was the little man with the nervous manner and steely eyes who had been in the hall. Llok. He was looking down from a window above the shop where they had bought their supplies, yet she had only a glimpse of him before Pizar pushed her into the carriage and shut the door. She was instantly plunged into deep gloom. She heard the thud as the bolt was slammed into place.

The carriage was small, little more than a wooden box. The only light came from a slatted window in the door and another tiny slit in the back of the carriage. Apart from these, there was nothing. No bench, no cushion, nothing.

She heard Pizar congratulate his soldiers. She heard him urge them to fulfil their duty on the morrow. She heard their resounding cry in answer, and then the carriage jerked forward. She looked through the slits in the doorway and watched the hall containing her bruised and bound friends move out of sight. They went over a wooden bridge, and then she could see nothing but hills and trees and the soldiers who rode beside her.

Shaeli sat on the floor in a corner and pulled up her knees. She wrapped her arms around her legs, dropped her head onto them, and gave herself up to despair.

\* \* \*

As Pizar was congratulating his troops, as they cheered him with full mugs, no one noticed the little figure scuttle between the horse's hoofs and disappear beneath the carriage.

\* \* \*

It was hard to tell what hour of the day it was. The gloom in the carriage made it impossible to tell if the day was almost over or if the afternoon was stretching as interminably as it seemed. Shaeli felt sick and bruised all over from the constant bumping, and she could not remember the last time she'd had a drink. She could see her water bottle on the floor back at the hall with her other belongings, and she knew it had been at least half full. As many times as she turned her thoughts from it, her dry mouth returned her mind to it.

She had alternated between sitting hunched in the corner, and standing near the door, clutching the slats to stop from falling over. Pizar kept his soldiers moving at a brisk pace through the afternoon, and when they finally stopped, she wasn't sure if she was relieved or not. There were the sounds of the soldiers talking, but they were somewhere in front of the carriage, and all she could see through the slats was the side of the road and the hills. Eventually, someone came and opened the door. It was the pock-faced soldier with the thin ginger hair, accompanied by the woman who had lost the fight over the boots. They would come for her many times on this awful journey, these two, but she would never know either of their names; they would only ever be the pock-faced man and the woman with the bruised face.

The man bound her hands together and tethered her to a rope. Leering, he pulled her off the side of the road and gestured to a clump of bushes.

"Do your business, if you have any," he said, the sneer and colourless eyes even more revolting than they had been back at the square.

He laughed at the look on her face, the woman with the bruised face and blackening eye grinning beside him.

Shaeli thought. She decided a disgusting escort was better than hours of discomfort, and she did not know when she would have the opportunity again, so she completed her "business" with her back turned and her cloak placed as widely as possible. She was hampered by the ropes around her wrists, and she had barely finished when he was tugging on the rope and pulling her back out.

They were stopped in the middle of the road, the soldiers eating as they stood beside their horses. The sun was low in the west and thunderclouds studded the sky to the north-east. As they pushed her back into the box of carriage, she knew it would be dark soon and her misery was to be accompanied by a storm. It was fitting that the god of storms, U'ee, was also the god of change. Everything had changed this day.

Before the door clanged shut, they threw in a small water bottle and a square of hard bread, and at least there was relief for her body, if she could find none for her heart.

She nibbled at the bread, and though she wanted to drink all the water, she made herself drink only half, saving the rest for later, for she could not know when they would next give her something. She sat down in her corner again, holding onto whatever she could to stop herself from being thrown all over the carriage as the time passed and the light diminished to almost nothing. She heard the rumble of thunder close by, and her trader's nose told her it would rain before long. When at last she was bouncing along in full darkness, the storm began, and at least she could be glad that she was sheltered from the rain, for the soldiers accompanying her must have been truly uncomfortable. The air was shattered by lightning bolts with unnerving regularity, and it was the only time she could see, when the white-blue light flickered outside the box. As the evening hours and the storm passed they went on and Shaeli dozed in her corner, yet she could find no comfort and was forced awake each time she drifted off by some bump in the road or too-close thunderclap.

It must have been somewhere near the midnight hours when they stopped. She was again led into the scrub, the leaves dripping with the end of the storm, and then she was put back into the carriage. The soldiers were unsaddling their horses, pulling cloaks around shoulders as they found some tree to lean against, and Shaeli knew that she would be the only one dry this night. When the door was closed upon her again, she pulled her cloak around her, curled up on the hard floor, and slept as if she was in her own bed on Purple Leaf.

\* \* \*

She woke to the sound of the bolt being pulled, and she sat up as the door swung open. She blinked in the sudden light and pulled herself upright. Outside stood the pock-faced man and the woman whose bruised face and eye was now turning a dull purple, the eyelid thick and red around the puckered eye. Shaeli was pulled outside, the rope was tied to her hands again, and for the third time she was led into the scrub.

The dawn light was thin around her, the trees dripped with the rain that had fallen, and her escorts seemed none too thrilled with their duties, for there was no leering, no jokes at her expense, and the hands that pulled at her bindings were rougher, the hands gripping her arms left bruises to add to those given her by the journey in the ugly carriage. Yet with the new day, her despair was given a brighter colour; some rainbow left by the storm grew in the corner of her mind, and she began to look about her with expectation. She did not know why, for her situation could not be more dire; the betrayal of Pizar hung heavily about her shoulders, the loss of everyone she trusted hung heavily on her heart – and yet she had hope. She could only think that the gods were lending her strength.

She had emptied the water bottle in the night, and when she was thrust back into the carriage, they threw in another and a piece of bruised fruit. The carriage jerked forward before she'd taken a bite of the fruit, the road bumped ahead, but she had almost grown used to the rolling of the vehicle, and her body rolled in time with the worst of it.

They had not gone far when she was suddenly pitched forward. She fell the length of the carriage, thudding against the forward wall. When she untangled herself, she found the carriage sitting at an unnatural angle, the floor sloping upward. Before the knowledge that a wheel had broken had entered her head, the door was being unlocked. Pizar stood outside, and he spoke to her for the first time since they had left the village.

"Get out," he said. "We have a wheel to repair."

She stumbled from the carriage and put out her hands, used to the fact that they would be tied. She wondered when it was that she had given in to captivity, but even as she wondered, she knew that she hadn't, not really.

The sun was halfway up the sky before they had repaired the broken spokes amid whispered conversations and darting looks at the trees, yet the job they did was in no way expert and the carriage lurched through the morning on its faulty wheel. Soon after midday they reached a village, and she was left in the carriage as the wheel was again removed and repaired. Through the slats in the door she could see the sun falling into the west when they finally left the village, and she could tell by the way Pizar berated his soldiers that he was feeling the strain of the journey. She smiled to herself, feeling better than she had since they'd walked into the village and disaster.

Shaeli passed the time in the thin light of the carriage throwing little light balls. She had hardly thrown a light without a stone since her Cave year, and she took pleasure in throwing a tiny ball up to hover near the ceiling, sending it spinning slowly, changing the colour. She wondered about their strength and fired a concentrated ball close to the wall opposite the door and found the spark left behind a small burnt spot, and the small glint of hope brightened. She spent the rest of the afternoon sitting before the wall burning little holes in an arc on the wall, not knowing if she could get through the wood, but trying just the same.

They stopped only once, just before dusk. The clouds were still lurking on the horizon, their bellies sullenly grey and full, and it began to rain again not long after dark, but they went on. When they stopped, it rained still, and she had no concept of the time or the space around them. She scanned the sky for some sign of a star as she was taken outside so she could see where she was, yet there was nothing, the rain drowned even the sight of the clouds in the dark night. She went damp and shivering back into the carriage, the hope that had burned with the dawn light now banked to a small ember.

In the light of another overcast day she woke with the clanging of the door. She went as wearily as she was led, but as she squatted in the scrub she heard a sound, the fall of some pebble in the dawn light around her.

She looked through the bushes at her two escorts. Both looked bored and disgruntled, but appeared not to have noticed the sound. It was probably some animal that had made the sound, but she could not help hoping it was something else. She composed her face, and followed the rope back.

They were leaving the foothills, and before she was put back into the carriage she could see the beginnings of the plains through a gap in the trees, and she knew that soon they would reach the wide road that led across the plains and around Lake Marnis to Marnissi. She sat and wondered, waiting for the carriage to jerk forward, wondered and worried; about the others, about Ebony, about her family, yet she was distracted from her worrying by raised voices outside.

"Well, where are they?" came Pizar's voice.

The voice that answered came from the pock-faced man. She had grown to know his voice well.

"Gone," he said. "I know not. Three in the night. Their horses and belongings left behind. If they have chosen to leave their duties they have chosen a strange way."

"And there is no sign of them?"

"None."

"Forget them," said Pizar. "Ride on."

And so the carriage was pulled forward once again, but Shaeli was left pondering. Three soldiers missing in the night. Gone. The ember of hope flared again.

\* \* \*

It rained off and on all that day, and she spent her time widening the arc of scorch marks on the wall, until one grew so deep she could see a small pinpoint of light through it. They stopped once during the day, but it was a long break, the soldiers sitting hunched on the sodden ground, the horses standing with their heads hanging low. As Shaeli was getting back into the carriage, she heard a noise over the sound of the rain, a snicker of a noise, coming from somewhere under the carriage. It was such a familiar noise that she stopped. She was pushed from behind by the pock-faced man and fell into the carriage on her knees, but before the door clanged shut she heard it again. A tiny snicker, barely audible above the sound of the rain. When the door shut upon her, her eyes were wide with surprise.

\* \* \*

It was late in the night when they stopped again. It wasn't raining, but it had stopped only a short time before, and the trees and bushes hung as heavily as the heads of the horses with the weight of it. She could barely see in front of her as she was led into the scrub, but she listened with heightened anticipation as she crouched behind a clump of trees. As she began to think she had imagined it earlier, the bushes trembled and something scuttled towards her.

She was filthy. Her fur was matted and dark with mud, her tail thin, her ears drooping, yet she fixed Shaeli with an unmistakable grin, and leapt upon her. Shaeli barely had time to think, for the rope which bound her hands was given a swift jerk.

"Come on," growled the pock-faced soldier. "Afore I come in and get you."

Shaeli shoved the dripping, muddy jevvi beneath her cloak and went back out. She kept her face down so they would not see the joy in her eyes.

\* \* \*

# CHAPTER FOURTEEN

When Shaeli had thrown Ebony into the lane and told her to find Kirrit, the jevvi had begun to do just that, yet as she'd rounded the corner, she'd looked back, seen her mistress struggling, surrounded, and she'd changed her mind. She rarely disobeyed, but this time she disregarded what Shaeli had told her, and when she went around the corner she'd ducked behind a pile of boxes stacked beside a door. After a moment, she crept back and peeked around the corner.

She was in time to see Shaeli's well-placed kick, and the amulet falling onto the road. She watched as the stones were retrieved and her mistress and the others dragged away, and when they had disappeared across the square, she crept out. She nosed around the place they'd been captured, scenting her mistress's fear. She picked something up from a crack in the cobblestones, pushed it into her tiny pouch, and scampered down the lane, following Shaeli's scent.

She dashed from shadow to shadow, over to the building where the scent led, scurrying beneath the steps, unnoticed by the soldiers milling upon them. Beneath the building she went, her little nose twitching. It was dusty under there and she sneezed a few times, encountering more than one cobweb on her way. When she smelt Shaeli above her, she scurried up to crouch on a rafter beneath the floorboards. She could hear her mistress's voice, muffled, and she sensed the distress in it. She recognised the scent of the other in the room above, remembered the pockets full of nuts in an indoor garden, and she chattered softly to herself.

When the voices stopped, she could still smell Shaeli above her, and so she began to sniff about for the others. She found them in the corner of the building, the scent of them mixed with the smell of blood and fear, yet she did not stay long, scurrying back to crouch beneath Shaeli. She pulled at the spider webs caught in her fur as she waited, rolling the sticky stuff into balls and wiping them off on the beam beside her. She was almost clean when she heard movement above and Shaeli's smell began to recede. She followed her back beneath the building and watched from the shadows as Shaeli was led down the steps. The one who led her was the one Ebony had smelled in the room with Shaeli; the one who'd had the nuts was the one who had caused such distress, and she bared her teeth at him. He was friend no more. She watched as Shaeli was taken across the street and thrust into a box on wheels.

As the one who was no longer friend was mounting his horse and speaking loudly, Ebony had taken a chance and scrambled across the open road. If any saw her, they thought her nothing more than one of the village rats, for she made it to the horses easily. Going between the giant, stamping feet was a little trickier, but within moments she was in the shadow beneath the carriage. She scrambled up a wheel, and found beneath the door a tiny space at the back of the step, and she had barely scrambled in when the thing with her mistress in it began to move. She was lucky the tiny space had a lip in the gap at top and bottom, otherwise she would have been bounced out. She gripped the lip with her tiny hands and her tail, and as the afternoon passed she bumped around the tiny space. When they stopped she had squeezed out, shaken the dust from her fur, and watched as her mistress was led out into the bushes and then back again. She had scrambled back into her space as the carriage moved again.

When the storm closed in, the little jevvi had grown truly miserable. The hooves of the horses and the wheels of the carriage threw up clods of mud that splattered against the underside of the carriage, and Ebony was soon covered in fine muddy droplets that coated every inch of her fur. For a while she had wiped at them, her dislike of being dirty still strong, yet by the time they stopped for the night she had long since given up. She waited beneath the carriage until she could see all the soldiers but one were still. The one who was awake had his back to the carriage, looking through the rain back down the road.

Ebony came out from beneath the carriage, sniffing at the rain that teemed down, and then she climbed up the wheels and leapt onto the door, but the slats were placed too closely together for even her tiny body to squeeze through. She climbed onto the roof and clambered over the carriage, seeking a way in. She hung outside the thin slat in the back, peering in, but she could see nothing, even with her huge eyes, she could only smell her mistress. She knew that Shaeli was sleeping, but she chattered through the thin gap. Again she called to Shaeli, and again, but Shaeli did not stir, and after a while Ebony leapt back down. She dashed into the trees, climbed up and drank the rainwater dripping from the trees. She nibbled on a few new leaves and sucked the nectar from rain-laden blossoms, and then she scurried back to the thing that held her mistress. She crawled into her little space, groomed herself as best she could, and then she curled her tail around her and slept.

She woke before the dawn and dashed out to eat and drink. As she was returning, she saw something crawl through the bushes, away from the carriage and the sleeping soldiers, but she could not catch its scent through the rain.

She had crawled back into her tiny space behind the step before the grey of morning had touched the sky. Soon the bouncing had begun again, yet before long the carriage thudded to a halt. She curled herself tightly into her little space as the soldiers climbed about beneath the carriage, her eyes wide and watching their every move, but none of them noticed her and soon they were on their way again. She lay tensely in her little hole as the wheel was mended properly in the village, and she dozed through the bumpy afternoon. When the rain began again, she resigned herself to the mud that splattered up from the wheels.

Again that night she had crawled over the little carriage, seeking a way in, chittering at the gaps, but Shaeli did not hear her over the loud voice of the rain, so she had grazed in the bush around the carriage and crawled back into her hole.

She woke once in the night. The rain had broken for a while, and she went out into the trees to drink. Beneath her had come two soldiers, a man and a woman, and Ebony had watched as they coupled beneath the trees. She smelt another scent on the breeze, a familiar scent coming closer. and she watched as the couple below were hit with something that flew swiftly and silently. Their movements ceased, Ebony smelt the odour of death, and then the one whose scent she knew had come and dragged the dead ones away. The jevvi had watched and listened for a while, and then she had gone back to her hole beneath the carriage.

She had woken before dawn with the familiar scent again in her nostrils, but she could see nothing, and later, she watched as Shaeli was led into the trees. Ebony sensed the veiled hope in her mistress as she was returned to the carriage, but she sat miserably in her hole. She began to chatter to herself, yet her mistress did not hear her.

When they stopped in the middle of the rainy day, Ebony watched again as her mistress was led away. When she came back, the jevvi had called to her once more, and this time she knew her mistress had heard her. When they finally stopped again, late in the evening, Ebony was ready. She leapt from her hole into the wake of the carriage before it had stopped completely. None of the soldiers had left their horses and she scurried into the bushes and waited. Through the trees, hands tied, led like an animal, came her mistress. Ebony could wait no longer. She remained hidden only until Shaeli was separated from the two who led her, and then she went through the bushes and leapt upon her beloved mistress.

\* \* \*

It was the first time Shaeli was eager for the door to close her into the box of a carriage. She stood back as it clanged shut, and then went to peer through the slats. She could see a few soldiers but they were unconcerned with her. She squatted down in her corner, and pulled out the jevvi. Ebony chattered loudly and grinned and Shaeli hushed her, but it was all she could do to keep from laughing out loud. She hugged the jevvi to her cheek, and then screwed up her face.

"You're a bit of a mess, aren't you, Eb?" she whispered.

Ebony screwed up her nose in reply, and rolled her shoulders.

"I know I'm not much better," smiled Shaeli. "Oh, but I'm so glad to see you." She hugged the jevvi to her again. "But how did you get here? Where are the others?"

But Ebony could only screw up her face and make the tiny shrugging motion. She could tell her mistress nothing, yet she had one thing to show her. She put her hand into her pouch and pulled out the thing she had found between the cobblestones in the lane where they'd been captured. She put it in Shaeli's hand and snickered.

Shaeli looked at it, held it up to the light, and then she hugged the jevvi to her again. "You wonderful, clever creature," she whispered.

In her hand lay the tiny green triangle. Somehow it must have been overlooked when they picked up the stones that had fallen from the amulet, and somehow the jevvi had found it. Shaeli's heart leapt, understanding that this meant she could escape, yet as she understood it, she knew she could not do it. Not yet. But having Ebony here gave her an advantage. As the soldiers began to settle into their accustomed positions around the carriage, Shaeli began to plan. She whispered to the jevvi late into the night. The sound of the rain that continued to fall drowned out everything else. When she finally lay down to sleep, she felt better than she had for days.

\* \* \*

She was ready when they opened the door the next morning.

The sky was still grey and overcast with a thick blanket, but the rain had stopped and the cloud blanket had a few holes here and there and sunlight was peeping through, yet its weak rays made the rain-soaked world glitter. They had almost reached the beginnings of the plains; open hills and fields stretched out to the west, the foothills and the mountains rising lead-green behind.

Shaeli kept her eyes down, so her captors would not see the glitter of the world mirrored within them. Her heart thumped, but when the moment came, all went as she planned and she released the jevvi into the brush without anyone seeing. She grinned, said a silent prayer, and returned alone to her little carriage. It was up to Ebony now.

All through that day she sat, stood, paced about the box, unable to be still, unable to think a whole thought through before another began. When they stopped mid-afternoon, she noticed something that she had not seen earlier that day.

Yesterday, Pizar's guard had led three horses, those three abandoned by the soldiers who had disappeared on the second night. Now, as she was led back to the carriage, she saw there were five soldiers missing. She counted nine, nine still on horseback, plus Pizar, but only four empty horses.

She looked more closely at the soldiers, saw many had their hands always on their weapons, saw that they looked about them with the unease of the stalked. She kept the smile from her lips as she went back into the carriage, kept it from them until the water bottle and some food had been thrown in, kept it until the door clanged shut and the bolt pushed home, then she pulled the verdena from her pocket and let the smile go.

That night, it was again late when they stopped. It had not rained all afternoon, and when she was taken out, she could see a few stars through the rips in the thick clouds. She was comforted by the sight of them, imagining her parents, her sisters, Koda and the others may well be looking up at those same stars. The moon had been growing behind the cloud blanket and its light shone silver through the dark clouds.

She listened to the sounds of the soldiers settling for the night, listened as they set a guard around the perimeter. She heard Pizar forbid any to leave camp, and as she settled herself into her corner to listen, she could not help the smile from coming again. She did not know where her companions were, but she knew that Kirrit had escaped, and would have reached Almarnoch. Almarnoch would not have let harm come to Williver, Ishaan and Flin, of that she was certain, and she knew also it was only a matter of the days passing until some effort was made to rescue her.

She sat late into the night, listening. She was nodding when she finally heard it. The little snicker, high up against the thin slit at the back of the carriage. She scrambled to her feet, and peered out. Ebony's nose was pushed against the slit, and Shaeli stroked it.

"All good?" she whispered, and the jevvi grinned. "Well done. Now take this," she said, pushing the verdena through the gap. She had made good use of it. "And back into wherever you've been hiding. I'll see you tomorrow."

Ebony snickered again and disappeared. Shaeli settled down to sleep.

She was woken the next morning by Pizar's voice. She barely recognised it as the smooth-toned man who had befriended her at Arinola's. He was cursing at his soldiers and there were the sounds of tearing and things thudding onto the ground. Then steps came closer and the door was unlocked and wrenched open.

Shaeli sat up and rubbed at her eyes as if she'd just woken. She did not need to pretend to blink as she was pulled out into the first sunshine she had seen for days. The light was thin, and it was still very early, the sun throwing warm arms through the mountains behind them. There were only a few clouds floating slowly by, and the sky rose high and brightly blue above them. Pizar's hand was rough on her arm as he pulled her from the carriage and thrust his face into hers.

"Where is it?" he asked.

She pulled her head back and frowned. "Where is what?" she replied, hoping she looked baffled.

Yet Pizar did not answer her. He began rubbing his hand across her pockets, over her bodice. She struggled as he felt every part of her, but in the end he thrust her away, disgust plain on his face.

"What are you *looking* for?" she asked again. "I *have* nothing, Pizar. You've already seen to that."

He ignored her and she was pushed back into the carriage. Before she went, she counted the guard. There were now eight.

\* \* \*

Ezebar watched from the trees as Pizar searched Shaeli. He did not know what Pizar searched for, but he knew the captain of the guard was worried. He watched as Shaeli was pushed back inside the carriage and then he scrambled back to where he'd left his horse. He and the black horse had become good friends since he'd left the village, and he gave the horse a pat as he waited for the sounds of the soldiers riding on.

They had been easy to follow, but now that they were entering the plains he would have to be more careful. When he heard the guard move ahead, he waited for a while before he followed.

He wondered where the Trader was. He had expected to see it before now, but thought the fierce storms of the last few days had probably delayed them. He grew impatient. Every day that passed and Shaeli was in that box made him more anxious, and he decided that tonight, Trader or no, she would not be in there another day

\* \* \*

# CHAPTER FIFTEEN

When Ezebar had left Almarnoch at the village, it had been with great trepidation. Leaving M'zena had been foremost in his mind, yet there was also the worry of leaving the old Warlock alone to release the others, yet he had done as he was asked, mostly because M'zena had told him to protect Shaeli.

He had ridden far into the night. The guard had had many hours start, but he bargained on them going more slowly and stopping at some point. He had pushed the horse as much as he had dared, and had finally come upon the guard and their prisoner just as the night was turning its thoughts to the sunrise hours.

It was lucky it was at a time when he was letting his horse walk, for he was almost upon them before he saw them. He turned his horse back, dismounted and led it into the trees, then he crept forward and looked at the soldiers and the carriage in which Shaeli was imprisoned. He had gone back to his horse for Williver's bow, thinking to pick off a few of the soldiers, yet as he reached his horse, he heard hoofbeats on the road. He grabbed the bow, and saw through the darkness two horsemen headed towards him. They had come from the same direction as him, and even in the darkness he could see the scarlet on their uniforms and the foam at the mouths of both horses. It was obvious the horses had been ridden hard through the night, and Ezebar could only guess why. They had a message to deliver – a message of escaped prisoners – and Ezebar was fairly sure he did not want that message received. Neither soldier saw the arrow that killed him.

Ezebar caught the two exhausted beasts, stripping them of bridles and saddles before releasing them, and then he had dragged the bodies and the saddles into the brush. He had never killed a person, and the necessity had been paramount, yet still it bothered him. He tried not to think about it too much, or of the fact he would have to do it again.

He had crept back, then, to see if all was the same as it had been around the carriage. Nothing had changed and he watched a while. He had thought to dispose of another soldier or two, but the first birds were beginning to stir and it could not be long before the soldiers mimicked the birds. Instead he had crept forward, sliding on his belly over to the carriage. He had crouched in the shadows of the ugly box, sawing at the spokes of one of the wheels. It took a while, for he dare not make too much noise. Four of the spokes he cut almost all the way through, and when the darkness had nearly left the sky, he crawled back into the bushes. He had led his horse out onto the road, walking it through the shadows past the place where the guard lay sleeping. He led it into the forest and let it graze as he dozed against a tree.

He had woken with the sound of the guard passing. He stretched and groaned, his back protesting the long ride and lack of rest, and then he mounted his black horse and followed the guard. To his satisfaction, they did not go far before the wheel broke. He watched from a ridge as Shaeli was taken from the carriage, bound, and guarded as the wheel was repaired, frowning as she was pulled roughly along by a weedy, red-headed man and shoved from behind by a stocky woman. He dozed again as they spent hours making the wheel usable, and then he trailed them into the village where they'd had the wheel repaired properly. He had eaten at a tavern across from the place where the wheel was repaired, listening as the locals speculated about who was in the carriage that was so closely guarded.

The captain of the guard – Ezebar thought him a fractious, self-important fop – marched about calling orders and looking as if he expected something unexpected to happen. When nothing did and the wheel was repaired without incident, he had driven his soldiers on into the afternoon.

Ezebar waited a while, sampling the fine ale at the tavern, and then he'd purchased a few supplies, found his horse and followed them through the afternoon and on into the evening. When the storm had hit after sunset, he had pulled up the hood of his cloak and gone on.

He reached their encampment that night, finding them by the sporadic bursts of lightning, the only way that he could see. The rain had stopped, but the storm still spun through the hills around him, and it would not be long before the squalls came again. He longed to sleep, yet the cover of thick cloud gave the perfect opportunity to slow the passage of the carriage again or reduce the number of soldiers guarding it. He prowled around the perimeter of their camp and his stalking brought great rewards.

He watched as two soldiers, a stocky man and a thin, flat-chested woman, snuck from the camp in the midnight hours. He followed them to a stand of bushes, and as they were distracted by each other, he pierced them both with one arrow. He took no joy from this encounter, nor any other like it as the days passed, yet he tried to turn his mind from it. It was necessary.

One more soldier he saw outside the camp, just after he had killed the amorous couple, one who had gone to relieve himself in nearby bushes. This one also felt the bite of the elf's bow.

Ezebar dragged the bodies away, covered signs of their blood with wet leaves, and then he went to hide his horse and himself for the rest of the night hours.

He woke to a grey dawn and made his way towards the guard's encampment. He watched from a short stony ridge as Shaeli was brought from the carriage, bound and led into the brush below him. Her two guards looked none too thrilled with their duty, and when Shaeli went behind some bushes, he could hear them grumbling under their breaths. He snuck lower down the ridge, closer to where Shaeli was, keeping his head below the line of rocks. His foot dislodged a stone and it rolled down the slope, breaking the morning silence with its passage. He froze, willing the tumbling stones to cease, and after a moment he poked his head back up. Shaeli was being pulled back to the carriage and the soldiers still retained their sullen faces. They had not heard him, yet as Shaeli was pushed back into the carriage, she looked back over her shoulder. He had a glimpse of her face before the door closed and she did not seem as frightened as she had before.

He waited as they looked for the soldiers who had not been there when they'd woken, and he smiled a grim smile to himself as the foppish captain blustered about. He saw the soldiers begin to look about them, the suspicion with which they regarded the trees, and he waited until they had mounted their horses and gone. He went back to his horse, saddled it, and ate something from the supplies he had bought at the village. He thanked the gods that he had carried some coin with him or his journey would have been a hungry one.

It was full morning before he began to follow the muddy tracks down the road, but the day was still a dull grey and the trees dripped with the rain they held greedily to their leaves. He was low in the hills now, and in the distance between the treetops he could see the beginnings of the plains. Far to the west they unrolled, wide flat lands, low hills creating green humps that continued far to the north.

A bird called nearby, a long hitching song, and he scanned the trees for it. It was a bird unknown to him, sitting high on a dripping branch, and, as he admired the bird's brightly-coloured plumage and cheerful song, he suddenly realised he was out in the World, at last. After all his years of wondering, dreaming what the Lands looked like, he was here, looking at them. Despite the dullness of the day and the desperation of

Shaeli's predicament, he could not help but smile at the sights around him.

Yet his smile did not linger, his mind had other tasks than appreciating the scenery. He trotted through the morning, now and then pulling up his hood against thin patches of rain. He stopped in the afternoon to eat and let the horse graze, and then he followed the passage of the guard and the carriage. It was not difficult; there was only one road with a few thin lanes branching off it, and the tracks made by the soldiers were muddily obvious.

He came upon them late in the night at the edge of the plains country. They had a fire, a small smoky fire, and Ezebar saw its white cloud hanging over their encampment from the hillside above. He was cold, damp and tired, yet he went down, tied his horse, and crept towards the encampment until he could see the carriage through the trees.

The soldiers squatted around the measly fire, the wood too wet to catch properly, and he saw others pacing the perimeter. They all watched the trees around them, and after a while he went back to his horse and led it further into the forest. He heard the tumble of water ahead and went towards it, and when he came out beside a little creek he followed it back into the hills until he came to a place where the creek fell down from the slope above. Beside the fall he found a depression within the rocks, a place not quite a cave, but a hollow deep enough that the rain had not reached into the back of it, and high enough for the horse to stand beneath the overhang. He unsaddled the horse, hanging its blanket over a rock under the shelter, tethering it so it could crop at the grass or stand beneath the overhang, and then he took it to drink from the creek and went back to the camp, taking the bow with him.

He circled the camp, found what he was looking for, and pulled out an arrow. He notched it, pulled it and waited until one of the guards walking the perimeter came into sight. He let the arrow fly, put the bow over his shoulder, and climbed quickly into the tree he had chosen as the first shouts went up. As he'd thought, the soldiers had dashed into the trees, looking for the assassin, yet by then Ezebar was high in his tree watching the fruitless search below. He waited there for a long time after the soldiers had moved back to their camp, and then he climbed down and made his way back to where his horse was tethered.

He drank from the clear water of the little creek again, filled his bottles and ate something. He looked up at the sky, and through a tiny rip saw a few stars. As he watched, the stars vanished and it began to rain again. He led the horse in beneath the overhang, lay down behind it, and slept.

* * *

He woke before dawn and went back to watch as the guard readied themselves for the day. The body of the slain guard had been disposed of, and he watched as the captain woke, looked at his pack and began to shout. Something was missing, that much was clear, but Ezebar did not know what. Shaeli was dragged sleepily from the carriage, searched and questioned, and he heard a little of her reply, but her tone was clear to him, even if her words were not. As she was pushed back into the carriage, he knew he could not let her spend another day in there.

It was then that he noticed the same thing Shaeli had as she'd been put back in the carriage. One of the soldiers was gone, he and his horse. Ezebar frowned. He pushed his way back through the brush to his horse. The black horse was cropping at the grass as he came through the trees, and it nickered softly. He ran his hand along its smooth neck and then saddled it. He was glad to feel the sun on his face again, and he could feel the heat that began to rise steamily from the ground. It would be a warm day, one of the last of spring, he thought, for already the air had begun to turn its thoughts to summer.

He waited for a while before he followed the guard. They were leaving the trees for wide open spaces, and he wanted distance between them. At midday he reached the last hill before the descent onto the plains, and he stopped to look at what lay ahead.

Below, the trees thinned and petered out as the land flattened. To the west the plains stretched, broken by low hills, so low that they were almost unworthy of being called hills. They were more like enormous mounds, humps beneath the flatness of the plains. The colours of a multitude of crops patterned the land like one of M'zena's quilts, and far in the distance a thin green line edged the horizon. Beneath him, the road unravelled from the trees and ran out into the plains, and upon it were the soldiers and the carriage. Ahead of them he could see the ribbon of another road that unrolled from the north and the place where the two roads met. There was a large town at this meeting of the roads, and Ezebar could see that only one road ran out the far side, heading west across the plain. From the town there came a large dark mass. A group of horsemen, mere specks in the distance. They were heading east, towards him, towards the carriage.

All this he saw in a moment, for his eye was drawn to something that shattered the southern sky with a score of colours. He heard the cry from one of the great birds, saw the Trader gather speed; saw it fly low over the distant carriage.

He looked no longer. He kicked his horse and galloped down the hill.

\* \* \*

# CHAPTER SIXTEEN

They had planned to leave the drell sanctuary at dawn, but as they prepared the Trader during the afternoon, thick clouds began banking the horizon, and it grew as dull as dusk. The thunder had begun soon after, lightning sheeting the sky and spitting long jagged forks down into the mountains. The rain did not come fitfully, but in one huge torrent that obscured the meadow in an instant. The storm concentrated over them as the dull day turned quickly to night, and they knew they would be not leaving the valley of sanctuary while the storm raged.

Tarkoda, Williver and Flin watched the storm shatter the sky far into the night. The valley holding sanctuary in its hand kept the harshest winds and lightning from the Trader, yet still they were lashed with gusty squalls, the rain pelting all around them. It seemed hard to believe that they had been swimming in the warmth of the midday sun only a few short hours ago. They went one by one to their beds, the rain beating against the balloon, the wind howling through the trees, the thunder and lightning clamouring to be strongest.

Tarkoda was up first, surveying the storm that still raged through the mountains. He checked the Zoi, and found them dry and quiet in the nest. He fed them, groomed them, taking comfort from their warmth and quiet eyes. By the time he reached the deck, Flin, Kirrit, Williver and Ishaan stood looking out at the storm.

Rain crashed onto the meadow around them, the sky hung so low it seemed as if you could touch it, thunder rumbled constantly. Tarkoda could barely believe the skies had betrayed him so badly. He dare not fly the Trader through the mountains in this weather, and yet he paced the deck all through that long stormy day, waiting for the break that meant they could leave and rescue his sister. Once he made Williver and Blenny accompany him across the meadow, under and through the waterfall track, thinking that perhaps the storm was less severe out in the valley. Yet when they had reached it they found the storm much worse, trees broken and torn through the valley beyond the waterfall, leaves and branches covering the ground. They had turned back to the safety of the sanctuary, and even Tarkoda had to be grateful for the protection it gave the Trader. The ancient spells of the drell still worked to hold this place in a bubble of magic, bringing in the rain and wind, but keeping it from the destruction that raged outside. All through that day he watched the skies and waited for the storm to cease, yet they went to their beds with the thunder still rumbling overhead.

That night Tarkoda barely slept. He woke so many times that eventually he took his bedroll onto the deck and watched the storm from beneath the shelter of the overhang. The rain danced through the night, misting beneath the balloon and coating his bedroll with a fine spray, yet as the sunrise hours crept almost unnoticed into the night, he began to sense a change in the air. As morning crept in, it too, barely noticeable, the rain still fell, the wind still blew, yet he felt the end of it coming, and he looked to the sky for confirmation. By the time it came, the others were with him, all of them sitting and watching through the long morning hours, waiting for the signs that they could fly. By afternoon the rain stopped. The clouds still hung low above them, yet by the midnight hours they knew the storm had broken, and the three-quarter moon appeared in the rents in the clouds to shed light over the land. Tarkoda would wait no longer, and Almarnoch did not argue with him. They flew from the sanctuary in the last of the moonlight, heading east through the mountains as fast as they dared.

*  *  *

Dawn found them in a valley far to the east.

They had left the sanctuary behind, leaving the little carriage inside the carved cliff castle and the horses to roam the vast meadow, and they had followed the path of the storm through the night, seeing the destruction in the torn trees through the grey light of the sunrise hours. Tarkoda kept the Trader high above the shattered valleys while night still covered the land, for there were many trees that were broken into giant spears by the storm. Between moon-set and the beginning of the sunrise hours he had had only starlight to fly by, yet the sight of the stars calmed him as they had so often calmed his father through long nights, and he flew confidently on.

When he could see the ground below, he further appreciated the protection the sanctuary had given the Trader, but as they flew on, the destruction in the valleys beneath the ship grew less obvious; the trees were less broken, the trails of run-off were thinner, and he knew the storm had not ravaged these lower ranges as it had higher up.

With the dawn came the relief of flying without danger, but also the knowledge that now they would be seen. When Almarnoch had told him of the queen's banishment of the Traders he had been furious, and now that the initial outrage had worn off he had begun to appreciate the dangers. He peered ahead for the sight of a village, wondering how he could possibly hide a Trader.

"Do not worry, lad," said Almarnoch. "Once your sister has been returned to us, we will worry about being seen." He smiled. "For now, we have only to find them. The storm will have delayed them, and perhaps Ezebar has also played a part in slowing them."

"But they have four days start on us, Almarnoch," said Koda.

"And we have already covered much distance," Almarnoch said quietly. "Do not despair. We shall find her."

And so Tarkoda flew swiftly into the east, and he found Almarnoch was right. The high ranges had turned to foothills by the time the sun had reached the shoulders of the mountains behind them. He kept the Trader as high as he could, yet from the villages they passed people came running to stare and wave at them. In some of the villages the scarlet and black of the guard patterned the colours of the villagers below, and twice a bell beckoned them down, yet he barely glanced below and flew on. At mid-morning he could see the last of the foothills dropping into the plain and he urged the Zoi on.

He turned and looked behind him, smiling at the others who were all clustered on the little deck with him.

"We're a little south of where the road comes out of the mountains," he said. "We'll go over the last hills to the plains and then head back north until we find the road and follow it to Mesbottee."

"Where is that?" asked Cheval.

"It lies at the crossroad where the mountain road meets the road from the north," said Almarnoch. "The great road that leads around Lake Marnis to Marnissi and beyond lies on the far side. They must travel through Mesbottee first."

"A fine town, Mesbottee," said M'zena. "I have stayed there many times on my travels."

"With luck they have not reached it yet," said Williver.

"There is a large guard housed at Mesbottee," said Tarkoda. "If they have already passed through, they may have gathered reinforcements before they went on."

"Whether they have reinforcements or not, we will deal with them," said Flin, touching the pocket where his stone lay.

"We have to find them first," said Kirrit, arms crossed over her chest.

"I'll find them," said Tarkoda, grim assurance in his words.

Over the last of the foothills they flew and he turned the birds to the north, the dark green of the mountains to their right, the patterned greens of the plains on their left. They all squinted into the distance, but none were surprised when it was the elves who saw it first.

"There's the road," cried Llianas, pointing ahead.

"I see it," said Williver, leaning forward over the rail. "And not far from the hills, something... can you see it, Llianas?"

"Not yet," she said. "Oh, yes I can. It's too big to be just one person."

None of the others could even see the road yet, and Tarkoda strained his eyes until the thin line of the road became visible. By then Williver and Llianas were fairly sure it was the carriage they sought upon it, and before the others could see the spot the elves were looking at, Williver and Llianas were picking out the black and scarlet of the queen's colours.

Tarkoda looked at Almarnoch.

"No use trying to sneak up on them, lad," said the Warlock with a shrug of his shoulders. "A swift approach would be best."

Tarkoda nodded and tugged imperceptibly at the lines in his hands. The Zoi had flown though half the night, yet they picked up speed immediately. Another subtle tug and they took the Trader lower until the heads of the crops were dancing beneath them, waving flower-topped stalks at their passing.

They could all see the line of the road now, the thick rope of it laying across the fields ahead, and the squat ugly carriage pulled amongst trotting horses. The faces of the horsemen were turned towards them, yet not all of the horses bore riders, and one of the wheels on the carriage rolled oddly.

"Take M'zena down," said Tarkoda.

Llianas nodded and took M'zena's arm to help her down the steps the main deck, but M'zena shook her off.

"I can manage, miss," she said. "I'll just go under the stairs where I can see."

Tarkoda smiled at her. "That was Shaeli's favourite spot when she was little," he said. He looked at the others and the smile waned. "We're almost there. Watch the balloon."

Llianas, Cheval and Kirrit followed M'zena down the stairs, Olando, Spotjaw and the drell behind them. They ranged themselves around the deck, weapons drawn. Tarkoda was left with Williver, Flin, Ishaan and Almarnoch on the upper deck. All but him held a weapon of some kind in their hands, and his own itched to take his sword and mow down whoever stood in his way, but his fingers held the lines gently as he guided the Trader across the fields towards the carriage.

It had stopped in the middle of the road, the soldiers grouped around it. One was on the ground, holding the heads of the horses that drew the carriage. The others were still on horseback, all with drawn bows raised at the Trader.

Llianas came back up the steps. "Ready, Williver," she said.

Tarkoda looked from the pretty dark-eyed elf to the tall, blond one beside him. "You're sure about this?" he asked.

Williver grinned. "Of course," he said. He clapped Tarkoda on the shoulder. "All shall be well," he smiled.

He turned and followed Llianas back down onto the deck. M'zena stopped him for a moment with a hand on his chest at the bottom of the stairs. She said something to him and Williver nodded and leant down to kiss her cheek. She patted his chest again and then he and Llianas went to the back of the Trader.

Tarkoda watched him go and then he turned forward. They had reached the road.

\* \* \*

Shaeli had sat bouncing through the morning with a head full of plans. She thought that as soon as she had a stone in her hand, she could escape. She could have tried that morning, she knew, yet they would have been ready. Pizar had expected her to have one, she knew that also, and she would not have been able to guarantee the outcome. No, she would wait until she had some control over the situation, some time when they would least suspect it. She would wait until dark and then...

She was pulled from her daydreaming by a shout, and though she heard the words, it took her a moment to comprehend them, so unexpected were they.

"Trader," came the cry. "Trader to the south."

She leapt to her feet and went to the window, threading her fingers through the slats to steady herself. She could see little of the sky or the fields around it, but in the distance, far across the fields, was the Trader she had longed to see. The score of patterns from a dozen broken balloons shone in the light, and as the Trader flew lower one of the birds let out a cry. Shaeli's heart let out a cry with it, but even as she rejoiced, she heard Pizar yell something to his soldiers that froze the joy instantly.

"If they come near, shoot the birds," he cried. "By the queen's order, aim for the birds."

\* \* \*

Ezebar could see nothing of the way ahead. He galloped the horse down the last slope and shot from the trees onto the plains. Still he could see nothing save the Trader flying in from the south, the road ahead wound through tree-lined fields, and he drove the horse on, knowing that somewhere ahead a battle was beginning.

\* \* \*

Tarkoda flew the Trader down over the carriage.

The soldiers below fired their arrows, but the ship was still too high and they dropped away, useless. Koda circled the soldiers, a wide circle, the arrows of the soldiers following them as they went around.

He looked behind him. Williver stood at the back of the Trader with Llianas, and he raised an arm as Tarkoda turned. Tarkoda nodded, turned forward, and took the Trader lower.

The fields were full of crops with gaily bobbing heads, and in several there were stands of tall trees. Crops and trees watched and whispered to each other as the Trader swept down.

Tarkoda pushed the Zoi lower as he banked around for another pass, gliding right over the fields and between the stands of trees. He flicked the lines and drove the ship again over the carriage.

This time some of the arrows thudded into the bottom of the ship. One flew up between the birds, and Tarkoda watched another fly up behind the harness and miss the balloon by a hand's length. Over and around they went, and this time as they passed over the fields, the heads of the waving crops swept the underside of the Trader.

"Did you see that?" Flin said.

"What?" yelled Tarkoda, not taking his eyes from the birds.

"It looked like Ebony," said Flin. "On the roof of the carriage."

"Look again," said Koda. "Here they come."

Flin held his stone in his hand, and this time as they passed he threw lightning-fast at two of the soldiers and they fell from their horses into the dust. One of the horses reared and took off back down the road towards the mountains.

The other soldiers continued to fire arrows at the Trader, but this time they did not aim at the ship, nor those upon it. Their arrows were trained on the Zoi, and Tarkoda watched with horrified disbelief as one of the arrows thudded into the bird at the rear of the pack.

The shaft hit the bird in the leg and it cried out and faltered. The momentum kept the Trader flying clear of the next arrows, but the bird was now flying awkwardly and the others were looking back, cries of distress echoing through the air.

For a moment Tarkoda wasn't sure what to do. The bird still flew, but he could see the crimson beginning to stain its feathers. The shaft hung from its thigh, and it continued to call to the others in short pained cries, yet Tarkoda set his jaw. He turned the Trader back and bore down on the soldiers again.

Beside him, Flin leaned forward over the rail, his arm outstretched, ready for the next strike. Tarkoda glanced over his shoulder, saw the others on the deck intent on the carriage ahead. There were four soldiers dead on the ground now, two more shot by the bows of Olando and Spotjaw. One of the dead was the woman who had held the horses pulling the carriage. Her body now lay between the hooves of the skittish horses.

"Their bows, Flin," Tarkoda yelled. "Get the bows. They're aiming at the Zoi."

Flin nodded and sent three tiny balls shooting from his stone. They curled around the Zoi and flew at the heads of three of the soldiers, hitting the arrows they held in their bows and exploding them into flames. The soldiers dropped their flaming bows and leapt from their horses, pulling other bows from the riderless horses, yet before they had notched an arrow the Trader was upon them, and arrows and bright bolts were raining down.

Only a few of the soldiers remained on horseback, and as the birds passed over, one, a man with thinning ginger hair, was plucked from his saddle by the lead bird. The man screamed as the giant male grabbed him around the chest and dragged him into the air. The Zoi cried out in reply.

Two more soldiers fell as the man was carried away. The male bird's talons had begun dripping blood, and when the man stopped screaming, the bird dropped him and he fell into a field at the side of the road.

Tarkoda watched, grim but unsurprised, as the lead bird picked up the man, crushed him, and dropped him, but he ignored the twisted figure in the field as they flew over it and he turned the birds for another pass.

There weren't many soldiers left, now. The few that remained were milling about in front of the carriage, looking towards the road to Mesbottee, their weapons still staunchly in their hands despite their dwindling numbers.

Tarkoda followed their eyes, and saw nothing but the fields waving in the sunlight, yet he could not see far, for he flew low to the ground and the road disappeared over the brow of the hill. He looked at the soldiers, wondering, and before he was past, he saw a wisp of greenish smoke curling over the carriage.

He checked on the injured bird, saw the shaft still quivering from its thigh and the scarlet stain that now reached to its talon, and though it still flew, the beat of its wings was becoming erratic. He must land and tend to it, but there would be one more pass first.

When they came around again the soldiers had dwindled to three. The horses pulling the carriage danced skittishly. Tarkoda looked down at the fields. Where was Williver?

Just as they were banking around for the final pass, there came the blast of a horn to the west, and over the brow of the hill between the serenely waving fields rode dozens of the queen's guard, their colours filling the road. The blast of the horn came again, and on its heels a shout, yet the shout came from the opposite direction. Tarkoda swung his head round.

A single horseman was thundering down the road towards them, a riderless horse trailing him.

Tarkoda looked from the horse bolting towards the carriage back down to the road. He saw with surprise that Shaeli was staring up at him.

\* \* \*

Shaeli had heard the order to shoot the Zoi and the mumble of assent from the guard. Pizar ordered them in the queen's name again, and she heard no more from the soldiers. She went to the thin slat at the back of the carriage, and put her lips to it. She eased a whistle between her tongue and the roof of her mouth, a high, thin whistle, and then she waited. Shouts from outside drew her to the door again, and she was in time to see the back of the Trader fly past. Her field of vision was small, but she could see one soldier dead on the road with an arrow through his throat and the fear on the faces of the few soldiers she could see.

"Shoot at the birds," she heard Pizar cry again, yet she could not see him, he was somewhere ahead.

The pock-faced man who had escorted her each time she'd left the carriage was closest, his ginger hair plastered over his forehead, and as she watched, the Trader must have been coming around again, for the man took aim. As the first of the birds flew over, he let his arrow fly. She did not see it hit, but she could tell by his cry and the scream from the Zoi that he had found his target. A noise drew her to the back of the carriage.

Ebony hung there, peering through the thin slit, and Shaeli whispered to her and the jevvi darted away. Shaeli went again to the door, peered out in time to see the pock-faced man pulled screaming from his horse by the lead bird on the Trader's next pass. She did not see what happened to him, but he did not scream for long.

Ebony was back at the thin opening, and Shaeli leapt over and took the tiny green triangle that the jevvi pushed through the gap. Shaeli whispered to her again, and the jevvi leapt away. Shaeli squatted down on the floor, took a deep breath, and then she took aim.

The line she drew in a shallow arch followed the holes she had already made with it and the light-sparks, and it sent a thin waft of green smoke up as it burned, but she ignored it and kept working. When she'd gone along the floor and met the place where she'd started, she had only to kick at the arch and the wood fell out onto the road. There were a few horses outside but they were riderless, and she stuck her head out and looked either way. She could see nothing, so she squeezed her shoulders through and pulled herself out. She dropped into the dust and crawled beneath the carriage. She almost screamed when she turned around.

Between wheels of the carriage was the body of the woman with the fading bruise, a black hole in her chest. The woman's sightless eyes stared at her, the yellowing bruise stark against her pale face, and Shaeli covered her mouth to stop the scream that wanted to push through her teeth. She shuddered and jumped as something touched her leg.

Ebony crouched beside her, the amulet she had stolen from Pizar's bag clutched in her hands. Shaeli swept her up and kissed her. She dropped the triangle into the amulet, pulled out her smoky quartz and tucked the pouch far down into her bodice. She put the jevvi onto her shoulder and told her to hang on.

Around her on the road were other bodies, and she tried to ignore them as she went back out from underneath the carriage that had been her prison, leaving the staring eyes of the dead woman to stare at nothing. She crept towards the front of the carriage, peered around the edge and could see only one soldier. There were shouts from at least one other that she could not see, but there was no sign of Pizar.

The Trader was banking around over the fields when she heard the horn and saw the soldiers galloping towards them from the west. She ran to the back of the carriage and looked up at the Trader.

They were still across the field, but she saw Flin and Ishaan and Tarkoda on the fore-deck, and though she longed to be with them, she knew they could not stop for her before the soldiers came. It was then she heard the shout, and saw with amazement that Ezebar was galloping down the road towards her on a huge black horse, another racing behind him. She did not know how he had come to be there, but she took one look back at the approaching Trader. She met Tarkoda's eye and she started to run.

* * *

It was well that Ezebar had befriended his horse over the last few days, for now it ran for him as if it were flying. On small rises he saw the Trader closing on the road ahead, and the last time he saw it before the fields swallowed him again it was over the road and circling. He came upon the bolting horse and managed to catch it without slowing too much and without knowing quite why he bothered, and then he galloped on. As he came around the last bend, he heard the horn, and saw far in the distance the dust of the approaching guard.

Just ahead was the carriage, surrounded by riderless horses, bodies, and three soldiers still on horseback. His eyes widened when he saw Shaeli hiding behind the carriage. She looked up at the approaching Trader and then she bolted straight at him.

One of the soldiers saw her and turned his horse to follow, but he was felled by an arrow from the Trader looming overhead. The two remaining soldiers took off up the road towards the oncoming guard.

The carriage was between him and the new group of guard, and he could not see them, but he could hear the hoof-beats that pounded the road. Shaeli was yelling up at the Trader as she ran, and Ezebar saw the shaft hanging from one of the birds and the scarlet stain on its white feathers.

"Go, Koda," Shaeli was yelling as she ran, the words bouncing with her footsteps. "Go, *go*. Go now."

The man on the Trader yelled something back, but Ezebar could not hear the words. He could see her face now, and he slowed the horse and then pulled it to a halt. She ran up and scrambled onto the horse he led.

"Alright?" he asked, and she nodded, breathless. "Good. Let's go," he said, and he threw her the reins and kicked his horse. It darted off the road and into the fields.

Shaeli took one look back at the Trader, and followed him. The crops of the field closed like a curtain behind them.

* * *

Tarkoda watched as Ishaan shot the guard who started to follow Shaeli and he yelled down to her, and heard her urging him to go as she reached Ezebar and climbed onto the horse he led. The guard was close now, but the two horses turned into the field before the guard reached the stranded carriage. Beside him Almarnoch waved his wand and muttered, and the signs of the horses moving through the field were erased behind them.

Tarkoda circled the road again, pulling the Zoi higher as the new guard reached the carriage. Dozens of arrows flew at them, but the Trader was over the fields and out of reach, yet the guard did not give up. Half the company began to follow the Trader across the fields, mowing the tall crops down and leaving a dark gash through the fields behind them. Koda looked down at the injured bird, had a quiet word with the gods, and flew back to the south as fast as he could.

\* \* \*

Ezebar led her through the field. He could hear the shouts of the guard behind them, but he did not hurry. He knew the soldiers had not seen which direction they were going, or even if they had seen them at all. He thought they probably didn't even know exactly what had happened, and with luck it would take them some time to work it out. He had seen the crops standing up behind them after they'd left the road, knew it had been by the old Warlock's hand, and he went forward hoping Almarnoch's magic followed them still.

His horse started when they came upon the twisted, bloody body of a man in the field. Ezebar had no idea how he had come to be there and he looked back at Shaeli. The hateful ginger-haired man lay sprawled on his back, the puncture wounds across his chest clotted with blood

"He was the one who shot the Zoi," she whispered, and Ezebar nodded and they went around the corpse and on.

The shouts of the guard grew fainter as they crossed into another field, and soon they could hear nothing. There was a stand of trees in the centre of this field, as there was in many of the others, and they stopped the horses in the shade. Both horses were sweating and breathing heavily and they let them rest for a while. Ebony scampered down and shook her matted fur, then she rolled over and scratched her back on the rough grass.

Shaeli smiled at her and looked up at the sun shining through the leaves and breathed the sweet air. It was scented with the flowers that bobbed on the roof of the field, and she could hear the sound of the bees that hovered over them. She breathed deeply again. She was free. She turned to Ezebar and grinned.

He looked at her and could not help but smile back. She was filthy, dirt smeared her face, her hair was dark and stringy. There were bruises on her cheeks and arms, but she looked so happy that he was glad he was here to share her freedom.

"What did the trader say?" he asked.

Her smile grew wider. "That was my brother," she said. "I couldn't hear him properly." She shook her head. "Something about Williver," she said. "I'm not sure. But where did *you* come from, Ezebar?" she asked. "How did you get here?"

"Almarnoch sent me," he said. "But I'll tell you everything later. We must go."

"Where are we going?" she asked.

"West," he said, looking down at her dirty face. "Though perhaps we better find you somewhere to clean up first."

She looked down at herself and screwed up her nose. "I'd appreciate that," she said. "And then?"

"And then we try and find the Proud Pig."

\* \* \*

# CHAPTER SEVENTEEN

Llianas had been standing beside Williver at the back of the Trader when they banked around for the third pass over the carriage. He had been looking down at the fields whipping beneath, a rope in his gloved hands. He had looked at her, winked, and then he had leapt from the Trader. She leant over and watched him fly out behind the ship, and when his feet had touched the crops he let go of the rope. He dropped down and was gone.

Llianas was worried. He shouldn't be down there alone. He might need help. She pulled her own gloves on and grasped the rope Williver had left dangling. It didn't look too difficult.

\* \* \*

M'zena saw Williver jump from where she stood beneath the stairs, and Llianas follow him a moment later. She did not think that that had been part of the plan.

\* \* \*

Pizar had seen things were going badly, and when the next man fell, he fell with him. Yet he did not fall heavily, he merely slid to the road and rolled beneath the carriage. He saw something fall from the back of the Trader, but he barely cared. He had failed. First that stupid amulet had been stolen from his pack, beneath his very nose, and now his soldiers were falling like flies at first snow. He crawled out from under the carriage and slithered into the field.

He went only a short distance and found a stand of trees. He climbed one where he could see back over to the road, watching dispassionately as his soldiers were picked off, wondering who it was who had killed the others in his party during the last few days. That they were dead, he did not doubt, and he had no wish to join them. When the last one had been killed and they could find no one, even though the man had been standing in full sight of them all when he'd been shot, then he had known he needed help. He had waited until the darkest hours of the night, and then sent a man ahead to the barracks at Mesbottee. He had expected reinforcements and then all would have been well, even without the stupid girl's stones.

It was then that he saw the elf creeping beneath him towards the road and he grew angry. As the elf passed beneath, Pizar leapt upon him. The blow he gave as he landed on the startled elf was enough to knock him senseless. Pizar kicked the blade from the elf's hand and saw a stubby wand in his belt. This he pulled out and threw a short distance away. It landed just inside the first tall crops, and he marked its position for later. Then he turned back to the elf sprawled on the ground.

Pizar drew a knife from his belt and crouched over the unconscious figure.

\* \* \*

Llianas dashed through the tall fronds waving around her, following the slim trail left by Williver. It was difficult to follow, for he had made little impression in the field, but she saw a bent frond here and a broken branch there and she knew she was not far behind him.

When she had leapt from the ship, she had been suddenly terrified. It had not looked so hard when Williver had done it, but when she was dangling from the rope, the crops slapping at her flailing feet, it had seemed particularly difficult. Yet she could not go back and so she just let go. She had tumbled down and been surprised when she stood up unscathed. Then she found Williver's path and scurried after him.

She came upon him beneath a stand of trees, yet not as she'd expected. He was lying on the ground, a soldier crouched over him. The soldier had a raised dagger in his hand.

Llianas did not think. There was a thick tree branch beside her foot. She picked it up and slammed the branch into the side of the man's head as hard as she could.

\* \* \*

When Williver woke he was lying in the dirt in the middle of the field, looking up at Llianas perched in the branches of a tree above him. He sat up. There was water on his face and an ache in his head. He felt the place at the back of his head where something had hit him and then he saw the soldier lying near his feet. There was a dagger near the soldier's open hand. He looked back up at Llianas, and she put a finger to her lips, and clambered lithely back down the tree.

She had rolled the soldier off Williver's legs, and though she did not think the soldier was dead, she did not think he would wake any time soon either. She had splashed Williver with water, and he'd moaned and his eyelids fluttered. She left him to wake while she saw what was happening out on the road. She watched the Trader circling the carriage from the same tree Pizar had watched from. It flew past so closely she could see each of those on deck, even M'zena under the stairs, yet she was hidden by the tree's thick foliage and none of them saw her. She saw the rear Zoi pierced with the arrow, and the lead bird's revenge on the next pass, she saw all that went on between the Trader and the soldiers around the carriage, but she was the only one who saw the tiny green light tracing a shallow arch on the side of the carriage; the only one who saw Shaeli push out the piece of wood and climb out onto the road. She heard the drumming of many hooves in the distance and watched Shaeli dash down the road and disappear with Ezebar on the horses through the fields, the way the crops hid all traces of their passing, and she watched the Trader fly swiftly in the opposite direction. The hooves in the distance quickly turned into many soldiers on the road, and half of their number trampled through the fields on the other side of the road in pursuit of the Trader. She did not wait to see what the others would do. Williver was sitting up, a hand to his head, and she leapt down and landed beside him.

"We have to go," she whispered.

"How did you get here, Llianas?" he said, frowning.

"I'll tell you on the way," she whispered, more loudly this time and tugging at his hand. She could hear them now, crashing like bulls through the crops at the edge of the fields. "But we have to *go*."

She pulled him to his feet, and he picked up his knife. He felt his belt.

"My wand," he said, scanning the ground.

"We haven't time to look for it," Llianas hissed, tugging at him again. "They're *coming*."

Williver ran his eyes across the ground again, but then he followed Llianas' dragging hand. The two elves went into the field, leaving the soldier sprawled in the dirt beneath the tree.

\* \* \*

They found Pizar when they were searching the fields, still unconscious beneath the tree. They carried him back to the road, but it was a long time before he woke, and when he did he could tell them little. When the Trader had attacked, he had seen something drop from it, he said. He had gone into the field, found elves were there, moving in on his men, obviously aiding the rebel ship. They had overcome him, he said, there were too many. They had beaten him and left him for dead.

Elves? questioned the guard, and Pizar had replied that yes, he was certain they were elves. He led them groggily to the place where they'd found him, and there, just inside the field, was a wand; short, stubby, and decidedly elfin.

When the soldiers had searched the fields and found nothing, they took the injured and the dead and went back to Mesbottee.

Other soldiers followed the Trader south, until they were stopped by a river, then they too, returned to the city. Soon after, the vines of rumour throughout the Land began to sprout tales, to say that now the rebels were in league with the elves.

\* \* \*

Llianas told Williver all that she had seen while he had been unconscious as they ran through the fields, leaving barely a trace of their passage. They broke no plants, their feet left no prints; they moved as wind through the afternoon, passing through the fields as if the magic of the High Warlock covered their path, too. They had found the slight marks left by the horses, and continued running, following the path taken by Shaeli and Ezebar.

"And you followed me down from the Trader?" Williver said as he ran.

"Yes," said Llianas.

"That was dangerous," he said. "You shouldn't have been so foolhardy."

"It wasn't *that* difficult," Llianas lied. "Besides, 'twas lucky for you that I did. That soldier was about to cut your throat." She would have crossed her arms, but it wasn't easy to look affronted while she was running.

Williver stopped, and she skidded to a halt a few paces in front of him. He came forward, and took her hand. His face was serious.

"You're right, Llianas," he said. "I'm sorry, and I thank you for following me unbidden." He grinned at her. "*Again.* May I ask what you did to the man?"

Llianas grinned back. "I hit him across the head with a bit of tree," she said. "He wasn't dead, but he'll have a sore head for a day or two, I'd wager."

"As long as 'tis equal to the ache he gave me, I'd say that's only fair," smiled Williver, feeling the back of his head.

"Let me look."

He turned around and bent his knees so she could see the place where he'd been hit.

"There is a fine lump," she said, moving his hair and probing the spot. "But little blood. I'll clean it later, but we'd better keep going."

"We shall have to run to catch them," he said. "You'll be alright?"

She nodded. "They'll have to stop sometime," she said. She clapped him on the shoulder, and dashed away. "Come on," she called, and Williver laughed and ran after her.

It soon became easy to follow the passage of the two horses. It seemed whatever spell Almarnoch had thrown after Ezebar and Shaeli had worn off after a few fields and they could easily see the hoofmarks the horses left. They followed them throughout the afternoon, north and then west, north again, and then back to the west and into the setting sun. They stopped to rest only a few times and then they went on, following Ezebar and Shaeli into the west and darkness.

\* \* \*

It took a long time for them to find somewhere that Shaeli could wash. They took a circuitous route around Mesbottee, keeping to the rows between fields.

The fields they rode through belonged to enormous farms, each run by many families who lived in a community in the midst of their crops. Corn, hemp and sugar cane they passed, wide fields of thick winding vines with melons plumping under the sun. They passed several of the farming communities, all with a huge central building and houses set around it like a wheel; the houses and central buildings were all round, with broad cone-shaped roofs. Each community was noisy with activity, and Ezebar and Shaeli took as wide a berth as they could around them.

The fields had irrigation ditches spreading out from the streams and shallow rivers, and they passed lily-covered dams, the blossoms pale lilac and the leaves deep green, but they were wary of being seen and so they went on. As dusk fell they approached another community, and they passed close to the back of the houses. Clothes flapped from long lines behind several houses, lights were coming on in the windows, and there was the soft lowing of cattle. Ezebar stopped and passed Shaeli his reins.

"Wait here," he said.

"Where are you going?" she whispered.

"I'll be back," was all he said, and he was gone.

It grew darker, but a slice of moon hung in the sky to the west, and by its thin light, she sat waiting. The crops – corn here – rubbed each other in paper voices, the cows had ceased their calling, and all she could hear was the screech of an owl in the distance. It was so quiet that when Ezebar returned, it was so silently that he startled her. He came through the field with a bundle of clothes under his arm, and leapt upon his horse.

"Come on," he said, and clicked to his horse.

"Did you just steal those?" she asked.

He looked back at her and shrugged. "I think we could both do with a change of clothes, don't you?" he replied.

"Well, yes," she said. "But..."

"They had plenty, Shaeli," he said. "I took only what was needed, and not enough that it will be missed. One or two things from each house."

She looked back over her shoulder. The lights of the community were lost now, and she thought how good it would be to put on something clean. She sighed.

"Alright," she said. "And you weren't seen?"

"No," he said. "I was careful. Now let's put some distance between us and the owners of these clothes, and then we'll find somewhere to swim." He looked at her. "You *can* swim?"

"I can manage," she said, with a laugh. It was a joyful laugh, a free, clear laugh, and it felt good in her throat and rolling across her tongue, so she let it flow.

Ezebar turned and looked at her. He had rarely heard her laugh, and the sound tugged at something inside him. Her eyes mocked him in some way and he frowned, frowned at the look in her eyes and at the thing which tugged inside him. He turned forward again.

Shaeli's laugh stopped with Ezebar's frown, and she employed a frown of her own, focussing it on his turned back and hunched shoulders. She was grateful to him for being there, for helping her escape, but she didn't know if she liked him very much. He was so moody.

They did not speak as the moon danced across its path between the stars, they did not speak when they came to a tree-lined stream, nor as they followed it to a place where it pooled. They were silent as they unsaddled the horses and tethered them where they could drink from the pool and crop at the thick grass beneath the trees. The frown had not left Shaeli's face during most of the ride, and she removed it now only as she pulled the sleepy jevvi from her lap.

"Time to get clean, Eb," she said, quietly, and she did not need to urge her.

The jevvi leapt from the saddle, glided to the ground and scampered down into the water. She tested the temperature, chattered softly to herself and jumped into the pool. She began to run her tiny fingers through the knots in her fur, and Shaeli felt the laugh bubble up inside again. She giggled as she dismounted, but she kept the laugh that had made Ezebar frown in check.

Ezebar came over and pushed a bundle at her. She barely looked at it, only thanked him shortly and went down to the water's edge. She put the clothes down on the grass beside a thick bush, sat down and took off her boots and socks. She wriggled her toes, wrinkly and pale in the silver light of the moon, and then she pulled off the dress she had worn since before she'd been captured. She was too tired and too dirty to be self-conscious about taking off the filthy thing. It was dark and she just wanted to feel the water on her skin.

Ezebar came over again, his eyes on the ground, and thrust something at her.

"Found it in the saddle bag," he said, and went back over to the other side of the pool.

She looked in her hand, and saw a small lump of soap. She looked at Ezebar's retreating back and shook her head.

She went to the water's edge where Ebony crouched and rubbed some of the soap into the jevvi's thick fur. Ebony chittered with appreciation and dove under the water, coming up a slick, thin creature, her white patches white once more. She grinned at Shaeli and Shaeli grinned back.

"Mind the soap," she said, putting the lump down on the grass, then she waded out into the water, testing the ground beneath her feet.

It was rocky, but the depth rose quickly, and soon she was up to her waist. The water's surface was silver in the light of the moon, and rippled with her presence. She judged the distance across and dove under. It was cold, but she did not mind. She swam underwater, arms outstretched in case there was some rock or log beneath the unreadable surface, and then she broke through, and swam with her clean crisp stroke across the pool. She went under again, surfaced and skimmed over to the bank on her back. Ebony handed her the soap and she sat in the shallows and lathered herself from head to foot, luxuriating in the tiny bubbles. When she had scrubbed herself she dove back into the water, rinsed off the now-grey suds, and inspected the different bruises that mottled her skin. Ezebar was swimming down near the horses and she took the soap and swam over to him.

"Thank you," she said, handing over the much smaller lump.

He nodded. "You swim well," he said, as he rubbed the tiny lump of soap over his body.

"I've always loved swimming," she said, smiling. "The water feels so good, but it's cold." She shivered a little, bobbing just beneath the surface.

He looked at her. Her arms were like alabaster beneath the water, the whiteness broken only by the shadows of bruises, her dark lashes framed her eyes in little wet clumps, and something shifted in him again. He covered the feeling with another frown.

"We'd better get some sleep," he said gruffly, and he turned and waded out of the water.

Shaeli watched his retreating back. The broad shoulders were stiff in the moonlight, and she decided that she'd seen far too much of his back and his frown.

She swam back over to Ebony and waded out of the water. She picked up her filthy dress, took it down and threw it in the water. She stomped around on it for a while until her annoyance and the dirt were gone, rinsed it, and hung it over a bush. Then she picked up the bundle Ezebar had given her, and went behind the bush to change.

He had brought her an entire outfit, underwear and a thin shift, as well as a summer dress. It was a pretty dress, dark blue, and it fit her almost perfectly, only a little long in the bodice. It was embroidered with tiny flowers around the neck and sleeves, and she wondered that he had taken the time to not only find something that fit, but something so pretty. And underwear. She felt a momentary pang for the girl who had owned the dress as she admired it, feeling the soft material swish against her bare legs, but she put the thought aside, and went back around the bush.

Ezebar had donned his new outfit – dark trousers and vest, a light shirt – and was squatting over the saddle-bags when she walked over, his hair slicked over his broad forehead, the shadow of thickening stubble dark across his chin.

"Nothing much to eat," he said, without looking up.

Ebony scampered over and stuck her head in the saddle bag. She came out pulling a piece of bruised fruit after her and Ezebar smiled at the jevvi.

Shaeli remembered the friendly open face that he had greeted them with when they'd landed on his island, and she wondered that she had not seen that face since. All she had seen was the frown, the worry, the concern for M'zena. She decided that she could not begrudge him those things – well, not the worry and concern anyway, but the frown, she still held a small grudge against that. It seemed he frowned mostly at her.

He passed her a square of hard bread and a piece of the bruised fruit, still without looking at her, and he bit into a piece of the bread. They were silent as they ate, and Shaeli found the silence uncomfortable. She tried to think of something to break it.

"Where are we headed?" she asked him.

"The Warlock said to go to Marnissi," said Ezebar. "If we head south-west in the morning, we should come to the road that leads around the lake."

Shaeli nodded. "And the Trader will be at Marnissi?" she asked.

"No," said Ezebar. "They won't be able to land. There *are* no Traders this year. I don't know where the Trader will go."

"What are you talking about?" she asked, thinking something had gone seriously wrong with his mind. "*How* can there be no Traders?"

Ezebar told her of the queen's ordering the Traders back to Cave, and she sat, stunned, as the information sunk in.

"But, the People," she said at last. "What will they do? How are they to go through the year without the Traders?"

"I know not," said Ezebar. "But we cannot worry about such things. We must worry about reaching Marnissi safely."

"But, how are they going to get there?" she said. "How are we to find them?"

"The Proud Pig," said Ezebar.

"I beg your pardon?"

"It's a tavern," he said. "In the city. Almarnoch said they will meet us there."

"That's all very well," she said, shaking her head. "If *we* can reach the city, because the guard are bound to still be looking for me. And if they can find somewhere to land, if they even make it to Marnissi."

He said nothing and she saw he wore the frown again. She knew he must be very worried about M'zena, and sought for something that would soften the frown.

"She'll be alright, you know," she said. "Almarnoch will look after her. And they'll find us, I'm sure."

"I'm glad *you're* so confident," he said, the words as sharp as claws. "For I'm not."

"It is not that I'm confident, exactly," she said, responding with a little tone of her own. "It's just that I know Almarnoch. If he said he will meet us in Marnissi, he will meet us. All we have to do is be there."

"That may be more easily spoken than accomplished," he said. "As you said, there are a few people looking for you. Probably me, too. I have delayed your passage by whatever means I could, and perhaps someone has discovered those... those means."

It was Shaeli's turn to frown. She thought about the things that had happened on her journey in the carriage. She stared at him.

"The wheel," she said. "The missing soldiers. That was *you*?"

He nodded and his eyes finally met hers. They were dark with the shadows of the night and grim determination. He shrugged and moved his eyes back across to the pool.

"So they hunt us both now," he said. "And they will be wanting to find us fairly badly, I imagine."

"Then we must do our best to see that doesn't happen, mustn't we?"

He did not reply, and she knew that instead of placating him, she had only deepened the frown that creased his forehead. She blew a breath out between her pursed lips and stood, annoyed all over again.

"Come on, Eb," she said. "Let's find somewhere to sleep."

She went over to the trees, taking her cloak with her. She laid it on the ground and settled herself onto it, doing her best to ignore Ezebar. Ebony sat beside her, grooming herself. Shaeli could not help but smile at the satisfaction on the jevvi's face at being clean.

"Come on," she whispered. "Let's go to sleep."

Ebony came and curled up next to her, and Shaeli pulled the edge of the cloak over them both. She wriggled on the hard ground, trying to find a comfortable place for her hip. The moon was low in the sky, and it would not be long before it set. She looked over at Ezebar. He sat where she had left him, staring out across the pool.

She was almost asleep when she heard it. It was downstream, a slight rustle, the crack of a twig. She opened her eyes and looked over at Ezebar, yet he was gone, and she could see nothing but the dark shapes of the horses standing quietly where they had tethered them. She wondered if it was Ezebar who had made the noise, but then she saw him. He was standing in the deep shadows beneath a tree, and it was only by the glint of the sword in his hand that she had seen him.

Another tiny sound broke the stillness of the night and Shaeli stiffened. She eased a stone from her amulet, saw the glint of the sword again as Ezebar raised it, and she held her breath.

A deeper shadow detached itself from the trees, and moved into the open.

"Stop there or die," she heard Ezebar say, his voice like gravel.

The shadow stopped moving and grew taller. She saw a profile outlined against the sky and a swish of pale hair. She threw back the cloak, leapt to her feet, and dashed across the grass.

"Williver," she cried, throwing herself at the elf. "How did you get here? Oh, I'm so happy to see you."

She hugged him again, hot tears rushing her eyes, and he laughed.

"'Twas not easy to find you," he said. "We have run behind you all afternoon."

"We?"

"Yes, we," came a voice from the trees.

"Llianas," said Shaeli, as the young elf came from the trees. She hugged her and looked over her shoulder. "Is it just the two of you?"

"Yes," said Llianas. "Just us. And when Williver said we've been running, he means we've been running. If I wasn't so hungry, I'd just lie down and go to sleep right here." She staggered over to the pool and drank deeply.

"But how did you get here?" Shaeli asked again.

"We jumped off the Trader," said Llianas, coming back and plonking herself down on the grass at their feet.

"You *what*?" Shaeli said.

"*I* was coming to rescue you," smiled Williver. "*I* jumped off the Trader. Llianas took it upon herself to follow me."

"And I'm sure we decided that it was lucky that I did," Llianas said, haughtiness creeping into her voice.

"Yes, Llianas," said Williver, still smiling. "We did decide precisely that."

"We have little to eat," said Ezebar. "But I'll pull out what there is."

"Thank you," said Williver. "Anything would be welcome."

"Is M'zena alright?" asked Ezebar.

"She fares well," nodded Williver. "And sends her love. She will see you when the gods deem it, she says."

Ezebar almost smiled. "That sounds like her," he said. "I'll get the food, such as it is."

"Come on," said Shaeli, pulling Williver down. "Tell me everything."

Williver recounted the journey to the sanctuary, and all that had happened since, the storm and the flight back through the mountains. He told her of finding the guard that held her, of Llianas clobbering the soldier, and of the two of them following their trail through the fields. When he had finished, Llianas, despite her hunger, was asleep at their feet, the bread Ezebar had given her clutched in her hand.

* * *

They were on their way before sunrise. They had only two horses, and Llianas, who had woken with legs so stiff that she hobbled down to the pool to wash her face, gratefully took Ezebar's hand and was pulled onto his big black horse.

"I'll climb up behind you, Williver," said Shaeli, handing him the reins.

Williver swung into the saddle, pulled her up behind him and they rode into the dusky morning.

The sky had disappeared under thick, grey cloud as they'd slept, and it grew more sullen as they rode into the west. The morning never quite came, and though it did not exactly rain, the clouds began to ooze a fine drifting drizzle that obscured their vision and left them cold and damp.

They were all hungry. Even Ebony had turned up her nose at what was left of the fruit, but she skimmed up a tree and nibbled on a few young leaves before they left. They were all jealous of her fresh breakfast, for they had been surrounded only by thick hemp fields and dry, grassy fields bereft of any produce, but as the drizzle about them turned finally to a thin rain, they passed into a few fields of tall corn. The corn was young, but when they cracked open the crisp husks they found the kernels almost ready, pale and sweet. They munched on the cobs as rain dripped from their hoods.

They saw no one, and each time they saw the tall pointed roofs of a community in the distance, they edged around it. By mid-afternoon they came to fields whose melons gave them more food, but the cover they provided was as low as the clouds above their heads, yet as wet and uncomfortable as they were, they gave thanks for the weather, for it kept the farmers from their fields. They headed west all day, and by the time the grey day turned into a black and dismal night, they could see the wall that was M'Zen'sclahr Forest rising darkly ahead. They had decided it was impossible to follow the road to Marnissi. They knew they were sought and they were better heading across the land to the forest. They thought to follow it around to Zuen and then take an inland route to Marnissi.

When night fell, the rain continued falling with it, and they continued on too, leading the tired horses now between fallow rows, for they could barely see. Williver went first, his keen eyes leading them faultlessly on, the others, heads bowed and shoulders slumped behind him.

They found a clump of trees to rest the horses through the small hours, dozing with their backs to the trees while the horses slept with their heads hung low, their manes and tails dripping. When the pale light of day finally pushed through the cloud, the forest loomed along the western horizon, the small trees under which they stood dwarfed by the trees ahead.

They were close to the end of the fields, the edge of the last one bordered by a low rocky wall. No one farmed the lands beneath M'Zen'sclahr's gaze, and past the rock wall a vast expanse of flat land stretched in either direction all the way to the forest's edge. The flat land was broken only by huge grey rocks that pushed themselves up through the scrubby grass, rocks the colour of the sky hanging wet and dull above; huge grey boulders hunched like brooding giants across the expanse, each covered with cloaks of ash-coloured moss.

They let the horses crop at the grass, and then they saddled them and rode to the edge of the last field. They stopped before they went onto the rocky ground, looking across the desolate place, such a contrast to the fields behind them, and then they went slowly forward, letting the horses pick their way between the boulders.

It had rained most of the night. Now another light drizzle enveloped them and they went through the ghostly land in a cloud, the rocks glowering at their intrusion, their moss pulled indignantly about them in web-like patterns. They spoke little as they went between the hunched boulders, their voices oddly muffled, their eyes suspiciously watching each monolith as it loomed and then searching beyond it for the next. Smaller rocks pushed from the pale ugly grass around the horse's feet like treacherous sprites, seeking to trip them at every step, and so they dismounted and led the horses between the huge boulders, feeling the brooding discontent of the rocks crowding close about them. Slowly they crossed to the forest's edge, and when they reached it they let out a breath as if they'd survived something truly awful.

They headed south, the forest looming on their right, the rocky land brooding on their left as they went on through the grey afternoon. Their saddle-bags held ears of young corn and a few melons, they hoped enough to last them until they reached Zuen, and as they went on through the drizzle-filled afternoon, they talked of what had happened to the Trader. Shaeli worried about the injured bird and where they'd landed, but she thought that Tarkoda would probably go back into the safety of the mountains.

She looked up at the sky. She thought it would rain for days. She believed her brother would not take the Trader into danger and was probably holed up somewhere safe. She had faith that they would reach Marnissi and meet the others at the tavern. The Proud Pig.

She was wrong about all three things.

The rain would cease during the night, Tarkoda was at that moment flying the Trader into danger, and the four of them would never reach the Proud Pig.

* * *

# CHAPTER EIGHTEEN

It had been easy to lose the soldiers who followed the Trader across the fields. The birds had easily outdistanced them and the guard was left in their wake, black-and-scarlet spots in the green of the fields. Tarkoda had headed them into the foothills, and as soon as he could, he found somewhere to land.

They passed over one of the farming communities, and Tarkoda saw they had a tiny Landing in the open space in the centre of the buildings. He took the birds down, circled the central building, and saw the surprised faces of the farmers and their families turned up in wonder. He signalled the birds and they went down to a faultless landing. He was down the stairs and at the wounded bird's side before the others had the ship tied. Flin was on his heels, his stone in his hand, calling to the people who had come to stare at them. Every one held a weapon of sorts; a spade, a scythe, an axe.

"We mean no harm," Flin called. "Our bird is injured and must be tended."

A thickly-muscled man holding a double edged axe stepped forward. "All loyal Traders have been taken from the Land," he said. "We have been told to report all sightings of others to the guard in the town. They are said to be aiding the rebels."

"None shall leave," shouted Flin, aiming the stone in his hand. "Not if they value their lives."

The farmer looked up at the Trader. Weapons were drawn, evident, but not aimed.

"You make threats against us," said the farmer, his fist tightening on the axe. "The soldiers are right. Traders *have* grown dishonourable."

"The queen's soldiers are the ones who shot the arrow through this Zoi," shouted Flin.

Tarkoda had unharnessed the bird, and now it staggered and dropped to the ground.

The farmer's people stared at Tarkoda and the bird, confused. To deliberately shoot at one of the great birds was to invite a noose around one's neck.

"Why should we believe you?" said the farmer.

"This is why," called Tarkoda.

He turned around and in his hand he held the end of the arrow. The feathers jutting from it were black and scarlet, the arrow of one of Queen Virrisian's archers.

"The other half is still in the bird," said Tarkoda. He turned back to it, and they could all see the broken end of the arrow jutting from the wound.

One of the women stepped forward and spoke quietly to the head farmer. They had a brief whispered argument, which she appeared to win, for her face was smug and his red with exasperation when he spoke again.

"My wife is a Faunist," he said, obviously begrudging every word. "She offers her services."

"I accept her help with thanks," said Tarkoda.

The woman came forward. She was not tall, her blonde hair patterned with thin streaks of grey, her eyes a clear, pale blue.

"I am Ceth," she said. She looked at the bird. "It won't hurt me?" she asked, looking up at it.

"No," said Koda, his hand in the bird's feathers. "She knows we will help her."

Ceth came and kneeled beside Tarkoda. The bird's eyes were upon her and she bobbed her head to it before she studied the wound. She took a breath and probed the spot where the point of the arrow stuck through the feathers and the place where Tarkoda had broken off the haft. The white feathers were dark and matted with dried blood and the bird trembled under Ceth's gentle probing.

She looked up at Tarkoda. "It has lost much blood," she said. "And will lose more when the arrow comes out, but that is not to be helped." Her voice was crisp. "I will mix the herbs and bring the bandages. It should not move after the arrow is removed for several days at least."

"I'll take it into the nest," said Koda. "We'll take the arrow out there."

Ceth nodded. "Ready it then. I'll not be long," she said. She looked at where her husband stood glaring up at the Trader, and then she looked back at Tarkoda. "And let the other birds rest also. You'll be safe here until tomorrow."

Tarkoda nodded and thanked her. She stood and went to one of the houses and her husband followed her, a low torrent of words flowing from between clenched teeth, but Ceth moved as though she did not hear him.

Tarkoda opened the doors of the nest and the bird managed to fly up to it. He leant one of the ladders against the side and followed it up. When Ceth came from her house, a large jug in one hand, and a small bag in the other, her husband followed silently, carrying a fat bundle of cloth over his arm. He followed his wife across to the Trader and helped her up the ladder, then he climbed up behind her and went into the dark nest.

He did not speak while they removed the arrow, merely held things and passed them to his wife as she worked, yet Tarkoda saw his face first soften and then grow awe-filled by the majesty of the Zoi.

The great bird barely flinched when Tarkoda pulled the arrow from it and Ceth stemmed the flow with wads of cloth. Koda soothed the bird as Ceth bathed the wound on the bird's leg, washing the blood from the glistening feathers. Then she tipped powder into the wound, padded it, and wrapped a bandage around it.

She stroked the feathers on its wing when she had finished and her eyes filled with tears when the bird crooned a soft note of thanks.

They left it nestled on the straw in the nest, its head tucked beneath its wing, its eyes closing. When they were climbing back down, Ceth's husband was assuring them they would be safe within his community as long as they had need.

* * *

They had unharnessed the other birds before they noticed Llianas was missing. Kirrit ran back up the stairs, calling her name. M'zena stood on the tiny Landing.

"No use calling for her," she said.

Kirrit stopped and looked at her. "Why not?"

"Because she followed the other elf," said M'zena. "She went with Williver."

"Off the back of the Trader?" said Kirrit, eyes widening.

"Yes, lass," she said. "Made it alright, she did. Saw her after, up and running."

"Why didn't you say anything?"

"Couldn't change it," said M'zena, with a shrug. "Saw my boy, too. A fine sight he was on that black horse. Lucky I made him learn how, three islands over, when he was a lad."

"Yes, I suppose," said Kirrit. "But... Llianas." She shook her head. "I guess you're right, it can't be changed, but I'd better tell Almarnoch."

She went back down the stairs to where the Warlock was talking with some of the farmers.

"Oh, yes," he was saying. "Best get one in, once or twice a year. Saves water, and topsoil when it's dry, gives you protection from the worst of the winds."

"But the price they charge," said one farmer. "Warlock magic is expensive."

"One must always look to the future," said Almarnoch. "We must nurture and protect the Land if it is to reward us. The more we give it, the more we look after it, the bigger shall be its bounty."

"I suppose you're right," said the man. "But it hardly seems worth it at the moment, crops rotting in the fields, rebels stealing. Still," he shrugged. "We'll think on the matter when things improve. If they improve."

"The gods reward those who treasure their gifts," said Almarnoch. "And things will not always be so hard. Now if you'll excuse me, I think my young friend has something to discuss with me."

The farmers nodded and left them. Kirrit told him about Llianas and the Warlock frowned.

"Silly thing," he said. "Tell the others and we'll decide what to do next."

Darkness fell and they sat in the bare room on the Trader discussing their options. They debated this way and that for a long time after they'd eaten.

M'zena dozed in a corner with her patchwork quilt over her knees. They had just about decided on their plan when she woke. They were going to fly south until they reached Lake Marnis, and then fly across it in the dark of night and land somewhere near the city. They could meet the others at the tavern that Almarnoch had told Ezebar about and fly them south.

"That's all wrong," said M'zena from her bed. She looked like a sleepy owl, blinking in the shadows in the corner. "We don't want to go there. Zuen is much better."

"Zuen?" said Almarnoch. "Since when is Zuen our destination? You said nothing of this."

"I'm not saying it now," M'zena said. "I said only that it is *better*. Besides, I see no need to say things before they need saying."

"But how are *they* to know where we go?" said Almarnoch. "They head for Marnissi."

"They'll know," said M'zena. "I gave the young elf a note, in case things didn't go as we planned. I'm sure he'll find it in his pocket before long. Probably has already."

"That changes everything," said Tarkoda, looking down at the charts spread on the only table in the room. "Zuen is much more difficult. It's close to the road and easy to see any Trader approach it. The Landing is outside the town, though, so that lies in our favour. There are no guard quarters, at least not the last time I was there." He mused. "We may be able to land without too much trouble. At least long enough to stop and pick them up. As long as they are there, ready to go."

"They need not be there, lad," said M'zena. "You need only stop long enough for me to leave the Trader. Then you shall fly on."

"Fly on?" echoed Tarkoda. "Without them? Without you?"

"Yes, lad," she said. "Without us."

"Why?"

"Because our paths run differently," M'zena said, as if that should have been very clear. She said no more, but closed her eyes against their stares and slept again.

\* \* \*

The Trader spent another night in the safety of the farming community. They had woken to leaden skies and it had rained as they'd had their first cup of tezz. The rain fell softly at first, and then more consistently as the day went on. Tarkoda thanked the gods for the protective blanket it threw over the World, and for the fact that there was no lightning in it.

Ceth tended the Zoi and changed its bandages, showing Tarkoda how to tend the bird after they'd gone, and they spoke with many of the members of the community during the day; people who spoke slowly and carefully, people who insisted on giving them supplies of fresh fruit, vegetables and cheeses. Their produce, like that of other farms and villages, would lie unused, much of it rotting in the fields, for there were no

Traders to distribute it through the Lands. Their crops had been sown early in spring, but by the time they'd started to bear fruit, the Traders had been ordered from the Land, and they had watched the crops grow to fruition under clear skies and soft rains, milked their cows and made their cheeses, knowing there was nowhere for it all to go. They condemned the queen in low tones, scared to speak aloud treacherous things even within the safety of their homes, yet all those on the Trader heard quiet words about the dark stain of Queen Virrisian which covered the Land. The farmers wondered aloud to the travellers about how those in the large towns and cities would eat without the Traders to supply them, and of how much produce lay rotting as the people of Zirrus starved. They spoke also of the rumours that Great Court had been closed to the people, of the throngs that flocked each day to the gates, of the delegates from other Lands said to be the most vocal amongst them. Now that summer was almost upon them, they speculated on how the throngs would eat, what the queen would do, and they spoke of the rumours of Tenelon's heir with small hope, but hope just the same. The travellers encouraged them in that hope, and the next day when they flew from the community, every member of it turned out to farewell them.

They left before dawn, the skies heavy above the balloon. The injured Zoi was recovering in the nest, yet Ceth said it would be a Moon before it recovered fully. Rain began to fall as they flew over the houses, the lead Zoi calling to the upturned faces below, and then the community was gone, lost in the worthless fields.

\* \* \*

It was impossible to avoid being seen. They flew beneath the low cloud through thin rain, back across the fields, heading west. They saw the spires of Mesbottee in the distance, and they flew on through the colourless day, far across the Land, the line of the road hidden in the grey World. They missed the keen eyes of the elves, squinting through the rain at the dark line of the forest growing closer and more immense with each hour that passed. The Zoi pulled them swiftly through the early afternoon, the rain their only competition in the skies. No other birds flew through the wet afternoon, no wind ruffled the fields and trees beneath them. The World was silent below, yet that did not mean that they passed through it unnoticed.

Lake Marnis appeared, stretching far into the distance on their left. The waters of the lake blended horizonless into the low skies, making it impossible to see where the lake ended and the sky began. On their right, the vast darkness that was M'Zen'sclahr Forest blotted out the land to the north. The road that led to Marnissi was a wide brown line between lake and forest, snaking its way towards them from the north, becoming wider and clearer as they came to the place it passed between the forest and the lake, and then they were flying high above it, following it around the edge of the lake.

Far back down the road was a long line of horsemen. It was easy to see the pace they kept, the way they rode steadily in pursuit of the Trader. Far ahead, the buildings of Zuen began to appear, and the place where the road passed within a league of the quietly pious town. As they flew closer, a large contingent rode from Zuen, scores of soldiers, heading towards them. Tarkoda looked at the faces beside him.

Flin, Ishaan and Almarnoch looked grimly back at him. Only Kirrit gave him a small smile of encouragement. He gave her one in return and he flew the birds into the thin light around Zuen.

It was not very late in the afternoon, but it was as dark as if night was falling. Lights were on in the windows of the plain buildings of Zuen, yellow flickers against the backdrop of the forest, yet the town was still a long way off and the guard was circling below.

Tarkoda flew the ship slowly above them, too high for arrows to reach, but low enough to see the weapons in the hands of the scores of soldiers on the road below. The soldiers from Zuen had been joined by the others that had come from the north, and they all rode directly beneath the Trader. They knew it would have to land sometime and it was clear they intended meeting it when it did.

The Zoi were tired from the long flight and Tarkoda let them fly slowly without pushing them, for he would have need of their strength later. He followed the road towards the town nestled before the great forest, and then, as the streets of Zuen were in sight, he turned the birds south, wheeling the Trader round and flying it past the town and on around the edge of the lake towards Marnissi.

The guards' shouts echoed through the rain. The scores of soldiers galloped their horses down the road, past Zuen, and around the lake in pursuit of the outlaw Trader.

Tarkoda let them keep him in sight. He pulled at the lead lines, slowing the birds even more, until they were floating not far ahead of the guard. They flew above the water still, but kept close by the bank where he could keep the guard in sight. The soldiers gained on the slow Trader, pushing their horses down the muddy road until those on the Trader could again hear their shouts.

The thin grey day was turning its thoughts to night when he saw the twinkle of Marnissi's lights ahead. Shadows crept across the land as the Zoi flapped slowly towards the city. They could see the lights, the spires and chimneys, the trees along the waterfront, when Tarkoda decided it was time. He turned the birds inland, taking them down over the soldiers who had pursued them from Zuen.

As they turned and flew overhead, the guard halted and began milling in the road. One or two arrows were belatedly fired as the Trader swept past, and then Tarkoda flicked at the lead lines and the Zoi immediately picked up speed and the Trader swept over the soldiers, flying quickly back to the north.

The guard turned their horses and began to follow, but Koda took the Trader out over the lake and the soldiers were quickly lost in the shadows. They would have a long ride around the shores of the lake before they made it back to Zuen.

Night grew thick about them as they headed to Zuen, and if they had not had its lights to guide them, they would never have found it in the dismal, rainy night.

Closer it came, and it was only by the different sound of the rain falling around them that they knew they flew over land instead of lake. The lights of the town became bright squares and Tarkoda flew towards the Landing on instinct alone. Over the dark land in the dark night they flew, past the town and across a small field to where the Landing stood apart from the town. Tarkoda turned the birds and they flew in for a perfect landing.

There was no customary light to guide them, but when the landing pole reared before them, Olando threw the hook and it sunk home with a dull thud. Yet they did not tie the ropes. A few bundles were put on the Landing, swift goodbyes were said as Olando ran back to release the hook from the landing pole.

Before the distant sound of hoofbeats reached them; before the landingholder had woken, taken a lamp and reached his door; before the feet of those on the ground had reached shelter, the Trader had lifted again.

It flew back into the rain, back towards the soldiers who had followed them from Marnissi, back into the dark night.

\* \* \*

# CHAPTER NINETEEN

"The World turns its thoughts to summer," said Taffka. "It will be a warm day."

Mareesha looked at him. She tried to dredge up a smile for the Fleet Leader, yet it was a pitiful attempt and she turned her eyes back to the dawn.

Taffka was right. Though the sun had not yet risen, the day's heat could already be felt. There was no breeze. The air hung listlessly beneath the pale morning sky, the last vestiges of pink and orange smudged across the horizon. Etched against the colour was the outline of Great Court, each turret clearly stamped into the sunrise, each flag hanging still and lifeless.

Below the Landing, the city was waking slowly, yet there was no bustle, no hurrying to the markets, no women shopping, no couples strolling. There were no markets to go to, no shopping to be done if there was nothing to buy, nothing but unneeded possessions, and there was no casual strolling. Anything remotely casual had been steadily denied them with each day of spring that had passed. The people who crossed the square below moved too slowly, or too furtively. The city was wasting away, a little at a time.

Supplies from the country were few and far between. The ships and wagons did what they could, but it was always too little to go very far. What did reach Palveron was bought by the highest bidder and sold for exorbitant prices; much of it was taken straight to Great Court. There was never enough to go around. Almost everyone went without at some time, yet the ones who suffered most were the ones who always suffer: those who could least afford it. The poor became poorer, the hungry became hungrier. Places were fought for outside bakers and grocers and butchers for the scraps that used to be thrown away and were now the only source of food for some families.

Thin men walked the streets seeking odd jobs for the wage of a few potatoes or a well-stripped bone. Children begged in the streets, using their younger siblings as sympathy cards, their arms white sticks poking from too-big sleeves, a parent watching from the shadows should some morsel be passed to them. They had all seen desperate mothers dividing a scrap of bread or a piece of fruit into bits and popping the pieces into her children's mouths, each mouth held open to her hand like the mouth of a baby bird.

The people who had thronged to the city had left, at first, yet those that had not left straight away had found themselves with families too weak to walk back to the farms they had left behind, the farms where the produce that would have at least fed them lay unharvested, much of it already rotting in untended fields, or taken by rebels to feed their own. Now those that were left still camped in the parks, dependent on those in the city who still had money and empathy enough to keep them fed, yet even these had diminished, for even those with means could find little on which to spend their coin.

Mareesha felt all these things in the city around her, just as she felt the breath of summer on the sunrise. The oppressive weight of both hung upon her, and yet she still tried to find a smile for Taffka before she looked back up at Great Court cutting into the sky.

"Summer does not hold the promise it usually does," she said, her eyes on the castle brooding above.

"No," said Taffka. "Yet we must continue to hope. And we must do what we can."

"What is there to do, Taffka, but hope?" Mareesha said. "We can do nothing for those around us. We barely feed ourselves. We cannot appeal to the queen. Every day it looks more like the other Lands will rebel against Virrisian's edicts. Every day that passes is one more day to worry." She did not need to say what it was she most worried about. The eyes she fixed on the castle would have told him, had he not known. She sighed. "Hope is all I have, Taffka," she said. "Hope and faith in my children."

"You can..." began Taffka, but a shout from below in the square cut him off.

They looked down, and saw people starting to run, run with a purpose that had been nonexistent a short time ago. The shouts grew louder and they spoke of ships pulling into the harbour. The scattered runners grew to a flock as the word spread and people rushed to the docks. Mareesha and Taffka watched them go, knowing that whatever was in those ships would reach few of the running people.

By the time the sun was shining on the Landing, many were back. Taffka called down and asked what the ships had carried. They had come from Wokk, he was told, but they said there was no food. It had not been believed, but they had been turned back by the guard. Hundreds of soldiers guarded the docks, they said. Rumours abounded about what the ships carried, yet they had moored far down the bay and nothing was taken from them.

They heard many and more increasingly wild rumours as the morning passed about what the new ships held, but by early afternoon other rumours had overtaken them. Word spread that the queen had ordered all houses near the wall beneath Great Court be vacated, several streets down. The houses and roads were to be cleared and any caught upon them would pay with their lives. A dusk to dawn curfew was also to be imposed with a similar penalty. This last was no rumour, for heralds went through the streets proclaiming the nightly curfew. The city trembled with speculation.

The traders stood on the Landing listening to the rumours that rolled around in the square.

"Why would the queen want the houses vacated?" asked Eenis.

"I'd wager she doesn't want people seeing who goes in and out," said Andos.

"Do you think it's true?" asked Renn. "There are always so many rumours."

"There is one way to find out," said Jarris. "Mareesha, shall we go and see the Lady Arinola?"

Mareesha smiled at her husband. He was returned to himself, though his memory was addled at times, this happened seldom, and his hair had grown long over the scar on his head. He still spoke little to outsiders, yet with them he was his usual self.

"A fine idea," Mareesha said.

"Andos, will you accompany us?" asked Jarris.

"I will," smiled his nephew.

"I'll go, too, if you wish," said Rafi.

"And me," said Rhubic.

The three had little to do and eagerly escorted Mareesha and Jarris up to Arinola's. It had become necessary to travel in groups, preferably with one of the large young men, otherwise one was harassed at every step. Similarly they could not leave the Traders unoccupied. Renn had returned to Golden Eagle one day and found a man rifling through her kitchen. She had offered him some of their meagre supplies and begged him to leave them something, yet the man had blackened her eye and taken whatever he could carry. Taffka had been furious, Rafi ready to do murder for the assault on his tiny mother, and Taffka had said that the women were to be accompanied everywhere and the two Traders were to be never left unwatched. The Zoi were the only things they did not have to worry about; no one would think of harming the birds of the Traders, for always they had been held as sacred creatures. The Zoi fed themselves, flying out of the city to forage in the fields, or circling the bay to fish in the waters between the scores of boats that also tried for a feed from the ocean. Fishing line and poles had become much sought after commodities in Palveron, and there was not a mollusc left on the rocks around the shoreline.

The five of them hurried up the wide road to Arinola's, the new curfew hanging over their steps. As they were about to turn into Arinola's road, they passed a cart piled with someone's possessions headed back down the road. They watched it head down the hill to Palveron, the people following staring stony-eyed at the mound of their lives.

"It's true, then," Mareesha said, watching the solemn people following the cart.

"Seems so," said Jarris.

"Look," said Andos. "There's another one."

This was a carriage, once meant to carry its owners to elaborate balls and up to Court, now stuffed with belongings, pulled by one thin horse. Its owners walked behind with bags and bundles, their servants, thin as the tired horse, trudging after them, pulling gardener's carts and pushing barrows piled with more bundles. The woman following the carriage – her head held as high as if she were merely taking an afternoon stroll – nodded to Mareesha as she passed.

They watched the carriage follow the cart down into the city and then they turned into the street and walked up to Arinola's drive. The gates were shut and two burly men with long spears stood outside. The men recognised the visitors and opened the gate with a friendly greeting. Six more men sat inside the gates, all with large weapons close at hand.

"Had any trouble lately?" Rhubic asked one as they passed.

"Not for a few days," said the man, with a grin. "But they like to keep trying every now and then."

"You're not having to leave the manor, then?" said Rhubic.

"Not as I know of," said the man.

"All them streets above us, they reckon," said another.

"A blessing, that is," said a third. "The gods know where we'd be without Lady A."

"Aye," said the first. "We owe her much. You'll find her in the gardens, bossing Sir V around."

"As usual," crowed another man.

They all guffawed and the traders left them to their guarding duties and went up to the house.

Arinola had taken in many of the families who had passed her street in the spring on their way up to stand at the gate outside Great Court. She had begun early on, at first merely feeding the people that flocked to the gates each day. She had taken her servants and Sir Vulcan, each with a basket laden with rolls and muffins for the children who trailed their parents. Slowly she adopted one needy family after another, and by the time the city had begun to grow hungry she had dozens beneath her ample roof.

The gardens through which they walked, once rich with flower beds, plush lawns and pretty bushes, had been given over to the planting of vegetables. The bushes had been pulled out, the flowers turned under, the fine grass dug up and replaced with beds of potatoes, pumpkins, and trellises holding all manner of vines. Only the trees remained recognisable in Lady Arinola's garden. Many people waved at them from the turned-over beds and tall trellises, children laughed between the rows, and Mareesha was struck by the sound. She seldom heard the gurgle of a happy child anymore.

Most of these people were farmers or small-town merchants, and while many had grown strong and gone back to their homes, Arinola always found another family with hungry eyes to take their place.

They found her in between tall rows of corn, inspecting the nearly-ripe cobs, and she waved at them when she saw them. She wore a faded skirt and her hair was tied in a scarf. Over her arm she held a basket brimming with ripe tomatoes. She looked strong and healthy for all her years; strong, healthy, and happy. She called a greeting and came out meet them.

"Arinola, you're a marvel," said Mareesha, kissing her cheek. "The gardens look wonderful."

"Nothing that many could have done as easily, given a little foresight," said Arinola. "I started planting as soon as the Traders were sent from the Land."

"And you share in your foresight," said Jarris, looking at the dozens of people who worked in the gardens.

"What little I can," she said. She looked behind her. "Where has... ah, there he is," she said, as Sir Vulcan came from behind the tall corn. "Vulcan," she called. "Bring the basket and we'll cut some of the squash."

"Coming," he said, and they smiled at Vulcan as he crossed to them.

He was an old man, but although he still trod with a firm step, the basket over his arm and the broad straw hat he wore made him a comical sight. The three young men tried to keep their laughter in check as Arinola called out again.

"Did you pick those herbs?" she said.

"Yes, Arinola," he replied.

"The ones I said to pick?"

"Yes. The ones you said. Afternoon, everyone," he said, planting a dry kiss on Mareesha's cheek.

"Come down to the rose garden, will you?" said Arinola. "I want some squash."

"In the rose garden?" asked Mareesha.

"Oh, yes," said Arinola. "You probably haven't seen it yet. I couldn't bear to dig up the roses, so we compromised and put the runners down under the plants. It works quite well, the squash and melons use all the extra water. Stops the roses getting wet feet. They've never looked better."

She led them around the house to where the conservatory jutted its glassy walls into the garden, and on the far side was a large rose garden, full of blushing blooms. The roses grew from thick trunks on long stems, or fell in lacy rows from vines climbing over arched trellises; soft pinks, blood-reds, creamy whites. The scent was wonderful, and the air buzzed with bees gathering the sweet nectar, a few hives scattered under the trees nearby. Between the trunks of the ancient roses, long vines wound between the thorny beds. The vines held a variety of colourful squash and melons, some already ripe, others with the tiny bumps of future fruit nestled beneath the leaves.

"The yellow today, I think," Arinola said. "Boys, you might like to help Vulcan gather them," she added.

"Yes, my lady," they said, obediently following Vulcan into the gardens.

"Watch the thorns," she called after them. "Such nice boys," she added, turning back. "So you've heard the news?"

"We heard the rumours and saw people already leaving as we came up the road," said Jarris.

"My dears," exclaimed Arinola. "They have only until the sunset hours tomorrow to be gone. There was guard knocking on every door at sunrise."

"And you're not affected?" asked Mareesha.

"No, but it's to our very doors," Arinola said. "All the street above mine. Those houses there," she pointed to the ones higher up the hill. "Those are all to be empty by tomorrow. I have made room for a few, I expect them first thing tomorrow, but I don't know where the rest will go."

"Was there any reason given?" asked Jarris.

"None," Arinola shook her head. "They would answer no questions, but the guard will search every house three streets down from the walls the day after next. No one will be allowed near the gates after that, and none are to be in the streets after dark." She looked at the sky. "So, I'll not ask you to stay for dinner, but come into the kitchen and I'll put some of these things in a bag for you to take home."

"Thank you, Arinola," said Mareesha. "Have you any other news?"

"No," she answered. "I shall be watching and listening, yet I fear we shall not see much of what happens at the gates of Great Court, at least not from here."

"That is as she intended," said Vulcan, coming from the garden, followed by the three young men. Andos held the basket brimming with yellow squash. "She has something planned," Vulcan continued. "That much is sure. It may have something to do with the ships that came this morning."

"The ships from Wokk?" asked Jarris.

Vulcan nodded. "I have no reason to think that, 'tis merely a suspicion. The ships moored in the bay. You can see them from the edge, if you'd care to."

They followed him around the rose garden and the thick hedge that bordered it. On the other side the lawn sloped down to the edge of the cliff. The bay stretched out beneath them, the Island of Dead Kings closest, its crypts and statues barely visible between the trunks of tall trees, the Faunist and Warlock Islands further away, sitting serenely green in the calm blue water.

Beneath the ragged cliffs, three ships were moored, far from the docks. They were oddly-shaped, almost square, their decks stained black. They flew Wokkii flags from their masts, but no one was to be seen upon their decks. They looked like empty, forgotten ships.

Down at the end of the bay, the docks and the waters around them were full of ships. Many were from other Lands, others were ships who sailed out for flour and sugar and other supplies. These never stayed long, for as soon as they docked their stores were stripped and they went out again. The ships were now the only line of supply to the city; wagons had become more and more useless, the rebels attacking each one as it returned the city, many wagons had never made it back at all, and eventually those that did would not be sent again, for there were few willing to drive them. It was the ships who tried their best to feed the city, but there were too few of them and too many people.

Jarris looked from the docks to the three Wokkii ships moored in the water below the cliff and he wondered at them, as Vulcan had.

The sun was falling towards the west, but as they turned to leave, five more ships entered the bay.

"Romynnii," said Vulcan, as they neared and the flags rippling from the mast could be seen.

"What do you think is in them?" asked Arinola.

"One is a cargo ship," said Vulcan. "The others are ships of battle. See the shields along the sides?"

"It looks as if the Romynnii have decided to send its message more forcefully," said Jarris.

"What will it mean?" asked Rafi.

"Perhaps nothing, lad," said Sir Vulcan. "But perhaps it means the other Lands have had enough of Queen Virrisian trying to rule the World instead of her own Land. They want the Fleet returned, and they want the question of Tenelon's heir resolved."

Here, he looked at Mareesha. Vulcan and Arinola had both been told about the twins and that they were at Great Court.

They watched the new ships from Romynn sail down the bay and moor just off the docks, and before they went back to the gardens, they saw a boat being lowered from one.

They went back to the house and Arinola wrapped some of the tomatoes, a dozen eggs and some of the yellow squash in a cloth and gave them to Mareesha. They walked through the house, and here, too, were the signs of the many people that now resided there. A group of children played in the entrance hall and the sound of voices and doors slamming came from the stories above. Half a dozen women sat out on the front steps cutting potatoes into huge trays while a gaggle of babies played at the bottom of the stairs. Across the grass a few nearly-grown girls herded a large flock of chickens towards their coop. The hastily built coop looked odd beneath the graceful trees, but Arinola looked around at the turned-over gardens beaming with satisfaction. Mareesha didn't wonder at the men guarding the gate, there would be many who would covet what lay behind these high walls.

Four men came past pulling a low cart on which there were several enormous cauldrons steaming with a dark, thin liquid.

"I'll walk down with you," Arinola said. "It is time to dole out the broth at the gates, and they become unruly if I am not there."

"No one would dare become unruly in your presence, my dear," Vulcan smiled at her.

Arinola returned the fond smile and they all followed the cart down to the gates.

"There is no further news of my brother, my lady?" Andos asked, as they walked.

"Arinola, please, my dear boy," she said. "No, there has been nothing further. I wish I could help, but my contacts aren't what they were."

"I thought as much," he replied. "But I know my mother will ask when I return."

"I know Eenis is concerned, but I'm sure the boy is fine, even if he is at Court," said Arinola.

There had been no news of Dari since before the Wintering. Shaeli and Kirrit had seen him the year before, here at Arinola's for the mid-Winter ball. He had been with a few other Warlocks and a couple of friends from the guard, the girls had said, but they had not seen him again. Lady Arinola had managed to find out that he had returned to the Warlock Island for his final training after the last Wintering, but it had been said he had left for Great Court again before autumn had begun, leaving his last few Moons of training unfinished. Now, with Great Court closed to all, they could not find out where he was.

None of those who lived in the white house on the bay had seen Dari, either. Mareesha's sister, Asheen, had retired from service at Great Court some Winterings before, and had had no contact with any of the Court Faunists for some time. Those that had been doing their service when the gates closed were there still, unable to leave. Iyri's husband, Meart, long a loyal member of the Court guard, had resigned his position in disgust soon after Asheen's retirement, unable to cope with the new and ever more belligerent young recruits entering the queen's service. It was well he had, because it was said that none had been allowed to leave the guard for several years, and deserters were hanged if they were found.

Arinola had told them the name of the young soldier who had come in the same carriage as Dari to the ball two Winterings before, a man who had befriended Shaeli on her first Wintering in the city. They had asked after Pizar, but were told he was on duty somewhere to the north, and so they did not know Dari's whereabouts and could only surmise he must be inside the castle walls. Eenis worried constantly about him, dreaming of him many times. He looked so pale, she said, and so unhappy in the dreams. She worried about the twins, about Koda and Shaeli, too, but everyone knew it was Dari she was most worried about, and they all knew Andos was right; Eenis would ask if he had inquired after his brother whilst they had been at the Lady Arinola's.

They had reached the front gates where the burly, friendly men from earlier were standing in a line in front of the closed gates without a trace of their former good cheer. Outside was a line of people, all holding a bowl or a cup or a small pot, waiting for what the men brought in the cart.

"How do you keep feeding all these people, Arinola?" asked Mareesha.

The old woman smiled. "One just manages, my dear," said Arinola.

"You'll run out of horses soon," said Vulcan, beneath his breath.

Mareesha gasped. "You make the broth out of your horses?"

"Only every now and then," said Arinola. "The people must have a little meat occasionally and a little horse goes a long way." She frowned at Mareesha. "Really, my dear, I would have thought you were much more practical." She looked at the people lined up outside her gate. "I don't think they will mind, do you?"

Mareesha looked out at the ragged line of people, each clutching their cup or bowl, licking their lips at the sight of the steaming cauldrons. She looked back at Arinola and shook her head.

"No," she said. "They'd not mind."

"You best hurry back down to the square, then," said Sir Vulcan. "The sun will not stay much longer."

They said their goodbyes, and as they left, Arinola was doling soup out with a big ladle, calling for order in her clear, forthright voice.

* * *

High above, at Great Court, Dari was drinking. He had drunk much in the last Moons, as much as he could. It drowned out his thoughts.

Garrit assured him that things were going well, that everything was alright, but he had increasing trouble believing it and he was not sleeping very well. His dreams were strange; things to be dreaded, jumbled and obscure, as if the dreams were not his own. He wanted to return to the Warlock Isle; he could not see how he was of any use here, and despite the lavish life, he wanted to use his magic, but none were allowed to leave. If he tried to voice his concerns, Garrit told him that he needed him; that everything was fine; that they would soon be free to come and go as they pleased; that the castle would not be isolated for long. There was a kind of masked glee in him as he reassured Dari, but Dari saw him less and less. When he asked where he was at these times, Garrit brushed the questions aside and poured him some more of the excellent wine. But Dari was still troubled. And he could not sleep.

\* \* \*

Eenis, predictably, was waiting for them, yet it was not to ask about Dari.

It was almost dusk. The afternoon had been long with the weighty heat of early summer, and it would be a while before full dark took hold of the city, but already the people were hurrying through the square to their homes. The guard were marching in knots through the streets, reminding people to be inside their homes before night fell.

A few birds called from trees, yet even these had become sparse in Palveron this year. The birds and their spring eggs had been too highly prized as a food source.

Eenis was almost hopping in anticipation as they came up the stairs. She was speaking before they were halfway up.

"Hurry," she called. "We have visitors."

"Who is it, Eenis?" asked Mareesha, wondering at Eenis' excitement.

"You shall see for yourselves," she said, ushering them towards Purple Leaf.

They were surprised to see who it was that awaited them. On deck, talking with Taffka, Renn and Jeth, were Sir Brudloc and Princess Crissita. They came forward and there were greetings and kisses all round. S'resh, Crissita's bird-like maid, stood shyly in the background.

Mareesha asked if they had come on the ships from Romynn. "We saw them arrive from Lady Arinola's," she said.

"That was us," said Crissita. "I couldn't wait to be off the thing. I begged Brudloc to bring me here."

"I've offered them our hospitality while they are here," said Eenis.

"Which S'resh and I will gratefully accept," said Crissita.

"And you, Brudloc?" asked Jarris.

"I will be unable to spend much time with you. We are here at King Balkus' request. As much as I might wish to be here on a mere friendly visit, my orders are clear," he said. "Romynn and the other Lands wish the Fleet to fly again, with or without the queen's permission."

"So they are finally ready to challenge her?" said Jeth.

"Almost," said Brudloc. "We shall seek an audience again, and we have missives to send if an audience is denied. There will be ships here from Ashkanna tomorrow. The Starisles send their representatives, also."

"And Wokk?" said Taffka.

"Wokk is strangely neutral," answered Brudloc, with a frown. "They support the return of the Traders, yet they are unwilling to engage in anything more forceful than sending delegates in protest."

"Yet their ships arrived before you," said Jarris.

"We passed them as we sailed down the bay," nodded Crissita. "Big square-looking things. Ugly."

"They are strange ships," agreed Brudloc. "We saw no one as we passed, but they did not look like ships sent for battle."

"So it has come to that," said Taffka, with a shake of his head. "There is to be battle."

"If she will not speak with us, if she does not let the Traders fly, if the rumours of the heir are not addressed, then, yes, we will be forced to battle," said Brudloc, grimly. "We will take the city first. We have people ready in Nebillonia Straits to take Meoro Village, the Pass, and then Serrat. Then the Fleet can fly again into the World."

"It will not be easy for them to fly on Zirrus, even if you manage to take Serrat and get word to them," said Taffka. "The landingholders are the queen's lackeys and the guard are everywhere."

"We have been speaking with those who head the rebels," said Brudloc. "They will aid us, when the time comes."

"The rebels?" gasped Eenis.

"Yes," nodded Brudloc. "They will protect the Landings and the Traders, and they are being supplied with weapons enough to take on the guard should the need arise."

"It seems much has been happening in the World while we are kept here in Palveron," said Renn. "The Lands have missed us and demand our return, just as you said they would, Jarris."

"Yes, yet I take no comfort in being right, Renn," he said. "Not when I also know what it means. Flin once said there may come a day when I have to make a choice to stand against Great Court." He looked sadly at Taffka.

"We do not have that choice yet," Taffka said, and at Jarris' nod, he looked back at Sir Brudloc. "For now, I can only follow her wishes."

"These excuses of Trader disloyalty are ridiculous and every Land knows it," Brudloc says. "She seeks more power, that much is obvious, and the Traders are a way to do that. No one blames the Fleet."

"If she would only speak with us," said Crissita. "The need for forcing her hand would not be so easy. Ignoring the World outside Great Court is no longer an option. Really, I think she's being quite stupid."

"And this issue of the heir," said Brudloc. "It needs addressing."

No one had a reply for this. They looked at each other, their shoes, the balloon, all clearly uncomfortable. Brudloc and Crissita looked at each other, both aware of the instant and obvious discomfort of all the traders. Crissita frowned and looked about the deck.

"Where are the others?" she asked, gazing about the quiet Landing. "Koda and Shaeli? Where are the twins?"

Mareesha looked at Taffka and then at Crissita. She took a deep breath. "The twins... the twins are in the castle," she said.

"At Great Court?" Crissita's frown deepened. "But..." she began.

"More I cannot say," said Mareesha. She looked at Brudloc. "We are forbidden to speak of them." She willed him to understand.

Sir Brudloc stared back at her. He remembered her closeness to his cousin, Queen Irinesta; remembered their first meeting – how Mareesha had taken him to see the newborn twins, how she had asked him to tell his cousin of their fine health when next he saw her. He had not seen Irinesta since Tenelon's funeral, save once when he saw her on the balcony in the tower of the Glade, but now Mareesha's words returned to him, her insistence, her odd manner. At once he understood and his eyes widened. Crissita watched his face and her mind leapt to the same conclusion, for he had told her of these things. She drew a short breath, but Brudloc was staring at Mareesha.

"All these years," he said at last.

Mareesha stared steadily back at him. She nodded her head just once. "We are forbidden to speak of it," she repeated.

Brudloc nodded. "I understand," he said. He looked at Taffka. "I understand the plight of the Fleet more fully also." He looked back at Jarris. "What of Tarkoda? And Shaeli?"

"We know not," Mareesha said.

"They seek to find a way into Great Court," said Jarris.

Brudloc nodded again. "I hope they find it," he said.

\* \* \*

By the next afternoon, all the houses three streets down from the wall were empty. Guard patrolled the streets, stopping anyone from going higher up. None were allowed to stand before the closed gates.

The diplomats from Ashkanna, Romynn and the Starisles approached the line of guard the next day. The soldiers had dragged carts and empty barrels across the wide road that led up to Great Court, even pulling some of the furniture from the abandoned houses around them, creating a thick barricade. When the dignitaries asked they be given an audience with the queen, they were met with shouts and laughter.

"She's tired of your whining."

"Go back to your own Lands."

"Queen Virrisian makes the rules on Zirrus."

"And we make sure they're followed."

There was more, including several lewd shouts at the ladies in the party. The diplomats did not stay long. They merely handed over several thick, sealed packages and asked that they be delivered. They left with more boasts and insults following them down the hill.

A runner delivered the queen's reply several days later. All the Lands received an identical letter. It was almost too short to be called a letter; it was more a note.

Queen Virrisian had considered their position, yet it did not change her own. She would address the rumours of an heir at Autumn's Eve and not before. The Traders would not fly until she decided they would. These things were not open to further discussion. Zirrus was hers to control as she saw fit. She suggested each of the delegates pack up their ships and return to their own Lands. She had not even bothered to sign her name to the papers.

The guard were everywhere, and in force. Thousands of them roamed the streets, they massed along the waterfront and in front of the castle. The city watched the ships from the other Lands to see what they would do next.

The representatives from the other Lands did not bother to go in person again. They sent runners who nervously passed more sealed parcels to the belligerent guards. Everyone knew they contained an ultimatum.

Queen Virrisian replied in a pointed and entirely unexpected manner.

The next day at dawn, as the people ventured into the streets, a shadow rose from behind the castle walls. There were few to see it, but Jarris was one of them. He had risen early, leaving Mareesha sleeping in their bed. He knew the day would bring something, yet he was unprepared for it when he saw it.

It rose slowly, detaching itself from the shadows around the wall and rising higher above the castle. There was a cry as someone down in the square saw it, other screams and shouts echoing from surrounding streets.

The black ship rose high above the castle, then cruised slowly over the city, circling it like some giant predator, and then it flew over the bay. Jarris did not see what happened there, but there were many who did and he heard the tale of it later.

The black ship gathered speed as it flew towards the bay. When it reached it, it began circling the ships.

It hit one of the ships from Ashkanna first. The red blast that flew from the black ship pounded into the deck, pulverising the wood and sending long lines of fire across the deck. One of the smaller, elegant ships from the Starisles was next, with two short beams hitting it forward and aft. It was burning fiercely even as the black ship banked, picked up speed and bore down on the ships from Romynn. Two of them took blasts as the black ship swept over, sending one into flame and leaving the other with a huge hole in the side.

The black ship swept at speed across the bay, and then it headed back over the city. It circled Palveron slowly, victoriously, and then it flew back up to Great Court and disappeared behind the wall.

The city was in uproar. Four ships burned in the harbour, one already beginning to sink, the smoke rising high into the air for all to see. Half of the city's population went to the shore to see the ships burning. The wounded were many, scores dead. The Faunists flocked to bring the burned and broken bodies to shore for treatment as three of the ships burned to the waterline. A silence hung over the harbour as the last one slipped beneath the surface. The last ship, one from Romynn, had a great black hole in one side, but the fires did not take hold, and it sat, a smoking wreck, out in the harbour.

The smoke hung over the city all day. There was no wind, only the heat of summer and the stench of smoke and death.

Crissita made them take her down to the docks. She insisted on going to search for Brudloc. Rhubic, Rafi and Andos took her and S'resh down, weaving through the streets where knots of people stood talking, shouting, pointing, crying.

The crowds were huge, the guard even huger, but Crissita managed to see someone from Sir Brudloc's ship. The woman was being carried from a small boat, her arm blood-covered and broken, and Crissita pushed through the crowd to the stretcher. Their ship had been holed but not sunk, the woman said, her face pale with pain, and Brudloc was seeing to his people. Crissita went back to the Trader relieved but very angry. She opened her mouth to rail against the destruction caused by the black ship, but then she saw the faces of the traders and remembered what it had done to their Fleet, and she did not speak. She kept the angry words for when she was alone, and waited for word from her husband through the long, hot, smoky afternoon.

She would wait in vain for word from Brudloc that day, and the next, for those from the ships were no longer allowed in the city. The queen sent heralds out at dawn, proclaiming all foreign dignitaries were to leave the city and clear her harbour. She would give them three days, she said, to gather their wounded and leave Palveron. Any foreign soldiers found in the city or upon the bay after that would be considered a threat and dealt with accordingly. The other Lands, like the Traders, had been banished from Zirrus.

The people of Palveron waited to see what the other Lands would do.

It seemed that they were complying, for many of those from other Lands returned to the ships left whole. Those that had been wounded hobbled or were carried down to the waterfront, the Faunists that had been tending them escorting them.

A huge contingent of the guard milled thickly along the waterfront, calling insults as they passed, sure that their queen had berated them suitably for their impudence. They reminded the other Lands as they passed that Zirrus was right, Zirrus was mighty, and their queen was the strength of the World. The people of the other Lands passed silently through the taunts, going to their ships with closed faces. It seemed they had given up, that Queen Virrisian had won.

Yet not all those from other Lands left the city. Some merely moved out of sight. Many moved through the streets as if they were locals, watching their mates return to the ships. Even more stayed hidden behind closed doors.

The morning before the queen's stated time, the ships from the Starisles left the bay, scudding slowly from the harbour under a soft summer breeze. The guard let out a cheer as they went, and another that afternoon when the ships of the Ashkannii sailed away. There were a few ships from Wokk in their wake, but the strange box-like ships stayed where they were, moored beneath the cliffs. When night fell, only the ships from Romynn were left in the harbour.

The city fell silent quickly. The streets were empty except for the always-present soldiers. Few of the Warlock-lit street lamps glowed; few were the Warlocks willing to light them for the guard to roam by. The houses brooded in the darkness, the curtains drawn tightly over the windows. The moon hung huge and blue over the dark, quiet city. Only the sound of the boastful, cocky soldiers could be heard echoing through the streets.

Those on the Traders did not sleep. They sat in the shadows on the deck of Golden Eagle, listening.

The night was still warm with the heat of the day. There was no wind; there had been little for days. There was only the first heat of summer blanketing the streets; the heat, and the feeling of expectation. Jarris wondered if the noisy soldiers felt it. He thought not, else they would not be so arrogant.

The moon climbed higher, and then it began to fall towards the west. The sounds of the soldier's voices had faded with the passing of the hours, but they still heard the sounds of their boots passing through the streets around them and in the square below. Eenis made them all tezz as the midnight hours passed, and then they waited and dozed and waited again. They heard the sound of another group of soldiers pass beneath them, and then a short time later, the sound of a bell.

It began far away, in the city's south, but soon other bells joined the first, coming closer and closer. More bells began clanging from the docks on the bay, others joined them from the west, and soon the city was alive with the ringing of the bells. Taffka stood. The others stood with him.

"It's time," he said, and they took their weapons and went down the stairs.

The guard had begun to shout to each other when the first of the bells rang out, yet the cries of surprise soon turned to cries of dismay. People began to pour from the houses, from the country around the city, into the streets, weapons in every hand.

The Starislanders landed on the beaches to the south, the Ashkannii came from the north. The ships from Romynn swept to the docks, spewing soldiers into the ranks of sleepy, unprepared guard.

The sound of swords clashing and arrows thudding and people shouting began to fill the city, accompanied, here and there, by the short flash of Warlock fire. Lights from flaming brands held high flew through the streets. The guard were set upon from every quarter. The people of Palveron raised arms against their own, joining with the soldiers of other Lands to free their city. For a while, it seemed that they might even win.

Virrisian's guard had been caught unaware, and the Starislanders coming from the beaches to the south met little resistance. They swept through the city, driving Zirrus' soldiers before them, and they were joined by the people of Palveron, even those from the parks who had walked to the city from all over the Land picked up stout branches and hammers and went after the guard who had taunted them mercilessly since their arrival. They followed the Starislanders, driving the guard back towards the bay.

The ships from Ashkanna who had left the bay had turned around and come back. Their sails must surely have been noticed from the castle in the moonlight, had any been watching, yet no warning was given to the soldiers in the city below. The Ashkannii landed to the north of the city, sweeping in their hundreds through the streets full of large estates along the waterfront. They, too, met little resistance, and found much support.

The Romynnii had the most difficult task. The numbers of guard along the docks were huge, and they met the Romynnii ships with determination. The soldiers of Romynn had to fight their way off the gangplanks, many falling before they gained a footing, yet others swept from the ships behind them with grim faces and swords held high.

The fighting was furious, swords turned crimson quickly, the sound of screams wrapped in agony tore through the air. Arrows flew at the guard from the rooftops around the docks, and the soldiers from Romynn pushed the guard back into the path of the arrows. More of the guard, herded by the people of Zirrus and the soldiers from Ashkanna and the Starisles, began to run back into the melee around the docks from the city's streets.

The moon was low in the sky now, its light slanting down onto the clashing swords and flashing shields. The arrows blurred through the night. Along the rim of the world, the sky began to pale.

Eyes turned to Great Court again and again, waiting for the black ship to fly up from behind the wall, yet it did not come. As the battle went on and the guard were driven back from the water, there came nothing from the castle, nothing until there could be seen a light, not from the castle, but from the wall. A short beam of light, shining from the end of the wall above the cliff. It shone brightly for a moment and then was gone. Few people saw the answering light from the bow of one of the ships from Wokk.

The soldiers had concentrated their forces at the eastern end of the docks. They could have retreated up through the streets to the castle, yet they would not give up so easily.

The soldiers from Romynn, Ashkanna and the Starisles had joined forces, closing off the city to the north, south and west.

The queen's guard were battling furiously when the things came from the water. They were no more expecting them than their opponents were, and when they saw them they were just as terrified.

They slid from the water, huge heads pushing up on the docks, followed by limbs as thick as trees and bodies like giant, elongated barrels. Out of the water they came, dragging long thick tails, the end of each massive tail a thick ball studded with long spikes, water dripping from their scaly hides. They opened their mouths as they gained the docks, letting a low roar belch from between yellowed, enormous teeth.

There were six of them, pulling themselves from the water between the hulls of the ships. Some of the smaller craft were crushed beneath the weight of the creatures as they dragged themselves up from the black water, and the docks trembled with their weight as they pulled their tails out of the depths. Their heads were huge, thick and stubby, the yellowed teeth protruding from lipless mouths. Along their backs were lines of spikes, the same wicked spikes as those on the rounded end of the thick tail. Between the spikes on the creatures' backs, sitting behind the stubby, ugly heads, were scores of Wokkii. Their white hair shone above the spines along the creatures' backs, the metal of their shields gleamed, their pale faces turned to the figures below. Those at the rear held long bows, those at the front held long lines that went to a ring in each of the creatures' noses. No one knew how the Wokkii had captured the Qotarr, the giant lizards from the island near their Land, but here they were, doing the bidding of the riders on their backs.

The people scattered before the creatures and their huge mouths, yet the streets around the docks were packed and there was nowhere for them to go. The Qotarr moved slowly from the edge of the water, urged by a pull at the ring through their noses. The people scrambled to run from them, and although the lizards moved slowly across the boards, they reached out for those running away with long flicking tongues, catching the running figures and rolling them back into their mouths, the now-screaming person thrown into the back of the creature's mouth, the screams cut off as they disappeared into the gaping throat.

Arrows were now directed at the lizards instead of the guard, yet the arrows bounced harmlessly off the thick hide, and few hit the Wokk soldiers sitting behind the thick spikes and round shields on their backs. The Wokk archers fired arrows down as the Qotarr pushed the fleeing people into frantic crowds trying to jam back through the streets. At first, those at the back of the surging crowd could not see what was happening, yet when the giant lizards moved into sight between the buildings, the crowd turned and began to run. Screaming and shouting they ran from the docks, their faces pale with terror in the first light of dawn. The soldiers from the other Lands gathered before the beasts, firing arrows at them and hacking at their legs, yet their swords barely reached through the scales covering the lizards, their arrows merely bounced off. Many fell to the giants.

The Qotarr pushed into the streets still packed with people. Many bravely hacked with a sword as one closed in, many fired arrows up, Warlocks threw fire from staffs held high, but nothing stopped the Qotarr. Into the streets they came, pushing the people before them, crushing some, eating others, clubbing still more after they had passed by. When the round spiky tail hit a building, the place trembled in its foundations and windows shattered into the streets, showering the wounded and the bodies with shards of glass. As the people found somewhere to run and the packed streets grew clearer, still the creatures snapped at those who ran before them. Two went around the bay to the north, chasing the people back through the streets, back into their homes, two more went up the wide road to Great Court, prowling through the streets above the city, seeking out those hiding there. The other two headed into the city to prowl between the buildings as the sun began to rise above the horizon.

\* \* \*

# CHAPTER TWENTY

When the bells had begun to ring, Taffka, Jeth, Jarris and Rafi had gone out into the streets, leaving Andos and Rhubic to watch the Traders. Mareesha and Renn both knew how to use a crossbow, and Crissita had her own longbow. Neither Eenis nor S'resh knew how to use a weapon, but no one thought that anyone on the Traders would need one. They merely took precautions.

They had talked through the long night, waiting for the bells to ring, taking turns dozing beneath the balloon. When the four men had left the Landing, they had gone straight to the wharves, knowing that the ships from Romynn would land there and it would be they who would be most in need of aid.

Others knew the same thing, for they soon became a throng that rallied to the bells tolling around the harbour. The Romynnii had barely gained a footing on the docks when they arrived, and they fell on the guard's rear, turning them from the onslaught on the Romynnii. More joined them and they drove forward, driving a wedge between the battling guard.

Jarris and Taffka were at the fore when they met the soldiers from Romynn, Sir Brudloc at their head. They looked grimly at each other and turned their swords to the soldiers, driving them back towards the end of the docks.

Jarris saw the light shine from the wall above. He had looked to the sky again and again, the fear of the black ship ever-present, but when it had not come he turned his thoughts to victory. He did not see the creatures until one roared behind him.

It was pulling its dripping bulk from the water, its spines glistening, its teeth huge. The swords of the queen's guard stilled in awe, but as the tide of people turned from the beast, the guard put up their swords again and began swinging at the terrified enemy.

Jarris dodged a sword as he ran towards Taffka. The Fleet Leader was close to where the beast was pulling its ugly tail from the water, Rafi and Jeth close by. He shouted at them, calling them back. The tongue of the creature swept out and grabbed the man beside Rafi, and, just as a frog grabs a fly, it drew the screaming man into its mouth. His body was bitten in two, his still-kicking legs falling to the ground with a wet thud.

Taffka, Jeth and Rafi ran to meet Jarris as the creature roared behind them. They felt the heat of its breath wash over them.

"This way," yelled Rafi, running to a small lane between the buildings.

They pounded through the frenzy, dodging some people, slashing at the guard as they ran, the creature slowly clambering across the boards behind them. The streets were jammed, the laneway less so. They reached its shadows and looked back out.

People were running, fighting, shooting arrows at the heads of the huge beasts clambering across the docks, but they were losing. Again and again they watched some poor soul gobbled down by a beast or crushed underfoot.

Across the dock they saw a group of Romynnii fighting a score of guard, Sir Brudloc among them, and they were outnumbered. Jarris looked at Taffka, and they ran together back out into the melee, Jeth and Rafi on their heels.

One of the lizards was closing on the group of fighting soldiers. When four more ran to reinforce the Romynnii, the guard turned and left them to the beast. Taffka led Sir Brudloc and the others back towards the thin lane, but as they reached it, the lizard swung around, sweeping its huge spiky tail at them. They threw themselves into the lane, tumbling in on top of each other, leaping away from the enormous studded appendage.

The creature's tail thudded into the lane, but it caught on the buildings on either side. The buildings rattled and they were showered with bricks and glass. There was a scream behind them, and they turned and saw Brudloc pinned through the leg by one of the spikes on the Qotarr's tail.

His soldiers ran after him as the creature slid away, dragging Brudloc with it. He hacked at the spike as the others ran at the creature, slashing at its legs. One was felled by an arrow from one of the Wokkii on the beast's back, another, a tall spiky-haired woman, was crushed as the tail swung again. Brudloc was swung with it and he screamed again as he was thrown off the spike. He flew through the air and thudded into the side of a building. They ran towards him as the lizard swung around again, roaring at them as they grabbed Brudloc and pulled him once again into the laneway. Other people pelted past them as they stopped to tie something around the wound in Brudloc's leg, and then they hoisted him up and ran with the others fleeing from the creatures on the docks.

The streets were a mess. Time and again they had to run around a mob that blocked the way, or dodge a creature or a group of the guard. Twice they had to fight their way through the guard who blocked the streets, joining with others to clear a path back through the city to the square. They carried Brudloc, blood seeping through the hastily bound bandage, towards the square, six Romynnii soldiers with them. The streets were awash with blood and bodies. The sounds of the lizards roaring diminished behind them and they ran towards the safety of the Traders. Yet when they arrived, there was more battle to be done.

\* \* \*

Mareesha stood on the top deck of Purple Leaf, the crossbow leaning against the rail beside her. On the deck near her feet lay a bundle of short arrows. She looked across at Crissita, who was toying with the string of her longbow across the deck.

"I hope we have no need of these," Mareesha said.

Crissita nodded in agreement. "Best to be prepared, just the same," she said. "The Zoi will be alright?"

"Jarris has closed the doors," she nodded. "And only a fool would enter a nest without knowing the birds."

"How long until sunrise, do you think?" Crissita asked.

"Not long," answered Mareesha. She listened to the bells for a while. "I wonder how Renn is going," she said, looking over at Golden Eagle.

They could see the shape of Renn standing on the foredeck, looking out across the city, and the shapes of Andos and Rhubic at the end of the Landing.

"We'll all feel better when Eenis and S'resh bring us some tezz," Crissita said, stifling a yawn. "It has been a long night."

Mareesha nodded, and yawned loudly, covering her mouth with her hand. Thudding steps from below drew her eyes.

There had been a lot of running when the bells had broken out, and they'd watched as the people and the Starislanders had pursued the outnumbered guard past them and on towards the bay, but they had seen little of the actual battle. She looked over the edge of the Trader and saw a group of people running through the square. Running away from the docks.

They ran wildly, arms askew, eyes wide with terror. Mareesha heard Andos call down to them, but they ignored him and ran on. Soon, more people began to run through the square, and Andos ran down the stairs and grabbed a man. She watched as the man answered Andos' questions, looking over his shoulder and trying to pull his arm away. Andos let him go and the man skittered across the square like a rabbit. He came back up the stairs, and spoke with Rhubic. Rhubic went over to Golden Eagle and Andos came up to Purple Leaf.

"It's not good," he said. "The Wokkii have joined the queen."

"What?" exclaimed Mareesha. "Why would they do that? They have been hurt by Virrisian as much as anyone."

"I don't know," said Andos. "But there's more. They have Qotarr."

"Qotarr?" Mareesha was incredulous. "But how...?"

"I don't know that, either," said Andos. "But they are swarming all over the docks. That man said there were dozens, slaughtering people by the score."

"Dozens?" cried Mareesha. "Oh, the gods, they won't have a hope against Qotarr."

"What are Qotarr?" asked Crissita.

"The giant lizards of Wokk," said Andos. "We flew over them once. Incredible, huge creatures."

More running drew their eyes, and at first the people came in knots. The knots of runners grew to a rope as more and more people fled from the streets around the bay. The chiming bells began to go silent, one at a time.

Eenis came on deck with a tray of mugs. Her eyes widened when they told her what had happened, and she looked over the rail fearfully as if there were one of the giants in the square below. Though it would not be long before she saw one, there were none there now, and she took tezz to the others with her tray rattling slightly. She stood with Rhubic and Andos at the end of the Landing while they drank their tezz, and then she brought the tray back, gathered Renn's cup as she passed, and she came up to collect theirs.

"Where's S'resh?" asked Crissita.

"Mixing up some kind of pie with the eggs Arinola sent," said Eenis.

Crissita nodded and opened her mouth, yet she did not say whatever she had been going to say, for there were more shouts and footfalls from below.

They had almost grown used to the people passing through the square, but the next group that came in drew every eye.

It was a group of Starislanders. They pounded into the square dragging several wounded companions. A few townspeople ran with them, a couple of burly men, a few women and two younger girls carrying bows. A man with blood oozing from his forehead and a young lad led the way. The man pointed across the square and the group swerved in that direction. They were halfway across when a large contingent of guard came after them.

The Starislanders turned as the guard came into the square, but continued pulling at their wounded, trying to reach the safety of narrower streets. The guard picked up pace, and those watching from above could see the others were going to be caught.

The guard were on their heels when the group stopped to defend itself, yet they were grossly outnumbered. They were close to the stairs of the Landing when the guard reached them, and the young archers let fly and several of the guard fell, yet the rest were on them instantly. The clash of swords shattered the grey light of dawn, and before Mareesha knew it, Crissita had taken up her longbow and was shooting arrows at the guard below.

She saw Rhubic dash down the stairs to help the Starislanders, and soon his big frame was wading into the fray. Andos was right behind him, and Mareesha heard him shout to the wounded to go up onto the Landing. She fit an arrow into the crossbow, took aim and fired at one of the guard and the bolt pierced the man's shoulder. He yelled, dropped his sword and crumpled, but he was only one of many. Mareesha notched another arrow.

Rhubic and Andos began shouting to them to go up to the Landing and slowly they edged towards the stairs. Mareesha, Crissita and Renn were firing down at the guard when they could take the chance of not hitting someone else. The Starislanders were tiring and it would not be long before they were overwhelmed, but they fought on as their wounded headed for the Landing, and then, with a shout from Rhubic, they all turned and ran for the stairs.

The guard were right behind them as they pelted up the steps. The wounded were already halfway along the Landing when the others reached the top, and Renn called to them to board Golden Eagle and they staggered towards the gate.

The Starislanders turned at the top of the stairs, and engaged the guard again, but there were too many and they were pushed back, two falling to the guards' swords. One fell with a cry from the Landing onto the cobblestones below as the fighting scattered along the Landing.

The wounded had reached Golden Eagle, the bloody-faced man and the young lad fighting two of the guard at the landing gate, and Renn dropped her bow and went to help the wounded into shelter. Rhubic dispatched the soldier he fought, and then he leapt the rail of Golden Eagle and ran to help the man and the lad at the landing gate. Crissita shot one of the guard who tried to follow Rhubic over the rail, notched another arrow into her bow and waited for another one of the soldiers to give her a target.

Eenis screamed, and ran down the stairs to the main deck.

Andos was fighting two soldiers at Purple Leaf's gate. Two Starislanders fought three more on the Landing nearby. Mareesha searched for a clean shot as Andos staggered back onto the deck, desperately fighting the two soldiers. He was giving ground, backing towards the stairs, but Mareesha could not fire, Andos was in the way, and the two soldiers, a thick, nuggety man and a tall, broad-shouldered woman, held blades that flew at his single sword with unerring regularity.

Andos was fighting hard, and losing, when his mother leapt from beneath the stairs with a broom raised above her head. She leapt at the soldiers and brought the broom handle down over the back of the woman. The woman faltered, and turned her eye to Eenis. The eyes narrowed and the woman raised her sword and went after the thin woman. Eenis screeched, threw the broom at the woman, turned and ran up the stairs.

Mareesha watched this in the space of a moment. When Eenis ran up the stairs she screamed one word at her.

"Dive," she yelled.

Eenis threw herself to the ground. The woman was two steps behind her, sword upraised when Mareesha shot her in the chest. The woman's narrowed eyes widened and she fell back down the stairs onto the deck in one even movement, the arrow still quivering in her chest. Eenis scrambled to her feet and they both rushed over to see the fight below.

The man Andos fought was not tall, but he was twice as thick as the young man, his sword enormous. The man had his back to the opening beneath the upper deck, and he was swinging his sword with mighty strokes, a huge grin on his face. Andos met each blow, but he was being pushed back, and then he stumbled and fell. The thick man grinned more widely and raised his sword for the blow. Eenis screamed.

Andos struggled to reach his feet and there was a loud clang. The grin left the thick man's face in an instant. He fell onto the deck, arms outstretched. His sword clattered to the boards. Blood began to run from his head.

Behind him stood S'resh. She held a thick frying pan in her hands. She looked at the frypan for a moment, and then dropped it onto the deck as if it burnt her hands. It fell with another loud clang and she looked at Andos. He looked back at her for the briefest of moments, and then he jumped to his feet and ran back across the deck to where the fighting still raged.

Rhubic was fighting on the deck of Golden Eagle, Renn and the wounded were nowhere in sight. The Starislanders and the people of Zirrus still fought on the Landing, and though they had killed many, there were still more guard than they. Another of the Starislanders fell, and the lad who fought beside the wounded man caught a blow to the head and fell onto the deck. Crissita and Mareesha could not fire without hitting the wrong person.

Mareesha had begun to despair when she heard a shout across the square. Coming at a run from the streets was Jarris; Jarris and Taffka and Jeth and Rafi, and behind them came Romynnii soldiers. They were on the Landing in moments and fighting what was left of the guard. A few escaped down the stairs to the square, but most fell to the already-stained swords of the Romynnii. It was not long until they all stood breathing heavily, surrounded by bodies.

The sky was stained pink and the streets were stained crimson when they dragged the bodies from the decks and the Landing. They took them and piled them around a corner where they could not see them. Eenis, S'resh and Andos washed the blood from the wood as Mareesha tended to the wounded.

Those who lived in the city went to their homes, the wounded man and the lad supporting each other from the square. The lad, the man's son, had woken from the blow that had felled him after the fighting was over, groggy but able to walk. The pair had thanked them and staggered off into the morning, the two young girls with bows following them into the shadowy streets. The Starislanders had been taken aboard Golden Eagle, the Romynnii onto Purple Leaf. Brudloc had been carried aboard unconscious, moaning and still bleeding from the wound in his leg, yet Mareesha had been able to stem the blood. She had bound and wrapped the wound and given him a strong draught so he would sleep more comfortably. One of the Starislanders was not so lucky. He had received an ugly wound to his chest, and despite Mareesha's efforts the man died. They were taking his wrapped body up on deck when they heard it.

The people running through the square had lessened with the rising of the sun. They had seen nothing of the guard since the ones who had followed the Starislanders, but now, in the distance they heard the low roar of one of the Qotarr.

The noise came closer. The lizard's roar was interspersed with dull thuds. As the roar came closer still, the thuds were accompanied by the crashing of glass.

When it was just streets away, they went into the Traders, crouching on the stairs and peering out from the shadows. Beneath them came sudden movements and the Trader began to jump as the Zoi moved about nervously in their nests. The roar sounded again and this time it was very close. From the shadows inside the Traders they watched one of the Qotarr lumber into the square.

The Wokkii on its back surveyed the buildings and headed the beast around the edge of the square. It circled the Traders, and behind it – a good distance from the studded tail – came hundreds of the guard. Behind the guard came carts and more soldiers, searching the bodies they passed for their wounded. The soldiers and the carts followed the huge beast through the square, their footsteps echoing down the empty streets. Every now and then the tail of the Qotarr thudded into some building or other and glass would fall from the windows onto the stones.

They circled the square twice, the Qotarr stopping and sniffing at Golden Eagle as it passed, and then they went down another of the streets, heading south towards the beaches. The roar and the thuds and crashes of the beast, the footfalls of the guard, all gradually diminished.

All through the morning the city waited. No one left their homes. There was no movement on the streets except the Qotarr and the guard. During the afternoon, carts came around and the guard collected their dead. They left the bodies of the people of Zirrus and the other Lands where they lay, bloating in the heat of the day.

Late in the afternoon the streets grew quieter still. There were no guard, no carts collecting the dead, no Qotarr roaming the streets. From the headland above the city there began a low rumble.

Before dark, in the last grey light of day, the people came from their homes. They went silently through the streets gathering their dead. This night there were no arrogant crowds of guard roaming the streets, and many took the chance to dig wide holes under cover of darkness. By dawn, there were no bodies in the streets. There was much upturned earth and a great pyre burned on the southern beaches. Another burned to the north.

During the next morning, the thuds and rumbles from up near the wall began again, but the people still did not leave their homes. There were none of the great lizards walking the streets, but the guard roamed in numbers. By afternoon, a few people began to venture from their homes, talking in tight knots on corners in low voices, watching for the guard, scattering when they saw them coming.

Far up on the hill, outside the wall, gaps began to grow in the view. Where once the large houses and estates of the rich had crowded the wall, there were now holes. Trees that had stood as sign-posts on the landscape began to disappear. The traders watched the familiar view change until it became too dark to see, and then they went back into their homes.

Rhubic had gone out several times during the afternoon, speaking to the small knots of people in the streets and carrying messages. He had knocked quietly on doors, passed packages and received others in return. He had snuck back to the Landing, dodging the roaming guard, asking whoever he met for news. His usually happy demeanour was grim when he returned the last time at dusk. Rumours were rife, he said, and none of them were good. Many were the dead who had been carried from the streets, most from near the docks, killed in the fighting or crushed by the Qotarr. The ships from other Lands had been boarded, and those who had died in the fighting had been thrown overboard and their bodies now floated on the waters of the bay and in the sea to the south. Those not killed had been locked in the holds of their own ships. The people of other Lands were stranded in Palveron, hiding in the homes of the people of the city, or held captive on their ships, and none could speculate on what Queen Virrisian would do with them, yet they had not given up. Here, Rhubic's face grew animated. There was already talk, he said, of ambushes to be set up against the roaming guard, plans to re-take some of the ships, yet in all this none could offer a suggestion of how to deal with the Qotarr. Shooting the Wokk drivers was the idea most discussed, but they did not know what the beasts would do without them; would the rampage be worse? Killing them seemed impossible. As to what was happening beneath the wall on the headland above, it was said they were demolishing the houses, but few had been brave enough to venture there. The streets on the hill were silent, empty, and the guard strode up and down the wide road constantly.

They talked late into the night and went to their beds with their next step already planned.

\* \* \*

Andos, Rhubic, Jarris and Taffka left at dawn. Mareesha insisted on accompanying them. Brudloc had wanted to send some of his people with them, but they decided they would be better off alone. It would be easy to explain themselves as escorting Mareesha to tend the wounded, should they meet the guard.

They were lucky, most of the way. They went down towards the bay, edging around the wide road that led up the centre of the hill, and then they turned and began to follow winding streets up. They saw the guard once, but they were far down a street and easily dodged. They came out at the edge of the cliff, and worked their way higher, passing through thin lanes and empty gardens. They came to Flin's house. It was silent, the shutters all closed, and they went through the overgrown gardens and out into the street. They checked the road, saw a large contingent of soldiers passing at the end, and waited until they'd gone. They dashed across the street, and ducked into a thin lane. The lane was overgrown with thick trees, soft purple flowers creating a lilac arch above the lane, but they barely noticed how pretty it was. They hurried to the end of the lane and looked out.

Arinola's driveway was directly opposite. The gates were closed and there was no sign of the men who usually guarded it. The street was silent. At the far end, near the main road, there was a pile of rubble, the remains of a high wall that had fallen into the street.

Jarris ran over and looked through the gates. They were locked, and he gave them a rattle and dashed back across the street.

"I couldn't see anyone," he said.

They were crouched in a garden opposite the closed gates, whispering about how to reach the gardens beyond, when there was a furtive movement between the trees. A man appeared at the edge of the gates. He looked over at them, up the street, and then he went and unlocked the gates. He opened them only a tiny way and signalled for them to come across. They ran over, ducked inside, and the man closed the gates and locked them again.

"Didn't expect to see anybody for a few days," he said.

"We must see the Lady Arinola," said Jarris.

"She's up at the house," the man said.

"Where are the others?" asked Mareesha. "Those who usually look after the gate."

"Most of 'em's dead, ma'am," said the man. "Those that managed to make it back are wounded. M'lady's seein' to 'em."

"How will you defend the gate now?" asked Taffka.

"We have them that have their bows trained on you now," said the man. "They spotted you as you came up the lane."

He pointed to the trees and they followed his finger with their eyes. In the foliage of the thick trees, half a dozen bows were trained on them. They were held loosely, but the faces behind the bows were unsmiling. They were the faces of women and boys.

"We put up the platforms a few days ago," said the man. "Gives us a good vantage point."

They went on up the driveway. Beyond the gates, the fields which had once been gardens waved serenely. The sky was white with the early sun, the heat already rising from the ground, and there were a few people about, but they moved slowly, with none of the joy they'd had days ago. They passed the girls releasing the chickens from their coop, but they did not smile and laugh as they had. They just shooed the chickens out and went in to collect the eggs.

As they reached Arinola's door, a thudding sound began higher up the hill. The sound was terrible, the thuds accompanied by the now-familiar shatter of glass and other crashing, grating sounds. The people in the gardens stopped and looked fearfully up, and then they turned back to their work.

The windows in Arinola's house trembled with the thuds and crashes from up the hill. Inside, they passed three Starislanders on their way down to the gates. Two young women in the colours of Ashkanna were coming down the stairs. One had a bandage around her head, the other walked with a limp. They asked after Arinola, were told that she was in the library with the wounded, and then the Ashkannii women followed the Starislanders outside.

The library had been turned into a Faunistry, the tables had been pushed back against the bookshelves and people were lying on couches and mattresses everywhere as the books stood silent watch over the room.

Arinola was spooning something into the mouth of a man from Romynn when they came in.

"Oh, Mareesha, my dear," she said, when she saw them. "Thank goodness you've come. You brought your bag?"

Mareesha had, but as the reason for them being in the streets, not because she thought Arinola would have all these wounded people in her home, yet she went straight to those Arinola said needed her most, tending their wounds, and then she checked all the others. It took a long time to see to them all, and she put a hand to her back when she was done.

"You have done a fine job, Arinola," she said. "The wounds have been cleansed well, and I have set the bones that were broken. Most will recover, but I would move that woman with the head wound into another room." She dropped her voice. "She should have peace and I fear she'll not last the night."

Arinola nodded. "I thought as much," she said. "I'll see to it. Go into the conservatory. I think Vulcan is there. I'll see to this lass and fetch us some tezz. Then I have something to show you."

They went down to the glass room, and found Sir Vulcan re-potting seedlings. Here, too, Arinola had cleared much space. Beneath the hanging pots with their stems of dappled flowers were tray upon tray of seedlings. Some trays were mere soil, others held tiny plants unfurling their first leaves, more trays held seedlings ready to be planted in the gardens. Vulcan greeted them, washed his hands and gently watered the plants. His face today was solemn, his steps slow. He suddenly seemed very old, yet his voice was brisk and held no trace of defeat when they discussed the battle and the coming of the Qotarr. Arinola came in with a tray of tezz and they drank it as they talked.

"They say we are to begin ambushing the guard as they roam the streets," Arinola said.

Jarris nodded, smiling. "How do you know of this?" he asked.

"We have many new people here," she said. "They have been sneaking out and talking to others in the city." She shrugged. "Much the same as yourselves, I expect."

"How did they all come to be here?" asked Taffka.

"We watched from out on the edge," said Arinola. "Of course, we knew what was to happen. Most of our men went down to the wharves, some of the women also. When we saw a light shine from one of the Wokkii ships, I knew something was afoot, but we never suspected Qotarr."

"How did they get them to the docks?" asked Jarris. "We know they were signalled from the wall, but no one saw the ships come. It is too far for the Qotarr to swim."

"Come and I'll show you," said Vulcan.

They followed him through the conservatory and into the rose garden. The lush flowers and vines unfurled in the morning sun, unmindful of the turmoil surrounding them. They went around the hedge and stood above the cliff.

The sun was now high overhead, the air thick with the heat of the midday hours, and the sunlight on the bay made the water shimmer as if scattered with diamonds. The Wokkii ships were still moored where they had been, but now there was a huge opening in the side of each.

"It was hard to see what was happening," said Vulcan. "The moon had almost set, but we could see the lights down the bay and the sound of the battle echoed across to us."

"An awful sound," said Arinola, with a shiver.

"We heard a scraping noise, loud, from the ships down there," said Vulcan. "And then a splash, as if something was being shoved in the water, something big. Then we heard the sound of them."

"That was even more awful," said Arinola. "I didn't know what it was, but Vulcan had heard them before."

"I have," he said. "Your father, my dear friend Povann, took me to Wokk and flew me over their island many years ago," he said to Jarris. "You and your brother were tiny lads, seems I was very young, myself. You probably don't remember."

"But I do," said Jarris. "Jeth and I never forgot. We flew our children over when they were small. 'Tis a sight not to be missed."

"Yet not something I ever thought I'd see in the streets of Palveron," said Vulcan. "We saw that they'd put out those barges you can see moored down the bay, and they pushed the Qotarr onto them. They had two of the creatures on each ship. We could see the hair of the Wokkii on their backs as they rowed them across the bay, and when they were close they took them into the water and swam them the rest of the way. We watched and listened as they climbed onto the docks." He shook his head. "There was nothing we could do." He smiled at Arinola. "Although my Lady did insist on trying."

"What did you do, Arinola?" said Mareesha. "You didn't go down there?"

Arinola sniffed. "Not all the way," she said. "Just to the bottom of the hill. We found some of our people, helped a few others, and were home just after sunrise. One does what one can," she said, and sniffed again.

Mareesha hugged her. "Thank the gods for you, Arinola," she said.

"As simple as she makes it seem, we barely made it back," said Vulcan. "The guard was everywhere. They brought one of those beasts into the street later in the morning. I saw it gobble up one poor fellow it found in a tree on the corner. A young Ashkannii. It knocked over the whole wall with its tail when it went."

"Where are they now?" asked Taffka, looking down at the ships with their open gaping sides.

"I can show you that, too," said Arinola. "Come with me."

She led them back around the hedge, past the roses and through the conservatory. She took them into a room near the library, checked the emptiness of the hallway before they went inside, and then locked the door behind them.

It was a small room, a few overstuffed chairs, a large desk, a small fireplace. The walls were panelled with a rich dark wood, interrupted only by a small bookcase and a few pictures of forested streams.

"This was my father's room," Arinola said. "And his father's before him." She sighed. "My grandfather was a grand old man, but rather wicked, I'm afraid. It was found, after his death, that he had been intimate with the widow in the next street for many years. He had built himself something where he could go to the woman's house whenever he pleased." She cleared her throat. "A way to visit without being seen coming and going at odd hours, you understand. The widow showed this to my father, after my grandfather died. She'd had a child, you see, and wanted it looked after, and, of course, my father was an honourable man." She smiled at them. "A lovely girl, was cousin Rous. Been dead these twenty Winterings, the gods keep her. Anyway, my father showed me this when I reached thirty."

She tugged at the edge of the bookcase, and it came away from the wall. Behind yawned a black square, a damp, salty smell coming from the blackness.

"Light the lamps, please, Vulcan," said Arinola. She smiled at Mareesha. "A thrower would be useful, but we shall have to make do with these."

Vulcan passed a lamp to Rhubic, took another, and went to stand before the gaping square.

"There's a few steps down," he said. "So be careful. And mind your heads."

He stepped through the square, and they followed him down into darkness.

The lamps cast a dull yellow glow on the walls as they went through the hole in the panelled wood. There were half a dozen steps down, and then they were surrounded by rock, pale gold and glittering slightly in the lamplight. They went along the passage and the bright rectangle that was the room they'd left grew smaller.

The tunnel was straight for a short way and then it headed to the left. It was wide enough for only one, and they followed Vulcan's lamp in single file, Rhubic bringing up the rear with the other lamp. The salty smell grew stronger and they felt a slight breeze. It grew lighter, dulling the yellow glow of the lamps, and then the tunnel opened into a natural cave in the side of the cliff. Another tunnel opening lay just to the right of the first, disappearing into darkness.

The cave was small, but there was room enough for them all to stand and admire the view, and high enough for even Rhubic to stand without stooping. A lip of rock pushed up at the front of the cave, and tucked in behind it there was a sandy build-up. The bay was framed in golden rock like a living picture, the gentle movement of the water and the sky, an occasional bird flying past, but apart from that the picture was still. No boats moved on the shimmering water, nothing moved along the shore. The little cave was a serene, hidden spot, sheltered from all but the windiest of storms. Arinola smiled around at the cave.

"It's lovely, isn't it," she said. "I imagine my grandfather and his widow spent a lot of time here. It's especially lovely in the moonlight. From down on the bay it looks just a tiny hole, one would never know it's here, but I'm sure my grandfather knew. That's why he built the tunnel like this, so they could have picnics and... whatnot here. But we must go on. Lead the way, Vulcan."

They went down the tunnel next to the one they'd emerged from, and they were back in the half-darkness, surrounded by rock in moments, walking back into the hillside. The tunnel ran flat for a while, and then it began to slope gently upwards. When it levelled again, it went only a short distance before they were at the bottom of another short flight of steps. Vulcan went up and jiggled something near one of the walls. A panel swung back, and light spilled into the tunnel. Vulcan went through the door.

"Leave the lamp here, lad," he said to Rhubic. "Leave them burning. We'll not be long."

He put the lamp on a small shelf just outside the door, and went into a tiny room and up a thin set of stairs. The staircase led up to the right, and they followed him through the tiny room that was no bigger than a privy and up the stairs. The thuds and crashes that echoed across the city were very loud here.

The staircase was very thin – Rhubic had to turn his shoulders sideways to make it up – and dim; what light there was filtered in through a series of vents set in one of the walls. There was a slight breeze through the vents and the smell of salt as they climbed, and ahead, Vulcan jiggled something else, and another panel slid open. The light brightened and they followed him into it.

It seemed bright compared to the staircase, but the room they stepped into was small, the drapes drawn at the windows. There was panelled wood on the walls, and pictures of pretty streams in thick forests. They were not surprised that the panel Vulcan had slid back held a small bookcase. The room was almost exactly the same as the one at Arinola's, upstairs instead of down, the desk smaller and finer, a soft chaise instead of overstuffed chairs, but essentially it was exactly the same. Jarris grinned.

"Your grandfather was a very wicked man, Arinola," he said, smiling at the old woman.

"That he was," she smiled back. "But come, we should not stay long. The house is empty, yet the guard think nothing of entering empty homes and taking whatever they like. This way," she said, going to the door.

She opened it a crack and peered out, then she opened the door all the way, and they followed her out onto a long gallery, the bedrooms on the right, a void going down to the lower floor on the left. At the end were the stairs to the lower floor and the doors that led outside. The big doors downstairs stood open, a bright slash of sunlight slanting across the floor. A lone chair, two legs missing, sat overturned in the middle of the room beneath them, and the white shards of a broken statue were scattered across the floor.

They went along the gallery, the rooms they passed a mess, clothes pulled from cupboards, furniture overturned, the pieces of the lives of the people who had lived there strewn about on the floor.

"This is how the guard treat the homes of the People," said Arinola, her lips tight as she stepped over a slashed painting. "They have taken whatever they fancied and broken things for no other reason than to see them ruined."

At the end of the gallery was a large room, a sitting room. The furniture was overturned and the cupboards and drawers open, the contents mostly on the floor. The curtains were drawn, the air was thick and over-warm. The sounds from outside were very close, and they all jumped as a particularly loud thud shattered the air. The windows rattled with the force of it and a fine dust sifted down from the ceiling. There was the sound of far-off cheering and they went to the curtained windows and peered out.

The drapes covered windows that looked down on the front of the house. Below, there was a circular driveway, the once-pretty flowers lining it lying parched and dusty in the sun. Down the short driveway, the gates were open, one hanging crookedly, and across the road was one of the Qotarr.

It was climbing over the ruins of the house that had once stood there. As they watched, it swung its tail and demolished a wall. The tall chimney was next. It fell in a long slow movement, the line of its bricks shattering on the rubble. A cloud of dust leapt from the site and there came another cheer from a large group of soldiers standing further down the road watching the destruction.

Other houses along the opposite side of the street showed signs of damage, and higher up they could see where more houses had been demolished, the roots of trees sticking up through the rubble. Between the houses they could see another of the lizards climbing across a lump of stones that had once been a grand house, and another nearby. This third Qotarr had no Wokkii on its back; it was tethered by the ring in its nose and lay basking in the sun atop a pile of rubble. Other thuds and crashes could be heard further along the headland; more Qotarr demolishing the homes of the rich somewhere out of sight.

Still higher, above where the Qotarr were ruining the houses, they could see the place where the wide road met the gate. The gate was partly open and the guard strolled in and out. There was no one now in this part of the city to beg for an audience; none who dared go beyond the barricade lower down. Few but the guard would have seen the sight they now looked upon, but they did not watch for long. They went back to the little room with the hidden stairs and tunnel.

Not much had been disturbed here, compared to the rest of the house. The drawers of the desk had been rifled through, the contents dumped on top, but the rest was undisturbed. Vulcan remarked that the guard would have little time for books, and he wondered aloud when it was that the royal guard had gone from being a noble profession to one filled with immorality and corruption. Yet it was a question they all knew the answer to; he did not need to be told it was Queen Virrisian who had made it so.

They went back through the opening in the wall, and Vulcan pulled the panel containing the bookcase across behind them. They went down the thin staircase in the light of the vents to where the lamps burned on their shelf, and on down into the tunnel. Vulcan covered this opening again too, and Rhubic led them back to the little cave. They did not linger to look at the view, but went straight on back down the tunnel to Arinola's. No one spoke until the tunnel had been closed from sight and the room looked like a small gentleman's study once more.

*** 

It was late in the afternoon when they returned to the Landing in the square.

Eenis watched for them from the top of the stairs, her agitation clear. Renn stood beside her with none of Eenis' angst on her face, yet when she saw them, her face showed a measure of relief equal to Eenis'. She had composed her features by the time they'd mounted the stairs, and accepted the kiss Taffka placed on her cheek with a calm smile. Eenis hugged Andos and asked him over and over again if he was sure he was alright, checking him to be sure that he had not hurt himself somewhere that he wasn't aware of, much to his embarrassment and Rhubic's amusement.

Arinola had given them a late lunch before they'd left, and she had also given them some of her produce to bring back to the Traders. Mareesha had promised to return there as soon as she could to check on those who had been wounded.

They had encountered a contingent of guard on the way back. They had been questioned, the soldiers listening with narrowed eyes to the explanation that they had been escorting Mareesha to tend the wounded, and Mareesha's bag had been searched. The soldiers had asked more questions; who had she tended, were they soldiers from other Lands? Mareesha replied that she did not know if she had seen anyone from another Land without dropping her gaze. She had not asked after their origins, she said, but had merely tended them. There were a lot to be tended to, she'd added defiantly. They had been given a stern warning they not aid any of the people from other Lands.

Jeth was waiting for them at the landing gate when they went aboard and they went below to tell Sir Brudloc, Crissita and the other Romynnii about what they had seen.

Brudloc's leg had sustained an ugly wound. The bone had been broken and the muscle almost shredded by the spine in the Qotarr's tail. He would walk on it again, given time, but it would never be what it was. Mareesha was giving him her strongest herbs to cope with the pain and she cleansed the wound every day. She had had an awkward time splinting it so it could still be cleaned, and she had wished more than once for Sahli'en's calm advice.

Brudloc and the others heard what Jarris had to tell with faces that had done little but look grim for days. The faces now became grimmer.

Taffka told the Starislanders on Golden Eagle too, and later, as night threw its blanket over the World, they met to discuss their plans. Later still, a few of them slipped into the night.

The moon was still big above the city, but thick cloud swept across its face, leaving the streets patchy with blackness. Through the patches dashed scurrying figures, slipping in and out of barely-opened doors, hiding whenever the sound of the guard came near. The city breathed secrets and hatched plots through the midnight hours and on towards dawn. Though few had roamed the streets of Palveron throughout the day, the city trembled with low whispers all through the night.

\* \* \*

Across the other side of the Bay of Islands, there were those who had watched the coming of the black ship, who had heard of the coming of the Qotarr with a strange mixture of horror and excitement. Spies with the gift of coming and going from the city had reported the destruction, the painful defeat, the plans to harass the guard from within, yet the messages from the battered city were becoming scarcer as the guard tightened their hold on its borders.

For Fezzik, while the news was grievous, it also brought him renewed hope. Many rebels had heard of the planned assault to regain control of Palveron and many had gone into the outskirts to give what aid they could, yet they had kept to the periphery, always sure they had means of leaving the fray. Fezzik had led an attack on an outpost outside the city at the place where he and Pelazarus had once rescued Kora and her husband from the soldiers. The small garrison which had been built on their land was easily overcome and the bodies of the soldiers lay where they had fallen. He had also found one who he had long sought.

The man who had once been the landingholder at Boccra was at the garrison. Qwintum was cousin to the woman who had once led the soldiers in the garrison above Boccra, the woman Fezzik had killed the night he had freed Verlie and Pemba. It had been Qwintum who'd spied on them; Qwintum who had told his cousin of seeing Verlie and Pemba hiding weapons beneath the chicken coop; Qwintum who had been instrumental in the taking of Verlie and Pemba, in the deaths of Pim and Zeffy beneath the wheels of the carriage that were taking their mothers. The weedy little man had cowered when Fezzik found him, had begged for his life just as the two little girls had begged for their mothers, and Fezzik had to admit to a grim satisfaction as he thrust his sword between Qwintum's ribs.

He had left the place with two score of rebels now in charge and taken shelter in an abandoned building on the edge of the bay with his brother and a few other rebels, gathering information to take back to their leader. The sunrise hours would see them gone. They did not expect much difficulty in returning to their stronghold.

The guard had been seeping from the Land as the summer had seeped into the World. To Palveron they had gone in their thousands; many more had gone east, it was rumoured to Serrat. This left the Land freer. Not bereft of guard exactly, but they were spread much more thinly across the countryside. Something formed in Fezzik's mind. He took one last look across the bay and then he and his companions rode north to seek the leader of the rebels.

\* \* \*

# CHAPTER TWENTY ONE

The rain had stopped during the night. Shaeli, Williver, Ezebar, and Llianas had slept huddled beneath their cloaks, dozing in uncomfortable snatches. Even though the rain had stopped, the remainder of the night had not passed more pleasantly; the trees dripped constantly and the ground was lumpy with rocks. They woke with the sky still thick and low above them, and trudged through the muddy morning expecting to be soaked again at any moment.

Shaeli picked her way over the rocky ground, each step caking her boots with more mud. Her feet had grown heavy with it throughout the morning, the hem of the dress that Ezebar had stolen for her was wet and brown with it too. The ground was so choked with rocks that it was impossible to ride, and so they led the horses, finding a path across thick muddy ground between the ragged grey rocks. The grey boulders ran right to the edge of the forest, and on into it from what they could see, yet they could not see far into the forest's confines in the greyness of the day and the mist that pooled amongst the trees, and, for the most part, they avoided looking there.

They skirted the edge of the forest through the dismal morning, stopping only to dislodge the mud from their boots and scrape it from the horse's hooves. Far away they saw glimpses of Lake Marnis, and sometimes signs of the road that passed between them and the lake, but they kept close by the trees, fearful of joining the road. Williver's keen eyes saw the glints of metal between the trees along the road every now and then, and so they kept as close to the forest as they could.

Beside Shaeli trudged Llianas, her eyes on the ground, seeking the smoothest path. Ebony sat on Shaeli's shoulder, her lip curled at the ground below; if she had not been averse to mud already, her journey beneath Shaeli's prison carriage would have made her so. Williver and Ezebar led the horses behind them, the two horses picking their way delicately over the rocks, finding soft ground on which to place their feet. Their legs, too, were coated with mud.

They went on through the long day, billowing grey cloud above them, rock-strewn, muddy ground beneath their feet, the forest dripping and gloomy beside them. A breeze came up during the afternoon, a soft wind from the south, cooled by its passing over Lake Marnis.

The lake was closer now, lying across the southern horizon like a piece of fallen sky. White tips appeared on the far off water and the wind grew stronger. The sky turned to ash, the clouds boiled, swirling around, thick with high peaks and deep troughs. The day darkened, lightning appeared in the sky to the south, thick jagged bolts leaping onto the water of the lake. The storm closed in on them, the wind ripping at their clothes and hair, lightning shattering the sky, the bolts coming closer and closer, the thunder booming incessantly, yet the rain did not fall. Across the rock-covered landscape the World disappeared, first the lake, then the land, as thick rain covered all from sight to the south and east and the sounds of the World were muffled by its fury, and yet they were hit with only a few fat drops. They went on with the edge of the storm buffeting them but never reaching them, the trees beside them leaping and tossing their heads with the wind's fury. Every now and then they would hear a branch crack and fall somewhere off to the right, but the storm swept past, boiling around behind them and heading further north, and they were left dishevelled and exhausted in its wake.

The sky was still thick with cloud, but a few patches cleared to show the edge of the sunset to the west, and they began looking for somewhere to spend the night. They would not traverse the rocky landscape once it grew dark, and they went into the edge of the forest, beneath the common trees, to see if there was some patch of ground where they could sit. Night was closing in around them when they came to a gap between a few trees where there weren't many rocks on the ground. They pulled the saddles from the horses and tethered them; the two would not eat the dry grass that grew on the rocky ground, but they happily cropped at the much greener grass that grew beneath the trees. The food they had left for themselves was meagre, and they munched on it as they sat on the damp ground. Past the common trees the thick trunks of the forest proper loomed like a wall, mist curling thick as soup between the trees.

They should reach Zuen the next day, and though they did not want to go into the town, their lack of food would make a trip necessary. Ezebar said he would go in; he was the least conspicuous. He grew a little embarrassed, but looked at them steadily as he spoke.

"I have no coin," he said. "All my things I left with M'zena. I had a little coin on me when I set out, but that's gone. I have nothing to buy supplies with."

Shaeli had not thought about the need for coin; Flin had always had an abundant supply. She looked blankly back at Ezebar.

"I haven't any either," she said.

"Well, don't look at me," said Llianas. "I don't have anything."

They all looked at Williver. He began to pat at his pockets.

"I don't believe I have any…" he began. "Wait a moment." He put his fingers into a deep pocket in his vest, and came out with a small wad of paper. "I don't know what this is," he said.

He unwrapped the paper. Inside were three bright coins and the paper was covered with fine writing. Some of the words had disappeared with the water that had reached the paper, and it was impossible to read it in the twilight.

"We can chance a small light, please, Shaeli," said Williver. "Crowd around."

They huddled in a small circle, the paper held in the centre in Williver's long fingers. Shaeli did not use a stone, she merely shot a tiny ball from her fingers and it hovered above the paper Williver held. The writing was light, spidery in the pale blue light from Shaeli's ball. Ezebar spoke.

"That's M'zena's hand," he said, leaning eagerly to see the words.

There were parts missing, run into faded blotches by the damp, but they could all read the words that remained.

*If you find this, young elf,* the note began, *then... unsuccessful. You must f... eli and my boy. We will mee... uen. Find the... red Do... ouse... safe there. Remem... Zuen.*

There was a large M signed with a flourish at the bottom. They looked at each other over the tiny fading ball. Williver looked back down at the paper. He quietly spoke aloud the words on the page, trying to fill in the blanks made by the damp.

"The first part is clear. 'If you find this, young elf,'" he read, "'then we have been unsuccessful. You must', I think it must say, 'find Shaeli and my boy'. And then I think it says they will meet us at Zuen."

"Zuen?" asked Shaeli. "Why there?"

"I know not," said Williver, turning back to the page. "This next part is difficult, just 'find the', and, I don't know, maybe 'red door'."

"Find something with a red door?" said Llianas. "That looks like 'house', perhaps?"

Williver nodded. "Perhaps," he said. "The words after that are 'safe there'. And then 'remember' and 'Zuen' once more."

"So we are to find a house with a red door, in Zuen," said Shaeli. "But the Trader will never be able to land there. The guard will be all over it."

"Nevertheless, that is where we shall go," said Williver.

"M'zena will have good reason to send us there," said Ezebar. "This place with the red door will be safe, just as she says."

Shaeli's light ball faded then. The paper disappeared from view and became just a small white scrap in the darkness.

Night had gathered close about them as they'd studied the note from M'zena. Though the wind had dropped a little, it still strode across the land with vigour, whistling around the rocks as it went. The sound of the wind's whistle was eerie, and they did not move far from each other to find a damp piece of ground to lie down on. Ezebar was pulling a couple of small rocks from a patch of soggy ground when he noticed.

"Where are the horses?" he said, looking into the darkness.

"They're right..." said Llianas. She stopped. "They were right there," she said.

Williver led the way to where the horses had been, but they were gone. The lines that had tethered them were still tied fast to the tree, but they had been cut through. They had not heard a sound, not a hoofbeat or footstep, but they did not look for long, there was little point. They went back to their little patch of ground, listening for the soft nicker from one of the horses, but there was nothing. They huddled together to sleep, hearing only the high whistle from the wind and the soft creak from the forest as they slept.

\* \* \*

Shaeli slept fitfully. She was damp and uncomfortable, and quietly frightened by the disappearance of the horses. She wondered where they had gone; what had happened to them, who had taken them so silently. She opened her eyes. The wind had dropped, and she was looking at Llianas' back. The fact she could see anything was amazing, for the last time she'd opened her eyes all she could see was her hand floating palely before her face, and she rolled onto her back and looked up to see the moon looking back at her. It was turning its face away from the World, but it was still plump and bright. It sat between a break in the clouds, serenely oblivious to the worries of the people sleeping below it. She looked at it for a while, and then rolled onto her other side to try and sleep again.

Ezebar was staring at her. He lay beside her, a hand's breadth from her, his dark eyes fixed upon her face. She drew a breath. Her heart fluttered in her chest.

"I'm sorry," he said, almost too quietly for her to hear him. "I was having trouble sleeping also. It's nice to see it." He hesitated. "The moon, I mean."

"Yes," she whispered back. She looked up it again for a moment, and then she looked back at him, tucking an arm beneath her head. "Perhaps we'll see the sun tomorrow."

"Perhaps," he said, smiling. "You should try and sleep," he said, after a moment. "Sun or rain or rocky ground, we'll be walking all the way now."

"What do you think happened to them?" Shaeli asked. "The horses."

"I don't know," said Ezebar. "But don't worry. You shall sleep safely."

His eyes were unreadable as he said this last, but something in his voice made Shaeli's heart flutter again. She hoped he could not see the pink blush which spread across her cheeks.

"Thank you," she said softly.

He looked back at her before he spoke again. It lasted only a moment, but the moment seemed to stretch, to last much longer than it possibly should have.

"Sleep well," he said at last, and then he turned over and left Shaeli staring at his broad back.

She looked at it for a while, feeling the last heat of the blush fading from her cheeks, and then she closed her eyes and tried to sleep.

She was breathing in a soft, quiet rhythm when Ezebar rolled over again. Shaeli slept on as Ezebar watched her face in the moonlight and listened to the sounds of the night.

\* \* \*

They woke early and began walking straight away, munching the last shrivelling cobs of corn as they walked. They had all slept badly, were wet and muddy and tired, and after a perfunctory look for the horses, they'd gone on. They'd seen the prints left by the horses, prints that led into the forest, but there was no sign of anything else, even the elves could find no sign of those who had stolen the horses. The two horses were just gone, and so they went too.

The morning was bright enough. The early sun warmed their backs as they walked, fat clouds scudded across the sky, and steam rose from the wet ground. The rocks that had peppered the ground began to lessen, and to the south the bright waters of Lake Marnis grew closer, yet so did the road that ran between lake and forest, and they hugged the trees, hoping they would not be seen. Occasionally, Williver saw a contingent of soldiers far across the rocky ground, and they would move into the shadows until they had passed. The forest proper, ringed by the common trees, was a darker curtain at their backs, silent and brooding.

By the midday hours, the fat clouds which had travelled happily north all morning began to bank again over the lake. The water deepened its colour, and by afternoon the wind had picked up and the familiar rumble of thunder sounded in the distance. The rain began again before dark, the afternoon shortened by the cloaked sky, and their path was lit by the ripples of lightning caught within the clouds. Their just-dry cloaks began to grow damp once more, but they did not stop. They had no food and another night beside the eerie forest was completely undesirable. Darkness also gave them cover, for the road and the lake had grown very close.

Between the patches of rain, Llianas and Williver saw lights ahead. It was many footsteps before Shaeli and Ezebar saw them too, but then they also could see the soft twinkles of far-off lights. Yet just as they saw them and began to hope, the lights began to go out, one by one, slowly at first, and then a few at a time as the people of Zuen went to their beds. The townspeople of Zuen did not linger long after the sun had left the sky, and soon the way ahead was unlit; every light in the town had been put out. They walked on, knowing the quiet town lay in their path somewhere in the darkness.

They stopped to rest once, but each time they dozed the rain began again, and so they heaved themselves up and walked on. The rocks had almost gone from the ground and walking had become easier, yet it was well they had the forest to guide them, for the night was very dark.

They edged away from the dark wall of forest now the night and the rain hid them from sight, walking as far from its border as they could without losing it in the darkness, for the eeriness of the trees grew with the lateness of the night, and none of them liked the silence that enveloped the trees, the feeling of dread that rolled from the shadows and the mist between the trees.

The rumble of thunder had ceased with the passing of hours, but they were doused in rain time and again. It hardly seemed to matter anymore. They plodded on, the interminable forest off to their right, scrubby open land on their left, the mud sticking to their shoes below and the rain falling on their heads. They almost walked into the buildings of Zuen before they saw them.

Ezebar was ahead. He tripped over something, and it took his dazed mind a moment to realise that it was a low fence. The others were clustered behind him as he rose to his feet. They were looking up at the side of a building, the windows blacker holes in the dark wooden face. Rain dripped from the gutters into his eyes, and he climbed back over the fence, barely feeling the sting on his shins. They went back, just a short way, wondering what the hour was, what they should do.

Ezebar and Williver wanted to go into the town alone, to see if they could find anything that looked like M'zena's red door, but Llianas and Shaeli staunchly refused to be left alone in the empty space behind the village and so close to the forest. In the end they decided they would all go. Shaeli knew the town well enough to know that few would stir from their beds before the sun, and none would leave their homes. If there were guard there, they would soon know.

The rain thinned to a drizzle as they crept along the fence that had tripped Ezebar, skirting the building and coming out into a cobbled street. The stones glinted with the rain and they went as quietly as they could through the streets.

Shaeli led the way, for she was the only one who had ever been in the town, and they went up and down the silent streets looking for a place with a red door, but finding nothing. On the far side of the town the houses were further apart, the gardens wider. When they had passed the last one, they had still seen no building with a red door; most of the town was coloured in muted tones, browns and greens and greys. They huddled beneath a tree in the last garden.

"There's not much past here," said Shaeli. "A few community fields and then the Landing."

She sighed, knowing that at any other time there would have been lights to show where the Landing was. Now there was only blackness ahead. They turned back into the town, circling the streets, checking each door again, finding nothing again.

They ended up in a thin alley near the centre of town, looking out across the town's small square. Above one of the shops a light came on and it began to rain softly again. The wind had dropped and here and there was the soft chirp of a bird. It would not be long until the town woke.

The building they stood beside was made of thick stone blocks with a large overhanging roof. They huddled, whispering, beneath the overhang, and they decided it was too risky to stay here while the town awoke. They would have to go back out and hide near the forest.

The light rain eased as they went around the front of the building, and the low moon broke through the clouds to the west, lighting the square and the front of the building. It was an inn, Zuen's only one.

Above the door hung a picture of a mouse dressed in waistcoat and trousers with slippers on his feet. He sat in an armchair, in front of a bright fire, sleeping. Beside him on a small table was a still-smoking pipe and a half-drunk glass. Above the picture hung another sign. Before the clouds took the moon away again, they all had time to read it. The Tired Dormouse, it said.

They looked at each other.

"The red door," whispered Shaeli. She choked on a laugh. "The Tired Dormouse."

The laugh threatened to bubble to the surface and she clamped her teeth upon it, fearing it would too easily become the cackle of hysteria. She looked at Williver. His grin was wide and she had to look away else the laugh would have come. Llianas was grinning too, and she turned her eyes to Ezebar. His eyes were dark in the shadows, but she could see the gleam of his teeth. They went, each struggling to contain their laughter, past the front entrance and around the other side of the building.

This side had a driveway that ran beneath low balconies to the stables behind the inn, and they followed it down until they could see the rumps of the horses in the stalls. The horses were the only ones who heard them give way to their swallowed laughter, but their mirth did not last long. Even though they had found M'zena's 'red door', they could not just walk through it; at least not until the sun had risen. Or so they thought.

As they went back beneath the balconies to the square – meaning to spend the morning hidden in the shadows at the edge of the forest, meaning for Ezebar to come in alone later and be sure they would be safe – everything changed. A light went on in one of the balconies above and a door opened. They stopped, huddling in the shadows beneath the balcony as someone stepped out onto it. Something was tipped onto the cobbles nearby, splashing their legs. A voice spoke. A tiny bell-like voice.

"Will you have some tezz?" it said.

Another voice answered. A faint, muffled voice from inside the room.

"I suppose so," said the second voice. "If I have to wake up at this ridiculous hour."

The footsteps above moved back into the room, the door was closed and the voices were gone.

Williver looked at Ezebar.

"Give me a boost," he said.

\* \* \*

Kirrit was looking grumpily at M'zena. The old woman pretended not to notice and went about preparing the tezz.

"You're not supposed to throw things off balconies," sniffed Kirrit. "You might hit someone." She yawned pointedly. "That's what my Mam says."

"Sounds like a sensible woman, your Mam," said M'zena, mildly.

"She is," said Kirrit. "She..."

Her words stopped in her throat as something thumped on the balcony. A dark figure was climbing over the edge. Kirrit thought she screamed, but only a small sound like the peep of a tiny bird escaped her.

"Someone's there," said M'zena, just as mildly as she had spoken before. She moved towards the balcony door.

"Don't," gasped Kirrit, untangling her legs from the sheets and jumping off the bed.

She was pulling her little crossbow from beneath the bed when M'zena opened the door.

"About time, too," she heard M'zena say.

Kirrit poked her head up and saw Williver standing in the doorway, grinning.

"My apologies," he said.

A hand appeared on the balcony, and Llianas was pulling herself over the rail. She, too, had a wide grin on her face.

"She'll need a hand," Llianas said.

Williver turned and went back to lean over the rail. Something tiny scurried up and between the rails, and then Williver was pulling someone else up, and it was Shaeli and Kirrit let out another little squeak. She dropped her bow on the bed and rushed across the room, grabbing her friend and pulling her into the room. She hugged her fiercely and then stepped back, her hands on Shaeli's shoulders. She looked at Shaeli, her face very serious.

"Shaeli, my friend," she said, her voice as serious as her face. "I love you dearly and am more than pleased to see you, but I am your friend, and if I don't tell you, then I'm not doing my job. You smell very, very bad," she said, and shook her head. "And your hair is a mess."

Then she giggled and hugged Shaeli again. Ebony skittered in and Kirrit scooped her up and gave her a tight little squeeze, too.

"Oh, thank goodness, Eb," she said, to the little jevvi. "I was so worried about you."

"We need a rope for Ezebar," said Shaeli. "He boosted us, but he can't reach."

Kirrit looked at her. "We haven't any," she said.

"Use my quilt," said M'zena.

They pulled it off her bed and lowered it down to Ezebar, who hauled himself up until he could grab the edge of the balcony. He was up in a moment, and as they closed the door they heard a rooster crow somewhere in the distance. Ezebar enfolded M'zena in a tight hug and the old woman almost disappeared entirely in the circle of his arms.

While Kirrit was greeting Llianas, Shaeli was looking about her. The room was tiny, just two beds and a small sink in one corner. She looked at Kirrit.

"Where are they?" she asked, brightly. "Where are the others?"

Kirrit's smile faded. "There are no others, Shaeli," she said. "There's just us. Just M'zena and me."

The four muddy travellers stared at the tousled red-head.

"Just you?" Shaeli said, the brightness gone. "Just the two of you?"

Kirrit nodded. "Just us."

"But why?" said Shaeli. "Where are Flin and Koda? Almarnoch?"

"M'zena wouldn't bring them," shrugged Kirrit.

Shaeli looked at M'zena. "Why?"

It was M'zena's turn to shrug. "I asked myself that a dozen times," she said. "Again and again I asked who would be needed on this journey. Time and again the answer came, 'just Kirrit'. I know not why."

"But what about Ishaan, Blenny? Surely Almarnoch should be here," said Shaeli.

"No Warlock is ever to be shown the way in," said M'zena. "This much I know. The others," she shrugged again. "I think their road lies elsewhere."

Shaeli's legs had a little wobble. She had been relying on the High Warlock's strength and wisdom to guide her, for Flin's throwing mastery, for Tarkoda's calming words, and again she was left without that which she thought would sustain her. She sighed and passed a hand over her eyes. Ebony scurried up her filthy skirt and nuzzled her cheek.

Williver took her arm. "She is tired," he said. "We have had little food or rest for several days."

"I shall make the tezz," M'zena said. "And there is bread and jam. Little else, I'm afraid, until the kitchen wakes."

"We must be careful," said Williver. "They will be looking for us."

"No," said Kirrit. "They think you are on the Trader. They knew it had landed here. The landingholder heard it but it was gone before he saw anything. They assumed it had picked you up and that you're long gone. They're searching the Land." She frowned. "I hope Tarkoda has managed to avoid them."

"Kirrit, how do you know all this?" asked Shaeli.

"I saw Pizar," said Kirrit. "He told me."

"Pizar?" Shaeli's face paled. Her knees trembled again. "He's seen you? He knows you're here?"

"Oh, yes," said Kirrit, airily, and then she frowned. "Shaeli, you look funny."

"Kirrit," said Shaeli, as steadily as she could. "Pizar was the one who caught us in the net back at that village. Pizar is the one who put me in that little box, that carriage, tied like a beast. Pizar is the one…" She could not go on.

It was Kirrit's turn for the colour to flee from her face. "We…" said Kirrit. She swallowed. "We had tezz with him yesterday."

"Far too eager to please, I thought," said M'zena.

"But…" began Shaeli. "But didn't Flin tell you?"

Kirrit shook her head. "No."

The word was barely heard in the silence of the room. Shaeli closed her eyes and sunk onto the end of the bed, her knees no longer able to support her.

"What did you tell him?" Ezebar asked.

"Only that I was here with my grandmother," Kirrit said, her voice high with angst. "I said we were travelling through the Land. One last journey for her, you know. I didn't tell him anything. I said I hadn't seen you since last year." Her voice trembled. "He doesn't know."

"Oh, he knows you were in that town, Kirrit," said Williver. "They saw you. He knows. Get dressed," he said. "Gather your things. We have to go."

"Where?" said Shaeli. "Where do we go?"

M'zena patted her arm. "Don't you worry, child," she said. "We are closer to the end than you think."

\* \* \*

# CHAPTER TWENTY TWO

They snuck down the stairs, Ezebar leading M'zena down the steep flight, her quilt bundled under his arm, the others behind. There were only a few lights on in the town as they emerged from the building and the cock was still crowing in the distance. A fine mist was rising from the ground to greet the rising of the sun.

"Hurry," said M'zena. "It will not be long until there are people in the streets."

"Which way?" asked Ezebar.

"That way," said M'zena, pointing to the north.

"But only the forest lies that way," said Williver.

"That is the way," said M'zena, and she began to walk in that direction.

They had only gone a short way before they heard the sound of footsteps in the distance, many of them, footsteps and the clanging of sword and shield. They started to hurry, going as fast as the short steps of the old woman would allow. From behind them came the crashing of doors and the shouts of angry voices. They went faster, almost carrying M'zena.

"They must have been watching us," said Kirrit. "Oh, how could I have been so stupid?" A sob caught in her throat.

The shouts from behind ceased, the footsteps began again. The buildings around them were thinning now, and ahead Shaeli could see the house where Ezebar had tripped over the fence. The forest lay beyond.

"Are you sure, M'zena?" she asked.

M'zena looked over her shoulder. She nodded. "It is the way," she said.

The footsteps behind them grew louder as they passed the last buildings. The forest lay across a scrubby field, brooding darkly in the thin light. The mist here was thicker yet it would not hide them. Shaeli looked over her shoulder. She could see the guard in the streets behind them. Her heart lurched.

"Hurry," she cried.

They left the town behind and stumbled across the grass. Shaeli pulled a stone from her amulet as she ran and she threw a couple of balls behind her. They fell before the feet of the guard, scattering them for a moment, but they quickly regrouped. Pizar was at their head, as she had known he would be.

She threw a few balls back, but they fell short and she stumbled on. She was just about to throw a third round at the soldiers when the edge of the forest loomed.

Williver and Ezebar hesitated at the first trees. The trees at the edge were natural enough for the Land, but the trees further in were thick, brooding hulks. They had spent so many days avoiding the forest, taking only sly glances into its depths – as if they were looking at something forbidden – that they wavered now, even with the guard at their backs.

The soldiers behind them were not hesitating. They ran across the misty grass swords raised, sure they had the fugitives captured, Pizar urging them on.

M'zena did not hesitate. She strode ahead, walking fearlessly between the first ordinary trees and on into the dark confines of the forest proper. The others hesitated only a moment longer. They took one final look at the soldiers bearing down on them and followed the old woman into the forest.

The guard reached the forest, milled on the edge for a moment, and then they followed them in.

* * *

The trees closed around them. The ground was covered with fallen leaves, the air became thick with the mist and centuries of silence.

There was no path, yet M'zena moved through the trees as if there was one. The trunks of the trees were thick-barked and gnarled with age, the branches low above their heads, the leaves a rich green. Here and there a low-flung branch crossed their path, and M'zena cautioned them not to touch the trees, going around or ducking beneath the hanging branch. The mist shrouded the ground and their bodies to their waists, making their feet indistinct, swirling as they passed through and closing eerily behind them. The sound of the guard behind was the only sound in the air and they hurried on, following M'zena on her unseen path, and, though the guard had been right behind them, perhaps fifty paces when they entered the forest, the sounds of their pursuit faded. After a while they slowed down, and M'zena looked behind them, satisfaction creasing her face.

"It seems we have lost them," said Williver.

"Perhaps they went back," said Kirrit. "It's pretty spooky in here."

"They did not turn back," said M'zena. "The Forest would not have let them pass as it has us."

"Why has it let us in?" said Llianas, looking at the trees. "I feel more watched in this forest than I have in any other. What's in here?"

"There is only the Forest and those it loves," said M'zena. "And it lets you pass because you are with me."

"What would happen if we weren't with you?" asked Kirrit.

"Many things are possible," said M'zena. "But it would not be likely that you would see the World outside again."

Kirrit shivered, Llianas copied her, and the two walked closer together, both darting glances into the trees around them. Ebony too, her tail curled tightly about her, sat quietly on Shaeli's shoulder, eyeing the trees and shivering every now and then. Nothing moved, and although the sun should be up, here it was still dim and shrouded in the swirling mists.

Shaeli began to stumble, Williver steadied her, and Llianas clutched at Kirrit's arm. They all walked slowly now, trailing the old woman between the trees. None of them were sure how much time passed as they followed M'zena through the Forest, for it never seemed to change; the trees stood huge and silent around them, blocking all sight of the sky above, the mist seemed as if it would never lift. It was as if time had stopped, and they merely walked through a frozen moment.

"Aah, good," M'zena said at last. "Many thanks," she added, and they wondered who she was talking to.

Shaeli shook her head. She had been stumbling along behind Kirrit and Llianas, Williver beside her, her mind as frozen as the Forest around her. M'zena's words brought focus back to her surroundings.

They were walking into an open space, and here the mist was suddenly gone, burnt off by the rays of bright sunshine slanting into the wide open space between the trees. The leaf mould beneath their feet turned to soft grass and there was the sound of water.

The trees opened out into a small meadow. On the far side ran a tumbling creek, and over the water was a tiny arched bridge made of patterned stone. They stared at the odd sight, the pretty arched-stone bridge crossing a tumbling creek here in M'Zen'sclahr Forest. On the far side of the bridge was another, much smaller grassed area, and then the trees began again.

They were still staring at the bridge when M'zena called them. She had walked off to their left, across the grass, and when they turned at her call, they were even more surprised.

She was walking towards a low stone building, huddled beneath the trees at the Forest's edge, the door open, a thin line of smoke curling from the chimney. They followed the old woman across the grass as she disappeared inside, Ezebar hurrying after her, calling her name, and when they reached the door they stopped, peering into the dark confines of the building.

Ezebar had stopped just inside the door, staring at a table laden with food. M'zena was removing her cloak. The small bundle she carried lay on one of several beds.

"Come in," she said. "It's all ready. Though I am very grateful, it took a little longer than I expected."

"Whose house is it?" asked Ezebar.

"'Tis the Forest's house, Zeb," M'zena answered. "It has been made ready for us."

The others came through the door. Williver had to duck through the low opening and his head almost brushed the ceiling inside, as did Ezebar's. The windows were low-set, open to the grassland and the creek, the little bridge framed through one.

"It's a drell house," said Shaeli, in wonder.

"That it is, lass," said M'zena. "And beautifully prepared, too."

At the end of the room were beds, each with a fat pillow and white sheets covering them. In the centre of the room was a table that was hard to ignore, so laden was it. There was bowls of fruit and vegetables, a tray of rolls covered in seeds, a joint of cold meat, already cut, and a variety of cheeses. Shaeli picked up one of the dozens of crusty rolls and found they were still warm, the just-baked smell filling her nostrils. A kettle bubbled over a low fire. There was a huge packet of tezz sitting beside a large pot and half a dozen mugs. Beside the fire was a bowl of eggs, a slab of thinly cut bacon, and a large frying pan. Hanging beside the door were six robes of varying colours and sizes.

"You lot best clean yourselves up and change out of those clothes," said M'zena. "One of the robes will fit. They're quite good at that. You'll find a pool a little way above the bridge. Kirrit and I will cook something for you."

"Is it safe?" asked Llianas.

"Oh, yes," said M'zena. "Just don't go into the Forest." She was already ladling tezz into the pot. "Or walk on the ground on the other side of the pool," she went on. "And don't walk on the bridge either. Apart from that you'll be fine."

Llianas took the soft pink robe Shaeli passed her and doubtfully followed Williver and Ezebar out into the sunshine.

Back in the Forest, the light was still dim, the mist shrouding the trees, but here they walked across the grass with the sun warm on their heads. They went to the little creek and followed it up to a small pool. Two trees like open umbrellas, covered in pale green leaves and bright red flowers, sat like tall mushrooms nearby, the lush grass growing right to their trunks. Beside the pool, on a wide flat rock, there was a cake of yellow soap, soft-scented, and a pile of thick cloths. They took off their mud encrusted clothes and leapt into the water. Ebony followed them in, swimming at the edge and chittering with pleasure. The water was not cold but almost tepid, and was incredibly clear, and they took turns using the soap on their bodies, hair and clothes, swimming with the sunshine warm on their shoulders. When they pulled themselves from the water it was with regret, but the smell of bacon called them across the grass, and they rubbed themselves dry with the cloths, donned the soft robes and followed the smell back to the little building.

The robes fit well, as M'zena had said they would, the material incredibly light and soft. Shaeli's was in shades of purple, embroidered around the neck and at the bottom of the long flowing sleeves. Williver's was deep blue, Ezebar's a rich claret. M'zena and Kirrit had donned theirs, too, Kirrit's in soft greens, M'zena's golden yellow. Llianas' soft pink robe, the embroidery in deep rose, fit her perfectly.

The bacon was sizzling and M'zena was dropping eggs into the pan when they entered. They ate their fill, sampling the soft fruits, the cheeses, making up for the days they had lived on raw corn cobs and melons. Ebony sampled many things with her delicate hands, piling discarded skins into a little stack before her, and when they had finished, wanting to eat more but unable, M'zena gave them mugs of tezz, but before they had finished they were taking turns yawning. Shaeli wanted to ask M'zena questions, about the house, the Forest, what had happened to the soldiers, but she could not form the words. When Kirrit led her to one of the sheet-covered bunks, she did not protest, she looked at the pillow, tried to remember the last time she had slept on one and couldn't. She simply lay down and slept.

* * *

Far away from the little building in the shadows and the mist, Pizar stumbled, terrified and alone.

His soldiers had followed him into the Forest, if not willingly, at least spurred on by his promises of riches, yet it had not taken long for them to question their choice. As the mist had closed in around them, they had followed Pizar, hacking at the many branches which barred their way. How the fugitives had disappeared so easily between the trees, they knew not, and by the time they had decided to go back it had been far too late.

Pizar had not argued when the soldiers stopped and milled about, eyes flicking at the trees, and he knew he wanted out of this place even more badly than they. Knowing they had lost those they pursued, knowing he had been a fool to try, he had allowed them to turn back to Zuen. It was then that they noticed that the soldiers who had brought up the rear were no longer there. At least a dozen were gone and their going had been unnoticed by those in front.

Their passage through the Forest when they turned around had stood out like a pathway, hacked branches, scuffed ground, and they had followed it back.

Thirty soldiers turned to follow Pizar back to Zuen. At first, the way had been easy to follow, but oddly, the signs they had made coming in slowly disappeared, and soon they found themselves in unmarked Forest. When they stopped again six more soldiers had disappeared. They panicked then, and although Pizar had done his best to keep them together, they had run, swords flailing at the branches around them, and he had run with them. The next time they had stopped, breathing heavily, the Forest a maze around them, there were thirteen left. On and on they went, and one by one, they had disappeared from around Pizar.

The last few he heard – a gasp, a cut-off scream, a thud – but still he saw nothing. And there were no bodies, no signs of the others, though he searched for them. He did not know then that he would never see another face.

He ran and ran, always in the mist, in the half-dark, branches tearing at his clothes, his face. Time passed and still he went on, stumbling at times, running at others, feeling something in the trees, something that watched him – watched him and waited.

In the end he was screaming at the trees, daring them to come and get him, come and finish it, but the Forest did not heed him. It seemed content to watch as he ran on, screaming, drooling, crying, hacking at the branches that slapped him, tripped him. Tortured him.

The day never seemed to end as he went on and on, running and screaming and hacking at the trees. When he finally fell unconscious into the mist, it would not be for long, for when he woke he would wander again, growing weaker and madder with every step – until the one time that he fell that he would be unable to rise again.

But that time was far off. There would be many hours, many days yet for Pizar to wander alone and terrified through the trees of the Forest.

\* \* \*

# CHAPTER TWENTY THREE

Shaeli woke with a start, but then she remembered where she was. She stretched and yawned, luxuriating in the feeling of the crisp sheets and downy pillow against her skin, thinking that she had seldom slept in so fine a bed. She scratched her head – her hair clean for the first time in a long time – and sat up.

It was dark outside, and the others sat at the table, eating the cold meat, salads, and cheese. A few tall, elegant glass lamps illuminated the room. Ebony chattered over at her, a tiny tomato in one hand, and Llianas grinned at her and said something around a mouthful of roll. She chewed, swallowed and tried again.

"I said if we started you'd wake up," she said. "They wanted to wait for you."

"I'm glad you didn't," said Shaeli. "I could have slept for a whole Moon."

She yawned again to prove the point, but threw back the sheets and stood up. The robe she wore fell creaseless to the floor, as perfect as if she'd just donned it, not slept in it all day. Her legs were stiff as she walked to the table, but she felt surprisingly well. Perhaps that was because she also felt safe. Kirrit passed her a plate and she was instantly hungry.

There was little talk around the table as they ate, but later, after Ezebar had made the tezz, they talked in the soft glow of the lamps.

"M'zena, you said this morning that this house belonged to the Forest," said Shaeli. "But then you said it was a drell house."

"So it was," said M'zena. "In long centuries past, when the drell still roamed the Forest, there were many such buildings here. Mankind was still a young race in this part of the World, elves and Ammerr lived far to the east, and the Forest had not yet closed itself from the Land."

"How do you know this?" asked Shaeli.

"She knows Blenny's mother," said Kirrit, eagerly. "She told us about it at the sanctuary in the mountains. She saved her life, and she's even met Almarnoch before. M'zena you'll have to tell the story again. Shaeli will be so interested."

"This is something I haven't heard either," said Ezebar. "And I thought I had heard all your stories." He looked at M'zena, a fond smile on his face, and she sighed.

"There are many things as yet untold, my boy," she said. "But I shall tell you what I told the others when we were in the sanctuary in the mountains."

She recited the tale much as she had then, telling how she had saved Blenny's mother and then gone to Great Court to see that the hunting of drell was outlawed. Kirrit prompted her to tell them about the young Almarnoch, and M'zena smiled as she did.

Shaeli shook her head; she could no more imagine the old Warlock as a young lad than Kirrit could. She was as intrigued by the story as Kirrit had known she would be, and she stored it with what she already knew about the drell.

"So, it was Blenny's mother who told you about this place?" she asked.

"No," said M'zena. "She was aware of its existence, of course, but it has been centuries since the drell used this place."

"Then how did you know it was here?" Shaeli said. "Why does the Forest let you pass? Why should they leave all this here for us?" She waved a hand about the room. "Who has left it here?"

"Those are questions with very different answers," said M'zena. "Yet I shall answer them as shortly as I can." She thought a moment, looked at Ezebar, and then she spoke. "I have spoken of the many lifetimes I have lived during this one life, of times long past, of places visited and people met. Zeb has heard much of these things. I have spoken of men also, and as hard as it has been for him to imagine such things, it was so." She looked down at her hands, and there was something coquettish in the smile she turned back to them. "My admirers were many, but few were as charming as King Tarkon."

"King Tarkon?" said Shaeli. "Old King Tenelon's father?"

M'zena nodded. "The time that I went to Great Court to ask for the outlawing of drell hunting was not the first time I had met Tarkon," she said. "Almarnoch imagined that I strode bravely into Great Court, but Tarkon and I had met many times before, most of them in private, and though it had been many years since it had been so, I was not wary of pushing my way into his court." She smiled that coquettish little smile again. "We met when Tenelon was a young boy. Tarkon had been widowed. His wife had died in childbirth and Tenelon was his only heir. Many nights I spent with him, and though he was a lovely man and I was fond of him, I could not wed him as he wished."

"He wanted you to wed?" said Llianas. "The king of Zirrus? And you said no?"

M'zena nodded. "I did," she said. "And though I often wondered what may have been if I had married him, I have no regrets. I was older than he, but I was still restless. If I had married Tarkon, I would have lived only one life, the life of a Zirrus queen, instead of the many other lives that I have been blessed with. There would have been no travelling through the Lands alone, no meeting the people who have given me so much joy." She smiled at Ezebar and he smiled back. "It was Tarkon who told me of this place. Tarkon who introduced me to the Forest so that I could travel through it safely."

"And Tarkon who showed you the way in?" guessed Shaeli.

"Yes," M'zena said. "It was to him I swore the secret would not be revealed unless in dire need. It is a promise I have heeded."

"Though I am grateful for its shelter, I wonder why you brought us here," said Williver. "And I wonder who makes us so welcome."

"We come to seek permission, young elf," she said. "The way in will be revealed only if the Forest deems it so. Though Great Court is far away, it is here we must seek for permission to enter. The way in is an ancient path, a path which must begin here. You are the first I have brought here. As to who makes us welcome, that will be revealed in its proper time. 'Tis not for me to say."

It was clear she would speak no more on the subject, but Shaeli had many more questions.

"How did you come to meet the king?" she said.

"I was on the Starcluster," M'zena said, proudly. "We had gone to Palveron on some diplomatic mission or other, I cannot remember now what for, but I remember feeling very important."

"Were you born on the Starisles?" said Shaeli.

"No," said M'zena. "I was not, though it has been my home many times."

"Where were you born?" asked Ezebar. He had never thought of M'zena as a baby; she had just always been there, just as she had always been an old woman. "On which Land?"

"I was not born on any of your Lands, lad," she said, quietly, her eyes steadily on his face. "I was born as my people journeyed across the sea from their own war-torn lands. I was found as a babe, on the sands of the island where the great ship broke its back. My family was never found, and I was raised by others, Irikai, like me."

There was silence in the room as they all stared at her. Everyone knew how long ago the great ship of the Irikai had run into the reefs of the Starisles. That M'zena should be so old

– still moving and thinking as she did – these made the other things that had already amazed them seem trivial.

Ezebar was shocked. He sat staring at the beloved old woman, even more worried now than he had been before, yet it was Shaeli who was most shocked. She stared, her mouth worked, but she was unable to speak.

Many things rushed through her mind, but mostly she remembered the time when she had heard parts of this story before. She thought of a tiny caravan, of Meoro Pass, of bright pots and new crockery, of baby clothes wrapped in soft paper; of a pregnant young bride who spoke the words of the family legend. The young bride who was setting off across the Land, who would eventually settle in Trilby, far to the north. The young bride who kept an heirloom in a box – a bangle that had now been reunited with its twin.

Shaeli goggled at M'zena. It took her three tries before she could form words. It was as if her mind had run out of them.

"You're the baby," she said at last, the words falling from her mouth like stones. "The one that was found by the grandmother of Ellirra's grandmother. The same one."

Now they all were looking at Shaeli. None of them knew what she was talking about. She looked at Williver.

"The bangle," she said flatly. "Shahlita's bangle. Ellirra said it came with the baby from across the sea. When the child grew, she left it with them when she went out into the World."

"I knew it would be looked after," M'zena said, her bell-like voice soft with memory.

They were all silent. Staring.

M'zena shifted, the coquettish look entirely gone. She pursed her lips and looked at them in turn. Her eyes rested at last on Shaeli's wide gaze.

"You best tell them," she said, with a sigh. "I would be interested to hear how you know something of this also."

And so Shaeli told them of when she had met Ellirra, of the tale that Ellirra had told about the babe left by the waves, alone in its basket, on the shores of the Starisles. She remembered Ellirra's face as she told the tale, of the shivers which had gone down her spine when she'd first seen the bangle – one of the very bangles that Williver had told her to watch for. She told of the dream where Williver had shown her which route the family's wagon would take and the place where they would settle; the place where the queen's guard would burn Ellirra's house to the ground and murder her husband many Winterings later. M'zena listened to all these things with an unmoving face, her eyes on her empty cup.

"The bangle we have," said Shaeli, at the end of the tale. "Though it was given at great cost and we almost lost it in Nebillonia Straits. The other I was given when I was twelve. They both now lie in safety at Cave. I suppose the wand is returned to the elves as they decreed."

"You are wrong, child," said M'zena. Her eyes did not leave her cup, although there were only the dregs of her tezz left. "The elves do not keep guard over the wand. Nor are the bangles at your Cave." She raised her eyes and fixed them firmly on Shaeli. "They are here," she said. "The bangles are here with me. The wand is in the hands of the High Warlock."

Shaeli blinked. "What?" she said. "But the elves..."

"The elves saw that the wand had chosen where it should be," said M'zena. "Ishaan repaired it at your Cave, this I'm sure you know, and he took it to the elves as they had requested. They saw that it was restored to its former self, and then they gave it to your brother before he left Lythnori. He gave it to the High Warlock for safekeeping when we reached the drell sanctuary. Seemed pleased to be rid of it, Almarnoch said. The bangles Almarnoch passed to me when he saw our paths ran differently. Happy I was to see mine again, and reunited with its twin."

"Why did he not come with you?" said Shaeli.

"Part of the promise to Tarkon was that I never show a Warlock the way in," said M'zena. "The rebellion by one of the

Warlocks and his cronies in his father's reign was large in Tarkon's memory and he had a distrust of them. Warranted or no, I would not break my promise to him."

"And Almarnoch took the bangles with him when we left Cave?" Shaeli said. "He never told me."

"The High Warlock does not reveal himself easily," said M'zena.

"He's not the only one," said Ezebar, looking pointedly at her.

M'zena ignored him just as pointedly. She stood. "Enough questions for tonight," she said. "I'm going to my bed. I suggest you do the same."

She left them looking at each other around the table and they did not linger. They went to their beds thinking of the questions that had now been answered, and of the new questions those answers had brought with them. Though each head reached its pillow all jumbled and busy, it was only moments before every one turned to thoughts of slumber. Soon the room was filled with the sounds of soft breathing.

When all had been silent for a long time, there came through one of the windows a tiny light, bright in the centre and lilac-grey at the edges. It drifted down and went slowly around the room. The light hovered over Shaeli's bed for a while, and then it drifted back through the window and out into the night.

* * *

They woke to sunshine and the smell of fresh-baked bread. On the table was a basket filled with still-warm rolls, a slab of golden butter and a pot of crimson jam. All the scraps from their previous meals had disappeared and the bowl of fruit was full again. Ebony was already picking up a tiny bunch of grapes when they were still yawning and scratching their heads.

"That smells lovely," said M'zena. "Many thanks," she said to the air.

"My thanks, also," said Shaeli, smiling sleepily at the ceiling.

"Yes, thank you," echoed Llianas, smelling the rolls. "It looks lovely." She looked over at M'zena. "Do you think they heard me?" she whispered.

"Yes, lass," said M'zena, smiling. "They hear everything."

"Oh," said Llianas, looking around at the ceiling as if the room held eyes as well as ears. "You'll want the kettle on, M'zena, won't you?" she asked, her eyes still roaming the ceiling.

"You're a good elf, Llianas," the old woman smiled.

Llianas grinned back and put the kettle over the fire. This, too, had been kindled from the banked embers and was crackling gaily when they woke.

After they'd eaten, they went to the pool. The cloths they had left hung on a low branch had been replaced with a fresh pile, and they took off their robes and swam. Even M'zena took off her robe and tottered into the water on Ezebar's arm. This time there was nothing calling them from the water and they swam until their fingers were as wrinkled as old grapes, then they lay on the cloths in the sun until they were dry, talking little as the sun rose overhead.

The Forest around them was eternally silent, but once they heard a far-off rustle, accompanied by a voice, a muttering whine of a voice, but both the rustle and the mutter lasted only moments.

When the sun was hanging huge and white over the clearing, they went back to the little house to eat. A large pitcher of fresh juice waited on the table, the glass beaded with tiny droplets, and they drank it gratefully and ate more of the rolls and fruit.

The afternoon was hot, even within the thick walls of the house, and they went out to sit in the shade beneath the red-flowering trees beside the pool. The trees dropped feathers of scent down to lull them, covering them in perfume and deep shade. The cloths were soft and the grass thick as sponge beneath them. M'zena was the first to doze off. Ezebar had brought cushions from the house, and she had propped herself against a tree. One by one they nodded off, lulled by the silence and the warm afternoon.

Shaeli did not know why she woke. It was as if someone had been calling her from far away. She sat up and looked around.

The sun was low and the clearing was filled with golden light. The grass and trees had taken on a richer hue, the water was given even more clarity, the sky was higher and bluer. The air was thick with the golden light, so thick she could almost taste it, and she breathed deeply. Everything looked even more beautiful, the colours deep and bright.

She looked at the others, thinking how good they all looked, their skin perfect in the golden light. Kirrit's hair was burnt copper against the grass, Llianas' like molten chocolate. M'zena looked like an oil painting leaning against her cushions, her dark skin unlined, her hair a soft cloud. Williver's hand stretched out on the grass, pale gold against the bright green; Ezebar's hair drifted over his forehead and she could see each one of the eyelashes resting against his cheeks.

She stared at him, his face soft in sleep, the customary frown erased. His chin was thickening with the beard growing untended and she decided she liked it. She was smiling, just a little, when the lashes fluttered and the eyes opened. The dark eyes opened upon her, as if that is where they had been resting before the lids had closed, and she caught her breath. She blushed and looked away from the depths of those eyes; from the things she had seen there.

She glanced back and still he was looking at her. She felt a little sick and she was sure he must be able to hear the heart which bumped so loudly against her ribs, sure he would see the pink spreading over her cheeks. She clutched at her knees, her hands trembling and sticky with sweat. She didn't know what was wrong with her. She felt stupid and self-conscious and excited and embarrassed all at once, and she never would have felt like that if it had been anyone else who had woken up. She would have just said hello, and talked about something; the light, or dozing off, or something. She rolled her eyes at herself, hoping the blush on her cheeks was not too obvious, and she looked out over the pool.

Something moved on the other side. Something tiny and high in the trees. She leant forward, sure she was not seeing what she thought she was seeing.

\* \* \*

Ezebar, almost despite himself, had been gazing at her. Staring at her. When he'd opened his eyes and seen her looking at him, he had been startled by the rush of feeling that had leapt from his belly. Like a flame it swept to his chest, burning with sudden, intense heat. The moment – like others he'd had when he'd looked deep into her eyes – had stretched. It seemed there was no need to breathe during such a moment, but the instant she moved her eyes from his, he had been breathless. He kept on staring, looking at the tilt of her nose, the blush on her high cheekbones, the fullness of her lips – finding himself wondering what they would taste like, those lips – then he saw her start. Her eyes widened and her shoulders straightened. She gasped, leant forward, and he sat up and followed her eyes across the pool.

Something was emerging from the trees. Something tiny that drifted from the leaves in a soft light. It flew into sunlight, and the light all but disappeared, yet by then he could see it clearly, and he blinked.

The tiny fairy flew slowly across the pool towards them, the lilac-grey of her dress bright in the golden afternoon.

Shaeli scrambled to her feet and Ezebar went and stood beside her. He took her hand, and she looked up at him. Her eyes were vivid, filled with delight, her smile wondrous to his eyes. She squeezed his hand, and turned back to watch the fairy approach.

He knew then.

* * *

Across the pool it came, through the sunlight and into the shade. It hovered before them, a drizzle of fairy dust falling from its wings. The wings were fluttering gently, the patterns in shades of lavender and lilac, and they shone like the wings of a dragonfly. It – she – was wearing a pale grey dress, the material light and flowing like cobwebs, tiny purple thread shimmering in its folds. Her hair was long and dark and it waved softly in the breeze of her wings. Her bare arms, as tiny as a child's finger, were open in greeting, and her beautiful little face bore a wide smile.

Another fairy, this in robes of green and orange with a cool yellow light, appeared between the trees and watched from across the pool, hovering just at the edge of shadow.

"We bring you greetings and the blessings of the Forest," said the lilac fairy. Her voice was light and airy, but easy to hear.

Shaeli bobbed her head. "We thank you," she replied. "It is very kind of the Forest to take us in."

She heard a gasp behind her and knew Kirrit had woken up. She would not let the others sleep for long.

Ebony scurried over, and she stood in front of Shaeli and pawed the air below the fairy, and the fairy laughed and flew down. Her tiny hand reached out and she scratched the jevvi behind the ear. Ebony chattered and put out a paw to the fairy, who laughed and shook it. She flew up to hover before their eyes again and Ebony watched her in adoration.

"I am Tish," she said. "'Tis my privilege to greet you." She looked back at the other fairy hovering across the pool. "That is Rem."

The other fairy bobbed in the air.

"We're pleased to meet you, Tish, Rem," said Shaeli. "We've been wanting to thank someone for the hospitality."

"We have heard your thanks," said Tish. "And those from the little elf. And you and I have met before, Shaeli."

"Met before?" Shaeli frowned.

Tish smiled. "You once watched a cluster at work," she said. "On the Forest's edge."

"I remember," said Shaeli. She had never forgotten watching the fairy cluster the year they had taken Princess Crissita to Romynn. She glanced over her shoulder, and saw the others standing there watching, and then she looked back at the little fairy. "That was you?"

"It was," nodded Tish. "And I have seen you since, whenever you visited Zuen. And before the last Wintering as you headed into the Drell Mountains on our western edge, and again, a few days ago, as you travelled between the eastern edge and the rock plains, with this man and the elves."

"You saw me, all those times?" said Shaeli. She shook her head, amazed.

The little fairy nodded. "Since we first saw your shenwa, we have watched for you."

"My what?"

"Your shenwa. The aura each person has around them, the colours of their mind and heart." Tish smiled at Shaeli's confusion. "You see the light coming from my wings, don't you?" she asked, and Shaeli nodded. "Fairies see the colours of every race," Tish went on. "As you can see my colours, so I can see yours, yours and the shenwa of each of your companions. We see who you truly are by the colours, and yours shine far more brightly than any other of your race that we have seen."

Shaeli stared at the little face. That she had been watched as she visited Zuen on the Trader, as she had fled to the Drell Mountains with the guard in pursuit, as she had walked through the rain on the other side of the forest; all this was incredible to her.

"Even if you had come into the forest without the old one, you would not have been harmed," said Tish. "Your shenwa shines like a beacon."

Shaeli looked behind her. Williver was looking at her. He had once said something very like that to her. He smiled and she looked back at the fairy once more.

"We must reach Great Court," she said. "We seek permission… M'zena said we must seek permission before we may use the way in."

"The old one speaks true," said Tish, smiling over Shaeli's shoulder to where M'zena stood before her mound of cushions. "And we shall grant permission. But not yet."

"But we must hurry," said Shaeli. "My sisters…"

"All is known to us," Tish said. "We know Tenelon's heir is held at Great Court with his widow and that you seek to free her."

"How can you know this?" Ezebar said.

"We know all things," Tish said to him. "We are everywhere, see everything. What one knows, we all soon know." She looked back at Shaeli. "There are happenings in the outside that you should know of before you go on. Your Land is in turmoil. Palveron lies in smoke, rubble lines its streets. The false queen's soldiers have brought Qotarr to the city and the other Lands are cowering."

"Qotarr?" Shaeli was horrified. "But how?"

"Those on Wokk have been forced to comply, but that matters not," said Tish. "That they destroy the city is enough. Yet all is not in ruins. Ashkanna has taken Meoro Village and the Pass. It is said Serrat will be next."

"Meoro Pass?" said Shaeli. "Serrat? But that means…"

"We shall wait for the Fleet to fly again in the World before we show you the way in," said Tish.

"But why?" said Shaeli.

"Because the black ship protects the castle," said Tish. "And you cannot fight it from outside."

"What do you mean, 'fight it from outside'?" asked Williver.

"Just that," said the fairy. "But that is not yet your task. Others are needed to find the riddle of the black ship."

The other fairy, Rem, flew across the pool and hovered behind Tish.

"We shall not speak of this now," Rem said, her voice light, her hair in long brown curls beside her pretty face. She tugged at Tish's arm. "We are all very pleased you are here, but we must go. Come, Tish."

Tish nodded, and Rem flew back across the pool.

"But how long must we wait?" asked Shaeli.

"Not long, so they say," said Tish, as she fluttered away.

The golden light of the afternoon had faded and the dull light of dusk now filled the clearing. Tish's wings shone more brightly and she fluttered higher in the air.

"Your meal awaits," she said. "We shall speak more of this tomorrow."

Her wings beat more quickly and she shot off across the pool. She stopped and raised an arm, and then she followed Rem between the trees, little trails of lavender and lemon left in their wakes.

Shaeli became aware that she still held Ezebar's hand, and she dropped it.

"I was wondering when someone would come," said M'zena.

"Why didn't you tell us it was fairies?" asked Shaeli, turning around.

"Because sometimes it isn't," said M'zena, turning back to the house. "I smell something and it smells very good," she said.

The lamps had been lit when they entered the house. Six fish lay in a pan beside the fire. A bowl of potatoes boiled above it, and the smell of fresh herbs filled the room. There was a bowl of several herbs on the table beside a pile of fresh salad vegetables, and there were even flowers in a vase on one of the windowsills. They looked around, as amazed as ever at what happened unseen in this house.

"Who does all this?" said Llianas. "It cannot just be fairies."

"They will reveal themselves when they wish, young elf," said M'zena, with a smile. "Now, who wants to cook the fish?"

\* \* \*

"Tell me of the Warlock who caused such havoc on Zirrus," said Williver. "The one who gave Tarkon a distrust of Warlocks. When did it happen?"

They sat again the next day beneath the trees beside the pool as the afternoon waned. There had been no sign of Rem or Tish, and they had done little but eat and swim throughout the day. Shaeli – her bruises fading and her strength returning – felt guilty about how relaxed she was when there was so much to do, so much occurring "outside", as Tish called it. She felt as if they had been completely removed from the World, and Williver had told her that last night he had tried to roam the dreamworld, but he had been unable to leave the Forest.

She looked at M'zena expectantly when Williver asked the question, pleased with a distraction. She was almost a little bored.

"It was during Tarkon's father's reign," M'zena said. "Before our ship came to these lands. Perhaps a decade, not more, before the Irikai arrived on the Starisles. The trouble began on Wokk and ended on Zirrus. The Warlock was a powerful magician, yet he became arrogant with it. He recruited many young Warlocks, naive, idealistic young men, and he taught of the superior knowledge of their kind. He said the People of the Lands were not clever enough to know what was best for them, that Warlocks should be more involved in the way they moved through the world; how they should dress, which of the gods deserved most worship, even when they should worship. This movement of Warlocks grew strong on Wokk, ever the most conservative of the Lands. Some of the nobles there were also convinced that the Warlocks knew more than the people, than their king even. No one knew how they gathered so much support so quickly, but soon half the people of Wokk were with them and they stormed the castle. The royal family only just escaped, fleeing to Zirrus. The Warlock, I believe his name was Virrek, then installed himself as ruler and he grew even more arrogant. He found a number of sympathisers to support his raid on Zirrus, yet he was defeated. The battle was long, but they caught him and his followers in the mountains and it is said that none escaped. Wokk was returned to its king and Tarkon's father brought in laws governing the apprenticeship and powers of Warlocks. Tarkon was little more than a boy when it happened, but he talked of it several times, and as I said, he had a distrust of Warlocks his whole life. It was he who had the Faunist and Warlock houses built outside Great Court. Before that they had been housed within the inner wall, inside the castle itself."

"It must be the same one," said Williver, when M'zena had finished. He spoke quietly, as if he talked to himself. "It must. The time is right."

"What time?" asked Shaeli. "The same as what?"

Williver did not answer her. He turned to M'zena again. "He had the gift of channelling stones, this Warlock?" he asked her. "The ability to walk the dreamworld?"

M'zena nodded. "I believe so," she said. "It was in these stories that I first heard tales of a black wind invading minds." Her eyes narrowed as she looked at Williver. "But why do you ask, young elf?"

Shaeli had never seen Williver look so grim.

"The Warlock who caused such havoc within your Lands," said Williver, his voice low. "It is the same one who caused even more havoc in ours."

Shaeli looked at him. Her brow furrowed, and then her eyes widened.

"The one who stole the wand?" she gasped. "Who killed the dragons and..." She could not finish the sentence.

"And Shahlita," Williver nodded, finishing it for her. "Yes. It must be the same man."

"Tell us, young elf," said M'zena.

Ezebar smiled at her. "Always ready to hear a new tale," he said.

He had smiled a lot that day. He had spoken little, but the frown they were all so accustomed to had been seen seldom.

"At my age, Zeb," said M'zena. "New tales are hard to come by." She winked at Ezebar and he winked back, and then she turned to Williver. "Many rumours of the lost dragons I have heard," she said. "When I was young, many people remembered them and spoke of them fondly. There were stories of a mad dragon, about the time the others disappeared, but they were few. As the Winterings passed, those who had seen the dragons in the skies grew to be old people, and when they had gone the tales of dragons in the World grew to legend. I asked many people as well as the drell and the elves I met over the years, but none could say. All I ever heard was that after one Wintering they did not fly the skies again, they simply vanished."

"We saw some of their skeletons," said Kirrit. "We went into their lair, and beneath it to Cave." She wore the journey almost proudly now that its horrors had diminished with time's passage.

"Did you just?" said M'zena. "You must tell me of it. But start at the beginning please, Williver. The elves I have met have been unwilling to give much information."

"They are forbidden to do so," Williver said. He told them of the man who had sought shelter in elven lands and the stolen wand of Shahlita, of the battle that she and the dragons must have had, of her disappearance and the loss of the dragons. "It is clear now that she managed to destroy the wand," he said. "The bangles must have been lost to the sea. One was found by the Ammerr, and eventually Shaeli, the other must have gone somehow to your lands, M'zena."

"Only to be returned here," she said. "The gods have seen that they are reunited, that the wand is restored."

"It's strange it should happen now, when the World is in such turmoil again," said Llianas.

"All things happen at their proper time, lass," said M'zena, then she looked again at Williver. "Why did the elves keep this a secret?" she asked.

"In the beginning it was thought the wand might be found," Williver said. "It was not known then that it had been broken, its magic dissolved, and it was feared it might have been sought, or found, by someone seeking to corrupt its power. Long did they search for it, on the mountainside, in the lair and the tunnels beneath, and by the time it was known to be truly lost, there were those from outside who wished to enter the lair, to make themselves rich on what the dragons had left in their nests. This became our focus then, keeping the lair safe, in case we should ever find out what had happened to them." His eyes flicked at Shaeli. "When Shaeli found the wand on the shores of Lake Marnis, it was almost ruined, bereft of its main stone and most of the lesser ones. Although we had searched the tunnels many times, it was not until we went down before last Wintering, when we were seeking a way to the Cave of the Traders, that something was found."

"You found it," said M'zena, turning to Shaeli.

Shaeli nodded, yet she did not speak. It was Kirrit who told them about Shaeli's fugue state and the finding of the stone while Shaeli sat uncomfortably in silence. And, unnoticed by all but M'zena, it was Ezebar who led Kirrit further on into the story of their journey beneath the mountain and away from Shaeli's discomfort.

As Kirrit and Llianas told of the blood-sucking bats that had attacked them beneath the mountain, Shaeli gave Ezebar a grateful smile and he smiled back. Neither heard any of the prattle from the girls during the moment their eyes met. M'zena noticed this also.

Shaeli heard her name spoken, and she tried to concentrate on what was being said. Regretfully, her eyes left the depths of Ezebar's.

"You should have seen it, Shaeli," Llianas was saying. "It must have been a huge tunnel once upon a time, an old Trader tunnel, because of the broken Zoi on one side. We couldn't tell what was on the other side, it was really ruined, but when the bats came out we knew it was the same tunnel we'd been in."

"Where was this?" asked Shaeli.

"On the north side of Zerrinius," said Kirrit. She said the words pointedly, as if this was something Shaeli should have already known. She turned back to Llianas. "What did Koda do, when the bats came?"

"He was a bit worried about the Zoi," Llianas said. "But the bats couldn't get in. We watched them come down the mountain, and after we'd closed the shutters they thudded against the gaps for the longest time." She shuddered. "And the next morning we looked at the old turret."

"Old turret?" Shaeli frowned.

"Near the ruins of the old tunnel," said Kirrit, again slowly and pointedly. "The one with the left-over bits of Zoi on one side. On the opposite side of the mountain to Cave." She shook her head. "How did you miss this, Shaeli?"

"I guess I was thinking about something else for a moment," Shaeli said, trying not to look at Ezebar. She could feel his eyes on her, and she fought to keep the blush from betraying her. "I wonder where it went?" she said. "The tunnel."

"Tarkoda thought maybe it was an old Trader route to Cave," said Llianas.

"Did he?" asked Kirrit. "What else did he say?"

"That it must have been centuries old, but he'd never heard anything about it in the Fleet," said Llianas.

"I haven't heard anything either," said Kirrit. "Have you, Williver?"

Williver shook his head. "No," he said. "We do not travel that far south. The land is treacherous, ravines and gorges and many avalanches in the spring."

"An avalanche almost hit the Trader," said Llianas.

"Where?" asked Shaeli.

"What did Koda do?" asked Kirrit.

And so Llianas was off again, telling of the wave of falling snow that had chased the Trader through the gorge.

The others asked questions, and although Shaeli listened, as interested as the others at the story of the Trader's journey through the mountains, at times she found it difficult to concentrate. She felt Ezebar's eyes on her, and when she met them with her own she could think of nothing but that.

\* \* \*

# CHAPTER TWENTY FOUR

To the east, a great battle raged.

Meoro Village had been unprepared for the assault upon it days earlier, the guard there small and easily overcome. Ships from Ashkanna and Romynn and the Starisles had landed at dawn, and by midday the village had been theirs. The people of Meoro Village had watched the ships come and joined the fray. When the soldiers from the other Lands had massed in their streets for the march up the Pass, they had been cheered on by the townspeople and many of them had taken up arms and joined the rearguard. They were halfway up Meoro Pass before they met resistance, but when it came it was fierce.

The queen's guard met them on a narrow bend, archers hidden high in the cliffs above, and at first they had been pushed back. Yet sure-footed Romynnii had scaled the cliffs, picking off the archers one by one, and when they had taken the cliffs, they turned their own arrows on the guard ahead. Slowly they had pushed forward, and in the end the guard had retreated and they had chased them to the end of the Pass. The soldiers of the queen had rallied again on the doorstep of Serrat, digging into the cliffs that sheltered it, and they managed, for a while, to keep the town.

Days passed with the guard holding the hills around Serrat, the soldiers of other Lands spreading out before them, and the other Lands were soon joined by the people of Zirrus. Several contingents went into the surrounding lands to clear the smaller towns and villages of the guard, but mostly they sat outside Serrat waiting.

Three days they sat at Serrat's doorstep, knocking on its door now and then, but the guard refused entry, and the door remained closed to them. Late in the afternoon of the fourth day there came a cry.

"Trader. Trader to the west."

The cry was taken up and passed through the crowd. All eyes turned to stare at the Trader as it flew closer. It had been a long time since any of them had seen one of the balloons, and as the Trader flew closer, a cheer went up from the soldiers spread out before the cliffs of Serrat.

\* \* \*

Tarkoda looked down at the massive crowd of people cheering below. He could see the colours of the Starisles mixed with the colours of two Lands and the clothes of the common people of Zirrus, and he grinned at Ishaan beside him.

Ishaan smiled back, and Tarkoda looked over his shoulder. The others were down on the deck, staring at the people below. Flin, Spotjaw, Wendll and Blenny, Qiren, Olando, Cheval and Almarnoch were all lined up along the railing, amazed by the throng outside the cliffs surrounding Serrat.

Tarkoda took the Trader up and over the cliffs. The faces of the guard on the other side turned up to them, the black-and-scarlet spreading over the land between the high hills and Serrat. Arms were raised here, too, to point at the Trader, but there was no resounding cheer accompanying them. Along the lines of soldiers were three massive slings, great piles of stone beside each one.

The city sat serenely in the afternoon sun, and Tarkoda took the Trader around the edge of it. The people of Serrat came into the streets to look up at the Trader as it circled.

Tarkoda looked with regret at the rough land that led to the Valley of Stones, the tumbling water of the stream that began in the spring pool inside Cave, and he turned the Trader away.

Over the guard huddled inside the hills they flew again, back over to the masses waiting to release the city from the guard's grasp. Another cheer greeted them as they flew back over the hills, and the Trader swept down, so close that Koda could see the faces behind the raised arms.

There was a Landing at the top of Meoro Pass and he flew the Trader down and took it in for a clean landing. The Zoi fluttered to a stop and let out a cry, for they had flown swiftly over long hours, yet they waited patiently as the ship was moored, watching Tarkoda's every move. When he unharnessed them they flew down to drink deeply of the water; it had been an exhausting flight and Tarkoda had pushed them as hard as he'd dared. Now he pulled out food for them and went to check on the injured bird in the nest.

When they had flown away from Zuen, they had easily evaded the guard; the night had been dark and Tarkoda had flown the ship out over the lake. They had gone back to the farming community on the other side of Lake Marnis that had sheltered them, staying only one night, fearing they would be found and bring danger to the people there.

Almarnoch thought they should head to Cave, to tell the old ones and the Fleet what was happening in the World, and so they had hopped through the foothills, landing in thin valleys and secluded grassland. Once they had flown low over a small town and the townspeople had called and waved and rung bells so fiercely that Tarkoda had circled the place. There was a small landing outside the town and the landingholder's hut was a pile of blackened ashes beside it. There was no sign of any guard, and after speaking with Almarnoch he took the Trader down.

The people had greeted them with whoops of joy. It seemed the whole of the small village had come out to greet them, and they all spoke at once as those from the Trader came down the stairs. There was much pumping of hands and claps on the back as they were welcomed, and it took some time before they could make sense of what the people were telling them.

It seemed that they had heard that the Land was in rebellion, and they had decided to join it. There had been few guard in their town, only a score or so camped near the Landing, and one night they had overcome them and the landingholder, burnt the hut, and chased the soldiers off. The people guffawed as the story was told, proud of playing their small part in the uprising.

"We thought you must be the first of the Fleet to fly over," said one.

"Aye, we hear they are taking Meoro Pass, and then Serrat," said another.

"The other Lands have had enough, they say," came another voice. "Palveron is under siege and starving."

They stayed there the night listening to the rumours of the townspeople; rumours of rebels joining arms with the other Lands, of black ships firing death and destruction, of Qotarr in the streets of Palveron. They had flown from the village in the sunrise hours, heading for Serrat.

Now, the Trader was surrounded by the cheering crowd, and the leaders of the rebellion came forward as the others came down the steps of the tiny Landing at the top of Meoro Pass. By the time Tarkoda came from the nest, Almarnoch was in earnest talks with them.

Crissita's father, Prince Davron, led the forces from Ashkanna. The head of his paladin, Malikk, who had once instructed Tarkoda during his stay in Djelda, stood unmoving beside him as he spoke, looking very like the boulder with eyes that Andos had once described. Davron told them of the failed diplomatic missions sent to Great Court and Queen Virrisian's reply. He told them how the black ship had decimated the ships and troops in the Bay of Islands. Word from Palveron had been scarce, and although the rumours of Qotarr in the city had been confirmed, there had been little word since their arrival.

The Lands wanted the Traders returned to the World, and the first step was the liberation of Serrat. With Serrat and Meoro Pass free, the Traders could fly safely again, at least to the other Lands. They could also aid in the battle for Palveron if they chose.

Davron could not understand how the Fleet had ever agreed to Queen Virrisian's command to leave the World. Almarnoch looked steadily at him.

"The heir of King Tenelon is of the Fleet," he said. "She is held as ransom at Great Court."

Davron stared back at him. He blinked, his lips thinned, and he nodded. "I see," he said. "Then the freeing of the Fleet is even more imperative. Queen Elenes heard rumours and hoped they were true. She has been ever more distressed with Queen Virrisian's treatment of her people. The Fleet will be needed."

"Then we must free Serrat," said Almarnoch.

Together they planned the assault. They made preparations through the night and at dawn they struck.

A massive wave pushed up the main road, aided by Qiren; archers scaled the hills while Tarkoda took the Trader to the sky and flew low over the hills into Serrat, two hundred soldiers crowded on the deck and in the open space below. As they flew over the town, bells began to ring out, and when they flew over the Landing, the square was crowded with people. Yet the guard were surrounded by the people of Serrat, and as the Trader flew down the people pushed the guard away from the Landing.

Tarkoda brought the ship down. People ducked as the rope and the hook flew out and dug into the landing post and he leapt down the stairs, threw a rope around the pole beside the gate and pulled the Trader in to the Landing. The soldiers had the gate open and were pouring down the stairs even before Tarkoda had closed the gap. It did not take long for them to leave the Trader and go down to aid the townspeople in turning the guard away from the square. Olando went down with the first wave and had the hook out before the soldiers had left the ship. He was back as the last few went down the stairs, and as soon as he was aboard Koda closed the gate and unhooked the rope. He was lifting as the soldiers below were pushing the queen's guard further back into the streets around the square.

He had seen the guard piling the huge slings with rocks as they'd flown past, and when they flew back over the town, he could see them working, the long arms throwing the deadly cargo over the hills into the soldiers on the other side.

Tarkoda looked over his shoulder and saw Flin looking back at him. Flin jerked his head towards the giant slings, and Tarkoda nodded and turned forward. The first of the great slings was near, and he took the ship down as they were loading the bucket with stones, and Tarkoda looked back in time to see Flin throw three fat balls from his stone. As the Trader wheeled around the balls hit. The guard leapt away as the three bolts hit the bucket and the arm of the sling, blowing apart the wood. Tarkoda looked away before the flame began to lick the rest of the shattered wood, turning the Zoi for a pass over the next one.

This one was flinging its stones and boulders over the hills as they flew past, but Flin decimated it before the stones hit the ground. Pieces of wood showered the guard underneath and they ran as the structure came crashing down. The third sling was hit with four mighty bolts, turning it instantly into a pyre. The guard scattered away from it, but reformed to fortify those fighting at the road.

Tarkoda took the Trader back over the hills, above the place where the fighting boiled. They went down to the Landing where others waited to be ferried over the hills into the city.

Three more times Tarkoda took people over the hills and into Serrat. The fighting had been fierce, but the last time they landed, the square had been nearly empty. When they took off again they flew slowly over the streets, seeing the last pockets of fighting.

At the edge of the city, they came upon a large crowd pushing the guard through the last streets, and when there was no more town around them, the guard turned and ran. Yet there was nowhere for them to go. The knot of guard holding the road had been breeched, the soldiers of other Lands and the people of their own had poured through the hills, and those that fled the town joined with those who were losing in the hills. The queen's guard had been split into two, and they were soon surrounded, yet they fought on.

It was afternoon before they finally surrendered, their numbers hugely dwindled. Their weapons were taken, and then the victors went through the battlefield, searching for the wounded among the many dead. By nightfall, a great pyre was burning in the hills before Serrat.

\* \* \*

There were celebrations in Serrat that night, even as the last of the dead were taken to the pyre and the Faunists tended the wounded.

The city had been in the grip of the guard for Moons, the people barely able to venture from their homes or walk safely in the streets. Some of the guard had made sport of the townspeople, delighting in baiting the men to fights they could never win, and preying on their mothers and sisters. The town breathed the air of freedom once again and rejoiced in its sweetness.

Tarkoda had landed the Trader in the square at Serrat and was greeted by cheers. His father's friend, old Billit the baker, pushed his way through the crowd and limped up the stairs to greet him. He leant on the arm of his daughter, Meri, and there were tears in her eyes as she smiled. They stayed the night in Serrat, but Tarkoda was up and eager to be gone before the dawn.

The Zoi let out a cry as they flew into the first rays of sunshine. Over Serrat they flew, and over the rocky land that led to the Valley of Stones. Never had he flown through the valley in full summer, always the Wintering had been at their backs, always it had been cold as he'd flown north to the Long

Lea, but now the baking heat of the valley blew up to meet them, and the birds soared on the hot currents. Tarkoda named each of the familiar rocky formations in his head, just as he'd named them aloud when he was a child, his heart leaping as each one came into sight.

It was midday when they flew up and over the last ridge, the falls tumbling down the cliff face, a rainbow sitting like a halo in its spray. Up they went and over, and the Lea stretched out before them, green and bursting with life.

They were all there to see it, standing on the deck beside him as they flew over the ripe fields and orchards, Blenny and Wendll, Spotjaw, Olando, Cheval, Qiren, Ishaan, and Flin, leaning over the edge, looking at the Long Lea unfold beneath them, Almarnoch pointing out the orchards and the crops as they flew over. They had all seen it before, but then the Long Lea had been brown with dead grass and then empty, snow-covered fields with the coming of the Wintering. Now the orchards were peppered with fruit, the fields swayed with a multitude of crops in the breeze and the little creeks gurgled; the stream that began inside Cave was full and dancing towards the cliff.

There were many people in the fields and the faces turned up as they flew over. Without exception every one stopped what they were doing and began running after the Trader.

Tarkoda took the ship down to the little Landing near the year huts where his father had landed Purple Leaf the year before, and by the time he'd opened the landing gate most of the Fleet were gathered at the base of the Landing. He waited for Almarnoch before he went down, suddenly nervous.

Almarnoch was not. Navez, Sahli'en and Llevvis came up the stairs, and he greeted them, then looked down at the anxious faces of the traders. Every eye was fixed on him. He knew each face, and every one was turned to him with hope shining in their eyes. He smiled and spread his arms.

"The World has need of you," he said, his voice rolling over their heads. "The other Lands have stormed Palveron. Meoro Pass has been taken and Serrat freed from the guard. The Fleet will fly again."

A cheer went up with his words, and they clapped each other on the back, hugged and kissed and whooped at the sky. Almarnoch held up his hands again and they grew silent.

"It is not without danger," he said. "Queen Virrisian still holds sway over most of our Land. She has unleashed the black ship on those outside, yet as the other Lands have aided us, now it is time to help them. There is safety here, safety on the other Lands, but unless the queen is overthrown there will be little safety on Zirrus. We have been asked to help. To ferry soldiers and information across Zirrus, to help free those in Palveron. Those who wish to remain here, those that wish to fly straight down Meoro Pass to other Lands may do so, but any that wish to aid in the freeing of our Land will fly with us."

"Where do you go?" came a voice.

"We go to Palveron," said Almarnoch. "We fly to Taffka."

* * *

Later that night, they talked in the meeting hall.

The room was very crowded. It had been built for old ones and children having Cave year to spend the warm Moons, not for an entire Fleet to meet in. They sat on the floor, the benches, and those who could not fit inside stood on the verandas running around the hall.

Navez had told them of their surprise when the Fleet had returned, and the difficulty they'd had in feeding so many. The repairing of the Traders still damaged from the coming of the black ship had come to a begrudging halt. Many were almost ready, but they had used all the wood available, and were now sending logging parties into the surrounding mountains. Yet the process was slow and a score of Traders still needed major work, and dozens more were waiting for more minor repairs. The ships too ruined by the black ship to ever fly again had been stripped of their wood – what little could be salvaged – and that had also been used in the repairs. Supplies of silk were also becoming scarce, but two dozen new balloons had been sewn and the weavers reported they would be able to make another dozen before the year was out.

The Traders that had flown into the World at the beginning of the year, only to be sent back, had been moored inside the darkened Cave, and they were only used to sleep in. No one had wanted to upset the glow worms as their cocoons had hatched into the giant courting moths, and the traders had spent their days weaving new balloons, repairing others, and working out in the fields. They had cultivated every piece of the Lea, even the cool western side of the stream, growing as much as they could. Several times one of the ships had ventured down to Serrat, but each had been met with a large contingent of guard and a hail of arrows, and even though the arrows had been easily avoided, the message had been clear. Now, there were many who were eager to fly into the World, yet there were also those who resisted the idea. Almarnoch left the decision up to each trader, telling them of the dangers they would face, but also of the dire need of many of the people on Zirrus, and the other Lands. Yet still there were arguments, and the talking went on until they were all hoarse and exhausted, but when they finally went to their beds, three-quarters of the Fleet that was able had decided to fly into the World. Two would ferry lumber from Ashkanna, so that when the giant moths flew from the tunnel they could finish the repairs to the ships and begin to build new ones. Many of those that would fly chose to go straight down Meoro Pass and from there to aid the other Lands, but some, Red Arrow, Green Arrow and Silver Hawk among them, would follow the High Warlock across Zirrus to Palveron.

Almarnoch watched the Fleet walk up the path to Cave. Despite the lateness of the hour, there was a lightness to many feet and the sound of laughter drifted back down to him.

Tarkoda and the others had gone to ready the Trader, for they would fly again at first light. Behind Almarnoch, Sahli'en and Navez were putting out the last of the lamps in the meeting hall, and he waited until they came down the steps behind him.

"You are sure this is the right path, Almarnoch?" said Sahli'en. "If the black ship comes again…"

"If it does, then it is best that the Fleet not be here," he replied. "Yet I think it is unlikely it will return. It took what it wanted and now it lies at the feet of Great Court."

"But it may fly at any time," she said. "Queen Virrisian will not let the Land go easily."

"No," said Almarnoch. "But her attention has been turned from us, and if we can help the Lands while she battles in Palveron, then that is our course. The time will come when the black ship shall be fought, but it will not be here."

"You leave at first light?" asked Navez.

"Yes," said Almarnoch. "We will spend a night at Serrat and see if there is news. Let them fly a few at a time the next day. Those at Serrat will greet them warmly, as will people everywhere."

"And Shaeli?" said Navez. "Where is she?"

"We know not," said Almarnoch. "We know only that she seeks to free her sisters."

"If they still live," said Navez, quietly.

"Navez," exclaimed Sahli'en, shocked.

"He speaks only what we all fear, Sahli'en," said Almarnoch. "While they were needed to ensure the Fleet did as she asked there was a reason to keep them safe. But now, with all the World against her…" He shook his head. "I know not. All we can do is go to Palveron and see to those in the city. To help those on Golden Eagle and Purple Leaf."

"But the Qotarr," said Navez. "What can they do against Qotarr?"

"I know not," said Almarnoch. "But we will find a way."

\* \* \*

As they readied the Trader the next morning, there came a fluttering, and they looked up to see the Zoi fly from the tunnel. The birds circled the Lea, and then flew into the mountains.

The Zoi had seemed unconcerned with their return to Cave. They slept in their own cave but fed themselves in the hills and streams around the Lea, perching in the cliffs above the fields or resting in the shade of the orchards through the day. Tarkoda and his companions watched them fly into the lightening sky, and then they turned back to say their farewells.

There were a few high clouds in the sky, the day was already warm, and Tarkoda was sweating as he waited at the bottom of the stairs for the last of his passengers to board.

The drell and the Ammerr were already up on the deck, ready for the journey. So, too, had the friends from Shaeli's Cave year joined them, and they stood at the rails calling final farewells to their families. They had not asked, they had just turned up at the Traders, gear in hand. They wanted to help, and he was glad to have them and their weapons aboard. Each was farewelled by their families, their faces staunch, but their eyes wet as they said goodbye. Only Lunn of Sky Lark was not there to farewell his daughter, Crylla, who had decided she had been wrong about Shaeli, who wished to make amends to her friend, yet her father would not overcome his bitterness and would not speak to her nor wish her goodbye. Beside Crylla were Bonn and Shylo, who had always been so quick to judge Shaeli, to find fault. Yet Shylo's sister, Driss, had been killed by the black ship and they would not be left out of the battle.

Spotjaw waited to free the landing hook and Flin stood by the rope on the little Landing, but Qiren was still saying goodbye to a tearful Illen, and Almarnoch was still talking to Llevvis.

Illen had remained at Cave when they'd flown out after first snow. The coming of the black ship had terrified her, and she had preferred to stay at Cave and help Wyshka look after Olver. The old storyteller had taken a long time to heal, and he would never walk straight again, but Illen had recovered her good spirits and been overjoyed with Qiren's arrival. Now she was devastated he was leaving again so quickly, yet still she would stay on the Long Lea. Qiren gave her a final kiss and walked over to Tarkoda. He looked at the last bird as he passed.

"It is ready to fly?" he asked.

Koda looked at the bird who had been shot by the arrow, and he nodded.

"It is fine," he said. "Sahli'en said the wound is almost healed." He smiled. "I gave it the option of staying here, gave it the formal farewell, but it wouldn't look at me. Just sat lower in its nest, pretending it couldn't see me. This morning when I came down, it was standing with the others, ready for the harness. Ah, at last," he added, as Almarnoch came towards them.

They lifted into the first rays shining between the mountains. Only Zerrinius was snow-capped at this time of the year, and of all the Fleet, only Tarkoda knew what it was like to fly over the great mountain. He had told the traders of his flight and the sights he'd seen on the far side; of the lost way he thought lay beneath the mountain, but these things must be left to future speculation; there were other tasks at hand. He looked up at the brightness of the mountain's cape as the Trader lifted into the sky.

They were all there to watch them leave, arms raised, voices calling farewell and good wishes. Five Traders came from the mouth of the tunnel to the Zoi's triumphant cries and followed them across the Lea; Red Arrow, Green Arrow, Silver Hawk, White Moth and Sea Mist, all ready to follow Almarnoch to Palveron.

Tarkoda flew low over the fields, following the spring stream as it meandered and was joined by others. When at last the stream fell away onto the floor of the Valley of Stones, he took one look back across the Long Lea, and then he took the ship down, heading through the valley, back to Serrat.

\* \* \*

It was afternoon by the time they reached Serrat. They circled the town, saw the colours of the other Lands waving to them from the square, and the place where the captured guard were held, and they took the ships down, mooring one by one at the Landing in the square. The people of Serrat were there to greet the six Traders, standing shoulder to shoulder with those who had freed the city.

They met with Prince Davron late in the day. He came to the Trader and they looked over the maps of Zirrus. There had been no news from Palveron, but there was word from a large group of rebels who now held most of the land around the western side of the Bay of Islands. Tarkoda unrolled a map and Davron showed him their position.

"The land between the Clahren River and the Royal Parklands is theirs," said Davron. "The rest of the Land still has large contingents of guard, but more and more people are joining the rebels. Their leader has their headquarters here," he said, pointing to a spot halfway between the Clahren River and Palveron. "There is an inn with a small Landing on the shores of the bay. You will be safe there. Conroi and Trilby have both been taken by the rebels, also some of the land around the Lakes' country, with the help of the Romynnii, but the rest of the Land," he shook his head, "I know not."

"We shall have to take our chances," said Almarnoch.

"Who is this rebel leader?" asked Tarkoda.

"That, I don't know," said Davron. "Only that this inn is their headquarters."

"I don't know how we're going to find it," said Tarkoda. "There are a lot of inns and small towns in that area."

"I think I know the one," said Flin. "Remember the place Purple Leaf dropped cargo?"

Koda nodded. "The one where you used to stop on the way to the house where Shaeli practised? In Boccra, wasn't it?" he said.

"That's the one," said Flin. "The inn was raided by the guard after you'd gone. They suspected rebels then. The innkeeper was killed, his wife driven mad, and the inn wrecked."

"I remember Shaeli telling me about it," Tarkoda said. "She said it was awful."

"A sorry sight it was," said Qiren. "Illen was very distressed by it."

"That must be the place," said Flin. "Do you think you can find it, Koda?"

Tarkoda nodded. "I'll find it," he said.

\* \* \*

"What time do we leave?"

Delphi asked the question and they all waited for Tarkoda to answer. He wondered when it was that he had become his father.

Delphi had regained much of her practical manner in the Moons since Baroz's death, but her face was lined with the grief it had brought her, and thick strands of grey were scattered through her dark hair. There had been no question of Red Arrow not following Tarkoda; each of his family wished to play some small part in avenging Baroz's death, and Green Arrow had followed them with similar sentiments. Silver Hawk had its own score to settle and they were eager to follow Tarkoda and Almarnoch. White Moth and Sea Mist had similar grievances.

Tarkoda looked at them all gathered on the Serrat Landing before him. Each looked to him to determine the way, just as they had once looked to his father. He felt a twinge at the thought of his father, the fine mind so addled by the blow from a rock, then he sighed and looked back at those waiting for his words: Delphi and her sons, all as red-headed as their father; Kaplan of Silver Hawk; Crylla of Sky Lark, whose mother had been killed and her ship destroyed by the black ship; Bic, whose Trader had been lost many Winterings before, standing with his cousin Jezzyn; so many others, all looking to him for answers.

"We leave before dawn," he said, at last. He glanced at Almarnoch. The old man nodded slightly, and Tarkoda looked back at the traders. "We shall go down the river," he said. "To Zerrin Crossing."

"There were many of the guard there when we flew back to Cave," said Bic.

"We know," said Koda. "Yet securing the crossing will be central to securing the region."

"And we have surprise on our side," said Almarnoch. "They'll not expect Traders."

"Nor anything else that we may bring," said Tarkoda.

\* \* \*

They followed Tarkoda down the river, flying the ships low over the water, the sun growing at their backs as they flew. Zerrin Crossing came into sight late in the morning.

The Landing was big enough to hold them all, but the others hung in the air while Tarkoda took his Trader down for a closer look, circling the buildings around the crossing. The wide punt bobbed on the waters of the river, and Savic, the fat owner of the tavern and inn, came waddling from his tavern to stare up at them. He had happily taken on the duties of landingholder when the queen had introduced them to the Land, ever eager to add to the coin in his purse, and now he waved them down.

Tarkoda looked at Almarnoch, signalled the other Traders, and took his own in to land.

They came from the tavern and the inn, from the huts and buildings as the fourth Trader flew down; scores of guard, weapons raised, streaming from the doors and rushing towards the Landing.

Tarkoda was at the bottom of the stairs when they came. He ran to the Trader and pulled open the door to the nest. The soldiers of Ashkanna and Romynn leapt to the ground, weapons drawn. On the decks above, archers from the Starisles stood up and began firing on the unsuspecting guard.

The battle was short and pointed. The guard thought they were attacking defenceless Traders, but each held a contingent from the other Lands who poured down the Landing stairs and from the nests beneath each ship. Before the last Trader had landed, the guard had been pushed back to the doors of Savic's tavern. They fought strongly, barricading themselves inside the building, but sheer numbers overcame them, and by afternoon those still alive were locked in the barn behind the inn.

Savic had trembled before them when the guard had been dealt with. His huge frame wobbled as he thanked them for freeing his pitiful establishment, offering them food and ale, yet when they searched the inn they found doors locked and the cries of women from behind them. The keys to the rooms were on Savic's enormous belt, and when the doors were opened they found dozens of girls and women, kept, for the most part, as unwilling participants in the entertaining of the guard. Two older women with eyes like snakes and mouths like cuts, were found cowering in the pantry. They were pointed out as Savic's accomplices, and the three were locked in the barn with the guard. Of the women found in the rooms of the inn, most would go back to the homes they had been taken from, but others had nowhere to go.

Almarnoch wondered if they might like to take over the running of the businesses at the crossing. He thought it fitting that Zerrin Crossing had a change of hands, he said, for it was about time the establishment had honest owners. The women looked at each other, and smiles began to crease the sad and dirty faces.

They took to the job with gusto, cleaning the kitchens and tavern before the day was out, and cooking a meal to feed their liberators. In Savic's room they found much wealth, coins and bags of jewels, and these they were given to divide amongst themselves, as some small payment for the trial they had endured. They donned the jewels and circled the barn where Savic was held, baiting him with their finery, laughing at his howls of protest, but none could dredge up any pity for the fat, slimy man.

When Tarkoda left the next day to follow the river to the west, it was with the two Arrow Traders and Silver Hawk; White Moth and Sea Mist would stay at the crossing. The Traders' ambush of the guard had been so successful that the other Lands wanted to use them again. When the four Traders flew from Zerrin Crossing, the others were already planning which town they would free next.

*  *  *

They flew west, following the River Zerrin, the bright ribbon of it unravelling before them, growing thicker with each passing league. They flew over smooth calm water flowing gently between grass-covered hills and grasslands, and they flew above white-flecked rapids between tall cliffs. They passed people standing on the banks, faces turned up, staring.

They landed at a tiny village, the people elated to see them, the guard non-existent. Even the landingholder was gone. There was only room for two Traders at the tiny Landing, and so the other two moored to the two ships moored at the Landing.

The people came hesitantly from their homes at first, but when they saw the Trader holding only friendly faces, they smiled and laughed. They had heard so many rumours from passing travellers that they were happy to have some real news. The townspeople also told the traders what the loss of the Fleet had meant to the Land, of the crops rotting in fields, of the people in big towns starving within their fine homes, and when the Traders flew from the village at dawn, it was with more determination than ever.

The next day, they saw a large contingent of guard on the road beside the river. The soldiers pointed and shouted, fired a few half-hearted arrows at them, yet they could do nothing but watch the ships fly on. Soon after seeing the guard they flew south, leaving the ribbon of river behind them, cutting across the land, heading towards the Clahren River. They found an isolated town to land in as the sun was setting, and here they met the first of the guard since Zerrin Crossing.

There was a score of them, and as the first Trader came down the guard ran towards it. Flin stood by the landing gate, and he threw a bolt into their midst before they reached the stairs. Two fell instantly, the others milled, and at another bolt from Flin's stone, they scattered. There were arrows raining from the second Trader as the soldiers began to regroup, and in moments another three of the guard had fallen. When armed traders began to come down the Landing steps they knew they were outmatched, and the rest surrendered quickly. They were taken and locked with the landingholder in his hut. The man had been asked to leave his post, but his oaths of loyalty to the queen saw him locked in with the others. The villagers disposed of the dead, tended to the wounded, and told of the increasing presence of rebels in the area. Again, they were gone before the sun had risen.

That afternoon, the four Traders saw the shimmer of the Clahren River in the distance. The Clahren split from the River Zerrin, and wound south to meet the water of the Bay of Islands, and when they reached it they followed its winding path towards the bay.

They had been told that the rebels held the land between the Clahren and the Royal Parklands far to the south, and when they saw the gleam of the bay before them, they crossed the river, flying over a small garrison on a bluff beside the water. The front wall of the garrison was a pile of rubble barely recognisable as a wall, and around the garrison, across several fields, was a great encampment filled with hundreds of people, their faces turned to the sky, cheers resounding in the air. Here and there a wide black hole marred the ground, and the people were camped away from the blackened rings; those on the Traders knew of only one thing which could cause such damage to the earth.

They circled the encampment, waving at the rebels in the fields below, and then they flew down the river to the little town of Boccra, near the sandstone house on the bay where Flin, Qiren, Shaeli and the others had so often enjoyed quiet holidays.

Tarkoda, remembering leaving Shaeli at the little walled house the Wintering she'd begun her apprenticeship, flew down over the house before he took the Traders into the village, and as they flew back over Boccra, there was much waving of arms and whistles and cries, and not a bit of black-and-scarlet to be seen, so the four Traders went in to land.

There was just room for them all at the Landing, and the people of the town waited for them to moor their ships and come down the stairs before they gave them a resounding cheer. There were gasps as the drell came down the steps, as there had been wherever Blenny and Wendll were seen, and the drell bowed graciously at the open mouths.

Almarnoch stood with his staff in his hand, and a man came through the crowd. He was a big man, broad-shouldered and tall, with a thick beard. On his forehead was an almost-healed wound, the skin just puckering around the scar.

"Greetings," he said, with a bow and a booming voice. "It is a wonderful thing to see the Traders back in the skies." He grinned. "So they have freed Meoro Pass and Serrat at last?"

"They have," Almarnoch smiled back.

"Good," said the man. "I am Fezzik. I head the rebels here, and it's happy I am to welcome you to Boccra, a free town once more."

\* \* \*

# CHAPTER TWENTY FIVE

Fezzik had been in the forge when he was told there were Traders in the sky. He had bolted outside, Verlie and Pemba on his heels, and when he saw the four Traders flying down the line of the river he'd picked Verlie up and swung her around. Pemba was given a hairy kiss and sent to fetch the children from the house. They would all greet the return of the Fleet to their town.

Fezzik could hardly believe he was sleeping beneath his own roof once more. When the black ship and the Qotarr had come to Palveron; when he had seen the guard beginning to drain from their garrisons, he had known it was time to strike. With the blessing of the rebel leader he had led the raids on the guard's outposts. The first to fall was the garrison to the south of the Royal Parklands, then he had set his sights on the one above Boccra.

He had used the same tactic he had employed to free Verlie and Pemba, filling the hill beneath the garrison with his people, striking the guard as they slept in the small hours. It had been one of the easiest of his victories, the guard taken before much blood had been shed and locked in their own cells.

From Boccra he had moved outward, taking back small villages and forcing the guard from their strongholds. Some were taken prisoner, others fled to join their brethren to the west or across the Zerrin River. With the taking of the garrison above Boccra, they also held the bridge and its access roads, and it was from the garrison that they directed where next they'd strike. They had spread through the countryside slowly at first, and then more quickly as the next village was freed and their numbers grew, for wherever the guard was defeated, the spirits and the weapons of the people were raised.

Those he had spoken to along the River Zerrin had begun their own offensive, attacking the guard's strongholds, spreading their own territories, until most of the Land along the west side of the Clahren was freed. Fezzik's brother, Fozar, had done the same thing to the south, pushing the guard back south of the Royal Parklands. People began to converge on the area to join the rebels, encampments sprang up, one to the south, one stretching beside the garrison above Boccra, others to the north and west. The encampments at Boccra and beside the bay to the south had both been attacked by the black ship within the last ten days.

Fezzik had been at the garrison when the black ship came swooping out of the darkness above the bay. He had eaten dinner with Verlie at the house that night, but gone back to the garrison to plan an assault upriver.

The first thing he had done after he had taken the garrison had been to send for Verlie, Pemba and the children, who had been overjoyed to leave the rocky valley where the rebel's stronghold lay.

His father had wept beside his sobbing mother as they walked up the path to their house behind the forge, and Fezzik's own sight grew cloudy when his daughter Florry's first act was to go and visit the place where Zeffy and Pim lay. The tiny grave had been tended in their absence with great care; a statue of two laughing children placed at its head, the ground covered with tiny purple and yellow flowers. Florry had knelt beside the grave and patted the ground, then she looked up at Fezzik.

"I miss Zeffy," she said. "Pim, too." It was the first time she had spoken their names since the day they'd died. She stood and took his hand. "But it's alright to, isn't it, Da? It's alright to miss them."

He had knelt beside her, and enfolded her within his big arms. "Yes, Florry," he said. "It's alright. It means we remember."

She nodded and wiped the tears from his cheek, and they had all stood in remembrance of the two girls, killed so senselessly, then they had gone into their home for the first time in many long days. It had become Fezzik's habit to spend a little time beside the tiny grave each evening; often with Florry, and they would talk of Zeffy and Pim, of the funny things and the naughty things they'd done in their short lives. With the return home, Florry also seemed to return to herself.

The night the black ship came, Fezzik had stood looking down at the carpet of pretty flowers that covered his youngest child and the child of his dead friend before he rode up to the garrison. He had ridden there with plans for the next raid on his mind, and he was greeting the men guarding the gate when one of them cried out and pointed to the south. A woman on the wall screamed as Fezzik turned his head and saw the thing fly up the line of the river and turn its lights towards them.

Across the little backwater and the road were camped hundreds of rebels. Men and women willing to fight for Zirrus were sitting in groups through the encampment or readying themselves for bed, small fires were scattered between the tents and wagons, horses were corralled on the far side. The black ship came at great speed up the river and a red light flickered on, shining from the front of the shapeless black ship.

Fezzik had heard of the thing, had watched from a great distance as it had circled the ships in Palveron harbour, but when he saw it moving towards the garrison he was frozen for a moment in silent disbelief. Then he yelled at his people.

"Off the walls," he shouted. "Sound the alarm. Take cover."

Bells began to peal and he heard shouts from the encampment, then the red light on the ship narrowed and shone on the walls and the archers fleeing from it. A red bolt flew from the ship and slammed into the wall above him, and he dived for cover as the rocks spewed out with a mighty crash. There was screaming inside the garrison as Fezzik rose to his feet, the body of one of the men with whom he'd just been talking lay beneath a piece of the shattered wall nearby.

Blood poured into one eye and he swiped at it with his sleeve as the black ship turned its red eye onto the encampment. It slowed its pace as it crossed the road and when the red light narrowed again, Fezzik braced himself.

There were three bolts, shooting from the black ship with immense power. They hit the centre of the encampment, turning it instantly into screaming, burning pandemonium. Fezzik bolted down the hill to the road as the ship circled the camp, then it belched one final bolt down into the melee before turning and flying south.

As Fezzik reached the road he saw two men running in terror across a paddock. The black ship slowed as it flew over them, almost hovering above the fleeing men. A white light snapped on from the belly of the thing, training on the two men, and Fezzik had stopped in terrified amazement as the two men were surrounded by the light and then lifted from their feet and drawn up into the belly of the ship, as if they had been eaten whole by some giant beast. The light flickered off, the men gone with it, then the black ship had picked up speed and sped into the night, leaving Fezzik standing in the road, blood pouring from the wound on his forehead, amid the shouts and screams of his people.

The next day he heard the ship had attacked the camp of his brother's band also, and many had been killed. Two score of his people had been killed the night the black ship came, many others injured, and the little garrison had taken a heavy blow, yet the determination of Fezzik had not wavered. Now, as he stood before the traders, his heart swelled with the hope that he had made a difference, and that with the return of the Traders they might yet have a chance. He smiled broadly and welcomed the traders again to the village of Boccra.

\* \* \*

"We are happy to be able to moor in safety," said Almarnoch to the big, widely grinning man.

"That you may do," said Fezzik. "All the way from here to the Parklands they will greet you eagerly. The Land has missed you. Where are you headed?"

"We seek the leader of the rebels," said Almarnoch. "We are told their base is an inn on the shores of the bay."

"That's so," said Fezzik. "And they will be happy to see you there. We could use a Trader or two."

"We have found them to be quite good for an ambush," said Almarnoch. "Perhaps one could stay here to aid you."

"Aye, that would be a great help," said Fezzik. "The guard tries to take back the land we have won, and having a Trader would make the battle that much easier."

"What is the word from Palveron?" asked Almarnoch.

"Not good," said Fezzik, the smile leaving his face for the first time. "The Qotarr prowl the city and the people there still go hungry. At first, we wished them to notice what the queen was doing to the Land, and so we made supplies scarce, but we could never wish them to starve. Those in the city still fight, but quietly, when the Qotarr are busy elsewhere."

"And the black ship?" asked Flin. "What of it?"

Fezzik's face grew grimmer. "It has been seen prowling the skies," he said. "Two of our camps were hit by its red fire. That is where I got this," he pointed to the scar on his forehead. "Two of my people were sucked into the belly of the thing before it left. Their bodies were found in a field leagues away."

Flin shook his head. "The quicker we get to the city the better," he said.

"You're not going to Palveron?" asked Fezzik. "That's madness. If the guard don't get you the moment you land, then the Qotarr will."

"Qotarr or no," said Almarnoch. "We go to Palveron."

\* \* \*

When they flew out the next morning, Green Arrow stayed behind to help Fezzik, and Red Arrow and Silver Hawk followed Tarkoda's many-coloured ship around the bay, but first Flin visited the sandstone house. It was much as he'd left it, the pantries had been emptied and a thick layer of dust coated every room, but everything else seemed the same. Fezzik, Ishaan and Tarkoda had accompanied him, and while Flin was closing up the house he heard Fezzik mention the many wounded who were in Boccra.

"Everyone helps," he said. "The whole village has taken someone into their homes, but they are all crowded and it makes it difficult for the Faunists."

"There will be more in the coming days," said Tarkoda, shaking his head.

"Why not bring them down here?" said Flin, closing the door of the house. "There are not many beds, but more could be brought in, I'm sure. It would be easier for the Faunists to tend them if they were all in one place."

Fezzik's brows rose and he came forward and clasped Flin by the shoulder. The thin thrower was dwarfed by the huge man.

"A generous offer," he boomed. "And one I will take advantage of, with many thanks."

Flin gave him the keys to the place, and before they'd lifted, the wounded were being moved down to the walled house.

Though they could have flown across the water, they went around the edge of the bay. It was good to fly over houses and towns without fear of the guard, and Tarkoda flew the Trader low over the roads and towns. Everywhere they heard cheers and waved back at the arms raised up to them, and as the midday hours passed, they began to look ahead for the inn. Flin told them of the many times they had stopped there for a meal, and how the owner had been killed and the inn ruined by Pizar and his men, the dead man's wife driven mad by the event. A picture of the hysterical Dorkit he and Shaeli had found in the garden shed was clear in his mind.

"And this was the same man who caught us in that town?" Ishaan said. "The one who had Shaeli in the carriage?"

"Yes," said Flin. "I began to doubt him after the inn, and it seems I was right to do so."

"Flin," Tarkoda called from the upper deck. "I think I see it."

Flin went up to join him, and Ishaan followed. On the edge of the bay was the inn, and as they came closer they saw tents pitched in the fields around the place, scores of them. Tarkoda headed for the landing posts, and when they neared they saw a new Landing had been built. It was large, uncovered, but easily had room for the three Traders to land. A dozen men were hammering boards into the top of it as they flew over. They circled the place before they went down, amazed at the hundreds of faces looking back at them, seeing that here, too, there were signs of the black ship. Shouts went up as the Traders wheeled around and came down to land.

People scattered beneath them, the hammering men ran down the stairs of the Landing as the birds brought the ships in to land, and by the time they moored, the Landing was surrounded by people staring at them as they looked down from the rails.

Almarnoch, Flin, Tarkoda, Qiren and Ishaan went down the stairs. A man stood waiting at the bottom. He was so tall and broad and bearded, so like Fezzik that they could only have been kin.

"I am Fozar," he said, and his booming voice again reminded them of Fezzik. "We had word we should expect you, and have been working on the Landing all day. This morning there were no stairs, nor boards upon it."

"You have done a fine job," said Almarnoch, and then he introduced them all.

Fozar bowed to them, and he looked up at the Traders. "When my brother sent word there were Traders in the skies again there was a lot of cheering," he said, confirming that Fezzik was his brother, as they had thought. Fozar grinned at them. "Also many toasts were made to you when we heard, and there were a few swollen heads to show for it this morning."

"Do you lead the rebels here, Fozar?" asked Almarnoch.

Fozar shook his head. "No," he said. "I follow orders. But let me take you in. She is anxious to meet you."

"She?" said Flin.

"Aye," said Fozar, walking towards the inn.

The crowd gathered around the Landing parted, leaving a path to the door of the inn, and they followed Fozar across the dusty courtyard. The last time Flin had seen the Fish and Field was when Dorkit's daughter had led her babbling and crying back to their home, but inside, the place was much as he remembered it before it had been ruined. The tables and benches had been repaired, the place painted, but here and there he could see the marks on the walls from the battle that had been fought there. The door to the kitchens were open, a variety of smells wafting through, and outside the kitchen doors there were huge cauldrons set over open flames, steam rising from them, people everywhere, cutting and stirring and cleaning. All turned bright smiles of greeting on the traders before turning back to their work.

"It takes much to feed such an army," said Ishaan, with a smile.

Fozar looked down at him. Ishaan was by no means short, yet Fozar looked down on everyone.

"It does," he said. "But there are many with unused produce who are happy to aid us. The Land lies filled with food while many starve."

"You have taken much of the Land back already," said Almarnoch. "People are free from the guard."

"Aye," Fozar said. "Yet only in our small part of it. There are many battles to be fought yet, and some that we cannot win."

"The Qotarr that roam Palveron?" asked Tarkoda.

"Them, and the black ship," nodded Fozar.

"You have seen it then?" said Almarnoch.

"I have," he said. "We watched as it blasted its red light onto the ships in the bay. It gave us our own warning recently, and if it comes for us with more purpose we are doomed." He shrugged, his huge shoulders rising and falling like lumps of wood. "Yet we shall do what we can. Come," he said. "She will grow anxious."

He led the way across the room and up the stairs. On the upper floor there were few people, but through an open door they saw a room full of beds, all of them filled with men and women sporting bruises, bandages, and splints, and two Faunists were there tending the wounded. Fozar led them past the room to the end of the hallway. He knocked, there was a quiet answer, and he opened the door and went through it. They followed him into the room where a woman stood by a table covered with maps. She turned as they entered, pushing a strand of grey hair from her forehead.

"Dorkit?" gasped Flin. "You? You are the leader of the rebels?"

Dorkit smiled. "I have that honour," she said, bowing her head once. "'Tis nice to see you again, Flin."

"But, you..." Flin began.

"The last time you saw me, I was, well... let us say unwell," Dorkit said, smiling a tight little smile. She held her shoulders stiffly, her hands clasped before her chest. "It was some time before I... returned to myself, and when I did, I would not let Borsal's death go unavenged." She looked out the window. "We were few, at first, but with time, we have become an army." She looked back at Flin, and then at the others. "But you forget your manners, Flin, and you used to have such fine manners."

Flin apologised and introduced them. Dorkit greeted them and she looked back out the window.

"There are only three?" she asked, looking across at the Traders.

"Yes," said Flin. "One has stayed with Fezzik at Boccra, two at Zerrin Crossing to aid the fighting there. Most will fly to the safety of other Lands, who are also in need of aid, some go to other strongholds held by the rebels. Trilby, Conroi."

"A pity," said Dorkit. "We could use them. My brother will make good use of the one at Boccra, though, very good use."

"Fezzik is your brother?" asked Flin, looking from the small woman to the big frame of Fozar standing inside the door, eyes crinkled in amusement. "Fozar too?"

"That's so," said Dorkit with a smile. "Half-brothers they are, the children of my father's second wife, both with reason to rebel against the guard, both pushed, as I was, to this path." The thin smile became a grim one, the teeth tightly clenched. "It is not an easy path, but the Traders will make it less hard, I think."

"We are at your service," said Tarkoda. "Yet ultimately our aim is to reach Palveron."

"The city is under siege," said Dorkit, frowning. "The giant lizards control the streets and the perimeter. Until we find a way to fight the Qotarr, Palveron is out of our reach."

"How are they controlling the Qotarr?" asked Ishaan.

"Wokkii soldiers sit upon them," said Dorkit. "They are tied through the nose and they direct them that way."

"Then this is where we must strike," said Flin. "In this I may be of some service."

"A thrower could be of great use," agreed Dorkit.

"What of the black ship?" asked Almarnoch.

"It has not been seen since the assault on the ships in the harbour and our encampments," said Dorkit. "Yet that means nothing. Even if we find a way of beating the Qotarr, we can never win against this black ship."

"I said the same thing," said Fozar.

"Even so," said Almarnoch. "These things we must do. But first, I must reach Palveron."

"We can't just fly in there," said Tarkoda. "They'd be all over us."

"Yes, lad," said Almarnoch. "That they will."

\* \* \*

# CHAPTER TWENTY SIX

Jarris knew just where to find Mareesha. She was standing on the upper deck, looking up at the lights of Great Court. The castle's outlines were indistinct against the night sky, but the lights in the windows shone like stars. Mareesha's eyes were fixed upon one light, high up and alone. She sighed as Jarris came up behind her and put a hand on her shoulder. She leant back against him and together they looked at the light atop the tower.

"Come," he said. "The dinner is ready."

"Alright," she said, but she did not move.

Gently he took her hand and led her down the stairs into the Trader. Inside the big room it was crowded and bright, and Mareesha took a deep breath as they entered and fixed a smile on her face as she went to help Eenis.

Jeth was taking platters to the table. Andos and S'resh were laying plates, Crissita sat with Brudloc. Other Romynnii and a few Starislanders sat around the table.

The meal was sparse, as most meals were, the talk the same. All were exhausted with the lack of food and constant harassment by the guard. The stalking Qotarr had become almost ordinary.

Each day brought sounds of battle, some distant, others closer, occasionally in the square beneath them. They crept up to Arinola's when they dared, twice going through her grandfather's tunnel to stare down at the rubble that lay between the empty house and the wall. All the houses had now been destroyed, the streets gone, only the wide road leading up the centre of the hill to the gates of Great Court, this barricaded and filled with guard. Where the soldiers slept and what they ate were things to be guessed at, but they were there in their thousands. At any time of the day or night they would sweep down the hill into the city, killing any they found on the streets after dark, pounding on doors and breaking windows. There was barely a whole pane of glass left in the city. And yet the guard did not have it all their own way.

The soldiers from other Lands and the people of Palveron were organised, and they led their own raids on the roaming packs of guard. Time and again the queen's soldiers would walk into an ambush where they fought for their lives. Sometimes they escaped, other times their bodies were left in the streets for the next contingent to find. Everyone lived with their breath caught in their throats and their hearts thumping, and now, as they sat over the remains of the meagre meal, there was a small thud on the deck above. Every hand went to a weapon, every eye leapt to the boards over their heads. Jarris, Jeth and Andos crept down the passage and up the stairs, swords in their hands. They stopped at the top and peered out into the darkness. A lone figure crept across the deck towards them. Jarris stopped him with a few terse words.

"If you value your life, stop where you are."

The figure stopped and raised his hands outwards. "'Tis I, Jarris," said a low, familiar voice. "I bring news."

He took a step forward and Jarris squinted into the night. The balloon fluttered above.

"Ishaan?" Jarris said, lowering his weapon.

"Yes," said Ishaan, coming towards them. His hair and clothes were damp, and he looked over his shoulder. "There are guard coming this way."

"Inside, quickly," said Jarris.

The sound of boots was coming into the square as they went down the stairs.

"Did they see you?" asked Jarris.

Ishaan shook his head, and glanced over his shoulder. "No," he said. "One group saw me on the docks, but I managed to hide. These I heard behind me. Luckily I had almost reached the square. I don't run well," he smiled.

"I've heard that," said Jarris, returning the smile. "Here we are."

They had reached the big room where every eye was turned to them. Mareesha sighed and put a hand to her chest when they entered.

"Ishaan," she said, coming across the room. "Where did you come from? How did you reach the city?"

"I came across the bay," he said. "Three Traders are moored at an inn on the shores to the north."

"Tarkoda?" said Mareesha.

"Yes," nodded Ishaan. "Red Arrow and Silver Hawk are with him."

"Shaeli, too?" asked Mareesha, taking a step forward in eagerness.

"No," said Ishaan. "She is far to the north. I'm sorry. Yet she is with Williver and free again."

"Free?" said Mareesha. "Again? Oh, Ishaan. What happened?"

"I shall tell you all I can," he said. "But I must return before sunrise. We have a plan."

"Did they not see your boat?" asked Crissita. "The bay is watched closely. No craft have been allowed on it since the coming of the black ship."

"They cannot see beneath the water," smiled Ishaan.

"Crissita, may I introduce you to Ishaan of the Ammerr," said Jarris. "Ishaan, Princess Crissita, formally of Ashkanna, now of Romynn."

Crissita goggled as Jarris introduced Sir Brudloc and the others to Ishaan.

"Do you know a Prince Davron?" Ishaan asked Crissita.

He had politely ignored the goggle, but his question only made Crissita's goggle work harder. At least it had company. S'resh's goggle was also working overtime.

"He is my father," Crissita gasped. "How do you know him?"

"We left him in charge of Serrat," said Ishaan. He looked at Jarris. "They have taken Meoro Pass and Serrat. The Fleet is flying."

"Fetch Taffka," Jarris said to Andos, and when he'd gone, he turned back to Ishaan. "The Traders across the bay, Tarkoda and the others, they are safe?"

"Yes," Ishaan said. "The rebels hold the land from the Parklands to the Clahren, and most of the land along the river. The Traders are with them. Two more aid the rebellion near Zerrin Crossing."

"Good," Jarris said. He shook his head. "I never thought I would be happy my children were with rebels."

"It is good to see you have regained yourself," smiled Ishaan, putting a hand on Jarris' shoulder. "Shaeli and Tarkoda have been worried. Tarkoda will be pleased when I tell him you have recovered."

"No more pleased than I," Jarris smiled back.

Taffka and Andos came into the room, followed by Rhubic and Rafi. Ishaan told them all that had happened since first thaw, yet time was short, much was left unsaid, and he asked for the news from the city. Taffka told all with as few words as Ishaan had used, and then Ishaan gave them Almarnoch's message. Taffka shook his head.

"And he plans to do this when?" he asked.

"Whenever you can ready the city," said Ishaan. "I shall be back in three days." He stood. "It grows late. I should return."

He said goodbye to them, and Andos and Rhubic offered to accompany him down to the docks.

"I'll accept, with thanks," he said. He looked at Rhubic. "The friends of your Cave year are with us too," he said. "They would not be left out of the fight."

Rhubic grinned. "They're probably just bored," he said. "It's been a slow year. For them, at least."

He laughed and followed Ishaan out the door. Andos took up a bow, kissed his mother's cheek and followed them.

Crissita watched them go. She had regained control of her eyes, but not her amazement.

"One of the Ammerr," she said. "Incredible."

She turned around to speak to Brudloc, and she did not notice that S'resh's eyes were still on the doorway.

* * *

Ishaan returned three days later, just as he had said he would. They were all waiting for him. Andos stood in the shadows on deck looking out across the square. When he brought Ishaan down, no one noticed S'resh slip in behind them.

This time Ishaan did not stay long. He confirmed Almarnoch's plans, discussed timing, and then he went back to the docks to slip into the dark water.

* * *

The sky was beginning to pale when Ishaan returned. Almarnoch and Tarkoda waited for him, sitting on the bank at the back of the inn. They stood as Ishaan came from the water. A frog creaked from a bush nearby, but was silenced when Almarnoch spoke.

"All is well?" he said.

Ishaan nodded, pushing the water from his skin. "They are ready, if a little concerned at your plans," he said.

"Where?" asked Tarkoda.

"We are to circle the city," said Ishaan. "They say we should go to the south first. There is one beside a park and they will be ready."

"I know the one," said Tarkoda. He looked down at Almarnoch. "You're sure about this?"

Almarnoch raised an eyebrow at him. "Not really, lad," he said. "But it's a start. And it keeps their thoughts from your sister."

Tarkoda looked back at him. He nodded after a moment and turned back to Ishaan. "When?" he said.

"Two days," said Ishaan.

"The gods be with us," said Tarkoda.

\* \* \*

When dawn broke over the city two days later, the streets were empty. The bay was silver glass, unruffled by even the slightest breeze, the air hazy and thick with the summer heat. The air was also thick with the plans being woven behind closed doors. Few people were seen outside, only the Qotarr and the guard roamed the shattered streets. The city baked through the heat of the day, the afternoon stretched painfully on, and when at last the sun began to fall towards the west, a breeze ruffled the air. The sunset was crimson and gold and was watched by many eyes through broken panes. Darkness brought little relief from the heat. The slight breeze disappeared with the sun and the city simmered through the evening. A half-moon rose, covering the roofs in silver. Eyes still looked through broken panes, and when what they looked for was sighted, a single bell chimed to the south.

The birds shone in the moonlight. They pulled the Traders low over the city, and those on the two Traders moored in the square watched them fly over with pride. And then they waited.

\* \* \*

Tarkoda saw the two Traders in the square in the city's centre as he passed over, knowing his parents would be there looking back at him, knowing his father's mind was whole, knowing his mother would be needing to see at least one of her children, yet also knowing it would not be tonight that she would see him.

He looked ahead and heard a bell chiming somewhere. There was a cry from below, and he looked down to see a large group of the guard. As the Traders passed, the guard began to run.

They should be close, and, as the thought went through his mind, a light began to glow from between the buildings ahead. The light became two, five, twenty, and more, and he took the ship lower and the lights ahead turned into a square, a leafy park framing a long Landing. He took the Trader down into the lighted square. Surrounding the lamp holders was a thicker, darker ring of people, all holding weapons in their hands and grim determination upon their faces. Every face was turned up to the Traders, yet there was no cheering, only held breaths as Tarkoda took his ship down. He looked behind him as they went down, saw all was ready, and went in to the Landing.

The first of the guard came just as Spotjaw sunk the landing hook into the pole, yet the crowd was ready for them, rushing to meet them, overwhelming the score of roaming guard, and the few soldiers not killed fled back into the streets. They knew it would not be long before there were more.

Tarkoda watched as they unloaded the sacks of food, handing them down the stairs to waiting arms, saw the boxes of bright new swords following them. Through the streets he heard the coming guard, this time no mere score, and he willed the others to hurry as the fighting began again on the fringe of the crowd and those with weapons surged towards it. The lights ringing the square began to go out.

He raised a hand to those that went down the stairs behind the food and weapons. Each raised a hand to him before they disappeared into the crowd. He signalled the birds to lift, watching the ropes coiled behind him. It was Bic and Jezzyn who coiled them now. Even Spotjaw had gone with the others. He suddenly felt very lonely.

The lights went out as they lifted, but the fighting went on. Silver Hawk and Red Arrow had circled while he had been on the ground, and now he flew up and joined them. Then he led them east, to find another Landing far across Palveron where people waited with lights and arms for the things to sustain the starving city.

The battle for Palveron had begun. Again.

* * *

The Traders landed at three different Landings around the city during the night, Tarkoda's first, then Silver Hawk and Red Arrow. Each time they unloaded supplies and weapons, but only from Tarkoda's Trader did people disembark. The drops did not last long. Each time, the Landing was lit by a ring of lights and guarded by many weapons. After the Traders had dropped their cargo, the lights were extinguished and the frustrated guard fought in the streets while the next Trader landed far from their swords and arrows. The Qotarr were used far too late to have any effect, the battles past and the crowds dispersed before they were near. The Traders flew back across the bay while the fighting still raged. They would fill their ships again for a raid the next night.

Those Tarkoda had dropped on the first landing were already reaching the square in the middle of the city. They had dodged many of the guard as they wound through the city, hiding in shadows, creeping through the moonlit streets. They had to hide in an alley just off the main square while it was patrolled by dozens of the queen's soldiers. The moment the guard had gone they dashed across the square to the Landing where the two Traders had been moored since early spring, to where those who had waited so long waited now for their arrival.

Almarnoch led them up the stairs. The drell, Ammerr, Qiren, Flin and Spotjaw followed him up through the shadows and across the deck of Purple Leaf. Taffka, Jarris, and Mareesha were waiting in the shadows at the top of the stairs.

"No one saw you?" asked Taffka, as they came into the stairwell.

"All is well," answered Almarnoch. "We are unseen. Yet we have only begun."

Taffka nodded. "And she will not like it," he said, glancing up at the castle brooding above the city.

"No," said Almarnoch. "But that is to be expected. And just as I planned."

"But is flaunting the Fleet across the city wise?" said Taffka. "My word has been broken and the queen will turn her anger upon us."

"If the city is fed and armed she will have other things to think about," said Almarnoch. "We plan to keep her very much distracted."

Mareesha's voice came quietly from the shadows. "You forget something, Almarnoch," she said. "You forget my daughters. If she cannot use them to control the Fleet then they will be of no further use to her."

Almarnoch peered through the darkness, looking at Mareesha as if he saw her clearly in the dim light.

"That is where we must trust in Shaeli," he said.

Mareesha met his gaze just as clearly. "But Shaeli is with strangers," she said. "And far away."

Almarnoch studied the words placed before him before he answered them. "Did not Irinesta trust her child to such circumstances, long Winterings ago?" he said at last.

Mareesha looked back. Moments passed as she tested the weight of his question, then she closed her eyes and dropped her head. "Yes," she said, quietly.

"Then now it is your turn to trust your child to follow the path the gods have chosen for her," said Almarnoch.

Mareesha raised her head. "Then so be it," she said. "I shall trust in the gods. The gods, and Shaeli."

* * *

# CHAPTER TWENTY SEVEN

Somewhere in M'Zen'sclahr Forest, Shaeli was waking to another hot silent day. They had sat and swum and talked through the days before, waiting for the return of the fairy, Tish, yet they had waited in vain.

Shaeli sat up and stretched. The others were still asleep; even Ebony did not stir when she pushed the white sheets back. She got up and crept out the door, taking a bunch of green grapes from the newly-laid table as she passed. They had grown accustomed to the bounty of the table, the fact they never saw anyone do it, the delights it held, the thanking of the air for it.

She nibbled on the grapes as she walked across the grass, still wet with the morning dew and cool on her feet as she wandered over to the little creek. A bird sang a melody in the trees somewhere on the other side, and she stopped to listen, a smile on her face.

There was seldom a noise from the trees surrounding them, though once, a few days before, they had heard a far-off howl; a cry of terror and despair that had frozen them all where they stood. They had been by the pool and the howling voice had come nearer, and through the trees on the far side of the pool had come Pizar, yet not a Pizar that they recognised. His clothes were torn and ragged, his hair matted, his face and limbs scratched and bleeding. He stood by the side of the pool, dribbling and crying, his head swivelling from one side to the other, yet he did not see them. Shaeli had called out to him, distressed to see him like that, even after what he had done, but he seemed not to hear her, and soon he had moved back into the trees, still moaning and calling out unintelligible words until the sound of his passing was lost back into the

Forest. She had begun to cry, but M'zena had patted her hand and told her the Forest had its own rules, and he must have been truly wicked for it to treat him that way. Shaeli had dropped her head, but she knew the old woman was right. They had not heard him again.

Now she listened while the bird rejoiced in the morning, not daring to move lest it stop. She stood in the dawn light until the bird had finished its song. The Forest sank again into silence, and she sighed.

"I'd almost forgotten the sound of birds at dawn," someone said behind her.

She knew it was Ezebar before she turned. She took a deep breath to still the rush of nerves that gathered instantly in her chest, and kept her smile and voice light – she hoped.

"Yes, I had, too," she said. "It was lovely, wasn't it?"

He nodded. "The grapes are good this morning," he said, picking half a dozen from a bunch in his hand, and putting them in his mouth.

Shaeli picked a couple from her bunch. "Yes," she said, chewing on them. "But everything is always good here, wherever it comes from."

They began to walk down the grass beside the creek towards the little stone bridge, their bare feet leaving dark green melted patches in the bright dew.

"I tried to stay awake the other night," Ezebar said, "to see if I could see anything, but it was useless. I drifted off, eventually, but I'm sure it wasn't for long, and when I woke up, they'd been."

Shaeli giggled. "I snuck up on the house yesterday afternoon," she said. "I'm sure I heard someone inside, so I leapt in, looking like a fool. I think I even said 'aha!'." She laughed. "There was no one there, of course, but there was a fresh jug of juice on the table."

Ezebar laughed with her. "I can't imagine you looking like a fool, Shaeli," he said. "You're much too pretty."

"Oh," was all she could say, nonplussed by the compliment. She searched for an answer. "Thank you, but... just the same, I'm sure it's possible to be pretty and look foolish all at the same time." She tried to laugh away the pink that threatened to cover her cheeks. "In fact, I'm fairly positive I've seen it done."

Ezebar laughed again. It was a nice big laugh. Her father had such a laugh, and she couldn't help but laugh with him. They grinned at each other, and while the laughter faded, the look did not. Shaeli realised that they had stopped walking, and were now just standing looking at each other.

Ezebar took her hand, and her breath went with it. Her skin tingled where his fingers held hers, and she looked down at their entwined hands, and then back up at him. Neither of them were smiling anymore. He took a half step closer to her, and his other hand reached up to brush a strand of hair from her cheek.

The fingers were light, gentle but work-rough, and she trembled as they stroked her cheek. Her eyes widened a little as she looked up at him, and his hand lingered on her face. His head lowered, coming closer to hers, and just as she knew that he was going to kiss her, she heard a noise; a snicker of sound from the other side of the bridge.

Ezebar heard it too and his head went up, the familiar frown creasing his brow as he looked across the water. His fingers left Shaeli's face.

Her face burned where his fingers had been, and, somewhere inside, she badly regretted that the moment had been lost, but she followed his frown across the water with her own, squinting into the shadows and the mist that pooled around the trees on the other side of the bridge. She could see nothing, and she looked back up at him.

"What was it?" she whispered.

He looked back down at her, the frown softening, and he shook his head. "It sounded like a horse," he said, his voice low.

"The one I..." He stopped, and his fingers gripped tighter to the hand he still held. "There it is. It is my horse. And look, yours is just behind it."

The two horses that they had ridden away from the guard – those that had disappeared on the far side of the Forest – were in the trees on the other side of the bridge.

Ezebar whistled. The ears of the black horse twitched and it moved from the mist-shrouded trees into the early light. The other followed it and both looked across the bridge. Ezebar whistled softly again and the horse looked back, mildly interested. Ezebar dropped Shaeli's hand and went over to the bridge, making soft noises to the horse, yet the horse did not seem inclined to come, it just looked back at them for a while and then it dropped its head and began to crop at the grass. The other horse, the one Shaeli had ridden, looked at them a moment longer and then, it too, dropped its head.

"I'm going to get him," said Ezebar, stepping onto the bridge.

"No," cried Shaeli. "M'zena said not to go over the bridge." She hurried after him, but he was already over before she'd gone two paces over the bridge's stone surface.

"I won't go far," he said, stepping down onto the grass on the far side. "I'll just... hey."

Before he had taken another step, three lights darted from the bushes and flew at him. Two of the lights stopped an arm's length from him, but the third flew at Ezebar and slammed into his arm.

"What the...?" he said, followed by a loud, "Ow," as the thing hit.

"Go back," said the fairy, for fairy it was, a male in leaf coloured trousers, with a red, angry light. "If you value your life, you will go back," he said.

He was shouting at Ezebar and Shaeli could hear him easily over the sound of the water.

"Come back," she cried, taking a few steps forward.

The male fairy looked at her. "You will go no further," he said, but more gently, his voice holding a note of respect in it when he spoke to her.

"Come on," Shaeli called to Ezebar. "Come back."

"But, the horses," he said. He was holding his arm where the fairy had hit him.

"The beasts belong to the Forest now," said the angry, hovering fairy. "I shall not ask you again. Go."

He fluttered closer to Ezebar's face and the other two also moved forward. Ezebar turned and came back over the low stone arch. By the time they were back over the bridge, the three fairies had disappeared. The horses stood still munching, unconcerned, on the grass on the other side. Ezebar held his forearm and looked at Shaeli.

"I didn't know they could bite," he said.

"I'm sorry?" said Shaeli, thinking she had misunderstood.

"It bit me," Ezebar said. "Or stung, or something. Hurts like fire, and my fingers are numb."

"Let me see," said Shaeli, taking his hand.

She pulled up the sleeve of his robe and looked at the angry welt that had spread over half his forearm. She held his hand with one of her own, the fingers of her other hand gently tracing around the edge of the raised angry wound. In the centre was a tiny spike, a prickle, and she grasped it between her fingernails and pulled it out. She held it up to the light. It sparkled, and she blew at it and it was gone. She looked back down at his arm and ran her fingers over it again. Ezebar watched her every move.

"I think we better put something cool on it," she said. "Come up to the pool."

Ezebar nodded. "Alright," he said, as she let go of his hand. "I think cold water sounds like a good idea. It already feels better, now you've pulled out the stinger."

"Fancy fairies having a sting," she said, shaking her head. "I never knew."

They reached the pool and Ezebar pulled the robe over his head. Now Shaeli watched his every move.

"Coming in?" he said, looking at her.

"I... alright," she said.

She waited until he had dived beneath the water before she pulled off her own robe and followed him in, wearing her thin shift. The water was the same mild temperature as always, and she dived under and came up in the middle. She swam over to the other side and pulled herself up on a rock, sitting chest-deep in the water. She looked around and could not see Ezebar, and then he came up beside her, the water beading on his shoulders and in his beard.

"That's much better," he said, standing before her and holding his arm out for her to inspect.

She touched the welt, still red but no longer raised and hot, and she smiled at him. "Good," she said. There was silence as they looked at each other across the water. She sought for something to say. "I suppose the others will be up by now," was the first thing that occurred to her.

"Probably," he said, but he said nothing more and his eyes did not leave her face.

He reached out beneath the water and ran his fingers up her arm. Shaeli shivered. His hand reached her shoulder, cupped it and squeezed. His other hand took hers beneath the surface and he pulled her closer.

Shaeli could barely breathe. His hands generated such heat wherever they touched her that all thought of breathing or talking, or thinking of anything but his hands and his eyes burning into hers was gone. There was nothing but this moment.

"Ezebar," called a voice. "Shaeli. Breakfast."

"Llianas," said Shaeli.

He nodded, but said nothing. His eyes left hers and moved to her mouth for a moment. She saw the regret she felt reflected in his dark eyes, and then he sighed and swam back to the bank. He picked up a towel and his robe and walked across the grass to the stone building, disappearing through the door without a backwards glance.

Shaeli watched his broad back go into the house, and then she sunk beneath the water, yet it was a long time before the heat left her face and she followed him across the grass.

\* \* \*

The four of them were inspecting Ezebar's arm when she walked through the door. Kirrit looked up at her as she came in.

"Fancy that, Shaeli, fairies have a sting," she said. "Ezebar says his fingers are still a bit numb."

Shaeli came and looked at his arm. The mark was pale pink now but still obvious.

"That's so much better," she said. "It was really red before, and raised."

"How big was the stinger?" asked Llianas.

"Tiny," said Shaeli, demonstrating with her thumb and forefinger.

"The water helped a lot," said Ezebar, looking at Shaeli.

"You're a lucky lad," said M'zena. "A few more and you'd not be smiling. Or breathing."

"What?" said Kirrit and Shaeli together.

"Aye, they'll kill you, if you get enough of them," said M'zena. "That numbness Ezebar speaks of, if the sting is to the chest, the throat," she shrugged. "There is little anyone can do. I believe their defences are usually used to deter birds of prey and such, but I have heard tales of people being stung for trying to interfere with a cluster."

They were surprised that such tiny gorgeous creatures could be so lethal, for though the elves knew of this ability, the others had never heard of it, and they talked more about it as they ate. Afterwards, when they went outside, the two horses were still cropping grass on the other side of the bridge. Ezebar whistled again and the black horse pricked up his ears and tossed his head, but then it went back to ignoring them and eating the fine grass, and so they walked up to the pool to swim.

Shaeli tried very hard to not meet Ezebar's eyes as she swam, remembering when they had been here alone just a short time ago. It proved an easy task; each time her eyes went unbidden to him, he was looking elsewhere. She swam across the pool in long slow strokes and sat in dappled shadows on the rocks at the edge where she had sat earlier, looking up at the strange green leaves on the trees. A branch wavered and full sunshine hit her eyes and she closed them against the sudden glare. When she opened them again, Tish was hovering in front of her, Rem just above.

"We have news," said Tish. "Shall you hear it here?"

"No," said Shaeli. The others were all looking at her and the two fairies. "Can we go to the grass?"

"As you wish," the hovering fairy said, her wings shimmering in the light.

She shot off across the water, Rem following her, and Shaeli swam after them. She looked at the others in anticipation as she waded from the water, grabbing one of the thick cloths and walking to where the two fairies hovered beneath the trees of red flowers. Ebony scrambled over the grass and looked up at them as the others came over. Ezebar helped M'zena sit down, and the others sat beside her.

Tish flew down and stood in front of them, her lilac light pulsing softly. Rem sat on a branch over their heads. Ebony ran over to where Tish stood and the fairy laughed and reached out a hand to tickle the jevvi's ears.

"We have word of the outside World," said Tish. "Serrat and Meoro Pass have been freed. The Fleet has regained some freedom in the World. Some have gone to Palveron."

"Then we must go," said Shaeli. "We are wasting time here, please, Tish, can we have permission to go on? We have a long way to go, and..."

"The way is not so long," said Tish. "And it is not I who will give the permission that you seek. They have said they will see you in good time, and that you are to look to the dark of the Moon."

"But the moon is still half full," said Shaeli, frowning. "The dark is days away. I cannot wait."

"Yet you must wait," said Rem, speaking in her soft voice for the first time. Though said softly, the words she spoke were also said firmly, and Shaeli looked up at her sullenly, lips pursed. "The city needs time to grow strong, as you grow strong," Rem continued. "Your shenwa shines more clearly each day. All of you grow stronger, and that strength will be needed when the moon grows dark. So they have said."

"But who are they?" said Shaeli. "Why must we wait?"

"We do not question them," said Rem, from her perch among the lacy leaves. Her face suggested Shaeli had said something completely ridiculous. "We merely bring word."

"All will be shown to you, Shaeli," added Tish. "You must be patient."

"But I don't *want* to be patient," Shaeli said, the sullenness on her face also clear in her voice. "I want to *do* something."

"It is not yet time," soothed Tish. "You are sought, still, outside. The coming of the Traders will distract those who serve the false queen."

Rem flew down. "We are to say no more," she said, looking sternly at Tish.

Tish looked at her, nodded, and she took off from the grass and fluttered before their faces. "We will return," she said. "Remember, gather your strength, for it will be needed."

They flew back across the pool and disappeared into the trees, and tears welled in Shaeli's eyes as they went. To be told to wait again when there was so much to be done, so much she didn't know, was too cruel. She stood up.

"Well, I'm not waiting," she said. "I want to go now."

"We cannot, Shaeli," said Williver, standing and taking her hands. "Even if I thought that was the way, we cannot leave this place."

"We'll be alright with M'zena," said Shaeli. "And they said before they wouldn't hurt me."

"Yes, that may be so, if I chose to go, but I'll not take you," said M'zena. The words were not said unkindly, yet they were said firmly. "And even though they would see that no harm came to you, Shaeli, can you be so sure the same would be true for your friends? I do not doubt they will follow you. Even Ezebar would choose to follow your path, this I know, but can you say that no harm will befall them in the Forest, or that the way out would even be shown to you?" M'zena's face was stern now, her dark eyes fixed on Shaeli's sullen face. "Remember the welt that one small fairy gave Ezebar only this morning for crossing the bridge, and then tell me you can lead them safely from this place."

Shaeli looked at her and knew that she was right. And yet she did not want her to be. She let out a groan of frustration, turned her back, and ran across the grass.

"Let her go," she heard M'zena say, as she ran down to the little bridge and across to the other side.

The horses had gone, but the little fairy that had stung Ezebar flew from the trees and hovered before her.

"You may go no further," he said, yet there was no threat in his voice. It was merely a request.

"Fine," she said, as though it wasn't fine at all, and frowning at him. "Can I sit on the bridge?"

"That will be permitted," the fairy said with a bow and a small smile, and then he flew back into the trees.

"Thanks a lot," Shaeli said sarcastically to his retreating wings, and she turned and went back to the little bridge.

She could see the others still talking on the grass beside the pool, and she turned her back on them, sat down, and leant over the other side of the bridge. The water flowed slowly beneath her and was the only sound she could hear, for the Forest was as silent as ever. There was mist hovering above the little creek at the place where it ran into the trees, and she could not see far in. All about the little clearing the trees rose, huge and dark, mist thickening around the bases, leaf mould carpeting the ground, and Shaeli knew that M'zena was right: she would not lead them into the Forest. She would have to wait, just as she had been told. And yet she resented it bitterly. She turned to go back with the frown still on her face.

Kirrit was sitting on the grass at the bottom of the bridge. "I told them you'd be alright after a while," she said. "But the frown isn't terribly becoming, I must say."

Shaeli shook her head, and smiled a pretend smile at her friend. "Better?" she said.

"Much," said Kirrit, taking her hand. "Come on. They've left the nicest lunch."

* * *

And so they waited. The hot days passed, the nights cool inside the little house. They lit the fire only as they needed it, often finding it already kindling for whatever food appeared needing it; fresh fish, smoky bacon, mushrooms pale-topped and dark-skirted. They swam and dozed and talked, and sometimes Ezebar would play his flute after dinner when the silence of the Forest grew too close. The woody tones and the soft melodies pushed the silence far back, and they would sit watching the melodies drifting off into the trees and the winking fireflies that greeted them. The fireflies were a source of delight, ringing the little clearing with their tiny blinking lights, sitting along branches or flitting from tree to tree. Shaeli sometimes sent a few low balls spinning across the grass, or butterflies or dragonflies fluttering above the water, but she dare not send any skylights up above the roof of the Forest. It still troubled her greatly that she had to use the deeper form of her magic against people, to wound and kill, and she knew she would have to again, very soon, so she delighted in the making delicate, pretty shapes; it seemed to her a long time since she had thrown mere skylights.

Sometimes they saw the two fairies, Tish and Rem, but mostly Tish came alone, to play with the little jevvi and talk to them. Ebony loved her, watching wherever the fairy flew, rolling over so Tish could tickle her belly, and Tish was the only one who could beat the jevvi at the game of hide-the-nut. Shaeli often asked questions of Tish during the first few visits about what was happening, and when they would be told something, but it obviously caused the fairy great discomfort to not be able to answer, so Shaeli eventually stopped asking and tried her best not to brood about it, but at times she failed miserably, and she would go off to sit by herself on the little bridge, contemplating the mist and the trees.

She watched the moon shrink with each passing day, a sense of anticipation growing with the waning light. She began to have trouble sleeping, her mind turning over and over even in slumber, and she woke early most mornings, going out into the last whisper of darkness before dawn to walk on the dew-wet grass. Ezebar did not join her again, and though she often wished he would, she was glad of the time to herself.

She did not know that he watched her from the shadows around the house or the pool on each of those mornings. She could not know that he had grown worried at the depth of feeling that she aroused within him.

\* \* \*

When M'zena had said that he would follow wherever Shaeli led, Ezebar had known it was true, and he had been ashamed. M'zena was the reason he was here, and it was she to whom he should give first thought, not Shaeli. That his feelings should make him so ready to abandon the old woman who had been almost his only family all of his life was appalling to him, and so he counteracted those feelings by spending no time alone with Shaeli. Ignoring the presence of his feelings would keep them in their place, he reasoned – and yet he knew where

Shaeli was at any moment of the day, heard her voice before all others, knew the moment she woke, and, though he did not join her, he would rise immediately after she'd left and follow her out the door. Sometimes he would sit just outside in the deepest shadows, other times he would go to the pool and swim, watching her across the water. If she came to the pool to swim too, he would speak as little as possible to her before excusing himself. He told himself it was right to do so.

\* \* \*

If the others noticed the strain between the two, they said nothing, but waited for the days to pass just as Shaeli did.

Shaeli would watch Ezebar's familiar, retreating back and sigh; he was impossible to understand, and she gave up trying to, or trying to meet his eye – this he avoided as studiously as he avoided a conversation with her. She watched his attentiveness to M'zena, the ever-present concern, and she went to talk to Llianas or Kirrit or Williver, trying hard not to care, trying hard to keep her mood from plumbing further depths.

Despite the turmoil in her mind, her body grew strong with the abundance of food and rest. Her wounds healed, the bruises were long-faded, and though her hand nervously fingered the stones in her amulet dozens of times a day, she regained her former health. Her belt, woven by her aunt so long ago, had been lost when the amulet had been cut from it, and she had threaded the pouch through a thick cord she'd found, wearing it around her waist every day and sleeping with it beneath her pillow at night. Her hand was upon it when she woke early one morning to near-darkness.

She blinked and the outline of the window came into focus. The sky above the trees was the deepest of blues, the stars beginning to pale. She yawned and watched the sky grow bluer, the stars struggle to keep their place, and before the last of them had gone, she had pushed back the sheets and gone into the morning.

\* \* \*

Ezebar watched her from the shadows of his bed. He tried to stay where he was, but his feet were on the floor and moving him across the room despite the fact that he had told them to stay right where they were. His rebellious feet continued to ignore him, and took him out the door in Shaeli's wake.

Outside, he took better control of his feet and steered them towards the pool, the promising warmth of the coming day already trembling in the air.

Shaeli usually went to stand on the bridge where the first rays came through the trees, and though he could not see her yet, he would have a better view from the pool. It stayed in shadow longer, and he could watch the morning, and Shaeli, from there. As he crossed the grass he still could not see her, and he turned to the pool, pulling the robe over his head as he reached it. Shaeli stepped from the thick shadow beside one of the umbrella-shaped trees into his path. She looked up at him, her face pale in the shadows, her eyes dark and unreadable.

"Good morning," she said. "Going in?"

He hesitated. He could hardly say no with his robe half-off. He pulled it all the way.

"Yes," he said.

He went past her and put his robe down. He dived into the water, and when he came up, she was standing up to her waist in the water behind him, the thin shift dampening as she stood looking at him. Her hair fluttered as she dove under and was a dark river when she came up nearby. He turned and swam into deeper water. Shaeli swam lazily after him, and when she drew closer, she stopped, floating before him. She fixed him with those eyes and now he could see how blue they were. The light through the trees and the water reflected off them, making her gaze intense.

"Have I done something?" she said. Her voice was flat, her eyebrows pulled together like tiny arched curtains.

He did not pretend that he didn't know what she was talking about. "No," he answered, flicking his eyes away from her unwavering gaze. "You haven't done anything. You're..." He stopped. "It's just... I'm here for M'zena, and..."

"And not me," she said. She looked back at him, and then she nodded. "I understand. She's your priority, as she should be." Her lips pursed, but before she turned away he saw the tears start in her eyes. "It doesn't matter," she said, before she swam away. She reached shallower water, and began wading back towards the bank, the shift clinging to her frame. "I've learnt that I only have myself to rely on," she said, her voice beginning to wobble. "Other people help, if they're there. But you think people are there and then they're gone, and you have to do it all by yourself." The voice cracked. "As usual."

She was wading from the water now, and he followed her as swiftly as he could. By the time he reached her, she was wrapped in a cloth, swiping angrily at the tears on her cheeks.

He didn't say anything. He just wrapped her in his arms and held her. She let him keep his arms there for only a moment before she broke free.

"I'm alright," she said, gathering her robe. "You don't have to worry about me."

She did not look at him as she went to the house. For once it was his turn to watch a retreating back.

\* \* \*

Tish came that afternoon.

She did not have to say anything. The way she sped into the clearing, her wings a blur, told them everything long before she was close enough for them to see the look on her face.

"It's time," she said.

They were gathering their things in moments. Ezebar and Williver were picking up their well-worn clothes when Tish followed them inside.

"You are to leave on the robes which have been provided," she said. "Bring all your things with you, for some may not return to this place."

"If we leave the Forest, then I think our clothes are much more practical," said Williver. "Comfortable as the robes are."

"You are to leave them on," Tish repeated. "Hurry now, time grows short."

"Ha," laughed Kirrit. "We've been lazing around for days and now time grows short. Typical. Come on, then," she said, taking up her bag and her crossbow. "I'm ready. Goodbye house. Thanks for having us."

She laughed again, and though they all laughed with her, the thanks each gave to the house before they left was heartfelt. They did not know that Kirrit would soon be returning to the little house in the clearing, yet none of them would be with her.

\* \* \*

# CHAPTER TWENTY EIGHT

When they walked from the house, they were all smiling. Tish led them down beside the little creek to the bridge and across to the other side. She hovered beneath the trees at the edge of the grass waiting for them.

Shaeli took one last look at the little building across the sunny clearing and the pool where they'd spent so many hours, and then she turned her back and followed Tish into the trees.

The shadows enveloped them immediately, the mist grew thick about their knees, swirling behind them as they walked through it. The smell of leaf mould drifted up with their footfalls. All sight of the clearing was instantly gone, as if it had been nothing more than a dream.

As before, the Forest appeared to have no pathway between the trees. They grew thickly together, many branches hanging low across the path, but Tish led them between trunks and beneath branches that seemed to move away to create a path only within the ground on which they were walking. Around them was only trees and mist and shadows, but once or twice, Shaeli thought she heard the gurgle of the little creek.

They knew not how long they walked in the cool mists between the trees, it seemed to not be long, but then it was no short time either, and when the trees opened before them all but M'zena blinked with surprise at the sudden light and the sight before them.

There had been no sound in the trees, but now it was if someone had opened a doorway, for the air was suddenly filled with sound. Children called, cows mooed, birds sang, women laughed, and men shouted.

Before them was a clearing, not a tiny quiet clearing like the one they had left, but a huge wide, bright space filled with odd-shaped buildings and odder-shaped people.

A grass-covered street opened out beneath their feet, and it led into a village with dozens of people on the street and in the gardens of the odd-shaped buildings. There were women leaning from windows, old folk at fences, and children crying out in doorways. All eyes were turned to them standing on the edge of the Forest.

Shaeli looked behind her, into the misty confines between the trees where nothing moved, and then back out into the village in the enormous clearing. Gardens and fields spread out around the odd buildings, the trees ringing the whole place, and she shook her head, sure that now she actually was dreaming. It seemed Kirrit was thinking the same thing.

"It's not real, is it?" she said. "Can you see that?"

"We can, lass," said M'zena. "And it is real, though I confess that the first time I saw it, I also thought I was within a dream."

Tish giggled and flew in a little loop in front of them. "Welcome to Forest Village," she said. "They have been expecting you, and are so excited for you to see them."

"For us to see them?" said Shaeli.

"Oh, yes," said Tish. "They have all seen you. They have watched you swim, listened to the music and watched the little skylights at night."

"They have?" said Llianas, her brown eyes fixed on the strange village.

"Oh, yes," Tish said again. "This way."

She flitted forward over the street, and they followed her. The voices of the village had grown quieter, but now there were even more people staring at them in anticipation as they reached the first buildings.

The buildings looked like they'd been stacked together by a young giant playing with blocks. There were turrets jutting at strange angles, chimneys coming from walls instead of roofs, rounded walls and triangular windows. There were tiny houses – one merely a turret on its own – others were enormous rambling structures with balconies jutting from them and a dozen chimneys on their roofs – or walls. Shaeli watched the smoke rise from the chimneys, and was unsurprised to see each grey tail of smoke disappeared as it reached the height of the trees surrounding the village.

    The people were even stranger than the buildings. They stood smiling and watching the strangers follow Tish down the street, some with eyes too big or arms too long, others with hair to their knees, some bereft of hair entirely, still others with strangely-hued skin. There were long fingers, huge feet, tiny people and tall, there were ears sprouting hair, chins down to chests, and people as thin as vines. Many of them wore strange costumes sporting leaves and feathers, strands of glittering beads, flowers or tufted reeds. All their feet were bare, in dozens of different shapes, and their hair – those that had it – was often braided with bright cloth or feathers or tiny blossoms. Several groups were dressed entirely in vines and flowers, the leaves and buds seeming to grow from their pale green skin. There was one group gathered in a garden with hair in different shades of blue, their skins, as pale as mushrooms, also tinged blue, their clothes like river grass. There were people scattered among the odd crowd who were as normal as those one would meet on the streets of any other village, yet they were easily outnumbered by the others, and all had one thing in common: every one of these people were staring at them, and all were smiling broadly and waving at them as they passed, talking and giggling to each other. Small children began to follow them, and when the strangers had gone a polite distance, everyone else followed them, too.

    M'zena strode down the street, a grassy, flower-lined street, calling greetings and waving grandly, and the three girls began to wave, too. Williver and Ezebar came behind them, nodding politely at the arms raised and returning the broad smiles to their owners. Tish preceded them all, her arm raised to the people gathered along the sides of the street, a smile on her tiny face.

At the end of the street there was a cross road and they followed Tish to the left and along another street. Here too, the street was grassed and lined with people and buildings, all just as odd as those they had already passed, but here, the people were joined by scores of fairies. They flew across gardens and between buildings, tiny lights blinking in every colour, to hover above the people's heads or stand on fence posts or in branches. They saw Rem as they passed one garden, with the male fairy who had stung Ezebar, both of them waving gaily. When the six people and the jevvi had passed, all the people joined the growing crowd who came down the street behind them, their odd-shaped faces wearing wide smiles of greeting.

There were more fabulous faces to be seen in the next street; pointed ears that were far superior to any elf's; noses that were almost non-existent or enormously bulbous; fingers more interesting than a drell's raised in greeting. Hair in every shade covered many heads, skins of yellow, rose-pink and soft green, a few more of the dappled blue people clustered before a bright purple house, a pale blue baby gurgling at them from its mother's arms.

Shaeli tried hard not to stare, and Ezebar and Williver tried with her, but Kirrit and Llianas made no effort whatsoever. They stared without reservation – and nodded and smiled and waved – and then they stared some more. They nudged each other and pointed with their heads as the next amazing person came into sight, smiling the whole time. They all felt they were in a parade as they walked down the street behind Tish, and when they reached the end of the street, the sight there did nothing to dispel the feeling.

This street opened out into what appeared to be the town square, except that it was a circle. The street went on around the edge of the circle, and the buildings surrounded the street. In the middle was a grassed area, the ground rising slightly in the centre.

Tish led them over the grass to where the ground began to rise and she stopped, looking up the short slope. The townspeople gathered behind them and grew silent.

Atop the mound was a building. It was an octagonal structure, open on all sides, the roof pointed. Beams stood at seven of the eight points of the octagon, and flowered vines grew up the posts and curled along beneath the eaves. Standing in the opening at the eighth point, looking down upon them, were two very different people.

The man was small, as small as a drell, but much thinner. His clothes looked like they were made of patterned bark, and his hair was woven with leaves and flowers. His hands and feet were very big, and so was the smile he wore.

The woman next to him was enormous, even more so for standing beside the thin little man. Her bare arms were huge and resting across the most pendulous breasts that any of them had ever seen. She was the colour of new leaves, her skin palest green tinged with pink, her eyes darkly brown, the colour of the bark on the trees of the forest. She wore a dress of leaves and a cape of flowers, and she opened her huge arms in greeting.

"Welcome to Forest Village," she boomed, her voice as huge as her bosom and as rich as honeycomb. She looked at M'zena. "It is long since we have seen you, old woman, for so you have become. If it were not for your shenwa, we would not have known you."

M'zena bowed her head and then looked up at the giant of a woman standing above. "I am most pleased to have this unexpected chance to see you again, Myrrabilla," she said. "And you, Filo," she said, bowing her head to the little man.

"We are pleased you have returned, Mizzy," Filo said. "We thought you had long returned to the earth."

The others looked at each other and then at M'zena. *Mizzy?*

M'zena ignored their looks. "No, Filo," she smiled. "I am fortunate to still be walking above the earth." She glanced at the others clustered silently beside her. "My young friends are impatient," she said. "But if there is time, I should like to ask if we may sit with you both awhile."

"We have until the darkest hours of the night," said Filo. "We think that will be the best time."

"The best time for what?" asked M'zena.

Myrrabilla spoke. "Why, for saving Shaeli's sisters from death, of course," she said, the broad smile still on her face. "But come, we have made you one last feast."

\* \* \*

# CHAPTER TWENTY NINE

Far to the south, Mareesha stared at the food on her plate. It was no feast, yet better than she had had in days. The drops the Traders had made during the last nights to Landings across the city were filtering through, and though none were yet full, neither were they hungry any longer. Yet Mareesha could not eat. There were guard surrounding the Landing in the square, and she knew that two more days would see them meet disaster. The black ship had returned, and she could only hope she could see the twins one last time before it was finished.

When the black ship had gone and where it had been were mysteries, but they all knew when it had returned.

They had begun the food drops with great hesitation, yet they had grown bolder with each landing the Traders made. When it was apparent that they could land, unload and lift again without the guard being able to stop them, and no black ship had appeared, they began making more drops. Soon they were coming in several times a night, even landing at dusk and dawn when they could be easily seen flying across the bay.

The rebels and those from the other Lands in Palveron aided them each time, ringing the chosen Landings, distracting the guard as the Trader landed. Tarkoda had managed to arrange to see his parents at one such drop, having time only for several hard hugs, a swift conversation, and a few tears from his mother before lifting again.

Those fighting in Palveron had also worried the Qotarr with increasing accuracy. Flin and Qiren had proved invaluable, if not in beating them, then certainly making them less of a threat, for they were able to reach the soldiers on the beast's backs with bolts and sever the leads the Wokkii used to direct them. This tactic was not without its own kind of danger, for the Qotarr, released from its reins, would go off on tasks of its own like an unruly colt, rampaging through the city without any reluctance to eat anything that crossed its path or crash through whatever stood in its way. The Wokkii and the queen's guard had managed to recapture all but one of the beasts released by the bolts, and were now using chains to guide them, something which made severing the lines more difficult, but not impossible. The one Qotarr still free had shaken off the Wokkii on its back and had stubbornly refused to be recaptured, and now it was as much a danger to the guard as it was to anyone else. Three days before, the free Qotarr had crashed its way into the square.

It was still early, the first heat of the day slow to wake, the sky still stretching its arms from the night's rest, the sun yawning above the horizon.

Andos was just coming down from the rigging when it arrived, watched by his anxious mother and his not-so-anxious aunt. Renn stood on Golden Eagle's deck smiling as Andos made his way back down. They had scattered when the Qotarr arrived, leaping for cover when the beast groaned its way into the square.

All the others had been gone before dawn defending a drop by Red Arrow at a Landing across the city, and only Crissita, Brudloc and Almarnoch were on the ship, they below decks. S'resh was also on board.

S'resh had been collecting the eggs from the remaining hens in the coop on Purple Leaf's deck. The chickens had been the source of much nourishment for them, supplying them with eggs daily; it was the only reason for their existence; any hen that had stopped laying had long since been eaten.

S'resh was coming from the coop when the Qotarr entered the square and she screamed at the sight of it. It had looked straight at her and sniffed the air. Andos bolted across the deck as his mother and Mareesha bolted for the stairs. He grabbed

S'resh and pulled her back into the coop, slamming the little door behind them.

The chickens began to fuss as they smelled the Qotarr, clucking in fright as the lizard crossed to the Landing and began to sniff its way around the Trader. It touched its nose to the balloon and snorted, drawing its head back. Perhaps something of the Protection Spell the Warlocks had placed upon the balloon was unpleasant to the beast, for it shook its head and sniffed lower, at the doors of the nest. The Zoi had flown from the city at dawn to forage, and so there was nothing but smell for the Qotarr there, and it raised its head back to the deck.

Mareesha and Eenis watched from the shadows beneath the upper deck as it sniffed at the coop. They could see Andos and S'resh cowering inside, and they knew Andos didn't have a weapon, even if one would have been of use. Mareesha and Eenis could do nothing but watch while the Qotarr sniffed at the chicken coop.

Suddenly the beast opened its mouth and ripped off the roof of the coop. The wood splintered and crashed onto the deck and the square below. S'resh screamed and the chickens fluttered up, panicked fully now and squawking. The Qotarr snapped at them. One it caught straight away, swallowing it with an audible gulp. The others ran screeching and flapping across the deck. The beast reached out for one, the top of its head coming dangerously close to the underside of the balloon.

This time it was Eenis who screamed when the Qotarr crushed the coop as it reached across the deck, pulverising the wood, yet it missed the hen. It snorted and pulled its head back, pushing at the remains of the coop, leaving it in a crumpled heap as it pulled its head out. A few ropes snapped as the great head was wrenched backwards and the lizard skirted round the Trader, snorting, chasing the hen which flapped up onto the top deck. As the Qotarr reached out to snap at it, there came the call of a Zoi in the distance.

The Qotarr looked up, and Mareesha and Eenis did too. They could see nothing, yet it seemed the Qotarr could. It reared its head and snorted again, and it moved away from the Trader.

Mareesha and Eenis came from under the top deck to see the Zoi swooping on the Qotarr, flying at its head and then shearing off at the last moment, taunting it – and leading it away from the Landing.

They ran to the crumpled coop, pulling at the splintered boards. Renn ran over from Golden Eagle to help them. Almarnoch and Crissita came from below, looked at the Qotarr, the swooping birds, Mareesha, Renn and Eenis pulling at the remains of the coop and they rushed to help.

They found them lying under the chicken's perches, huddled together, shaken, scratched and bruised, but basically unharmed. S'resh was crying as they led her back to the safety of the stairwell, watching the birds taunt the beast. Crissita hugged her and patted her back.

"Andos saved me," S'resh sobbed. "That thing..."

"There, there," Crissita soothed. "It's only fair. Payment for that frypan episode. Now you're even."

S'resh cried harder at that, and pushed her face into Crissita's shoulder.

* * *

The birds were still circling the Qotarr's head when the others returned through the streets.

It was Jarris who saw them first. They were heading back to the Landing after the dawn delivery when he saw a Zoi fly up and then dart back down between the buildings.

"What's the matter with the Zoi?" he said.

There was a large group of them returning to the Landing, but only those who had seen the Zoi fishing for the giant stinging eels in the black lake beneath Mount Zerrinius recognised the bird's behaviour.

"Hurry," yelled Flin, and he began to run.

The Zoi had the Qotarr backed into a street when they reached the square, and Flin fired at it, blasting intense beams at its face. His fire barely dented its tough skin, but it threw its head, moving its eyes away from Flin's beams. It turned, knocking a chunk out of a nearby building, and went down a street and away. They could hear it snorting and crashing through the streets as they went up the stairs of the Landing.

S'resh had finished crying when they came across the deck and Mareesha was inspecting her and Andos' wounds. Both had ripped clothing, long scratches and a plethora of bruises, but there was nothing more. Mareesha took them down and bathed the scratches, and then Crissita took S'resh off to change.

Eenis was fussing over Andos, but Andos was busy watching Crissita and S'resh disappear down the hall.

* * *

That night, there were more drops of food to Landings across the city. Silver Hawk had the last run just before dawn. Those that had defended it brought news to the Landing in the square soon after sunrise.

Iyri's husband Meart was with them, and said that those on Silver Hawk had seen large contingents of the guard coming down the coast from the Lakes' country, and they were massing in the land between Palveron and the Royal Parklands. The rebel leader feared an attack, and had called for help from the north, but it would be days before they could come and it would also leave those borders unprotected.

Meart had other news, too. Zander had been injured in the fighting at a Landing during the night. Asheen was worried that he would not live, and there were certain herbs she had run out of. When Mareesha went to make up a parcel for him to take back to her sister, Meart said something else worrying. He said they had captured a few of the guard that morning, and they had been given a chance to leave the queen's service. Meart said that they had been spat upon for their trouble, the oaths of loyalty to Queen Virrisian were strong, but then one said something else: that if any of the guard deserted, there was a group especially formed to hunt them down and kill them. And not only them, the deserter's two closest family members would also pay with their lives for a soldier's disloyalty to the queen. They were horrified and talked long on the matter after Meart had gone and the hot afternoon passed.

The black ship returned with the night. It came stealthily, unseen.

The city had heard of the massing of the guard around its outskirts, but they still came to defend the Landings for the Traders. Silver Hawk was the first to come.

Dusk was falling as it flew across the bay, heading for a Landing near the docks. In the streets the guard milled, waiting to see where the Trader would land, and the people also waited, huddled in the buildings near the chosen Landing, brands ready to light the way. They came out to defend the Landing as the Trader flew down across the water, eyes expectantly turned to the sky. They had a clear view of it as it flew above the dark bay, but none saw the black ship come across the water until it loomed up beside the Trader.

It must have come low across the bay, its black shape a thicker wave flying above the night-thick water, for those on the shore saw it only as it reared up before the Trader and the red light blinked on.

Silver Hawk turned to avoid it, circling around. In the last grey light of the day, those watching on the ground saw the people on the deck scatter as the red eye of the black ship narrowed. A beam flew from it and struck the Trader mid-centre. The side of the ship flared and flames began to lick across the wood. The black ship's eye narrowed again.

Three people were cutting at ropes on the fore-deck as the second blast hit the Trader in the rear. They were thrown to the ground, but before the flames had begun to grow along the back of the ship, they were up again and hacking at the ropes.

Other figures began to drop over the sides of the Trader into the bay.

The last light had drained from the sky, but now the scene was lit by the light of the flames from the burning Trader, and those on the shore realised what the three figures still on the deck were doing, for suddenly the Zoi detached from the ship. They flew away from it, wheeled around in uncertainty and then they headed back across the bay, leaving the burning Trader hanging in the sky, at the mercy of the wind and the black ship.

The breeze was from the north, and it caught the balloon and began pushing the Trader slowly towards the docks. A trail of smoke began to drift from it. The cries of the Zoi echoed across the water as the black ship circled the burning Trader.

A gust blew the ship closer to the docks as the red eye on the black ship narrowed for the third time, and when this beam struck the far side of the Trader, there was a loud thud, and wood splintered out and showered down onto the water. One huge chunk, already on fire, fell onto a small boat moored below. The burning hunk of wood crashed onto the smaller boat, breaking it in two, and a great splash swallowed the pieces whole.

The back half of the Trader was covered with fire now, the flames swirling up the ropes to the balloon. As the fire reached it and the material began to burn, the Trader sagged in the sky. The three figures left on the Trader were huddled together on the fore-deck as the flames devoured the ship, slow licks of fire threading their way along the balloon.

The black ship circled the Trader once more and then it flew off into the night, heading towards Great Court.

The Trader drifted closer to the docks, falling slowly towards the water. It hit not far from shore with a terrific splash, the flames hissing as they met cold blackness. The balloon and the deck were well alight now, and the three figures on the fore-deck leapt into the water, two dragging the third over the side. Their heads could be seen outlined against the flames for a while, and then they were gone.

Some raced to the docks to see if they had made it to shore, others followed to watch the burning Trader sink beneath the water. It did not take long. What the fire did not consume, the water quickly did. There was little left of the balloon when the ship went under, the last of it pulled beneath the waves with a long gurgling sound. There was white foam on the waves for a moment, and then nothing. Silver Hawk was gone.

The soldiers came then, and those on the docks had to fight their way back into the darkness of the streets. The guard did not see them pull people from the water and spirit them away into the night before they went.

They brought three to the Landing and up the stairs with the guard two streets behind them. Two figures staggered along by themselves, the third was carried along behind. Up the stairs they went, and over the deck of Golden Eagle. There was no sign of them when the guard entered the square.

Beneath the decks, those who had brought the three waited until the guard went on, and then they took their leave and went back out into the night. Rafi followed them, going over to Purple Leaf to fetch Mareesha, and Jarris went back to Golden Eagle with her.

They had known of the drop by Silver Hawk, and had themselves been preparing to leave for one by Tarkoda's Trader to the south when the three were brought aboard.

Kaplan and his wife, Narla, of Silver Hawk were unharmed, but both were so shaken, so distraught at the loss of their ship, that after they'd told Taffka what had happened, Mareesha gave them a strong draught and ordered them put to bed. They protested, but soon Mareesha's draught began to work and their words of protest slowed, and Jarris and Taffka helped them to a bed.

The third of the figures who had been aboard was Rennan, Renn's nephew and Shaeli's Cave Year boyfriend. His leg was broken, and though he'd managed to make it to shore with Kaplan and Narla's help, he had lapsed into unconsciousness soon after and was carried to the Trader. Mareesha set the leg and stitched a long wound on his arm. He woke as she was wrapping the arm and he cried out in pain.

"There, lad," said Taffka, leaning over and taking his uninjured hand. "I know just how you feel."

Rennan looked back at him, his face puckered, but he clamped his teeth on his pain while Mareesha prepared him a draught. It was much stronger than the one she had given Narla and Kaplan, and he slept again within moments, his hand still clasping Taffka's, Renn hovering over him. She moved a bed-roll into the room and they eased him onto it, and he slept through the night.

The next morning, word came from Great Court. It was brought by an enormous contingent of the guard. They filled the square below the Landing and a lone soldier came up the steps.

Taffka met him at the top. He was handed a rolled parchment, and he brought it back to where the others stood on the Landing between the ships. The drell remained out of sight, but the rest were there to hear what the parchment held. The guard remained in the square and the soldier at the end of the Landing did not move.

When Taffka unrolled the parchment, two locks of hair fell out.

Mareesha snatched them up with a cry. It was the twins' hair, she was sure, and these were no small swatches either, but long, thick chunks of hair. They all listened as Taffka read aloud.

The Traders were to be given one last chance, by the queen's grace, the parchment began, for it seemed the word of the Head Trader held little honour. Taffka cringed as he read this, but he went staunchly on. Queen Virrisian knew the High Warlock Almarnoch had brought something of great value to the city. She was willing to exchange it for the two girls and their promise to fly immediately from the city and not return. No further aid was to be given to the rebels, else all other Traders would befall the same fate as the one destroyed over the harbour. She awaited their immediate reply, stating a time for the exchange.

Now, as Mareesha sat looking down at her plate, she remembered how Taffka and Almarnoch had looked at each other first, and then at her, before the High Warlock had spoken. Then he had looked back at Taffka, and nodded.

"Tell her we agree to her terms," he said.

Mareesha had hugged him, weeping. As he'd patted her back, she heard him murmur, "May the gods be with us now."

As she sat now, poking the unwanted food with her fork, she added more prayers to his.

They were to go to the gates at dawn, two days hence, and there, she would either see her children or they would meet disaster. All she could do now was wait. Wait, and ask the gods to watch over them all.

\* \* \*

# CHAPTER THIRTY

In the Forest far to the north, Shaeli was also poking at her food. Yet it was in impatience.

They had been taken to a nearby house, where fresh new clothes, fitting each of them perfectly, lay waiting for them. By the time they had changed, the scene outside had altered completely.

Food had appeared with amazing speed. Bright platters filled with meats and bread, fruits and cheeses, jugs filled with pale wines and cool juices were set on colourful rugs, and lights had been set around the octagonal building on the small grassy hill in the middle of Forest Village. The golden light of afternoon thickened with the setting of the sun, and now, in the dusk, the lights the people had set and the lights of the fairies began to glimmer. A sliver of smiling moon hung over the western horizon, the outline of its fullness a mere shadow.

A patterned cloth had been set for them beneath the pointed roof of the octagonal building, and they sat on thick grass ringing an enormous variety of food. The scent of the hanging flowers wafted gently down around their heads, and the people of Forest Village picnicked on the hill around them. The feast was as sumptuous as promised, but Shaeli's appetite had been erased when Myrrabilla had mentioned the death of her sisters. Her questions had been waved away by Myrrabilla's fat hand and wide smile until after the feast.

M'zena sat talking with Myrrabilla. Williver was in earnest conversation with Filo; Kirrit and Llianas sat eating and talking with two girls, looking down on the crowd of amazing people surrounding them. One of the girls was pale as a summer sky, her hair so darkly blue it was almost purple. The other had soft pink skin, her brown hair covered in tiny red flowers which curled up their petals as the sun set. Ezebar sat beside M'zena, eating and looking about, and Shaeli caught his eye. The brown eyes were dark in the lamplight, and she looked away. She would expect no help from him, even if she wanted it. He had made it clear she was no priority of his. And so she waited while the smiling moon set, while they talked and ate and the crowd around them laughed and frolicked as if they were at a fair, and in the end she could not stand it. She stood up, her hand on her amulet.

"Can we go now?" she said loudly.

Conversation stopped. Eyes turned to her. Myrrabilla spoke.

"It is not yet time to go anywhere, child," she said, calmly. "We are far away, and can do nothing until the Forest deems it. Be patient."

"Can you not ask the Forest to let us go on?" said Shaeli.

"There is no need," said Filo, frowning slightly. "It knows all. It feels everything."

"Come and sit beside me," said Myrrabilla, patting a patch of grass next to her. "We will talk of when Mizzy was young and visited often."

Conversation quietly resumed, eyes were averted. Shaeli begrudgingly went around and sat beside Myrrabilla. Tish came and sat on the edge a plate nearby. Ebony came and sat beside Tish.

Myrrabilla talked of the times when the young M'zena would come walking into the Forest, how she and the king would stay in the little cottage.

"And your name was Mizzy?" asked Llianas.

"It was," smiled M'zena. "I used to stay at the Tired Doormouse, and sometimes the people of Zuen saw me enter and emerge from the forest. It was they who first began to call me M'zena, after the Forest itself. I liked it," she said. "And decided to adopt it. There are few outside this place who would remember Mizzy."

"And Forest Village has always been here?" asked Ezebar.

"Yes, Zeb," said M'zena. "And it has always looked just the same."

"It is a very... unusual place," said Williver. "I have never seen anywhere like it."

"There is no other place like it," Myrrabilla smiled proudly. "The people here are of this World, and yet we are not part of it. We bring life to the World, but we are separate from it. We are of the plants, the waters, the animals. We are of the Forest. We are of Merrom."

"But some are... like us," said Kirrit. "From outside."

"Many are those who have come to this place, and for many reasons," said Filo. "Some the Forest deems unworthy, and they are not seen outside again. Others may be permitted to return to their lives; those who love deeply or who have great deeds still to complete, and sometimes, those who wish it, who have a clear shenwa, may be permitted to join us in serving the goddess Merrom and the Forest. With time, we all take on aspects of the things we serve."

Shaeli sat stiffly as they talked. Normally she would have been enthralled, yet she sat with her lips pressed firmly together, her fingers touching her stones through the soft leather of her amulet. She just wished they could just get on with it, she wished...

Suddenly a light flared through the trees, a thickly golden bloom which shone brightly. The crowd instantly hushed, looking towards the light. Myrrabilla looked down at Shaeli.

"The Forest deems it time," she said, the smile gone from her face for the first time. She rose to her feet, and addressed the crowd. "Come," she said. "I know you are all eager to lend your strength. Now is the time."

They rose instantly, looking up as Shaeli and the others gathered their things. Filo stopped them.

"Take only your weapons," he said. "Leave the rest."

"But we may need them," said Williver.

"You will have all you need," said Filo.

They left their baggage beneath the octagonal building on the hill, M'zena's patchwork quilt laying on top of their meagre belongings. The crowd parted as they followed Myrrabilla and Filo down the slope and through the streets. The people followed them, and, like Myrrabilla, they were no longer smiling either.

They went through the town, the crooked buildings dark around them, and when they left the town there was only the light of the fairies and the distant stars to light the night. When they entered the Forest, there was only the light of the fairies.

The light that had flared through the trees was gone, and they followed Myrrabilla and Filo through the dark silent Forest, followed by the colourful silent crowd.

Rem and Tish flew just ahead of Myrrabilla and Filo, the other fairies flying at intervals over the heads of those that followed. The Forest was intensely black around them, the great trees looming like brooding giants as they walked between them. Kirrit and Llianas moved closer together.

After a while they stopped. Myrrabilla and Filo turned to face them, and the silent crowd kept moving on around them, into the trees. A few stopped behind Shaeli and the others, some stopped in the trees a short distance away, one or two seemed to melt into the trunks of the trees. Only those with pale wispy clothes could be seen, most drifted away into the darkness and the mist. Only the fairies could be seen clearly, like giant fireflies.

Myrrabilla looked down at M'zena. "You remember?" she said.

M'zena smiled and nodded. "It is not something one could forget in a thousand years," she said.

"Very well," said Myrrabilla. "Rem, Tish, Zod," she called. "You will accompany them."

Rem, Tish and the male fairy who had stung Ezebar came forward to hover around M'zena's head. Myrrabilla took Filo's hand, and they moved a short distance away. M'zena walked over to Shaeli, pulling a wrapped bundle from her sleeve.

"'Tis time you used the gift granted you," she said, unravelling the cloth.

Inside were the dragon-scale bangles, laying together and shimmering in the light of the hovering fairies, and Shaeli found her hand reaching out for them before her mind had registered the fact. She had never meant to wear them, but she was pushing them up her arms in a moment. She looked up at Williver, unsure. He nodded, eyes alight with his smile.

"It is as M'zena says," he said. "They were always meant for you."

Shaeli looked down at her arms. The bangles glimmered above her elbows, the gem-encrusted scales throwing tiny flashes into the trees, a perfect fit. They were cool, at first, but then they grew warm with the heat of her body and the flame of her magic. She looked at M'zena and nodded, but she could say nothing.

M'zena nodded back at her, and then looked at Myrrabilla and Filo and bowed her head to them. She turned and went a few steps forward. She looked back over her shoulder at Shaeli, Ezebar, Kirrit and the two elves.

"Ready yourselves," she said. "For anything," and she turned her back on them and raised her arms.

She began to sing softly, her voice tremulous at first, but growing stronger as she went on. The song was wordless, but beautifully melodic, and around them the people of the Forest began to echo M'zena, to harmonise with her.

The trees trembled as if swept by a wind. The leaves rustled. Before the tiny old woman's arms, a light began to grow. It seeped through the trees, softly at first, as if a door was being slowly opened, and then the light grew brighter.

Between the trees in front of M'zena, a small clearing began to emerge, a tiny, perfectly round glade.

\* \* \*

In a tall mountain to the west, within the abandoned nests in the dragon's lair, the gems that had been lit with a tiny spark before the Wintering began to blink. Each tiny light started to beat in a soft pulsing rhythm, slowly at first, very slowly, but as time passed, the pulsing of the lights grew more regular. And stronger.

\* \* \*

The little glade emerged gently, the light seeming to come from its centre, to emanate from the very grass. Brighter the light grew, rich golden light, like the thick light of afternoon in the Forest; gold with shimmers of silver at its edges. The light shone more brightly still, illuminating the trees surrounding it.

Across the glade, the faces of the people of the Forest began to appear as the light grew stronger. Around the edges of the clearing the people of Forest Village stood singing, ringing the tiny glade, their faces bathed in the soft silver-gold light. Behind them, here and there, other shapes fluttered, flickering glimpses between the trees and the people of the Forest. They were the shapes of drell, of elves, of Zoi; of the peoples and the animals of the World. The creatures of Merrom.

M'zena's voice grew louder. The voices of Myrrabilla and Filo rose in harmony.

The glade grew brighter until each blade of grass could be clearly seen and the trunks of the trees were dappled in rich hues. Faces seemed to emerge from the shadows on the trunks, calling to the singing people of the Forest with silent voices. Nothing moved in the glade, but it shone with vibrant colour; the colours of the Forest and the masses of flowers that grew at the feet of the trees seemed impossibly bright.

Shaeli looked at the shining glade. It was very like the one she had once sat in with Williver, in a dream. She glanced at him and knew he was remembering the same thing, and she looked back at the people around her, at those on the far side of the little glade, their mouths open in song.

Something shimmered, a figure stood outlined against the trees on the far side, and was gone.

M'zena stopped singing, but the people of the Forest sang on, their harmonies rich and strong. The old woman dropped her arms, and looked over her shoulder. Her dark face was in shadow, yet her eyes gleamed as if they had caught some of the golden light from the glade.

"It is time," she said.

She stepped forward, walked a few steps into the shining glade, and disappeared.

The three fairies flew after her, and they also vanished.

Shaeli jumped. Kirrit let out a cry, and was echoed by Llianas. Ezebar uttered an oath and strode forward. He, too, disappeared when he walked into the light of the shining glade.

Williver was with him before Shaeli had finished jumping. He had gone into the light of the glade and disappeared as Shaeli was pulling a stone from her amulet and following him.

Kirrit looked at Llianas, each notched an arrow into their weapon, and they followed Shaeli into the glade.

\* \* \*

Shaeli went between the trees, running out onto the bright grass and into the golden light. The trees before her shimmered again, shadowed figures emerged, and when she took another step, her foot hit hard stone and the golden light dulled instantly to the yellow of lamps. The trees disappeared, the sound of singing faded to the whisper of an echo. The clash of swords replaced it.

Shaeli blinked. There was chaos before her.

She was in a room, a huge round room, with large windows looking out at the dark night. M'zena was to her left, and across the room, Ezebar and Williver were fighting four of the queen's soldiers, the three fairies swooping the heads of the guard. Another soldier was standing at the doorway yelling, and one lay moaning on the floor.

To her right was a huge bed and standing beside it, eyes wide, were her sisters. An old woman with a long silver braid stood in a nightdress before them, a knife in her hand.

The girls cried out, and she rushed over to them. Both had short hair, cropped close to their heads, their faces pale, and they were both babbling, saying her name over and over.

Just as she reached them, a dozen more soldiers came through the doorway. Ezebar had felled one of the soldiers already in the room, and another stood against the wall gasping, his arm held before him, stung by the fairies, but Williver and Ezebar backed off when the others burst in, badly outnumbered.

An arrow flew across the room, another followed, both hitting two of the soldiers coming through the door. Shaeli looked behind her, and saw Kirrit and Llianas standing before a huge mural, Llianas with a bow, Kirrit with her crossbow. The mural covered the whole wall, a fabulous scene of a forest glade, braided with faces and animals and birds, and it shimmered softly. It was the glade they had walked into in the Forest, the faces shimmering between the trees the faces of the people of Forest Village, yet she had no time to wonder at it.

"Get behind me," Shaeli yelled to her sisters, and she fired a beam across the room. The bangles on her arms grew warm, and the magic that came from her stone was more intense, more refined. The heat generated by the dragon scale bangles throbbed in time with her heart.

Two soldiers fell, but more filled the room, and she fired again. Ezebar and Williver were fighting fiercely, but losing ground, backing towards her. Kirrit and Llianas, standing side by side before the mural, had time to loose a few more arrows as the soldiers poured into the room. M'zena watched from the far side.

"Kirrit," Shaeli yelled, firing her light at the unending stream of soldiers that were pouring through the door. "Kirrit, get the girls. Take them back."

Kirrit looked at her and nodded. She fired one more arrow and dashed over and grabbed the girls.

"Go," Shaeli said to them. "I'll be right behind you."

The old woman with the braid came over as Shaeli threw again. Her beam knocked out the frame above the door, and it fell, showering the soldiers with wood and stone. Neesha took the hand of the old woman and pulled at it.

"You come, too," she said, and the old woman with the braid nodded.

"Go," yelled Shaeli, knowing the woman must be her mother's dear friend, the old queen, Irinesta. She pulled Ebony from her shoulder and launched her towards the mural. "Go with them, Eb," she cried. "Go with Kirrit."

Ebony bounded over and Shanna scooped her up from the floor. Kirrit led them back to the mural, and they disappeared as they touched it. Shanna and Neesha were looking back over their shoulders, eyes wide with fright, as they vanished.

Shaeli fired at a soldier who had Williver against a wall, and saw M'zena still standing nearby.

"You, too, M'zena," she called. "Go back."

M'zena moved towards the mural and Shaeli turned back to the fighting.

Llianas was still firing arrows, but as Shaeli turned a soldier leapt at her and knocked her bow from her hands, throwing her to the ground.

Shaeli fired at him and he fell away, and Williver ran across the room and pulled Llianas to her feet. Ezebar was fighting two soldiers nearby, and Shaeli hit one of them with a short sharp bolt as he raised his sword to strike.

Rem and Zod flew back through the battle, stinging whoever they could. One of the soldiers took a swipe at Zod as he passed, and Ezebar kicked the legs out from under her. The woman fell with a thud and Zod zipped by, unharmed. He looked back at Ezebar and bobbed in the air.

"Go back," Ezebar yelled to the two fairies. "We'll follow."

Rem and Zod zipped across the room, and vanished into the mural.

"Williver," Ezebar yelled, throwing his head towards the mural of the glade.

Williver nodded, slashing at the guard he fought, and he and Llianas took a step back, but two more soldiers climbed over the dead at the door and ran at them.

Shaeli stood near the bed, and she picked off one of them, and then she fired at two Ezebar fought. Both crumpled and he ran over to her.

"Come on," he said.

She nodded, but a cry from Llianas took her eye and her arm across the floor. The soldiers had grabbed Llianas, Williver had lost his sword, and both were struggling. Shaeli fired at the ones who held Williver, and as they fell, Williver threw himself at those who held Llianas.

They were dragging Llianas towards the door when one was hit by an arrow. Shaeli looked over and saw M'zena standing there with Llianas' bow. Ezebar yelled at her.

"Go back, M'zena," he yelled, and she nodded and dropped the bow.

Shaeli fired at the other soldier who held Llianas, and as he staggered, Williver rushed over and took Llianas' hand, pulling her away from the door and back towards Ezebar and Shaeli.

More soldiers appeared at the door, followed by a tall woman. She held a sword in her hand, but she was wearing long robes. Behind her in the shattered doorway was a taller figure, standing in the shadows. Shaeli had seen the woman at Autumn's Eve Hunt. She knew that this was Queen Virrisian.

The queen stepped into the room, and more soldiers poured through the door behind her, rushing at Williver and Llianas, overwhelming them. Shaeli fired at them, but Ezebar was pulling at her arm, dragging her towards the mural. The tall figure who stood in the shadows outside the broken doorway spoke.

"Get the girl," he said.

"Capture her," cried the queen, pointing at Shaeli.

The soldiers rushed at her. Ezebar dragged at her arm. They reached the mural and Shaeli struggled.

"No," she yelled. "They've got Williver."

She threw another beam that crashed into the wall above the soldiers' heads, but she could not fire at them, for they held the two elves before them.

"We have to," Ezebar yelled.

He pulled at her. The other soldiers were closing on them now and Shaeli fired at them. Two fell but the others kept coming. She threw again. Williver yelled at her.

"Go, Shaeli," he shouted. "Hurry."

"No," she cried, firing again.

More and more soldiers came through the door. The floor was littered with their bodies and still they came.

Ezebar and Shaeli had reached the edge of the mural. It still shimmered, but the ripples were slowing. Shaeli could hear the distant echo of singing, and she glanced along the wall.

M'zena still stood watching them at the far end of the mural. Tish hovered over her shoulder.

"Take her out, lad," M'zena said, and she began to sing.

Ezebar looked at M'zena, at the soldiers dodging Shaeli's fire, and back at the old woman.

"Hurry," M'zena said, and she kept on singing.

The mural shimmered, and Shaeli struggled, firing at the guard. Ezebar grabbed her, picked her up, and threw himself backwards into the mural where he stood, right at its very edge.

The last thing Shaeli saw was Williver and Llianas struggling within the grasp of the guard, the soldiers only paces away from her. Queen Virrisian stood beside the shattered door, the tall figure in the shadows outside it. M'zena was still singing, Tish fluttering over the old woman's head when Ezebar pulled her backwards. There was a flash of golden light, the sound of singing grew very loud for a moment, and she thought she heard one of her sisters cry out her name. Then everything went dark and she fell on top of Ezebar with a thud.

* * *

She scrambled to her feet and turned around, furious.

"You *left* them," she said, her voice thick with rage. "You left them behind. Even M'zena."

He stood up and looked down at her. She could barely see his face in the darkness.

"I had to," he said. "It was what she wanted. They would have had you otherwise."

"But they have them, in the castle, and we're..." she stopped and looked around, suddenly aware of her surroundings. "Where are we?"

Ezebar shook his head. "I don't know, but I don't think we're in the Forest anymore."

They stood on thick grass, and it was very dark, only the pale starlight to see by. Around them was a stand of trees, growing thickly together, but there was no glade, no Forest people, no singing. There was only the sound of the sea close by, and the tang of salt on the air.

"These trees," said Shaeli. "They're like the ones in the Forest."

Ezebar touched the bark of one, and then held out his hand to her. "Come on," he said. "Let's look around."

"Shall I throw a little light?" she asked.

"I don't think so," he said. "Let's see what's outside these trees first."

She ignored the proffered hand and went through the trees ahead of him, following the sound of the waves. There were not many trees, only a few dozen, and she wound her way between them, old leaves scrunching beneath her feet. The thin starlight grew a little as she emerged from beneath the trees. She stopped, gasped and stepped back, colliding with Ezebar.

She had stepped out onto a ledge. Below there was a drop, she didn't know how far, but she could hear the waves crashing onto the rocks below. Ezebar went forward and looked over the edge and Shaeli's heart lurched. She closed her eyes and shuddered. Ezebar came back and took her arm.

"This way," he said, leading her down to the left at the edge of the trees.

They went down a slope and came out onto open ground. Ahead there were the dark shapes of buildings, squat plain buildings, trees huddling in lumps around them. They crept towards them and they began passing tall statues, some enclosed in low rock walls, others surrounded by thick bushes. The nearest building was dark stone, cold and damp to touch, and they crept around the edge of it until they found a columned opening at the front, yet when they went up the steps they found there was no door, it had been sealed by a great stone.

"I don't like this," said Shaeli. "Lets see what's further on."

Ezebar nodded and they went back down the steps. All the buildings were the same. Squat and coldly dark with no openings, but richly carved. Here and there were more statues, unrecognisable in the dark, and more trees, none like those they'd emerged from. They went on through the buildings until they came out the other side. Here the sound of the sea grew louder again. They walked to where the ground fell away once again into dark waves.

Far across the dark water there rose a great headland. Atop it was a castle, its turrets lost in the night sky. Below the castle, a city spread out, they could tell by the lights that were scattered far around the bay; not many lights, but enough to see the city was large.

They were standing on the Island of Dead Kings, alone with the graves of the dead rulers of Zirrus.

* * *

# CHAPTER THIRTY ONE

"Well," said Ezebar. "It looks like we missed the Forest somehow."

Shaeli looked at him and cocked her head to one side. "Do you think so?" she said, her lip curling. She flung an arm out. "That's Great Court over there. We're on the Island of Dead Kings in the middle of the bay. The gods know how, but we're a long way from anywhere, anyone." She shook her head at him. "Since your powers of deduction are so finely honed, what do you propose we do next?"

He looked mildly back down at her and shrugged. "Well, I guess we'll have to swim," he said.

She snorted. "Swim? Into Palveron?" She snorted again. "I don't think us drowning ourselves is going to do anyone any good. Do you know how far it is?"

"I can see how far it is," he said. "If we go with the tide, I don't see why we couldn't." He looked around. "I don't think we're going to do anyone any good out here either, do you?"

"You're serious?" she said, shaking her head again.

"If we find a good log, I reckon we could kick our way there. I'll help you," he added.

She ignored his last statement. "Kick our way?" she mused. She turned her back on him and started picking her way down the hill.

"Where are you going?" he said.

"To see what the tide's doing," she called back over her shoulder.

He stood for only a moment and then followed her down into the shadows.

They went slowly, for it was very dark, almost feeling their way down the hill. The ground flattened and the sound of waves grew louder. They could see a small pale half-moon of sand ahead and the blackness of the water beyond.

The beach was small and the sand made squeaking noises beneath their feet as they walked across to the water. They reached the tide line, and Ezebar took a piece of driftwood, walked a few paces over damp sand and threw it a short way out onto the water. The waves were tiny, rolling onto the sand with their tops white against the black water, and the driftwood rolled around for a while and then drifted out into deeper water. It took only a few moments of watching the water to see that the tide was on its way out. Shaeli sighed.

"We'll have to wait," she said. "Let's see if we can find a good log."

Ezebar nodded and turned back. They went back to the tide line and walked across the sand, squinting into the darkness. They criss-crossed the white sand, seeing in shadows stout branches, but finding only hollows or mounds, or small piles of flotsam clinging together. When they had searched the beach and found nothing, they went to a nearby clump of trees. It was much darker here, and Shaeli tripped on a rock and fell full-length along the ground. Ezebar helped her up, but she shook his hand free. She fumbled in her amulet and felt for the smooth surface of the amber.

"I'm going to throw a light," she said, pulling it from the pouch.

"Do you think that's wise?" he said, looking at the castle far across the water.

"If anyone sees it, they'll think it's one of the dead kings or queens out for a midnight stroll," she said. "I almost hope someone does."

She threw a low beam of light ahead, and the golden glow lit up the ground beneath the trees. They found a sturdy log, and while it was not as thick as they would have liked, it was long enough for them both to hang on to, with the splintered remains of a few branches jutting from one end. As Shaeli's beam faded, they each grabbed one of the branch stumps and began hauling it back down to the beach.

They were both hot and sweaty when they reached the sand, but they kept dragging the log down to the water's edge. The tide had receded since they'd been there and they took off their boots and dragged the log down into the water. It floated easily and they pulled it back to the edge of the waves where the surges left it sitting in wet sand as the tide continued to drain.

They collected their boots, and went to sit at the edge of the sand on the thick tufty grass.

"I guess there's no point putting them back on," said Shaeli, putting the boots down on the grass beside her.

Ezebar shook his head. "No," he said. "We'll have to tie them onto the log, or leave them behind."

She could not see his eyes in the starlight and she was glad of it. She looked across at the castle. The lights on inside it were fewer now, as were the lights along the bay and in the city. The hour must be late. She looked up at the stars and nodded to herself. The midnight hours were passing. She looked back at the castle, to the turret that held the mural of the glade. No lights shone there.

"What do you suppose they've done to them?" she asked.

"I don't know," he said. His eyes also rested upon the castle. "But..."

"But, what?"

"I cannot imagine they will find them of much use. Two elves and an old woman." He shrugged. "I don't know," he repeated, and he shook his head. He dropped it to his chest for a moment, and then he looked down at her. "At least your sisters and Kirrit are safe."

"Yes, and the old queen," she said, thinking. "That must have been how she brought the baby to the Trader, through the glade mural. The girls were born at the Landing in Zuen. One of them anyway. Oh, I wish I'd had more time with them, but you're right, at least they are safe. And Eb."

She sighed and looked up at him, then she remembered she was angry with him, and she frowned. Ezebar pretended not to notice.

"We should try and get some rest," he said. "The tide will not turn until the sunrise hours, and we have a long way to go. With luck we will make it before the sun is too high."

He looked at her and she was glad it was too dark to see his eyes. She became suddenly aware they were alone, safe, and far from anyone. She looked away.

"I suppose you're right about that, too," she said.

She lay down on the grass and turned her back on him. The grass was thick, but tough and spiky, and it prickled her skin. The clothes they had been given in Forest Village – light trousers and vests, thin shirts – did little to keep the spiky grass away. She wriggled and looked across the water. The lights along the bay were few now, and she could no longer tell that a city lay spread out beneath the castle. She closed her eyes, trying not to be aware of Ezebar laying down behind her.

There had been no wind as they'd explored the island, but now a slight breeze picked up, ruffling the water. She breathed deeply, enjoying the tang of salt. She was thankful for the cool breeze, for it was a hot night, and dragging the log had made her sweat. She closed her eyes against the sight of Great Court against the sky, wriggled into the grass, and tried to sleep.

She woke shivering. She opened her eyes, and looked up at the stars. The night was passing but it was still a long time until the tide turned. She shivered again, and sat up, her teeth chattering. The breeze had grown stronger and the warmth of the day was long gone from the grass.

Ezebar shifted beside her. "Move closer to me," he said.

She turned around and looked down at him. "I'm sorry?" she said.

He sighed. "If you move closer to me, it won't be so windy, and you'll be warmer. I will too. We're going to be cold enough in the water. We should at least go in warm."

She considered this. "I suppose you're right. Again."

She sighed, and begrudgingly moved closer to him and lay back down. He was right. His bulk protected her from the worst of the wind. She wriggled, and looked around at him. His nose was very close to hers, she could see the subtle patterns of colour in his beard, and for the first time his eyes were lit by the starlight. She blinked, and her eyes widened as he looked at her.

"I'm sorry," he said.

She blinked again. "What for?"

"For the pool. For letting you down. For leaving them."

She almost forgot why she was angry with him. It seemed a distant memory. "Oh," was all she could think of to say.

And then he was leaning towards her and there was nothing to stop him, this time, from reaching her lips. He kissed her softly, a long, gentle kiss, his lips soft and warm, cupping her face in his hand. He stopped for a moment to look at her, and then he kissed her again. His whiskers brushed against her, softer than she would ever have expected them to be. She shivered, but she was no longer cold.

His arms had gone around her and he was stroking her hair and her cheek. She began to feel breathless. He stopped and looked at her, breathing heavily, then he lay back down beside her, and held her close. Her head was on his chest and she was surprised that the thudding of his heart matched her own. The wind fluttered but she was glad of it now, for it cooled the heat in her cheeks.

"Try and sleep again," he said, his lips brushing her hair. "I'll wake you when it's time."

"I'm not sure I can," she said, turning her face to his.

"Try," he said, smiling gently.

He kissed her again and then she closed her eyes and turned her face into his chest. She could feel his heart beating against her cheek and wondered if he could feel how hard hers was bumping against her ribs. She sighed, and snuggled closer to him. His arms grew tighter about her, and she drifted into sleep in the warmth of his embrace. Yet her last thought was not of him, but Williver, caught with Llianas and M'zena in the castle.

\* \* \*

The dream was swift and pointed.

She was wandering a dark passageway, looking through barred doors into rooms filled with the bones of long-dead people. Then, through one door, she saw M'zena, lying beside Llianas on a thin hard bench, her head on the elf's lap. Llianas had her arm around the old woman and Williver was hunched on the floor opposite. They were all sleeping. She called through the small barred hole to him. His head rose, and he blinked at her.

*Shaeli?* he said, looking at the others and then back at her. *How did you reach this place?*

*Williver, are you alright?*

*Yes, but you must go. He will hear you.*

*Who?*

*He who brought the black wind. 'Tis he who wants the wand. Don't let him have it, Shaeli, you must...*

He stopped as a wind shuddered through the small cell. It ruffled Williver's hair, but not Llianas' or M'zena's.

*Go, Shaeli. Quickly,* he said.

*I'll come back for you,* she said, pressing her face to the bars, and then she turned and fled back down the long dark passage, past the doors holding shadows and old bones.

The wind that had risen in Williver's cell pursued her down the passage. She could hear it whining through the passageways as she ran, could feel it pulling at her hair, her mind...

\* \* \*

She woke up gasping, bolt upright.

Ezebar was sitting beside her, one hand on her arm, the other about her shoulders.

"You're dreaming, Shaeli," he was saying. "It was a dream. It's alright."

She stared at him, and then looked around. Her breathing slowed and she swallowed the fear left in her throat from the dream.

"I saw them," she said. "Something chased me."

She told him of the dream; how different it was from the way she and Williver usually met in the dreamworld. She told him of the black wind and how it had sent her out to drown on the sea.

"And that's when you came to our island," he said.

"Yes. Ishaan said I was past your island when he found me, drifting out onto the Endless Sea."

Ezebar whistled. "It's a wonder he found you at all," he said. "And you think this dream now was really them, that they are still alive?"

"Oh, yes," she nodded. "It chased me again, the black wind." She shuddered.

"And Williver said it is he who wants your wand, the one who brings the black wind?" She nodded again. "Why hasn't he sought you again, in the dreamworld?" Ezebar said. "If Williver can find you, why can't he, this other one? It seems to me he could have sent you mad a hundred times over if he almost succeeded once."

"It isn't that easy to find someone in the dreamworld," she said. "Williver has always been able to find me, but he can't go into the dreams of anyone he chooses unless he knows where they are. When he contacted Llianas at Lythnori, he was actually trying for Qiren or Tarkoda."

"Another elf and your brother?"

"Yes, you'll like Tarkoda, I'm sure," she smiled. "When you finally meet. Anyway, whoever it is must have known, somehow, where I was, almost exactly, when they found me in the Starisles."

"Then Williver sought you out tonight?"

"Well, no," she said, and frowned. She thought for a moment. "He seemed really surprised to see me."

"Then you must have found him," said Ezebar.

She wondered at this and shook her head. "I don't know," she said, slowly. "I've never travelled the dreamworld before."

"Perhaps your worry for them led you to them somehow."

She thought about this for a moment. "Perhaps," she said, and then she sighed. "Is it time to go yet?"

"Almost," he said. "Let's tie our shoes on to the ship and push her down so she's ready to launch."

"Ship," she laughed, shaking the dream from her shoulders and grabbing her shoes. "Some ship."

She stood up and he was right in front of her, a small smile curving his lips. He kissed her, just once and quickly, cupping the back of her head in his rough-gentle hand, and then he took her by the hand and they went down to the beach. They found their log well above the softly curling waves, tied their shoes to it, and dragged it down to the water-line. They took off their heavier clothes, wrapping them beside the shoes and tying them on with Ezebar's belt, and Shaeli re-tied her amulet on beneath her clothes, and tucked it tightly into her waistband. The bangles she thought were safest where they were, on her arms.

The bay was as still as a lake. The wind had dropped to a whisper, and the tide would sit contemplating its lowest ebb for a while before turning its thoughts to rising again.

They watched the last drag of the current, and as the tide reached bottom, they dragged the log into the water. It easily took their weight, and they pushed it into deeper water, Ezebar near the stumps of broken branches, Shaeli at the other end.

Before they took their feet from the sandy bottom, they looked at each other. Shaeli took a deep breath.

"Here we go," she said.

He nodded. "So it seems." He gave her another of those light, quick kisses. "Let's go," he said.

Shaeli took her feet from the bottom and grabbed the log, then she and Ezebar began to kick their way across the bay to Palveron.

\* \* \*

When the sun rose, she was aching in every muscle she possessed. Even her eyebrows hurt.

At first it had seemed easy, even though it was dark and slightly spooky, she had Ezebar there and the water wasn't cold. They felt the tide turn beneath them; the sudden surge, the push from behind. The tide pushed the water in from the deeper water of the sea, and they were swept by cooler currents, yet the rising tide helped push them further into the bay.

Far, far ahead, above the water, a light had shone through the last hour of darkness. Shaeli imagined it to be some old person whose sleepless night had been given up for a little reading, or perhaps some sewing.

Across to the right loomed the black shape of the Faunist's Island, and every now and then she looked over at it, yet it was a long way across the water. Closer, on their left, though not by much, grew the base of the headland. There were three squat ships moored beneath it, and as the world faded from black to grey, she could see the place where the wall divided the castle grounds from the city. The view looked odd to her, as if there were fewer houses near the wall. The side of the cliff was dotted with tiny caves, and she peered up at them occasionally as the day grew slowly around them, but mostly she just aimed at the light belonging to the imagined old one.

They kicked and kicked, and one of them would swim beside the log every so often, just to exercise their arms, but it was so much easier to hang on and kick. They seemed to be moving through the water alright, but the far-off light did not seem to come any closer, and then it was gone altogether. By the time the sun had risen, they were already tired, their legs kicking with leaden weights attached, and the wind began to pick up again. It was then that they noticed that their log was getting lower in the water. The shoes they had tied to one of the broken stumps was sitting below the water, their clothes just above it. As the day grew, they began to see the shore ahead, and though it was a welcome sight, they realised how far they still had to go. The ships moored in the bay and along the docks were tiny, the buildings behind all running together above the bobbing of the waves. To their left the cliff loomed, still a long way off, and now Shaeli could see the obvious gap beneath the wall more closely, but the sharp rocks at the cliff's base kept them from going closer. They kicked on, and soon the sun was burning the backs of their heads and their arms as they swam, just to add to their misery.

It was mid-morning when they abandoned the log. It had grown so water-logged that it had become like pushing a cart through the water in front of them. Instead of keeping them afloat, it had slowly become a burden. They left their things tied to it, too tired to care about them, and they struck out for the shore. It seemed to hang tantalisingly close for a very long time and then it began to creep nearer, but far too slowly. Ezebar swam close beside her, his eyes filled with concern, flicking between her and the shore. They swam, they floated to rest, trusting to the tide to take them closer, and they swam again. They were both sunburnt and tired, their faces crusted with salt, struggling, almost beyond caring when Shaeli felt it. A brush against her legs. Something touching her. Ezebar cried out.

"Something tried to grab me," he said.

Shaeli felt the hands encircle her waist. She saw the grey streak of a dolphin's back arc through the water nearby. She smiled at Ezebar, relaxing in the waves.

"Let it grab you," she called to him. "We are safe now. 'Tis the Ammerr."

* * *

# CHAPTER THIRTY TWO

Jarris had spent the morning looking down on the guard in the square. Since the queen's last message there had been a large contingent surrounding the Landing; they had not been allowed to leave the Traders, nor had anyone been allowed aboard. The men and women of Queen Virrisian's guard now stood steadfastly in the square day and night, but few paid attention to the man with the addled mind sitting on the stairs carving at a piece of wood; Jarris had heard many useful pieces of information as the days had gone by.

He shook his head, yet it was not at the rows of guard standing beneath, but at what had happened during the night. If the others had not seen it, he would have thought his mind truly addled. There had been many strange visitors to his Trader over the last Winterings, elves, drell, Ammerr, but last night had come a creature he had never thought to see on his ship.

The hour had been very late. He had watched Mareesha pretend to eat her dinner, sit afterwards not looking at the book she held on her lap, and he had made tezz to distract her after almost everyone else had gone to bed. The big room was filled with bed-rolls and mattresses, and only Almarnoch and Ishaan were still awake, talking quietly at the table when he left. Mareesha had gone to sit in their room, and she still held the unlooked-at book upon her knee when he brought the mugs into the room.

The lamps were low, the windows open to let in the cool night air, and Jarris was passing Mareesha her mug when something flew in through one of the windows. He thought at first that it was a huge moth. It had fluttered through the window and come erratically across the room. He took up a cloth to flick the moth back out the window, and then it spoke to him.

"If you wish to hear the news I bring, threaten me not," said the moth, and then a light sprung out from it, a soft lilac light. The light drizzled down in a tiny glittering rain from rapidly beating wings.

Mareesha gasped. Jarris dropped the cloth and his jaw.

The fairy made a tiny curtsey mid-air, and then it flew down to stand on the table before Mareesha. The drizzle from her wings puddled around her tiny feet.

"I am Tish," she said. "I have come from the Forest."

"Which forest?" asked Jarris.

"There is only one Forest," Tish said, giving him a pitying look. "You are the parents of the girl whose colours shine so brightly," she said, she turned to Mareesha. "Shaeli?"

"Yes," said Mareesha, leaning forward eagerly. "Yes, we are. Have you seen her? Is she safe?"

"She was safe," said the fairy. "Yet they missed the way, and did not follow the others back to the Forest. I know not where she is now. Others have been caught in the false queen's trap, but the twins who are not sisters are with the girl with dark copper hair, safe on the other side."

"Twins who are not sisters?" repeated Mareesha. She looked at her husband. "Jarris. The girls." She turned back to the fairy. "You say they are safe, with a red-haired girl? Kirrit? Are they with Kirrit?"

"That is her name," nodded Tish. "They returned to the Forest. The little creature, too. But some were caught and Shaeli missed the way."

"Tish, you speak in riddles," said Mareesha. "Who was caught? Shaeli missed the way where?"

"Forgive me," said Tish. "They tried to catch me, and I lost my way on the journey down from the castle. I forget your kind know so little."

"The castle?" said Jarris. "But did you not say you came from a forest?"

"I have," said Tish. She sighed. "The telling will be longer than I thought. Have you some water or nectar?" she asked. "I am very dry."

"Of course," said Jarris. "I'm not sure if I have a cup small enough, though."

"Some small leaf will do," she said. "Bring in the old one who sits sleeplessly when you return. He should hear the tale. Bring the Ammerr also."

Jarris came back holding a small cup of water and a variety of leaves. Almarnoch and Ishaan followed him into the room. The Warlock's eyebrows quivered when he saw the fairy.

"I wasn't sure which one to bring," Jarris said, putting the cup and some herb leaves down on the table.

"I thank you," said Tish.

She took up a small leaf, rolled it into a cylinder and dipped it into the cup. The leaf filled as if a drop of morning dew had been caught in it, and Tish drank from it, filled it again, and drank deeply. Her tiny light grew brighter as she drank, her wings fluttered more gently. When she had finished she told them what had happened in the tower of the Glade. They listened to the tiny lilting voice, and when she had finished, she drank from her little leaf cup again.

"I don't understand," said Mareesha. "How did you get into the castle? How did they return to the Forest?"

"It is not my place to say," said Tish. "These things are not spoken of on the outside."

"It must be a portal," said Almarnoch. "I have heard there are ancient paths through the Lands, unknown and long lost."

"You are as wise as your colours decree," said Tish.

"A portal?" asked Ishaan.

"Like a window from one place to another," said Almarnoch. "Distance has no relevance."

"I always wondered," said Jarris, slowly, staring into the past. "I wondered how she brought the babe to us. It always seemed so impossible." He brought his gaze back to the present and was met by the eyes of his wife. Jarris and Mareesha stared at each other for a moment, and then he turned back to the fairy. "And the twins are there with Kirrit, on the other side of this portal, in M'Zen'sclahr Forest."

"Yes, they and the one who was kept from the World," said Tish. "But the old one and the elves were taken in their place."

"Irinesta?" said Mareesha, and at Tish's nod, she sighed. "Oh, thank the gods she is with them. But Williver and Llianas were taken?"

"Yes," said Tish. "They, and the old one."

"She must mean M'zena," said Almarnoch.

"Mizzy. Yes," nodded Tish.

"Yet Shaeli escaped?" said Mareesha.

Tish nodded again.

"But she is not with the others?" asked Jarris.

Tish shook her head. A little more dust fell from her wings. "She went with the man with dark eyes," she said.

"Ezebar," said Almarnoch.

Tish nodded once more.

"And you don't know where they are now?" the Warlock asked.

Tish shook her head again. A little more dust floated down. "The edges spin strangely," she said. None of them knew what that meant, but Tish did not give them time to ask. She lifted off the table. "I will find out what we know," she said.

"Find out from who, about what?" said Mareesha.

"The others will have word from the Forest, those of my kind that live here in the city," Tish said.

"Fairies? Here in Palveron?" said Jarris.

Tish's face held that pitying little smile again. "Of course," she said. "We are everywhere. We know all things."

"But I've never seen one here," said Mareesha.

"If you had, we would not be doing our job properly," said Tish. "I shall return when I know what we know," she said.

Her little pale-purple light extinguished, and as she flew out the window, she looked again like the moth Jarris thought she had been when she'd flown into the room.

Mareesha had been overjoyed with the news of the twins' release, but Almarnoch stilled her enthusiasm quickly.

"It changes nothing, Mareesha," he said, quietly. "With no other hold over us, they will have to take what they want. This was never about the girls, the heir, it is about the wand. About power."

"Then what are we to do?" Mareesha said.

"We do nothing," he said. "Nothing more than is already planned. If we do not go to the castle, we will be taken. She will have no other choice."

She looked at him for a moment, and then she nodded.

Tish had returned at sunrise, yet if she knew anything more, she would not say. She had merely yawned and flown into the cupboard, where she had curled up on Mareesha's handkerchiefs and gone to sleep.

She was still down there sleeping soundly as Jarris sat on the Landing steps looking down at the guard ringing the Landing and being amazed by the fact there was a fairy asleep in his room.

He looked over at Golden Eagle. There was no one on the deck, but he knew it was as crowded below their decks as it was beneath his. Many were those who were stuck below, unable to show their faces to the guard. It was hot below decks, and stuffy, and there was little for them to do, so they spent their time sharpening weapons and fletching new arrows. Jarris feared that tomorrow there would be too much for them to do.

The day was bright. The sky had become the high, white-blue of summer and the clouds were few, floating far above the ground, drifting lazily north on a light breeze. He gazed up at the endless panorama of the sky stretching itself to show off its summer finery, and he sighed deeply; he missed the sky sorely, even fighting the god U'ee and his storms. If he was never stuck in another city again, it would suit him happily.

He frowned as he looked back down at the guard. They must be hot in their scarlet-and-black, but he could barely dredge any sympathy for them, even knowing that some now served by force instead of choice.

Something caught his eye. Something in the shadows of a thin lane opposite. He blinked. A tiny light ball rolled out from the lane and dissolved in the sunlight. He squinted. A figure stepped out from the shadows. It was there for the barest moment and then it was gone, but he saw and he knew. He dare not raise an arm, dare not acknowledge the one he had seen, he merely raised his face again to the sky in thanks. He stood, slowly brushed the curls of wood from his trousers and walked back to the Trader. He dithered at the gate, forced himself to amble across the deck, and then he went below to tell them he had just seen Shaeli.

\* \* \*

She went back to where Ezebar waited in the shadows of the thin lane.

The Ammerr had pushed them in to a small beach surrounded by chunky dark rocks under the brow of the great headland. Shaeli and Ezebar had staggered to the sand and turned around. From the water behind them came a tall bearded figure.

"Rizar?" gasped Shaeli, wading back to greet him. "Oh, I'm so glad to see you."

The old Ammerr she had met in Qorientae smiled at her. Behind him in the water rose other heads, some familiar – friends of Ishaan's – others unknown to her. The heads kept rising from the waves, more and more, until the water was dappled with them. To one side rose huge majestic heads, like the heads of horses, but covered with slick, colourful skins and huge eyes. Ammerr rode their backs, long pikes held in every hand, and Shaeli knew these must be Ammerr from Wokk, for only there were the giant seahorses found. A pod of dolphins rose and fell in unison behind them. Ezebar stood on the beach, eyes fixed in amazement at the heads rising from the water.

"I did not expect to meet you in such circumstances," Rizar said.

"I thank the gods you did," Shaeli said. "We were lucky you found us."

"The tide was almost ready to turn, child," he said. "Why were you so far out on the water?"

"We came from there," said Shaeli, pointing across to the island they had left.

Rizar followed her hand. His eyebrows rose. "So far? Why?"

"We were stuck there," she said. "There was no other way. But, Rizar, what are you doing here?"

"We have come to aid those who would free the World from the shadow of the false queen and her black ship," he said.

"But why?" Shaeli asked, shaking her head. "Why would your people do this?"

"Because Qorientae was attacked by the flying ship that wields red fire," he said. "Many were killed. Lythnori was also attacked. Aneris will not let it pass. We shall let the World know we are still here and we are mighty. We are many, and we seek revenge."

"Oh, Rizar," Shaeli said, her eyes widening with the news. "I'm so sorry."

"The fault is not yours," he said. "But we must go. You will be able to reach your city from here?"

"Yes," she said. "But where are you going?"

"Across the bay, to where a great army gathers," he said. "Your brother is there, I'm told."

"Tarkoda?" she said. "Oh, tell him…" she began, but there was so much to tell him, too much, and she stopped. "Just tell him his sisters are safe," she said. "All three of them. Just tell him that."

Rizar nodded. "This I shall do," he said.

He went back to the water, and when it reached his waist he turned and raised an arm, then he dropped below the waves and all the other heads disappeared with him. The giant seahorses were the last to go. There was a swirl of bubbles, and they were gone. Shaeli waded back to where Ezebar stood on the sand.

"That was a sight I would have never even imagined I'd see," he said.

"They're amazing aren't they," she said, looking back over her shoulder. There was no sign of the Ammerr.

They had rested on the beach for a while, and then they'd clambered bare-foot over the rocks until they came to the first buildings. First, they found a well, for they were both very thirsty, their throats thick with the taste of the salty water. They tipped some of the cool clear water over their heads, soothing the redness the sun had burned into their faces, and then they crept through the streets. Shaeli led Ezebar eagerly to the square, but they had to dodge roaming soldiers several times and when they finally reached it they found the Landing surrounded by guard. There was no way they could board the Traders.

They huddled in the shadows of a thin lane, looking up at the ships moored so tantalisingly close, and she saw her father sitting on the Landing steps. She studied him, heart swelling with the sight of him, wondering if his mind was still addled, and even though he appeared to sit vaguely carving a piece of wood, something in the set of his shoulders and the eyes flickering over the guard gave her hope. She had said a prayer to the gods, and rolled out three little balls before he noticed one. She jumped out in the street, smiled at him, and jumped back. She turned to grin at Ezebar.

"He saw me," she said.

"Now what?" he asked. "We cannot reach them."

Shaeli thought. "I know," she said, taking his hand. "Come with me."

She led him back through the streets, gasping at the ruin the once-fine city was in; the broken windows, the rubble, the holes in the buildings. They dodged guard several times, and once, far down a wide street, they saw one of the Qotarr.

Ezebar stared at the beast, the city around him, the castle above, amazed he was seeing so fabled a place with his own eyes. All around him were things he had never seen, and as he followed Shaeli through the broken streets, he shook his head time and again in amazement. Shaeli passed through the streets quickly, determined only on reaching her destination.

When they came to the gates she sought, they found them barred and guarded by surly men and women. They were let in, but were not allowed to go up the driveway until word was sent to the house. Shaeli and Ezebar stood uncomfortably, squirming under the arrows trained on them from the trees, until the runner came back.

"Lady A says let 'em through," said the man. "Though she's doubtful she's who she says she is," he added, jerking his head at Shaeli. "They's waiting for 'em at the top."

"On you go, then," said a large woman holding a doubled-edged axe.

Shaeli led Ezebar up the driveway, shaking her head and gasping at this sight, too.

"Are you sure about this?" asked Ezebar, looking around at the bobbing fields of produce in the middle of this huge city.

"I think so," said Shaeli. "Oh, there they are," she added.

As he came from the trees flanking the driveway, Ezebar saw an enormous house with tall gables topped with leering gargoyles. There was a group of people standing in front of its broad steps, and many of the people stood threateningly, weapons in their hands. A gaggle of children peered out from the doorway, a white-haired man with a long staff standing protectively before them.

An old woman standing at the front of the group let out a cry as she saw Shaeli and she rushed forward. A very tall elderly man followed her. Ezebar breathed a sigh and followed Shaeli up to the house.

"Oh, my dear, how did you reach us? They have been so worried about you and the little ones," the old woman was saying when he reached them.

"Arinola," Shaeli said, embracing her. "It is so good to see you, although it looks a little different since I was last here. Hello Vulcan," she added, hugging the tall man.

"'Tis good to see you also, child," said Sir Vulcan. "Arinola speaks truth when she says they've been worried about you. And who is this young man?"

"This is my friend, Ezebar of the Starisles," said Shaeli, taking Ezebar's arm and pulling him forward. "Ezebar, this is Lady Arinola of Palveron and Sir Vulcan of Conroi."

Ezebar bowed his head to them.

"Happy to meet you, lad," said Sir Vulcan.

"Welcome to my home," said Arinola. "Though, as Shaeli has pointed out, it does not usually look so much like a farm. Come in, come in. Are you hungry?" she asked, leading the way through the group of curious people and on up the stairs.

The children scattered as they reached the doorway, but the tall man remained where he was, and Shaeli introduced Skeltom, the house Warlock, to Ezebar. Skeltom nodded his head, shyly said how happy he was to see Shaeli safe, and then he went and followed the children into the house.

"He has been so good with the children," Arinola said, watching as Skeltom chased the children down the hall towards the conservatory. "Now, did you say you were hungry?"

"Yes, Arinola, we are," said Shaeli. "But why have you ploughed up the gardens? Why are all these people here?"

"People were hungry," Arinola shrugged. "They were sleeping on the streets and in the parks."

"And you took them in and fed them," Shaeli said. "Mam always said you were a very determined woman."

Arinola ruffled. "I only do what is right," she said. "Vulcan, take them out into the rose garden where it's cool and I'll fetch something from the kitchen."

Vulcan led them through the house, and Ezebar did his best not to look like he was staring. He had never been inside such a house, and when the old gentleman led them through the garden enclosed in glass, he shook his head. Shaeli smiled at him and took his hand.

"Isn't the conservatory amazing?" she said, looking up at the lacy fronds spilling from the hanging baskets. "The first time I came to Arinola's, I walked around with my mouth hanging open for about three days." She looked down at the trays of seedlings which had replaced many of the ornamental plants. "There were no vegetables here then, though."

He returned her smile, yet he was feeling overwhelmed by his surroundings.

They went through the room and out into a garden filled with roses of every colour. Ezebar let Shaeli's hand drop as they went outside, but she hardly seemed to notice as she gasped at the rose garden. Winding along beneath the thorny plants were vines laden with ripening fruit and vegetables. To one side, beneath a tall, wide-branched tree, there was a table and chairs. Skeltom and the children were just disappearing around a corner of the house.

Lady Arinola was coming from a doorway, followed by a small man carrying a tray. Shaeli stared at him. Arinola began speaking before she was halfway across the lawn.

"We closed Flin's house and brought all his people up here when things grew bad," she called out as she crossed the grass. "Yorrow has been most helpful."

Shaeli smiled at her and the little man who followed.

Flin's cook set his tray down on the table and met her eye with a short nod. The greeting was without the slightest trace of a smile, but Shaeli didn't think it odd; she couldn't remember Yorrow ever smiling at anyone. A pot maybe, or a dish he was particularly pleased with, but never a person.

"Hello, Yorrow," she said, smiling at him despite the fact she knew it would be unreturned.

"Young lady," Yorrow nodded, as economical with his words as with his smile. "Safe, I see. Good." He nodded again, and then he turned back to the kitchen.

Arinola laughed nervously. "He has been such a help," she said, again.

Shaeli looked at her, trying not to laugh. "He won't be mad, Arinola," she said. "Flin is the most generous man I ever met, and he would be happy his people are here." She let the laugh go. "Though I'm sure he'll want them returned, especially Yorrow."

"Yes, well... that will be up to Yorrow, I suspect," Arinola said vaguely, smoothing her hair. "But there is a fine pie left from last night and a jug of fresh juice. I must say, you two look like you could do with the benefit of a bowl of water and a comb. And your faces are very red."

Shaeli felt her cheeks. They were hot, and her arms were bright pink. She looked at Ezebar. His cheeks were red as apples above his beard, the whites of his eyes very bright against the sunburn. She was lost in those eyes for a moment as Ezebar smiled at her. Arinola prattled on.

"I have something that will take the sting straight out of that sunburn," she was saying. "Your mother showed it to me. I'll fetch some after you've eaten. And washed?" she added hopefully.

"That would be nice, Arinola," Shaeli smiled, taking a long drink from her glass. "And then we must find a way of getting to the Traders. Have you seen them? My parents?"

"Oh, yes, many times," Arinola said.

"They're alright?" Shaeli said. "My father. Is he...?"

"Your father is as well as he's ever been," said Vulcan. He leant forward and patted her hand, smiling kindly. "He was... most unwell when he reached Palveron, but you may be at ease, he has regained himself."

Shaeli's eyes filled with tears and she looked down at her glass. She had not known how much she had dreaded that her father might still be lost within himself until she found that he was alright. She drew a breath and stopped the tears.

Ezebar watched her, and Arinola watched Ezebar. She looked at Vulcan, raised an eyebrow, and the old man smiled back at her.

Shaeli looked up at Vulcan. "Tell me everything," she said.

Vulcan told her all that had happened in the city since the Traders had been forced back to Cave. She listened carefully, and beside her Ezebar listened even more carefully; much of what they spoke about was information he had not heard before. He began to wonder, to look at Shaeli with growing fear in his eyes. She did not notice.

"So they're all down there at the Landing?" Shaeli said. "Almarnoch and the others? Flin, too?"

Vulcan nodded. "Yet we have not seen them, nor spoken to any of them for several days, since they have been confined to their ships. The rumour is that they are exchanging something for your sisters at dawn."

"The wand," Shaeli said. "They'll want the wand, but there is no need now. The twins aren't there any more."

"What do you mean, child, not there?" said Vulcan.

"Oh, my dear," cried Arinola, putting a hand to her chest. "You don't mean...?"

"No, Arinola, they're fine," Shaeli said, with a small, grim smile. "They're safe now and far from harm. But others are in danger in their place." She thought for a moment. "We must find a way of reaching the Traders," she said.

"We may be able to help," said Vulcan.

"That's just what I was thinking," said Arinola, rubbing her hands together. "A small diversion, perhaps. Something to distract the guard from the square."

"Do you think you can?" said Shaeli. "Long enough for Ezebar and I to get up the stairs?"

"I believe so," said Vulcan.

"But first, as you've made short work of Yorrow's pie, perhaps you'd like to wash and change," said Arinola. "I'm sure we can find you something to wear, and some shoes," she said. "And perhaps a comb."

\* \* \*

Arinola found them both fresh clothes and by the time they'd washed and changed – and combed their hair – the afternoon was beginning to drain from the sky. Shaeli was aching all over when she came back downstairs, but her face and arms felt much better with the soft gel from the inside of the spiky leaf Arinola had given her. She found them showing Ezebar through the conservatory.

"Ezebar was just telling us about the old woman who raised him, and the elves who were captured inside the castle," Vulcan said, as she joined them.

Shaeli sighed. "I don't know what we're going to do," she said. "The girls may be safe, but the others…" she shook her head. "I don't know. We have to get to the Landing."

"I still don't understand how you got them out," said Arinola. "Or how you got in. And who is this older woman Ezebar says is with them?"

"Oh, Arinola, it's the old queen. She is with them," Shaeli said. "I'm sorry, I should have told you earlier, but it must have been her."

"Irinesta?" Arinola cried. She looked at Vulcan and she began to weep. "Oh, Vulcan, she is free."

Sir Vulcan patted her back as she dabbed her eyes, and then she looked at them, sniffing.

"Come," she said. "There is something I want to show you."

She took them into a small study that Shaeli had never seen before, and explained about her wicked grandfather. Shaeli tried not to laugh, and she dare not meet Ezebar's eye, but when Vulcan pulled a bookshelf aside and lit the lamp, she was intrigued. They followed him down into the tunnel and to the little cave overlooking the bay. Shaeli admired the view from the shadows further back, knowing she was in one of the little caves she had been staring at from the water that morning. Ezebar went right over to the little lip that curled up from the bottom and leant over it and looked down. Shaeli's heart lurched as he leaned over, looking at the waves crashing on the rocks below, and when he pulled himself back in, she breathed a sigh of relief, and grabbed at his arm when he came to stand beside her.

They went on through the second tunnel to another house, creeping up a thin staircase and coming out in a study too similar to the one they'd left for it to be coincidence. Vulcan looked out the door before he led them out onto a long gallery and down to a room overlooking the street and the devastation caused by the Qotarr. One of the beasts was lolling in the afternoon sun just outside the gates of the house, and there were two more further down atop the mounds of rubble that had once been fine houses.

"One of the Qotarr escaped when Flin broke its reins, and they couldn't recapture it," said Vulcan. "He had some success breaking the leads they use to direct them, but they're using chains now, so it's more difficult."

"What happened to the one they couldn't recapture?" asked Ezebar.

"It left the city," said Vulcan. "They say it's somewhere to the south. Causing problems, I'll wager, for some poor souls."

They did not stay long, but returned through the tunnel to Arinola's house. Ezebar looked again at the view as they went through the little cave, out across the bay to where the Island of Dead Kings sat silently.

When they were back in the little study and the tunnel was again hidden behind the bookcase, they began to talk of their plans for the night. Shaeli impatiently waited for the sun to set, her hand on her amulet, blinking like an owl. She was tired, and though Arinola kept asking if she'd like to rest, she could not, for there was far too much to think about.

Ezebar listened to the plans made, and though the wait seemed agonising to him also, the time eventually passed and he found himself standing back at Arinola's front gate.

There were many people with them, and as they went through the streets, the crowd thickened. Scouts went forward, looking for the guard who roamed the streets looking for those who were breaking the curfew. A few times they had to detour, but they reached the area near the Landing with no trouble. The moon was a thin sliver low on the horizon and the stars were brightest over the dark and silent city. The people waited in the darkened streets, their weapons gleaming in the starlight. Shaeli looked at the large woman wielding the huge axe who walked beside her, and the woman nodded at her and grinned. Two of her teeth were missing.

Shaeli took Ezebar's hand as they went through the streets, creeping through thin lanes and thick shadows until they were on the far side of the square. She waited only a few moments before she pulled a stone from her amulet.

The long finger of smoky quartz began to pulse in her fingers, and she could feel the answering pulse from the bangles on her upper arms. She looked out at the Traders wrapped in the night, and drew a deep breath, and then she threw a beam up into the sky, high above the square. It flew invisibly into the night and then burst into a hundred balls that began to drop down onto the guard surrounding the Landing. Shouts went up and she threw another invisible ball into the sky. This one shattered lower and the soldiers cowered beneath the balls. She had left some fire in them and when one of the dropping balls hit a soldier, it burned. Cries of pain began to rise over the shouts, the guard milled, some ran to the edge of the square. Light and noise suddenly erupted as people ran yelling into the square, weapons held high, attacking the confused guard.

They waded in with vigour, catching the guard still cringing from the burning light-balls. Shaeli waited for the right moment, and then she took Ezebar's hand and they ran across the square and into the shadows beneath the Landing. She had seen people emerging onto the decks of the Traders as they'd run, and her heart thudded, knowing they would be watching the fight below.

There were still half a dozen soldiers standing at the foot of the stairs, but most of the others had gone to join the battle. Shaeli saw the large woman swinging her axe as she strode through the soldiers, and in a few moments, the six at the stairs had gone to aid the others.

Shaeli went around and dashed up the stairs, Ezebar on her heels. She ran doubled over along the Landing, looking down at the fighting, waiting for one of the guard to spot them and come in pursuit, but they were well occupied, and she reached the landing gate without being seen. She jumped through it and ran across the deck.

They were waiting for her in the shadows beneath the upper deck. She fell straight into her father's arms, unable to see his face for the tears that crowded her vision.

"There, Mouse, there," he crooned. He looked at Ezebar standing behind her and smiled. "We best get you downstairs, there's a lot waiting for you."

Jarris waited as Shaeli hugged her mother and then he shooed them below, taking a look back down at the square before he followed them. The people who had attacked the guard turned suddenly, on some unheard or unseen signal, and they melted back into the streets, leaving dazed, dead, and injured guard behind them.

* * *

Shaeli walked into the big room to be confronted by many faces. There were bedrolls stacked around the room, and they were all there; the three Ammerr, Wendll and Blenny, Spotjaw, Flin and Almarnoch, her aunt and uncle, Andos sitting near S'resh, Crissita and Brudloc, some she did not know. Each of them wanted to greet her, and Ezebar almost lost sight of her as she was surrounded.

Almarnoch came through the crowd to greet him. They had not spoken since the night he had followed Shaeli after she'd been captured in the little village in the foothills far to the north.

"You have done well, lad," he said. "M'zena and the elves, they have been captured?"

Ezebar nodded. "They have been taken," he frowned. "They are somewhere in Great Court."

"Yet the girls are free?"

"Yes," he said. "They, the old queen, Kirrit and the jevvi have escaped." Ezebar frowned harder. "But how do you know of this?"

"We had a visit," said Almarnoch. "A lilac fairy."

"Tish?" said Ezebar. "I wondered what happened to her. I'm glad she's safe."

Almarnoch nodded. "She was most helpful," he said. "Now, come, you must tell us what you can. We have only until dawn."

More came over from the other Trader until the room was crowded with bodies. The windows were closed, curtains drawn and lamps lowered, and as the hot night passed the room grew stuffy with the heat and the plans that were woven. When at last they had decided, they dozed.

Before dawn had even thought of turning the sky pale, they were up again, readying themselves to go to Great Court.

* * *

# CHAPTER THIRTY THREE

The day before, at about the same time as Shaeli and Ezebar were clambering over the rocks beneath the headland, Tarkoda was standing at the water's edge far across the bay. He was looking towards where the city lay, wondering what to do. The sun was high and the bay sparkled, but there were no craft riding its waters, no boats fishing for a feed. The bay was empty, silent but for the sound of itself and the birds that called overhead. Behind him, the two Traders bobbed in the sun, ruffled by a slight breeze, and around them thousands of people readied for battle. The Land shimmered behind the crowds, trembling with the summer heat.

He had not taken the Trader into the city since the loss of Silver Hawk. He had just lifted for the flight to Palveron when the birds of Silver Hawk had flown back to the inn. He had turned around and landed straight away. The Zoi were still in their harnesses and tethered to each other, their cries of distress echoing through the dusk. It was hours before he found out that the black ship had destroyed the Trader, though he'd guessed as much, and much longer before he heard that the people had made it to shore, most of them anyway, but he still didn't know who was safe, who was wounded, who the dead were. He dare not put his Trader or Red Arrow into such a position, and so the food drops to the city had ceased.

He looked from the shimmering land back to the sparkling bay, wondering for the hundredth time what to do. Out on the bay, the water swirled. The swirl appeared again, closer to shore, and he saw an odd line of bubbles. It reminded him of something, and as the memory surfaced, so did a dozen heads. They came from the water, Rizar at their head, and the dozen turned to a score, the score to a hundred, then hundreds. They rose from the water, weapons in every hand, standing in the water behind Rizar, their faces grim, their weapons dripping. Behind them a line of giant seahorses rose, the riders on their backs holding long pikes.

Tarkoda went down to greet Rizar, saw some of Ishaan's friends behind him, and hundreds more he did not know.

"Rizar, what are you doing here?" he said. He glanced back and saw people had begun to line the slope above the bay. "They'll see you," he added pointlessly, knowing they already had.

"It matters not," Rizar said. "We come to join you, lad."

He told of the coming of the black ship to Qorientae and Lythnori as the Ammerr came from the water. The giant seahorses tossed their heads as their riders dismounted and then disappeared beneath the waves. The people on the bank watched with varying degrees of amazement as the hundreds of sea people came to shore.

"It came with the sun, rising up above the cliff from the Straits," Rizar said. "It circled the city, and then a red light shot from it. Many were the homes it destroyed. The tower was the first to go, and three of our Elders were killed there." He shook his head. "Many escaped into the water, but dozens were killed. Aneris will not let this go on. Ammerr from all Lands were told, and each has sent their might."

"How did it know where to find you?" said Tarkoda. "Qorientae is hidden from sight."

"We know not, lad, but find us it did."

"And what of Lythnori?"

"They, too, felt the might of the black ship," said Rizar. "It flew from our lands high over the mountains. Luckily it did not attack our inland settlement." Rizar's face was grim as he continued. "But Lythnori took a mighty wound, and it is said many were killed, almost half the houses burnt. Before the black ship left, it flew up and circled the mouth of the lair. Xyrrol and Mithrina are incensed."

"What will they do?"

"The elves are coming from the mountains," Rizar said. "From the north and the south they come. They will be here by nightfall."

"Nightfall?" said Tarkoda. "They come to help us? You come to help us?"

Rizar nodded. "We do," he said. "Such destruction is intolerable and cannot be allowed to continue. If Zirrus' queen wishes to own the World, she will have a fight on her hands." He shook his head, but then he smiled. "I have just met your sister," he said, taking Tarkoda completely by surprise.

"Shaeli?" said Tarkoda, and when Rizar nodded again, "Where?"

"Out on the bay," said Rizar, smiling more broadly at the look on Tarkoda's face. "She was swimming with a friend." He told Tarkoda of finding Shaeli and Ezebar struggling to reach shore, and the aid he had given them. "She says to tell you that they are safe, not only she, but all of your sisters. I'm sure this means something to you?"

Tarkoda nodded, and his face slowly creased with a smile. He didn't know how, but they'd done it; they'd saved the twins. Suddenly he knew what to do.

"Come, Rizar," he said, clapping the old Ammerr on the shoulder. "Come, there are many who will welcome you back to the World."

He led the man up the slope and the other Ammerr followed them. The crowd at the top had grown large, the faces all showing the same open-mouthed stare. Dorkit stood at the front of the crowd, Delphi and her family behind her. As Tarkoda was introducing them, there came a cry from the Landing.

"Trader," came the cry. "Trader to the north."

Tarkoda turned and saw the ship in the distance. It was too far away yet, to see who it was, but then he saw another flying in its wake, and then another. Soon there were a score of

Traders flying towards them, the voice of a Zoi echoing across the summer afternoon.

As dusk closed the afternoon, the sound of singing came from the north, and across the plains came line after line of elves. Williver's friends, Ky and Jocovar, walked proudly at their head, Williver's father and Qiren's beside them.

As the midnight hours passed, the army of men and elves and Ammerr began to move south, towards Palveron. Their weapons would be stained with blood by morning.

\* \* \*

# CHAPTER THIRTY FOUR

Night still lingered above the city. The last stars struggled to glimmer in the western sky. The day would be hot; already the air was heavy with the sultriness of the coming morning. There was no breeze, and the land, grown cool with the passing of the night hours, readied itself for the day's heat. A flock of sea-birds wheeled above the surface of the bay, the water still dark with the last of the night. Dawn trembled beneath the edge of the World, turning the clouds dotting the horizon to crimson and pink and gold.

In the streets of the city, there was movement. Through the half-light strode great crowds of swaggering guard, and when the guard had passed, scores of dark figures scuttled through the shadows, the glint of weapons in every hand.

As the clouds along the horizon lost their colour, the sun drew a line of light along the sea and then burst golden from the water. Its head now exposed, the sun lost no time in rising, and the clouds drew back in respect. The water of the bay began to glint with light, and soon it was a shining sheath beneath an indigo sky, the sun white-hot and growing bigger with each passing moment.

Shaeli was unaware of the beauty of the sunrise as she stood at the top of the Landing stairs. She looked past Almarnoch to the mass of guard that waited below. On the far side of the square, one of the Qotarr snorted and shifted its weight. The lines of Wokkii on its back rose and fell with the scaly wave.

Beside her stood Flin, Qiren on her other side, and she was reminded of how often she had stood like this with them before a performance. She tried to smile when Flin looked at her, but the smile felt crooked upon her face.

Behind them were Blenny, Ishaan and Ezebar. All the others stood on the decks of the Traders, and she took one last look at them before she followed Almarnoch down the stairs. He held his staff in one hand and a wrapped bundle in the other.

The guard parted as they reached the bottom of the steps, and when they had passed through, the queen's soldiers began to follow them.

They went through the dim, silent streets with the guard and the Qotarr behind them, through the shattered city and on up the wide road to the gates of Great Court. As they went higher the number of guard around them grew. The soldiers lined the street on either side, and when they came to the place where there had once stood houses, the scarlet-and-black lined the road six deep.

They walked silently past the piles of rubble and the hundreds of guard, and, though Shaeli saw in the soldiers the same righteous belligerence as ever, here and there, she also saw faces with lines of doubt creasing their brows.

As they neared the great wall she looked up, and was unsurprised to see the top lined with archers, their arrows already notched and trained on the little group below. The gates loomed ahead and as they walked closer, the great gates cracked open.

Almarnoch stopped, and they waited as the gates heaved open. On the far side of the gate, inside the walls, the road was also flanked with guard. Upon the road stood a small open carriage, the horses nervously pawing the ground. Between the black-and-scarlet rows of soldiers, four people walked out to meet them.

Queen Virrisian stepped first from the shadow of the wall into the morning sun. Her gown glittered with a thousand jewels, and her still-black hair hung to her waist in a thick braid.

On her left stood the man who had been beside her at the Autumn's Eve Hunt, the year the man had slit open the maggot-filled pheasant, the man so quick with a knife, Sir Azeron of Maxx. His handsome face was hardened, the lips thinned with their lack of compassion. He looked at the group before him in the same way as he'd looked at the remains of the pheasant and the man who had killed it, with undisguised contempt.

From the shadows came another man. He came to stand on the queen's right, and Shaeli knew this was the man she had seen in the shadows outside the door in the tower of the Glade.

He was very tall and wore robes of black, symbols in bright scarlet slashed across the chest. His hair was dark, too dark against the sallow face that was cracked with a thousand wrinkles. The skin across his crooked nose was pulled tight, but the rest of his face was as cracked as shattered eggshell. His lips held no colour, and his eyes were set back beneath heavy brows. There was no touch of emotion in the gaze with which he pinned them. Shaeli knew this was the man who brought the black wind; the man who wanted the wand.

The other person to join the trio standing before the gate was the one who surprised Shaeli the most. He came grinning into the sunlight, the only one of the four to show any glee at the meeting.

Garrit strode forward to stand beside the other three, his grin triumphant as he stared at Almarnoch. He wore fine robes and he had grown fat. Shaeli understood then how the queen and the tall cracked man had known about the wand.

"It grieves me to see you here, boy," Almarnoch said.

"That doesn't surprise me," sneered Garrit. "You were always unhappy when someone reached greater heights than yourself. As you see I have."

"You deceive yourself," said Almarnoch. "All I see is that you have grown fat while the city below starved."

"Enough of this prattle," said the queen. "You have what we asked?"

"We do," nodded Almarnoch. "But where are those we seek in exchange?"

"They will be brought out when we see that you have what we want," said the queen.

"Very well," said Almarnoch.

He unrolled the bundle in his hand. Beneath the cover, Shaeli saw the worn and faded wine-velvet cloak that had wrapped the wand for many Winterings. The tattered cloak fell to the dust as Almarnoch pulled the wand from it and held it up. Those of the guard who could see what Almarnoch held gasped, and she drew a breath with them.

The wand shone in the bright morning sunlight, the pink tones in the golden haft glowed, the gems outshining the thousand on the queen's robes, but it was the stone at the tip which drew every eye. The great stone gleamed, rainbows shining from every face.

The tall man with the cracked face took a step forward, but Almarnoch drew the wand back.

"There are those we would see first," said the High Warlock.

Virrisian's lip curled. "I could fell you all with a word," she said.

"Yet you would be the first to fall," said Almarnoch.

Qiren, Flin and Shaeli drew their stones and aimed them at the queen. She laughed.

"I could have had you all killed on the Trader any time I chose," she hissed. "But I wish to make more of a spectacle out of you than that. Yet I shall indulge you," she said to Almarnoch. "For now." Her smile was as cold as her voice. "Bring them out," she called through the shadows of the gate.

Other figures came from beneath the wall. Williver, Llianas and M'zena were pushed forward, their hands tied before them. Shaeli heard Ezebar gasp at the filthy condition they were in, but she did not turn. Her eyes were fixed on the fourth person the soldiers were pushing through the gate.

It was Dari. His robes were clean but his face was sallow, his arms thin, poking from his sleeves as if they had been stripped of the flesh beneath the skin. His eyes were hollow and did not leave the ground as the soldiers pushed him along behind the others.

"These are not the ones we thought to see," said Almarnoch.

The tall man spoke for the first time. His voice was as cracked as his face, rasping between sand-dry lips.

"Do not lie, old man," he said. "You know the two girls taken from the Cave of the Traders have been freed, but you are welcome to these. We have no further use for them."

"How would we know this?" said Almarnoch.

"You were visited by a fairy after it flew from the tower," he said. "We know everything that the loyal traders have been doing for many Moons."

"How could you know?" said Almarnoch.

"This one," the man said, pushing Dari. He fell to the road and made no attempt to rise. "He was eager, at first, to aid us in regaining the wand, but even when he became less eager, he was still useful." Garrit stood grinning beside him, enjoying the words. "His mother dreamt of him often, and was happy to tell him all her news. Even as she dozed last night."

"Do you think we don't know this snivelling city is about to strike?" said Queen Virrisian, with that same cold smile. "They will fail, this time, as they have every other. Cut them free," she said to the soldiers, and while they cut the bindings of the four, hauling Dari back to his feet, she looked contemptuously at the group. "Your little stones and your weapons have no power against the black ship," she said. She looked at the tall man beside her. "You have waited long for this day, Virrek," she said to him. "Let me give it to you."

She pushed at Dari's shoulder, and he and the other three came forward. Dari did not look at Shaeli as he passed, but Williver came to stand beside her, his eyes bright. Llianas, showing a mean bruise above her right eye, went with M'zena to stand between Ezebar and Ishaan.

"Hello, little one," Williver said, quietly. He looked at the others. "Be ready," he said, even more quietly.

The queen stepped forward and stood before Almarnoch. She put out her hand. Almarnoch did not hesitate. He handed her the wand.

Queen Virrisian held it triumphantly above her head. The great stone shimmered in the sunlight. The silent guard watched. The queen looked around at the soldiers.

"Kill all but the girl," she said loudly. "Then go and burn the Traders in the square and feed those you find there to the Qotarr."

She turned her back on them and walked to the tall man, Virrek, the wand held out in both hands.

The guard surrounding Shaeli and the others moved forward, their weapons low. The circle of weapons was closing when Almarnoch looked at Shaeli. He nodded.

Shaeli pointed her fist at the queen. The stone in her hand trembled, the bangles on her arms shivered with it. Shaeli fired.

The deep-purple beam she threw leapt from her fist, yet it did not hit the queen. Shaeli's aim, as ever, was perfect, and she wrenched the wand from the queen's hand just as she was handing it to the tall man. The wand leapt into the air above their heads. The queen screamed in frustration and spun back around.

"Kill them," she screamed.

The guard closed on the little group. Then the city exploded.

From down the hill, there came shouts and the crash of swords. The Qotarr in the middle of the road was suddenly sprayed with arrows. From the rubble around them rose hundreds of figures with long bows and broad swords in their hands. Rocks began to pelt down from the buildings still lining the street further down the road, showering the Qotarr and the soldiers. The guard ducked and turned to defend themselves.

Swords crashed around Shaeli as she drew the wand over the heads of the guard, yet she concentrated only on pulling it closer. Over the heads of the soldiers she drew it, out of reach of the many hands that grabbed for it, and just as it hovered above, she was shoved from behind and her beam disconnected. The wand crashed to the ground near her feet.

She grabbed it, but as her fingers closed over the shining pink-gold metal, she almost dropped it again. Sudden, intense sparks leapt from it, slamming into her fingers. The bangles on her arms grew warmer.

All around her the others were fighting the guard. She could no longer see the queen and her cronies, but M'zena was beside her. The old woman looked at her, her black eyes rich with feeling. She nodded her head, just once.

Shaeli grasped the wand tighter. She rose from the ground and held it above her head, the huge stone pointing at the sky. The bangles on her arms throbbed, the power of the wand, restored by the elves at Lythnori, rippled through her arm and she pushed the magic out into the sky, not knowing what would happen.

The bolt roared screaming from the wand, straight up. She pulled on it and it erupted into a ball of white fire, exploding above their heads in a huge ring. There was a tremendous boom as the ring exploded outwards, shattering the sky with a vast umbrella of silver-white fire, the edges coloured like a rainbow.

The battling crowd around them halted, staring up at the sky in disbelief.

Shaeli lowered the wand and spun around, pointing it at the guard surrounding them.

"Stay back," she cried. "Stay back or die."

\* \* \*

Far across the Land, the echo of the white light from the wand vibrated through an almost-dark cavern. The dots of light that had pulsed there for long days and nights flickered into bright flame. Each flame began to grow. And grow.

\* \* \*

Tarkoda was flying across the bay when the white light exploded in the sky above the castle. He tugged on the lead lines and urged the Zoi to greater speed.

\* \* \*

Down at the docks, the Ammerr were pulling themselves from the water. They had swum swiftly across the Bay of Islands, their weapons ready, their minds firm. They would not have chosen to come thus back into the World, but when the time came, they went quickly from the water onto the docks of Palveron to attack the guard there. A pod of dolphins watched as the Ammerr were joined by the people of the city; watched as their weapons were covered in the blood of the queen's guard.

\* \* \*

Fezzik's sword was also dripping with blood. He had joined the others who had gathered around Dorkit's tavern, arriving at the head of hundreds of people come to do battle for their Land, Bekerra and Bithani and Fozar beside him. Darkness had hidden the multitudes from him, yet by morning he had found himself striding beside a band of elves, heading towards the guard who massed between the Royal Parklands and the city. There were Traders flying above them, each filled with elfin archers, and by the time the sun had come up the battle had already begun. When the great white light had shattered the sky, he had looked at it, as stunned as the rest, then he had turned his face and his sword back to the fighting.

\* \* \*

Sounds of battle began again before the silver-white ring had disappeared from the sky, yet the soldiers around Shaeli and the others did not move. Nor did they lower their weapons. Shaeli took a few steps forward.

"Go back," she shouted again.

An arrow thudded into the ground at her feet. She looked up and saw the soldiers on the wall firing at them. Others were picking off those who were coming from the rubble. Flin fired up at them. Two fell and Shaeli aimed the wand.

Again, sparks flew up her fingers and trembled in the bangles upon her arms before she threw a bolt at the high wall. She thought she had pulled at the magic, reduced it, yet the bolt she threw took out dozens of the soldiers and a chunk of the wall.

This made the guard ringing them do as she'd asked. They took a few paces back. She lowered the wand again, pointing it at them, and took a few paces forward. The soldiers stepped back. She started to walk slowly up the hill, moving towards the gate, and pace by pace the soldiers moved away from her. The others followed her, weapons pointed out.

Of the queen and the three men, there was no sign, and the gates in the shadows beneath the wall were moving back together, the opening growing smaller. She knew that now the black ship would come and seek the queen's revenge and she looked at Almarnoch.

"We have to go in," she said, and he nodded his head.

She kept on walking forward, the silent guard ringing them, the cries of battle filling the streets below.

The gates were almost shut now, and she raised the wand again. The soldiers ahead of them scattered, and she took aim and threw. The silver-white bolt leapt from the stone and hit the gates at head-height with a thud, and the thin line between them widened again instantly as they flew back. The gates opened onto fleeing guard. Two charred bodies lay in the middle of the road.

Shaeli shuddered at the sight of them, but between the running guard she saw a carriage driving away, the horses galloping up to the castle. She looked back down the hill.

They were still being watched by a large contingent of soldiers, but all around was chaos. Swords clashed, rocks and arrows flew through the air. In the road below, the Qotarr was writhing and snorting beneath an avalanche of rocks and arrows. None penetrated its thick skin, but the bodies of the Wokk soldiers on its back flew about as it spun around, trampling the guard in its confusion. Two Wokkii were still alive above its head, pulling at the half-broken chain. The chain snapped as she watched, and the Qotarr snorted and shook its head, throwing the two from its hide. Their bodies thudded to the ground and the beast began to lumber, roaring and snorting, down the hill.

Across the bay, there came a cry, and Shaeli looked over to see Traders in the sky, flying low across the water to the city. They were still far away, but the sight of them swelled in her chest, for there must have been at least a score. The Trader her brother flew was at their head.

Shaeli looked at the others, then she turned her back on the final battle for Palveron and went through the shadow beneath the wall into Great Court. She did not see the two Traders rise up from the square in the city.

* * *

Across the rubble, from the deserted house at the edge of the cliff, Sir Vulcan and Lady Arinola watched the tiny figures go through the gates.

The two old nobles had been up all night. There had been a constant stream of people flitting up Arinola's driveway and through her doors. In single file they had gone through the passage in her grandfather's study, swords and pikes and bows in every hand, down through the tunnel and up through the hidden staircase until there were hundreds in the empty house overlooking the rubble. They had waited, packed into the ballroom and along the gallery upstairs through the night. Before dawn they had begun to leave, sneaking out to hide amongst the fallen walls and chimneys, to wait until they were needed. Many more had stayed in the house, and in the day's first hour they had watched as the queen came from the gates. When she had given the signal to attack Shaeli and the others, they had all heard her, and they had run from the house, charging past the houseless gardens to begin an attack of their own.

Arinola could tell that Vulcan itched to be with them as they watched the battle from the safety of the empty house, and she patted his arm. He glanced down at her, returned the pat to the hand resting on his sleeve, and then his eyes returned to the scene outside.

Shaeli and the others had disappeared inside the wall, but the battle raged on outside the broken gate. Swords flashed in the early sun, arrows flew like raindrops through the air, Warlock fire flashed sporadically, distant cries and screams filtered into the abandoned house.

There was a rush of movement at the edge of their view, at the place where the road led further down into the city. Splashes of rich green were seen as the fighting surged up the hill.

"Look, Vulcan, elves," Arinola cried.

There, amongst the crowd of people who were pushing the soldiers back up the hill, were the tall figures of elves, dozens and then scores and then hundreds, battling side by side with the people. Above the buildings and the battling men and elves, a Trader flew from the city, another beside it; Golden Eagle flying proudly over the buildings of the city, and beside it the colours of Purple Leaf glowed against the high blue sky. The ships rode smoothly above the battle-filled road and the rubble, and many people stood on the decks of both Traders, their weapons glinting.

A shadow suddenly blocked the sun, and they looked to the east to see the side of another Trader flying past them, close enough to see the weapons in the hands of the people on the deck. The rainbow feathers on the underside of the Zoi's wings shimmered as they pulled the Trader up and over the wall, two more Traders in its wake. It was only a short while before they saw the black ship rise up to meet them.

* * *

When Shaeli went through the gate, she expected some resistance and she was right. The scores of guard that had lined the road inside the gates were waiting for them, and Flin and Qiren were firing before they even reached the shadows beneath the wall. The gates had been pushed halfway back by the force of Shaeli's bolt and they ran to shelter behind one.

Shaeli had a light bow and quiver on her back, and she passed these to Llianas, who began picking off soldiers who stood on the roofs of the buildings. Ezebar was at the rear, firing arrows at those brave enough to try and follow them beneath the wall. He stood in front of M'zena, and he was the only one who saw the Traders flying up from the city. Beside M'zena, Dari leant against the gate, his hands wrapped around his chest, paying little attention to his surroundings.

Llianas and Ishaan shot arrows and Flin and Qiren threw beam after beam at the soldiers inside the gates, but to venture out from the shelter of the gate was impossible; they were trapped in the shadow of the great wall.

Almarnoch stood against the gate behind Flin, Shaeli was next to him, and Blenny stood behind her. Almarnoch peered around the gate, and then looked back at Shaeli.

"There are many," he said. "You must clear a path for us."

She nodded and gripped the wand tighter, stepping past him to peer around the gate. There were scores of soldiers, on the roofs of the buildings, behind the thick walls, and she knew there were more on the wall above, waiting for them to step out. She pulled the wand up, and pointed it at a dozen archers on the roof of the first building.

As the magic was building, a body fell from the sky and landed a short distance away. She gaped at the broken, black-and scarlet figure crumpled on the ground. An arrow stuck out from his neck, and she looked up.

A Trader was gliding over the wall, and she knew the patterns of the wood as well as she knew the lines on her palm. It was Purple Leaf, and there were arrows flying from it, aimed at the soldiers who walked the wall and those who blocked the entrance to the castle.

The soldiers on the roofs ducked as the arrows rained upon them, and another Trader passed over, the colours of Golden Eagle joining those of Purple Leaf inside the castle walls.

The soldiers scattered as the two Traders circled and came back, lower this time. Ropes dropped from the sides of the Traders, and as they came across the fields beyond the buildings, people began to slide down the ropes. They were running as their feet hit the ground and the guard turned from the gate and went to meet them.

They inched forward, peering around the gate as the guard were distracted by the Traders.

The cry of a Zoi turned Shaeli's eyes to the east, and for a moment she could not see the shape of the thing that flew out of the sun, yet as she squinted, the shapes of the birds and the balloon it pulled became clear, and she could see her brother on the top deck of the Trader that swept up from the bay. Ropes dropped from this ship, too, and before it was halfway across the headland there were people sliding down them, ready for battle.

Inside the walls of Great Court there was now chaos, as there was in the streets they had left behind. No longer were the guard focussed on the few trying to come through the gate, for they were busy fighting the many that were coming from the skies.

Out from behind the gate and into the fighting they ran, Flin and Qiren first, then Shaeli and Almarnoch, and Ezebar and Williver flanking M'zena, Llianas, Blenny and Dari.

Another Trader flew up from the bay, and then another; Sea Mist and Red Arrow bringing reinforcements to those already on the ground. As they came closer, Shaeli could see the green-clad figures swinging from the ropes.

"The elves are with them," she cried. "Williver, the elves."

The elves swung lithely down the ropes, leaping to the ground when they were still far above it and running to join the battle. The decks of the Traders were filled with them, swinging down as the Traders criss-crossed the ground. The castle above watched impassively as its defences were crushed.

Flin and Qiren led the way. There was fighting all around and several times they were attacked as the went up the road. Shaeli pulled a stone from her amulet, more secure in her wielding of the smaller stone, and she picked off those that still threatened them from the roofs. They moved quickly along the road until they reached the last of the buildings before the gardens began, stopping beside a smithy. They ducked into its dim interior to look out at the fields being trampled by the battle.

Everywhere they looked there was fighting. Shaeli saw Rhubic across a field with some elves, his face ablaze as he fought two soldiers. Near him were Andos and Olando, wielding broadswords with a group of Starislanders. She looked up as her father flew over, archers picking off those still alive on the wall; yet these were much fewer now. Across the fields there were flashes of elf-light, and they could see Qiren's father, Tyllerin, standing amid a group of elfin archers, his wand gleaming in his hand.

Ahead, up near the elaborate gardens, abandoned in the middle of the road, was the carriage that had held the queen and the three men. The horses stood stamping and snorting at the noise behind them.

"Where are they?" Shaeli said, scanning the gardens.

"I don't know," said Almarnoch. "Wait. There they are."

Queen Virrisian was coming from the trees, her master-at-arms beside her as they boarded the carriage, but there was no sign of the tall man, Virrek, or the fat figure of Garrit. The queen took up the reins and slapped them across the horses' rumps, and, already nervous from the shouts of battle, they bolted up to the castle. The carriage flew past the Warlock and Faunist houses and went inside the inner wall. A moment later the gates closed Great Court off from the rest of the headland.

From the trees in the gardens rose the black ship. Slowly it lifted from the treetops, floating as if on a gentle updraft. It hovered over the trees, its black shape leeching light from the sky around it. It turned, pivoting slowly in the air, turning its pointed face to the Traders flying above the battle. It rose higher and the red light flickered on.

"We have to stop it, Almarnoch," cried Shaeli. "The Traders." She gripped the wand tighter. "We have to try."

"Yes, lass, we will," he said. "Williver, Ishaan, Flin, come with us. The rest stay here, use your arrows to protect us."

They stepped out from the building, Almarnoch with his staff before him, Shaeli with the wand in her hand, Flin with his stone, and Williver and Ishaan with long swords. Qiren, Llianas, Blenny and Ezebar came to the door to give them protection from the guard as they went out to meet the black ship, M'zena peering out from behind them. Dari hung back in the shadows, hunched on the ground, his arms still wrapped about his chest.

The black ship was coming slowly across the headland as they stepped out into the sun. The red light at its peak shone brighter, and it turned, surveying the Traders flying over the fields. The light narrowed as Sea Mist crossed its path.

The black ship suddenly shot forward. The red light grew redder still and a bolt flew out and hit the Trader in the rear. The ship lurched in the sky, the birds cried out, but regained their control. Sea Mist turned, flames beginning to spread along the boards, those on deck beating at them as they licked at the ropes leading up to the balloon. Sea Mist headed back towards the cliff, away from the black ship, yet the light from the ship was still trained upon the Trader and again the red eye narrowed.

Shaeli raised the wand and threw a silver-white bolt that hit the black ship just as it fired on Sea Mist, slamming into where ragged chunks like chewed wings thrust out, and although the bolt did not penetrate the ship, it rocked it, pushing it across the sky. The red beam that flew from the black ship merely skimmed the Trader, and a moment later Sea Mist flew, still burning, over the cliff and down out of sight.

A group of the guard came swarming towards them. Some dropped with the arrows that came from the shadows of the smithy, and Williver and Ishaan turned back to meet the rest. Ezebar and Blenny ran from the blacksmith to stand with them, and before Shaeli turned back to the black ship, she saw Llianas standing with a bow in the door, M'zena handing her arrows. Qiren stood beside them firing from his short wand. Dari was invisible in the shadows.

The black ship was swinging around, turning its face to them as Almarnoch began to mumble. The gem in his staff grew brighter, and as the eye of the black ship reached them, a great streak of light flew from his staff, thudding into the front of the thing.

Flin followed it with a series of small intense blue balls that thundered into the place where the red light shone, yet the light did not flicker. Shaeli aimed the wand again, throwing a huge bolt in the wake of Flin's, and still the red light did not flicker. The ship was rocked by her blast, but the magic of the others did not seem to touch it. None of their beams marked its surface.

Behind them the clash of swords came closer, the guard pushing Ezebar, Ishaan, Williver and Blenny towards them.

Llianas had few arrows left and she shot them more slowly, choosing her target carefully. The light in Qiren's wand was fading and he thrust it into his belt, pulled out his sword and joined the others. Blenny hacked at one soldier and the man fell into the dirt, blood gushing from his belly.

"You cannot penetrate it, Shaeli," Blenny yelled, running to them. "It is drell metal, drell made. Even the magic of the wand cannot touch it."

She looked up at the black ship. It was turning its light away from them, disregarding their weapons. Its light sought another Trader, and it did not linger in choosing one.

The Trader her brother flew was flying across the road behind them, and when the red light shone upon it, the Trader turned to fly across the fields. The red light followed it, narrowed, but it did not seek the ship itself. The red bolt hit the balloon that was made from the pieces of others, and a huge hole bloomed first in one side, and then the other as the bolt shot right through. The balloon buckled on itself and the Trader dropped to the ground.

Shaeli gave a cry of frustration and pulled the wand up with both hands. She threw four white-hot bolts at the ship, and though they pushed the ship through the sky, they did not mark the surface. She had not veiled any of the magic, pushing the bolts with the redness of her anger, and she had barely touched it, no more than if she were a gust of wind. She imagined the cracked face of the tall man inside the black ship was even more crinkled with mirth at her puny efforts.

Tarkoda's Trader thudded into a field at the edge of the cliff. The balloon fell burning onto the deck, far-off figures scrambling off the sides. People ran across the fields towards it, some to help, some to attack those who leapt from the flaming balloon. The light of the black ship turned from the downed Trader, seeking one of the others.

Golden Eagle flew close to Red Arrow, Taffka gesticulating wildly. Red Arrow swung away and flew straight towards the cliff edge, disappearing down over the lip, the red heads of Kirrit's brothers turned back towards them as they went.

Golden Eagle turned back. It flew low over Tarkoda's felled ship, and then it headed down to where Purple Leaf circled above the wall. The red light of the black ship followed it, swinging between Purple Leaf and Golden Eagle as if in indecision.

Shaeli looked back to the fighting outside the little smithy. The guard in the road had lost a of few of their numbers, but Qiren was bleeding from the shoulder and the others were tiring. Llianas had no arrows left, and she stood in the doorway of the smithy, holding a small dagger and standing between the soldiers and M'zena.

Something caught her eye down at the broken gate, a glint of light. She blinked and there were more of the tiny glints, dozens, scores, hundreds.

The lights came streaking through the gates hanging ajar beneath the wall, scattering out in little clumps, darting at the soldiers who battled across the fields. Soon there were oaths of surprised pain rolling across the field to mingle with the cries of battle, for the fairies lost no time in loosing their tiny barbs. The sight of them jiggled at something in her mind, and even as she saw Tish streaking up the road ahead of a swarm of fairies, she was remembering what the lavender fairy had said to her in the Forest.

"Almarnoch," she said, swinging around. "We have to get inside it. We can't touch it from out here."

She turned and ran up the road towards the black ship, leaving the others battling the guard behind her. She knew what she wanted it to do, and she bolted up the road, ignoring Almarnoch calling her name. As she drew closer to the ship, it seemed it had finally picked its target. The red beam narrowed. Shaeli pushed the wand into the sky and fired.

She was close enough now to see the ragged shapes along the sides of the black ship, the point at the front, the thicker, rounder back, and she saw the moment that the red bolt flew from it. Her beam connected with the ship at the same moment, pushing it up and across the sky. The red bolt missed Purple Leaf by the width of a tezz leaf, streaking past the Trader and slamming into the top of the wall. Shattered blocks and dying soldiers fell over into the rubble on the far side. The black ship turned and flew lower, closing in on the figure of Shaeli standing by herself in the centre of the road.

She was not alone for long. As the black ship reached Shaeli, hovering over her head, shadowing the road in an obscene parody of a cloud, Almarnoch reached her also.

He had followed her instantly but she had outrun him, and he had struggled to catch her. Blenny was on his heels. Williver broke from where the others were still battling the guard and sprinted towards them.

There were fewer soldiers left fighting now, Flin's beams took their toll, as did the swords of the others and the barbs of the fairies. Across the field, many of the guard were lowering their weapons and raising their arms.

Shaeli knew none of this. She stood looking up at the black ship as it covered her with its shadow. She glanced at Almarnoch as he joined her, flicking her eyes at Blenny as he ran into the shadow beneath the ship with them, and then the three of them turned their eyes up. Williver bolted in from the sunshine, took Shaeli's arm, met her eye and looked up at the black shape above. Another figure skulked into the shadow behind them.

A light began to glow in the base of the ship. It came from an opening in the belly of the thing, and it grew brighter until Shaeli had to shade her eyes. They were surrounded by the white light when the skulking figure bolted into the bright circle with them.

Dari ran in as the light surrounding them intensified. Streaks of purple and black began to run up and down the edges of the light circle.

Outside Flin ran up and tried to leap through the light wall, but he was thrown back. The others came to stand around the light wall encircling them. M'zena, Ezebar, Llianas, Tish and the others stared in at them as they were flooded with the white light.

Ezebar threw himself at the wall and Shaeli watched helplessly as he was thrown back. She met his eyes and shook her head sadly. He was shouting to her, they were all shouting, she could see their mouths moving, but inside the circle of light she could hear nothing. Ezebar threw himself again at the wall of light and again he was thrown to the ground. He stood up, the sword in his hand clutched tightly in his bloody fist, staring at her as the light grew brighter still. The air trembled, the hairs on her arms and neck stood up. As her feet lifted from the ground she looked at Dari. He met her eyes for the first time since she had seen him outside the gate.

"I'm sorry," he said, almost too quiet for her to hear.

She looked at his sallow, haggard face, and all she could feel for him was pity. He had always felt so unloved, and he had been so badly used. She gave him a little smile, took his hand, and then she turned her face up and they were drawn into the light.

As Shaeli's feet left the ground, Ezebar gave a howl of frustration. He circled the bright, black-purple streaked light shaft that imprisoned Shaeli and the others, his heart beating in his ears, drowning all sound of the battle surrounding him. Yet in the end, all he could do was watch as they were drawn slowly up, into the belly of the black ship.

\* \* \*

# CHAPTER THIRTY FIVE

The ground dropped away beneath their feet, the air around them tingled, the scene outside was filtered through black and purple streaks. The faces upturned to them grew smaller, the underside of the black ship grew closer, and they began to hear voices.

Garrit's was the first one she recognised. The answer came from the dry rasping voice of the tall man who had stood beside the queen, Virrek. As the black ship grew close enough to touch, there came another voice, a soft voice, spoken in a droning mumble. The sound of it made Blenny catch his breath. He looked up eagerly into the light, hands clenched tightly on his sword.

Shaeli wondered at the look on his face, and then she remembered.

She remembered the room that had taken them to the top of the falls before they'd entered the drell city; the dark metal disc lowering drell to the ground in the field the day they had looked at the drell mines; the drell that had gone missing over many Winterings, Blenny's wife amongst them. She remembered his quest to find his queen; how he had stopped Flin firing at the black ship when it had attacked their little boat in Nebillonia Straits; and she remembered what he had said just a short while ago, about the ship being drell metal, drell made. She looked down at him.

"Blenny," she whispered. "Are there drell in there? Your wife?"

His brows were low as he returned her whisper, yet his eyes were bright with hope. "That is her voice," he said. "Though altered somehow."

"Do drell control this ship?" whispered Almarnoch.

Blenny nodded. "That is my fear."

"We're about to find out," said Shaeli.

The light surrounded them still, but now all sight of the world outside disappeared behind the black and purple swirls, replaced by dark, pink-edged shadows and dim shapes. As their feet were drawn up into the shadow, something was pushed beneath them, cutting off the circle of light below their feet. The ring of light surrounding them abruptly ceased, and the five of them dropped down onto a cold hard floor. The drop was not large, yet none of them but Williver retained their feet. Shaeli gripped the wand tighter, scrambled back to her feet, and squinted into the dull surroundings.

They were in a kind of pit, a shallow circle, looking up at spear points and dull eyes. There were dark-robed men and women standing around them, a pike in every hand, the points directed at them. All had the white-blond hair of the Wokkii.

Behind them on a higher tier sat a circle of drell. They sat in torn robes, their faces staring blankly, their hands gripping the arms of the low chairs they sat on. As Shaeli's eyes adjusted to the pink half-light, she could see the drell's chairs were part of the ship, the same black metal, growing from the floor. Each of the drell, at least a dozen, were strapped into the metal chairs, their hands clutching balls set into each of the arm-rests. The red rims of their eyes glowed like distant fire.

Behind the drell, on the highest tier, there were only two figures, a leering Garrit and the tall man whose face was cracked with age.

Virrek sat bathed in red light. Behind him, a red gem was set in the centre of a six-sided wheel like a blood-red spider, the spokes holding it in place like thick legs. Between the legs of the spider, the red stone was surrounded by thick crystal, and through it she could see the blue of the sky. This was the only source of light inside the black ship.

"Take us higher," the tall man said.

"As you say, my lord," said one of the drell.

It was the soft droning voice they had heard before and Shaeli looked at Blenny. He was staring at the drell sitting directly below the tall man.

Her robes were thin, her hair matted, her arms poking twig-like from torn sleeves. Her eyes stared dully across the room above their heads, her fingers gripped tightly to the balls set in the arms of her chair. One of Blenny's eyes flicked at Shaeli, the other remained fixed on the drell sitting below the tall man, and she knew that this was the one that Blenny sought.

"Mahra," said Blenny, softly. "Mahra, it's me."

Mahra blinked once, but her eyes did not shift. They remained dull and fixed on the shadows across the room.

"She does not hear you," came the voice of Virrek. He grunted a short laugh. "She is mine. They are all mine, but worry not, you will join her shortly. Some grow weak and 'tis not as easy to catch drell as it once was."

"You are the one who has taken my people," said Blenny, his voice dull as a rusty blade. He took a step forward and the pikes wielded by the Wokkii were thrust towards him.

"You are not as stupid as you appear," the man replied. "When I found your kind had the power to shape this metal and give it flight, I worked long to exploit it. It took many years before I conquered their minds, yet as you see, they work uncomplainingly for me now."

"You have bewitched them," said Blenny. "They do not serve you by their own will."

"Perhaps not, but they *do* serve me, though some grow weak and will need to be replaced. You will do for a start, and the other that came with you to the city shows great promise." The cracked face creased. "Yet I like the idea of flying right into the city of the drell and picking up a few fresh ones. We shall have to see about it, eh, Garrit, when we finish with this rabble?"

"A fine idea," Garrit agreed.

Blenny opened his mouth to reply, but the High Warlock stopped him.

"You'll not find this rabble so easy to destroy," said Almarnoch, putting a hand on Blenny's shoulder and ignoring Garrit. "Your time is done, old man."

The grunt of laughter came again. "I will be around a long time yet," said Virrek. "I have lived far beyond the years intended for me, and will live many more Winterings yet."

"Our magic was not meant to sustain our own lives," said Almarnoch. "You have used your gift for a purpose for which it was not intended. Your face shows you have lived too long and Warlock magic has sustained it."

"I am not governed by your boundaries," rasped Virrek. "As you see, I make my own rules." He waved a hand about. "I needed drell, I took them. I wanted to live long, and I have. I want to rule, I make it happen, though it has taken longer than I expected."

"And more than one attempt," said Almarnoch.

"Oh, yes, but I did not allow for such stupidity," Virrek said. "This time I have been very sure of my people. Some I have trained their whole lives for this moment. Others I have gathered as their talents became known."

Garrit preened at this, the sneering grin growing wider.

"What do you mean?" asked Almarnoch.

"The first time I was young, and did not plan fully enough," said the man sitting high above. "Later, there was my son, Periqol, groomed for greatness. Yet he grew impatient and thought he could bully his way to that greatness. He tried to *pillage* his way up. He was killed, of course. Such a waste of the fine elfin mother I had taken to bear him. If I'd known he would grow to be such a disappointment, I would not have killed her so hastily." He shook his head. "One just cannot rely on one's children to listen." He sighed and shook his head again, as if saddened by the thought. "Ah, but Vermona, she did just as I asked."

"Vermona?" said Almarnoch. "Tarkon's second wife, Queen Vermona?"

"Yes, yes, a fine daughter, obedient," Virrek said. "Always so eager to please. Such a shame I had to ask Virrisian to give her a potion. Vermona was still relatively young, but I had little further need of her and she had become tediously sentimental. Proud of her position, eager for her daughter to be a young lady." That sad shake of the head came again, as if he had been very poorly done by. "I didn't want a young lady, I wanted a ruler, so I had Virrisian deliver her mother a potion, just as she had delivered one to her father some Winterings before." His teeth gleamed in the pink light as he smiled, as if the memory was a fond one.

"You had her murder her parents when she was just a child?" Blenny said the words with undisguised disgust.

"Oh, yes," said Virrek. "It did not bother her nearly as much the second time. She was angry with Vermona for some trifle, I forget just what it was, but my, she was an eager child," he said. "Eager and ambitious. Such a pity her brother took so long to leave us, though it was not from trying. Very lucky man, was Tenelon. It took many Winterings before that arrow at the Hunt. Yet we stopped him from having an heir, at least until the end." Here, he looked at Shaeli. "And we found her, too, even though it mattered little, by then."

"You stopped the king from having heirs?" asked Shaeli. "How?"

"Come now, girl, your mother is a Faunist," Virrek said, as if Shaeli was being particularly stupid. "There are things easily slipped into a meal or a drink. The last time, Irinesta was extremely vigilant about what went into her mouth, and the child lived."

Williver spoke. His voice was colder than Shaeli had ever heard it.

"There is something you forget," he said. "You do not mention something when you speak of your own pitiful attempt to incite the Warlocks, to take Wokk and invade Zirrus. Something that happened after your defeat by Tarkon's father." Williver's eyes narrowed. "You do not mention the Lady Shahlita, how you murdered her and took the dragons from the skies."

Virrek snorted, and rolled his eyes. "I do not deny the elf's death was mine, yet it was her own fault," Virrek shrugged. "She refused to give me the wand and chose to challenge me. I had no other choice." He waved a hand as if an insect had fluttered in front of his face. "But the loss of the dragons was not due to me. Oh, some I killed, yet it was only a means to an end. It was she who sent them away."

"You lie," said Williver, through clenched teeth.

"Now, why should I do that?" Virrek sneered. "The dragons cowered once I had what I wanted. Three I killed outside their lair, more inside as I took from their nests. Others grew maddened with the bolts I threw at their heads. Shahlita and the others could not stop me."

"What did you want so badly that you should betray her so, that you should kill so many dragons?" said Williver.

"Why, the dragon's wealth, of course," Virrek said. "And a stone greater than any other." He waved a hand at the red stone set in the circle of crystal above his head. "This I found, this and enough riches to buy whatever loyalty I desired, but as I came from the lair, those stupid elves confronted me." The cracked face sneered again. "Yet it mattered not. I was far too powerful. The three wielders who had come with Shahlita were easily dispatched, and she stood alone against me." He stopped, pondering the memory. "Her wand was powerful, everything I desired, but she knew I would take it, even though the dragons defended her as I backed her into the lair. I don't know what she did inside that cavern, but when she came out to meet me there were only two with her, the rest I never saw again. Once more she tested the wand against me." He shrugged and smiled. "She was no match, of course. She was mortally wounded and knowing she had lost, she had the dragons rip the wand apart. One took the gem into the lair, and although I sent a mighty blast after it, it kept going. Shahlita took the remains of the wand and flew away on the other dragon. Beam after beam I sent after them, and I know they hit that dragon, but she kept going, east towards the sea. The dragon was seen again, crazed and dangerous, but she never was. I had long given the wand up for lost before young Garrit here made its existence known, albeit unknowingly, to one of the queen's loyal guard, who in turn reported it to his cousin, Azeron, master-at-arms. Garrit was most eager to help. He was instrumental in guiding us to your Cave and pointing out the brats for us. He was most pleased to aid his queen when she asked, weren't you, Garrit?"

Garrit nodded, the gleeful grin stamped on his face.

"The queen. Your granddaughter," said Almarnoch. He did not even spare a glance for Garrit with the news of his betrayal of the Fleet.

"That is so." There was satisfaction in the nod. "I have also kept *her* youthful with my magic."

"But why should Shahlita destroy the dragons?" said Williver. "Her own wand?"

"Perhaps because she knew I would not settle for just some of the riches that lie in the dragon's lair. She knew this because I told her I would not." The gravel of his laugh came again. "I suppose she thought to protect them somehow. It matters not. The elves of Lythnori have kept my people from the cave for many years, yet the taste I gave them of what this ship can do should keep them in their place from now on."

Williver's face paled. "What have you done?"

"Only showed them a token of my power. They and the sea urchins who sheltered you," he said.

Almarnoch stepped forward. "Neither has taken your attack lightly," he said. "Even now they are coming through the gate to aid the people of the Land."

The man above seemed unconcerned. "They will die with the rest," he said. He stood and put his hands on the edges of the crystal ring holding the red stone. "Enough chatter, it bores me," he said. "Let's burn another Trader, shall we?" He turned his back on them and looked out through the crystal. "Take us down," he said.

"As you say, my lord," droned Mahra.

"No, Mahra," cried Blenny, but she merely blinked and the ship dropped lower.

They went down at an angle, and suddenly the ground came into view through the crystal.

They could see pockets of fighting across the fields, the bodies that lay on the ground, the road, the wall. And they could see Golden Eagle as it came into view, flying into the sights of the black ship.

"Follow it," he said.

Shaeli clutched the wand tighter, and the man turned and looked down at her.

"You may be tempted to use your magic, girl," he said. "But know this, I have woven a Protection spell tightly around me. Your magic is no match for it, and know this too; all those that stand with you will be dead before you throw. That wand was not my equal with the strength of the elf Shahlita wielding it. You have little hope."

Shaeli looked a the pikes surrounding them, and then she looked back at him, her eyes unwavering. "You're wrong," she said. "There is always hope."

He turned away and the black ship followed Golden Eagle as it banked around over the fields. Great Court came into sight, but they could see no sign of Purple Leaf. Virrek spoke to Garrit, and Garrit walked around the top tier to the back of the ship. He pulled on a latch and a seam appeared in the smooth lines of the black metal. Garrit pulled and a square of daylight appeared. In the patch of blue sky behind them flew Purple Leaf, the lead bird flying just above the back of the black ship.

"It's here," Garrit called.

The other man did not turn, merely nodded his head curtly. "Stay there," he barked.

He followed Golden Eagle through the skies, ordering the slack-jawed drell to greater speed. Again Mahra followed his orders in the monotone voice and Blenny called to her softly, over and over. Each time she blinked, yet her eyes did not focus.

Shaeli watched as the black ship followed Golden Eagle, seeing it now in the window of the crystal, then gone from view. Her eyes flickered between the crystal window and the hatch at the back where Purple Leaf followed them.

Virrek's hands gripped the edges of the crystal wheel, and she saw the moment the red light began to build. Brighter it grew as it focussed on the ship, and when the beam began to narrow she knew the bolt would soon follow. Virrek cackled as the bolt flew, hitting the back of Golden Eagle with tremendous force. Bits of wood flew through the air and the Trader ricocheted forward, a gaping hole in its rear. Tongues of flame began to lick the wood. The red eye narrowed again.

A cry from the Zoi took her eyes from the red light, and she turned in time to see Purple Leaf veer sharply away. A moment later, something slammed into the black ship and she was thrown to her knees. The others fell around her.

The people with the pikes were thrown about also. Some fell into the pit with them, the rest onto the tier on which they stood. Garrit was thrown backwards and fell heavily. The tall man stayed upright only because he held the crystal ring so tightly. The bolt that was flying from the red stone grazed Golden Eagle but hit the balloon. It too began to burn and the Fleet Leader's ship fell, arcing down towards the wall and then slamming into it, fire engulfing it. It ploughed through the ramparts and fell over the wall.

Williver was on his feet first, slashing at the hooded people before they regained their footing. Almarnoch's staff was also swinging at the hooded figures, Blenny's sword slashing beside him. Dari cowered, his back to the wall.

Blenny cut a swath through the hooded people. Their reactions were slow and he pushed through them, leaping onto the tier above, and going to Mahra's side. None of the drell had moved when the ship had been hit, but now some were blinking slowly. Virrek turned and yelled at them to turn the ship. Those that were blinking stopped and returned their dull-eyed gazes to the wall.

All except Mahra. She kept blinking, and though she answered affirmatively, her voice was hesitant. Blenny was standing before her, calling her name and fighting off the pikes turned towards him when the ship was struck again.

Once more they were knocked from their feet, and this time Shaeli fell heavily. She thought that Flin must be firing at them, for he was the only one powerful enough, yet she had never seen his beams rock the black ship so strongly. She scrambled up, her hand in her amulet seeking one of her gems. In such a small place, she was frightened she could not control the strength of the wand, but the tiny green triangle she pulled from the pouch easily took care of two of the hooded people who kept Blenny from Mahra.

Almarnoch was making good use of his staff, thudding it into the people who came near him, striking the pikes from their hands. Williver was at his back, his sword flying. Dari was still on the ground, watching as the others fought for their lives. Garrit was clutching the wall above and Virrek cried out in frustration.

Shaeli aimed the little green triangle at the crystal window and fired. One of the pieces in the ring exploded out into the sky, and Virrek turned, saw his people losing below, and Shaeli with her fist pointed at him. He cried out again, but his voice was swallowed by a roar. Shaeli caught a glimpse of something streaking past the square at the back of the ship, and then they were struck again. She had wondered if Purple Leaf was somehow hitting the black ship, yet what she had glimpsed looked nothing like a Trader.

Williver shouted to her and she turned in time to fire a tiny green bolt at one of the hooded figures who pointed a pike at Dari, still huddled on the ground. She threw quickly and the man fell with a cry, a wisp of smoke rising from his chest. Shaeli turned to Blenny who was standing before Mahra with a pike at his throat, and she hit the wielder of the pike and the woman dropped to the floor. Blenny turned again to Mahra, cut her bonds and pulled her to her feet, yet she was not eager to stand, to let go of the arms of the black chair. He struggled with her, pulled her harder, and with a cry she rose.

Where her hands had clutched the arms of the seat, two balls of swirling black and purple were set. Two balls of vistrella. The ship lurched as Blenny pulled Mahra from the seat. She blinked again as Blenny shook her, calling her name softly, but she closed her eyes as if she did not see him.

Something flew past the crystal ring where the tall man stood and Shaeli heard him cry out, yet this was not a cry of frustration or anger, it was one of fear.

"Take us down," he shouted. "Take us down."

None of the drell answered him, but the ship began to sink back to the ground.

Virrek gripped the sides of his wheel and the red light began to glow. The beam narrowed quickly and a few short bolts flew from it.

Shaeli threw another light from her triangle, aiming squarely at Virrek's back, yet the green fire disappeared as it touched his robe, and she knew that the Protecction spell he'd spoken of had sheilded him from her magic. She shifted her aim, threw one light, and another, and two more pieces of the crystal wheel shattered outwards.

She was aiming again when something flew past. This time there was no mistaking what she had seen, and she looked at Almarnoch, eyes wide. She opened her mouth to speak, but the ship was hit again, this time a roar accompanied the thud and again they lost their footing. The drell began to blink again.

Blenny and Mahra were thrown to the ground, but when Blenny pulled her to her feet, Mahra's eyes began to lose their cloudiness. She blinked, and looked at him with eyes that truly saw him.

"Blenny?" she said. Her voice was no longer flat and dull, but hesitant, uncertain. "Blenny, is it you?"

"Yes, it's me, so it is," he answered softly, drawing her into his arms.

She fell against him with a cry, but pulled back quickly. She looked about her, the red rimming her eyes burning like flame.

"Cut them free," she said, looking at the other drell. "Oh, quickly, cut them free. He has their *minds*." Her voice was filled with pain, and she took up a fallen knife and began cutting at the bonds of the nearest drell.

The black ship was still dropping to the ground. Most of the hooded people were dead or wounded. Garrit still clutched the wall above, and Williver scrambled up to help Blenny and Mahra cut the drell free. Shaeli climbed up and turned to help Almarnoch when something slammed into them from above.

Many of the drell had been cut free, and several fell from their seats with the impact. Virrek lost his grip on the crystal ring and fell to the ground. The ship shuddered and a moment later it hit the ground with a jarring thud, and all those who had not already lost their footing fell crashing to the floor.

Outside, there was a distant roar. It was answered by another great roar, closer still. Yet another roar, this from right outside. A shadow covered the broken crystal ring.

Shaeli had fallen back down into the pit beside Almarnoch when they hit the ground. She looked up when the shadow covered the light. She was looking into the face of a dragon.

\* \* \*

# CHAPTER THIRTY SIX

Tarkoda was fighting with his back to the smouldering Trader when he saw them coming.

When the black ship had downed his Trader, it had fallen heavily, covered in moments by the burning balloon. He had helped the others off the side, throwing the rope ladder over, and before his feet were on the ground the guard were rushing at them. He ran forward to cut the Zoi free and then turned back to the fighting. Others ran to help him, Andos, Rhubic, Bic, and more, and for a while he had no time to see what was happening overhead. When he did look up he saw the black ship following Golden Eagle, Purple Leaf flying close behind it.

Something in the sky to the north caught his eye. He thought at first that it was more Traders flying to the city, but as the far-off shapes flew across the bay, he heard a distant rumble, like a short burst of thunder. Closer the shapes came, and he caught his breath when he realised what they were.

"Dragons," he shouted. "Dragons to the north."

Eyes turned, shouts echoed his own, weapons were stilled as they watched the dragons come, dozens, scores.

Some rode high in the sky, their wings and bellies glittering, others flew low across the water, their great dark shadows sailing across the bay. All were headed to Great Court. That sound came again, the sound like the distant rumble of thunder, and Tarkoda knew the sound was the roar of the dragons.

Each was covered in dark green scales, but each dragon shimmered with a different hue. A glint of blue, of gold, emerald green or deep red coloured each of them, the colours rich and thick on their hides. Their wings were massive, their tails curling behind them like giant asps.

The guard turned back to the fighting, but they were few and soon those around the smoking Trader began to put down their arms and turn their eyes back to the sky. All across the fields, people were scattering as the dragons swooped towards them.

Tarkoda saw his father riding the air behind the black ship, and Golden Eagle circling the wall. The red light began to glow from the black ship, but Tarkoda's eyes went back to the dragons circling in the sky and he did not see the bolt hit Golden Eagle.

Three flew ahead of the rest. As they closed on Purple Leaf and the black ship, the Trader suddenly veered away, wheeling away towards the south, the voices of the birds drowned by the voices of the dragons. As the red light came again from the black ship, one of the dragons, a shimmering cobalt dragon, put down its feet and thudded into the side of the ship. He sent a silent prayer to the gods as Golden Eagle was hit and crashed through the wall, falling over into the rubble beyond with a terrible noise, aflame.

Tarkoda watched, amazed, as the dragons attacked the black ship, and when it began to sink to the ground, the blow the dragons gave it made it drop from the sky. When the black ship hit the ground, he started to run.

\* \* \*

Jarris was so intent on following the black ship that he did not see them coming. He had seen Shaeli and the others sucked into the belly of the thing and had swept around to fly hard on its tail. When the red light had begun to shine, he had flown closer and seen the opening in the back of the ship, the pale spot of a face peering back at him.

A cry from the deck turned his head and he saw them, scores of dragons flying towards the castle, the ones in front flying across the cliff edge even as he turned. The Zoi cried out, and Jarris swung the Trader away as the first dragon swooped towards the black ship. He flew out over the southern cliffs and turned the ship towards the city where other Traders circled, away from the dragons. He had no need to urge the Zoi to go quickly.

Golden Eagle was flying back towards the wall when the beam narrowed and destroyed its rear.

Jarris looked back as the first dragon hit the black ship with a thud. The ship was pushed through the air and the second bolt skimmed Golden Eagle and hit the balloon. Jarris flew towards Taffka as Golden Eagle hit the wall and fell with a crash onto the the far side, looking back as another dragon slammed into the black ship.

Far above the balloon, dozens of the great dragons circled, their bellies glittering in the early sun. Three of the creatures circled the black ship, and as he turned the Trader, a series of short bursts flew from it. They were aimed at one of the dragons, and it reared in the sky and roared as the beams flew harmlessly by, and then it swept around and thudded into the side of the black ship again. He took the Trader over the wall where Golden Eagle was splintered on the rubble, a few people dragging bodies from the broken, burning ship, and his heart lurched at the sight of it, but he pulled on the lead lines and the Zoi flew back over the wall, above the buildings to the Landing near the stables.

On the ground, the fighting had stopped. Those of the guard who had not already surrendered were staring in awe at the sky. Jarris looked down to see Tarkoda, Andos, Rhubic and some others near the smoking Trader, also staring into the sky. He took the Trader down and landed on one side of the little Landing. They moored quickly, the birds crying out to the giants flying above, and they looked up in time to see one of the dragons crash into the black ship from above. The black ship seemed to be landing when the dragon hit, but the force of the blow thrust it downwards and it slammed into the ground.

The three dragons circled, roared at each other, and then one landed on the front of the black ship.

\* \* \*

Shaeli was looking out into the face of the dragon.

Its scales were thick and green, but tinged with deep blue. Its eyes were golden, patterned with amber and emerald, the pupils diamond-shaped, black and enormous. Its breath blew through the cracked crystals, fogged on the unbroken ones. Virrek skittered backwards as the dragon roared and thrust its face through the ring, reaching for him. The rest of the crystals shattered and the red stone fell to the ground. Virrek grabbed it as the dragon pulled its head back, and he crawled to where Garrit leant trembling against the wall, his eyes fixed on the beast outside.

The ship had fallen at an angle, the nose pointed into the sky, the square hatch at the back looking down on grass.

The others had fallen in a heap with the impact. The drell blinked like baby owls, their eyes still unfocussed. Mahra was speaking to them, shaking the stupor from their faces as Shaeli regained her feet. She looked at Virrek, but his eyes were fixed on the dragon trying to thrust its face again into the ship. Virrek raised his fist, the glint of red between his fingers, and he threw a bolt across the ship as the dragon pulled its face back for another blow. The red bolt exploded, and the dragon roared and disappeared from view.

"Out, boy," Virrek said, pushing Garrit towards the hatch.

Garrit backed away, shrinking into the wall, shaking his head furiously. Virrek pushed him, and Garrit went backwards, his eyes fearfully on the opening where the red stone had once rested, but there was nothing there, only the sky.

Shaeli and Williver started to scramble towards them.

"Stay back," Virrek called, aiming the red stone at them, and pushing Garrit to the edge of the opening.

"No," Garrit cried, but Virrek pushed him on.

Shaeli and Williver had reached the last tier when Garrit almost fell out the hatch. Virrek turned, threw a blast down at them and climbed out after him.

A dragon roared close by.

Shaeli and Williver leapt out of the way of the red flash, evading it easily; the beam had been fired hastily and crashed into the wall opposite. They scrambled up, raced to the opening in the back of the ship, and looked out. Garrit had reached the ground and was cowering beside the ship. Virrek was climbing down steps set in the side. On the ground were the shadows of the dragons that flew above. As Virrek's feet touched the grass, one of the dragons roared again.

Almarnoch scrambled up behind them, and looked out. He looked back at Blenny.

"Stay with them," he said, and he turned to Shaeli. "He'll try and reach the castle," he said. "We must stop him." He looked at the wand in her hand and back into her face. "Will you try?"

She nodded and went to the hatch. "Come on, then," she said with a grim little smile, and she put her foot over the edge.

She looked down as Virrek took Garrit's arm, and they ran up the road beside the gardens towards the Faunist house. She scrambled down the steps and leant back into the side of the ship while Williver and Almarnoch followed her down.

The shadow of one of the dragons grew larger on the ground. It grew and grew, covering the running figures of Garrit and Virrek.

Garrit looked up, and cried out. Virrek aimed the red stone over his shoulder and fired it into the sky. There was a roar, the shadow skittered across the ground, and a dragon thudded into the road in front of the black ship, its shoulder smouldering, its roar cracking the sky.

Another shadow covered the running pair.

They had almost reached the Faunist house when the dragon swooped. They heard Garrit scream as Virrek pushed him, tripping him. Garrit thudded to the ground. Virrek ran on. The dragon swooped.

It was the blue-tinged dragon who had broken the crystal ring, and it landed with one foot on Garrit's back. Its mouth came down and Garrit went head-first inside it, his screams cut off as his head disappeared. His legs still hung from its mouth, kicking feebly as the dragon raised its head. The dragon opened its mouth and Garrit was gone.

Shaeli put her face into Williver's shoulder as the dragon swallowed, and the air was filled with its triumphant roar. She shuddered, and looked back out.

Virrek had reached the Faunist house, yet he did not seek shelter there, but ran straight past towards the castle gates. They cracked open, but he was still a long way from safety.

It seemed the blue dragon knew this, and it hopped into the air and flew towards him. The other dragon, whose shoulder still billowed smoke, took off and flew over the edge of the cliff towards the waters of the bay. Another, this one patterned in golden tones, swooped down from above and landed in front of the Faunist house while the blue dragon flew over the running figure of the tall man and landed in front of the castle gates. Virrek stopped and raised his arm. The dragon leapt into the air, and the bolt Virrek threw skimmed its foot before slamming into the gates. The gates leapt inwards and the dragon roared in pain, wings flapping, hanging above the broken gates. Soldiers scattered along the castle walls.

Virrek raised his arm and fired at the dragon again. The blue dragon dodged in the sky, and the bolt passed close to its tail, just missing one of the turrets before shooting out over the water.

The golden dragon in front of the Faunist house roared, and the tall man spun around and threw a bolt at it. It leapt away, but it was hit near the throat and it screamed, its head thrashing about in agony as the bolt burned into its flesh.

Shaeli could not stand it. "He'll kill them," she cried, and she ran out from beneath the shadow of the black ship.

She bolted into the sunshine as Virrek threw a second bolt at the gold dragon. She pulled the wand up and threw her own beam as she ran, hearing the footsteps of Williver and Almarnoch behind her. The white bolt from the wand connected with the red in front of the dragon, exploding the beam before it hit the dragon in the chest.

The gold dragon turned towards her and roared. The blue hovering before Great Court flapped its wings and rose higher, watching her run forward. The other dragons circled overhead, their shadows peppering the ground.

Virrek turned towards her, and although she was too far away to see his face clearly, she knew he was sneering at her. He turned the red stone towards her.

When the bolt came she was ready for it, and she hit it with her own when it was still far away. It exploded in the air, but there was another coming before she had time to draw breath. This one, too, she hit easily, and the third. She was closing the gap now and as she neared the Faunist house, the gold dragon flapped its wings and rose into the air. It flew up to the roof and perched there, looking down. She hesitated, stopping in the middle of the road, looking up. Williver was with her, Almarnoch still behind.

She only saw the streak of red from the corner of her eye. It was well her reflexes were good, for the beam she threw to meet the red bolt stopped it only a body length away. The colliding beams shattered, showering her with fiery sparks, but she stood firm though her heart beat like a drum in her ears. She was close enough to see Virrek's face more clearly now, and there was no sign of the sneer. There was only boiling, caustic anger in the cracked face.

"Do you think you can save them, you stupid girl?" Virrek shouted at her. "When I have dealt with you, I shall kill them all, one by one, as I always intended. I don't know how you freed them, but they will die this day. All of them."

He threw a bolt at the dragon perched on the roof of the Faunist house. The dragon leapt into the air and the bolt passed beneath it and demolished a chimney and the top of a nearby tree. The tree began to burn and the bricks fell clattering to the ground. The dragon fluttered back down to its perch on the roof again, watching. Virrek turned his red stone back to Shaeli.

She was expecting another bolt, but the beam he threw at her was a solid, unending stream of red. She wrenched power from the wand, and met the red beam with silver white. The two beams crashed together and she felt the force of it to her shoulder. The place where the two beams met was a blaze of light, the magic crackling in the air around it. She could see his face above the crackle of light, filled with superiority and confidence. She felt a push through the wand and she staggered back. Virrek sneered a smile. The red light snapped off. She let her own stop. The bangles surged heat. Her arms throbbed.

"Just give up, now," he said, his rasped voice soothing, reasonable. "You need not sacrifice yourself. You cannot win."

"Perhaps not," she said. "But I think I'll try, just the same."

She threw a short intense bolt at him, knowing it would never reach him, but giving emphasis to her words. Her heart was pounding, her hand trembled, but she raised her chin.

Virrek dealt with her beam easily, and followed her bolt with six short sharp bursts. She almost caught them all. Five she met and stopped, one flew past her, missing her face by a hand's width. She heard a cry and spun around, knowing Almarnoch was still behind them. He stood unharmed in the road, but he was looking back. Dari was writhing on the ground in the road, his arm ablaze. Almarnoch ran to him, covered the flames with his cloak and slapped at them as Dari screamed in pain.

Further down, there were people beneath the black ship and hiding in the gardens, others were running towards them from the battlefields. Every one of those people were looking at them, their eyes flicking skittishly at the sky where the dragons circled, but mostly intent on the battle outside the castle gate. Purple Leaf had landed down by the wall. A coil of smoke showed the place where Golden Eagle had fallen. Dari lay screaming in the road, smoke rising from his clothes.

Shaeli's face paled and she glanced at Williver, but he grabbed her shoulder and pulled her to the ground. The bolt flew over their heads and went on down the road to where the people clustered around the black ship, exploding into the side of it. People scattered.

Shaeli had the wand up as she rose from her knees, a deep frown creasing her forehead. She threw a series of answering bolts even as she stood, her arm straight, a cry of rage in her throat that she did not hear.

Virrek answered each bolt with one of his own, the confidently sneering smile still on his face. When he fired at her again, the beam did not end, but pushed in an unbroken stream at her magic, reaching for her.

She thrust back at it, grasping the wand with both hands, she pushed at the red beam. The beam from the wand grew brighter and thicker, rainbows began shooting through its silver-white depths. The bangles on her arms crackled and sparked with magic.

Virrek was pushed back a step and the sneering smile disappeared from his face. His eyes narrowed, the red beam grew brighter, and Shaeli gasped at the force that shuddered through her hands. She pushed harder, dredging all the magic she could, seeking deep inside for some strength she may have missed.

The red beam wavered, the confidence in Virrek's face wavered with it, and Shaeli took a step forward. Virrek's brows lowered, and his arm rose slightly. The red of his light grew even more intense. It pushed at her light, thrusting it back at her.

Shaeli staggered and Williver's hand steadied her. She felt a rush of magic from his fingers and she grasped at it with her own.

Williver gasped as he felt Shaeli draw the magic from him, yet he did not try and fight it. He gripped her shoulder tighter, opening his magic to her, and the silver of her beam glowed a little more brightly, the rainbows shot faster through the white glow.

Virrek's confidence had shone again for a moment when Shaeli staggered, but was gone when the magic of the elf was drawn into her own.

Shaeli pushed, and regained some of the ground she had lost. A hand grasped her other shoulder, and she felt Almarnoch's strength flow through her. She drew it down too, sucking the Warlock magic from his fingers and turning it into her own.

The streak of silver light from the wand grew longer; the red stream from the other's stone grew smaller. Virrek's face had lost the confident, sneering smile altogether now. It had been replaced by tendrils of fear.

Shaeli pushed again, but she could not shrink his red light any further. She could feel Williver's magic was almost gone, Almarnoch's was quickly draining, and she knew she could not hold him alone. She drew a breath and tried again.

Something grasped her ankle, something that held magic in its grasp and she drew it into herself and pushed again, drawing on everything she had and thrusting it through the wand. The red beam narrowed, fear shrivelled the cracked face of Virrek. As Shaeli's light reached him, he dropped his stone and threw himself back.

The red stone exploded into a thousand pieces with the force of the silver light from the wand, the pieces showering the figure of Virrek, tumbling through the air like drops of blood.

Shaeli stopped the flow and lowered her arm. She looked at Williver. His face was pale, but his eyes were vibrantly blue. On the other side Almarnoch still had his hand on her shoulder, but now he leaned there, breathing heavily. Behind them in the road lay Dari, one arm outstretched, the other a blackened mess. She looked back at Virrek as the dragons began to roar.

Virrek scrambled backwards as the blue dragon flew down and landed before him. He put up an arm as the dragon lowered its head, yet the arm and the scream for mercy did little good. The dragon grasped him in one huge claw, and with a roar, flew the still-screaming man into the skies. Up it went and up, Virrek's struggling body growing smaller as the blue dragon flew its prize up to the others. When it reached them, they flocked to it, and then the dragons began to squabble over the struggling thing in the blue dragon's claw. Shaeli looked away as the body was torn to pieces high above the castle.

* * *

# CHAPTER THIRTY SEVEN

She slumped, lowered her head, and turned around. Almarnoch straightened his back, his breath coming more evenly now, his brows quivering and his lips curved.

"Well done, child," he said.

He shimmered and she swiped at the tears threatening her sight. She looked at him, Williver smiling at her too, his face pale, and then she squatted down to Dari.

When she had stopped her magic, his hand had fallen from her ankle, and now he lay in the dust, eyes closed, one arm burned, blood seeping from his nose. His magic had been the thing which had given her the strength to overcome the red stone; to stop Virrek once and for all. Without Dari, she could only wonder at what would have happened, and she took his hand, and called his name softly. He did not move.

There were shouts from the road, and through the crowd clustered around the black ship came figures, all running towards her. She saw her parents, uncle and aunt, cousin and brother, her Cave year friends, and more, yet her eyes sought for another. She saw him at last pushing through the crowd, M'zena sheltered beneath his broad shoulder, and she smiled.

She lost sight of him as they all reached her. She was enfolded in her mother's arms, and then Mareesha crouched beside Dari and Eenis was calling his name and crying. Shaeli's eyes filled with tears at her father's strong arms, and then Tarkoda was there, a bruise streaking his cheek, but his grin intact. She was surrounded by smiling faces, but many kept glancing nervously at the dragons swirling in the air above.

As Ezebar and M'zena reached the edge of the crowd, the dragons began swooping back down.

"To the Faunist house," called Almarnoch, and the little crowd clustered around Shaeli began to run.

Dari was picked up and carried across the grass to the Faunist house. The door there opened, a group of Faunists came out and stood on the steps, peering into the sky and down at the black ship laying in the gardens down the hill. As the dragons streaked down from the sky, people scattered across the fields and gardens, sure the dragons were coming to feast on them.

Shaeli rushed over to Ezebar, and helped M'zena across to the Faunist house. Their eyes met over the tiny woman's head, and he shook his head at her and smiled. She smiled back, the tears again prickling at her lids. A shadow covered them. She took M'zena's arm and together they propelled the old woman up the stairs beneath the shelter of the covered front entrance.

Most had run straight through the doors into the Faunist house, but Shaeli stopped in the doorway and looked up.

The dragons were swooping to the ground, all of them, raining from the sky, landing in the trees, on top of the black ship, on the roof of the Warlock house, and on the ground outside. The roof of the Faunist house thudded as one landed on it, and someone in the hall behind them screamed.

The blue dragon landed right in front of the Faunist house, its massive form stretching across the circular driveway, the blue sheen on its scales reflecting the sky above. It roared at them clustered in the doorway, and Shaeli could see right down its throat. Her heart thudded and she shrunk back.

The dragons surrounded the Faunist house, looking at her. The eyes of the blue dragon met Shaeli's and she was drawn to their golden depths.

Something happened as she stared into the richness of the dragon's eyes; something amazing. The fear stopped clutching at her chest, and some of the golden warmth coming from the blue dragon's eyes replaced it. She took a step forward.

Tarkoda took her arm, and she turned and looked at him.

"It's alright, Koda," she said, and she turned back to the dragon.

Again they stared at each other, and she began to smile. She walked forward, out into the sunshine to stand at the top of the steps, looking across at the dragon. She looked up and saw a reddish dragon perched on the roof directly over her head, but she was not frightened. She looked back at the blue dragon, and bowed her head.

When she looked back up, the dragon was staring at her, and then it raised its head and roared at the sky. One by one the others joined it, until they had all raised their voices to the sky. The noise was deafening, the windows of the Faunist house rattled, and Shaeli ducked her head, yet she did not move. She knew they would not harm her.

When the roar of the dragons ceased, each lowered its head to the ground.

From the shadows of the doorway they began to come out behind her, watching as the dragons bowed to the one who had released them back into the World.

Shaeli looked very small as she stood at the top of the steps, and she felt it. When the dragons raised their heads her face glowed, and she raised the wand and fired a silver white ball high into the sky.

The dragons roared again as the skylight exploded, and as one they leapt into the air. Some flew down over the city, others streaked across the bay, most flew up to ride the sky high above the fading skylight.

The blue dragon looked at Shaeli a moment longer, then it bowed its head again and leapt into the sky. It flew up and circled the castle, roaring, and then it landed on the tower of the Glade. It threw its head into the sky and roared again.

\* \* \*

Shaeli went down the steps and looked up at the dragon sitting on top of the tower of the Glade, and then back to the people at the top of the stairs.

"Great Court must also be freed," she said.

"And so it shall," said Jarris. "Come, we shall rally an army for one last battle. But first we must see to Golden Eagle."

He came down the steps, put a hand on her shoulder and looked into her eyes for a moment, then he smiled and they followed him back down the road.

Golden Eagle had fallen amongst the rubble on the other side of the wall. A few had scrambled unharmed from it, dragging the bodies of the dead and wounded with them as the flames crept hungrily through the Trader. What was left of it was now almost consumed. Beside it lay the body of Taffka, Sir Vulcan sitting on a rock beside him. Taffka's head was tilted unnaturally, his eyes closed. Next to him, the Lady Arinola crouched over Renn. Her chest, caved in on one side, was rising, but barely, and as Jarris sank to his knees beside her, a soft sigh came from her and she breathed no more. Dead too was Rennan, sheltered on Golden Eagle since he'd been injured when the black ship sank Silver Hawk in the bay. He had been in the back of the ship when the first red bolt had hit, and what remained of his body was covered in a cloak, only one leg poking from beneath it. Almost a dozen others were also dead on the ground, covered with grit and ash from the smouldering hulk. Rafi was still on his feet, a blistering burn covering one cheek. He stood looking down at his parents, and as his mother sighed her last breath he crumpled to the ground at their feet. His tears were mirrored by every trader clustered about him, and then Rhubic pushed through the throng and took Rafi in his big arms and held him as he sobbed, his own face wet, his eyes on the body of Rennan, his best and most loved friend from their Cave Year, and on the still forms of Taffka and Renn, who had become his family too with his time spent on Golden Eagle.

Others were dead, many others, bodies littering the ground outside the gates and down the wide street that led to the Landing in the square; people with ugly sword wounds, with arrows through their throats, their backs; elves and Ammerr crumpled and bloody; a Warlock with his arm in the road beside him, the hand still clutching his staff. And more. So many more. Shaeli followed the contingent carrying the bodies back through the gates to the Faunist house, tears clouding her vision.

Blenny and Ishaan stood beneath the black ship, guiding the shattered drell to the ground. They blinked up at the sun, at the gardens around them and the great castle filling the sky. Mahra followed the last one from the black ship, embracing Blenny as she reached the ground.

From the fields littered with the refuse of battle came Wendll, followed by Spotjaw, a bandage wrapped around the tall man's head. Wendll bowed before Mahra, who smiled and placed a hand upon his head. When she took her hand away, Shaeli saw there was a small stone set into her palm, a stone the colour of dark honey. She caught only a glimpse, for Mahra put her hands in her sleeves as they neared. Blenny put an arm around her shoulders, and bowed his head to Shaeli.

"You have given the drell a future, my friend," he said, one eye flicking to the woman beside him. "I give you our thanks, so I do. You shall ever be welcomed in drell lands."

"Oh, Blenny, without you I would never have made it," Shaeli said. "We all do our part. I'm just so happy you found them."

She smiled at Mahra, and turned around, scanning the crowd. Her father was rallying whoever he could for the assault on the castle, Tarkoda by his side. Ezebar came with M'zena, gently elbowing a path through the people to her. The old woman hugged her, her face creased.

"You have done well, child," she said.

"Thank you, M'zena," Shaeli answered, looking over her head at Ezebar.

He took a step forward and took her shoulders. "You had me worried," he said.

"I was a bit worried myself, for a while," she said, quietly.

Time slowed around them as they looked at each other. Voices stilled. He smiled and pushed a strand of hair from her face.

Time and noise began again as her brother ran up and grabbed her hand.

"Come on," Tarkoda said, pulling at her. "I need you."

Ezebar dropped his arms instantly, the smile disappearing.

"Wait," Shaeli said, pulling Tarkoda back. "Wait, I want you to meet someone. Koda, this is Ezebar, and you know M'zena. Ezebar, this is my brother, Tarkoda."

Tarkoda dropped his head to M'zena, and looked at Ezebar. He stuck out his fist.

"We have heard much about you," said Ezebar, taking it.

"My sister always did talk too much," grinned Koda.

"Most of it was from our friend Kirrit," smiled M'zena.

"Kirrit?" Tarkoda's brows rose. He looked at Shaeli. "Where is she?"

Shaeli laughed. "She's safe, Koda," she said. "She's with the twins. Somewhere."

"Somewhere?" Tarkoda repeated, frowning. "But..."

"Did you want me for something?" Shaeli interrupted.

"Yes," he said. "Da wants you and Flin on the flanks." He looked at Ezebar. "We could use all the help we can find," he said.

Ezebar put a hand on his sword. "Stay with the drell," he said to M'zena. He looked back at Tarkoda. "Where do you want me?" he said.

They were walking over to where Jarris stood when a horn sounded from the wall. They turned as a column of people walked through the broken gates. At their head strode a big, dark-bearded man, battle weary but smiling. He was surrounded by rebels and elves, Ammerr walking among them, and at his shoulder was a huge woman holding a Warlock staff.

The people of Palveron followed them victoriously through the gateway.

Williver went to meet his kindred, his smile broad.

\* \* \*

Fezzik was weary, but he was more content than he had been for a long time as he walked through the gates of Great Court. He had battled half the night, cutting a swath through the guard who surrounded the city, taking first the Royal Parklands and then the outlying villages. Many had fallen, his brother, Fozar, had been injured terribly, but they had pushed on, determined, and the guard had fallen slowly back.

He had been fighting in the city's streets when the Traders began circling the castle and the city, and he had seen glimpses of the black ship, yet he had not seen the dragons until they were swooping around the castle, and for a moment he had stood, mouth open as the dragons filled the skies. When he saw one hit the black ship, he had known then that they would win, and his battle cry was a triumphant, joyful sound.

Now, as he walked up the road surrounded by people and elves and Ammerr, Bekerra at his side, he saw other legends clustered before the fallen black ship. He bowed to the drell before he joined the army who sought to free the castle from the dark stain which the Queen Virrisian had cast upon its glory, his eye going again and again to the dragons above. He wondered as he waited for the battle if Verlie, Pemba and the children could see them.

\* \* \*

As greetings were made under the midday sun, the dragons rode the skies.

The blue dragon perched on the tower of the Glade, waiting and watching the army gather below.

Beneath its talons, in the shadows beyond the balcony, Queen Virrisian also waited.

\* \* \*

The last of the queen's guard waited for them also. They had pushed the damaged gates closed and archers lined the walls, but the faces of the guard showed none of the assurance they had swaggered about the city with for so long.

There were many introductions made as they planned their assault on the castle, and Shaeli stood in the sunshine with dragon shadows peppering the ground, Ezebar's arm around her, and she raised her head and looked up at the tower of the Glade, ready for the battle ahead.

\* \* \*

Fezzik, already known among the elves and Ammerr for his bravery as well as his stature, asked where his people were needed; all were eager to aid them in this final battle to free their Land. He had been surprised to find many faces in the gardens before the castle that he already knew, and was greeted as a hero by Flin, an accolade he modestly brushed aside. He had fought his way into the city expecting to be met by a wall of guard and the giant lizards. Soldiers they had found in plenty, but they had found few of the lizards. He told them the city had been taken easily after the coming of the dragons and the defeat of the black ship, and the last guard had surrendered their arms, but, amazingly, the Qotarr had gone.

Rizar told them what had happened. He was fighting with other Ammerr on the docks, and they had seen the dragons come and the black ship thrown from the sky, and two of the Qotarr had been swum out to their barges by their Wokk riders and rowed over to the square ships. After the dragons had landed in the castle grounds, they had been fearful, he said, of what was happening, but when the dragons had flown again, a few had gone down into the city and attacked the remaining Qotarr. As fearsome as the giant lizards were, they were no match for their larger, stronger cousins. Wokkii bodies had rained from the backs of the lizards as the dragons picked them up and carried them away, writhing, dropping them onto the rocks beneath the headland. Their bodies now lay broken, a feast for hungry dragons. Several feasted upon them now, he said, pointing to the south. As he pointed, five dragons streaked up from below the cliff edge, flying up to join the others high above. Four more dropped down and flew beneath the cliff to feast on the dead Qotarr.

Shaeli shuddered at the thought, and as she turned to her father, there were gasps and exclamations from the rear of the gathered people. She turned around again just as a cloud of fairies flew above the upturned faces and came to hover over them. One lilac spark detached from the glittering lights and flew down to hang in the air before her face. Ezebar stood quietly behind Shaeli; he had shadowed her every move since she'd shattered the red stone.

"Hello, Tish," Shaeli said to the light hovering before her face.

The fairy curtsied in mid-air. "Greetings," she said. "You have achieved much since I saw you last."

"My sisters are safe," Shaeli nodded.

"And more," said Tish, looking up at the sky.

"I don't think I had much to do with that," said Shaeli.

Tish laughed, the tinkle of a small bell. "They have waited long for the wand to be whole," she said. "When you made the wand your own, they were free."

"You knew this?" Shaeli said.

"The Forest knows all," Tish nodded. "But the Forest knows 'tis best one learns the greatest lessons for oneself. Now," she said, looking around at the array of amazed faces watching her. "There is one more battle to be won. May we be of service?" she asked, turning to Jarris.

"Ah, why... yes," he stammered. "The, ah, archers could be a problem."

Tish nodded. "We shall wait for your signal," she said.

She flew up to rejoin the cloud of fairies and they flew over to a nearby tree to wait. Rough, battle-dirty men watched them with faces like small boys. Women weary from Moons of despair smiled in wonder as they passed. Jarris looked at Shaeli.

"It seems you've made a few new friends since the Wintering," he said. Shaeli smiled and Jarris put an arm about her. "Come, Mouse," he said. "It is time to rid the World of the blight the queen has thrown over it."

Shaeli shook her head. "She was used, too, Da, just like…" she hesitated. "Just like Dari." She looked to the Faunist house. "Will he be alright?" she said.

"I don't know," Jarris said. "Eenis and your mother are still with him. If having two score of Faunists around him does not help him then only the gods can."

His arm tightened about her shoulders, and then they walked over to stand before the battle-ready crowd.

When all were assembled, he raised an arm, but not before wishing that it was Taffka, not he, who commanded this final battle. The loss of the Fleet leader and his strong, tiny wife was an open wound in his heart.

The fairies flew from the tree and spread out before them. The sun hung high overhead, dragons circling beneath it as Jarris turned and began to walk between the elaborate gardens, past the silent Warlock and Faunist houses, to the wall surrounding the castle. Behind him, the lines of people and elves and Ammerr raised their weapons and followed him. Inside the castle walls, a trumpet sounded.

From the roof of the tower of the Glade, the blue dragon watched.

Shaeli walked past the Faunist house looking at its windows, her brother on one side, Ezebar on the other. Faces stared back at them as she passed, and she knew her mother's face was one of the small white spots she could see pressed against the window panes. She raised an arm, and turned forward once more.

On the far side of the crowd she could see Flin and Qiren, and across the face of the crowd that advanced upon the castle many others who she held dear; Andos, Spotjaw, Wendll and Blenny, Williver, Ky and Jocovar, others she had met at Lythnori, Llianas walking proudly with them. Many were the Ammerr, too, striding along beside Ishaan, Cheval and Olando. Members of the Fleet mingled in the front line; Kaplan of Silver Hawk, which now lay beneath the waters of the bay, Rhubic, Tajindi and the rest of Kirrit's brothers, Bic, Jezzyn and more. Fezzik and his rebels strode forward in the centre of the line. Jarris led them all, men and women, elves and fairies, drell and Ammerr. He stopped an arrow's flight from the gates, and they stopped silently behind him.

Black and scarlet lined the walls before them. The closed gate sported a blackened hole, yet it was barred tight against them. Hundreds of arrows were poised in bows, ready to strike. They could not know how many more waited inside. Jarris signalled to the fairies, and as they took off for the gates, he raised an arm and leapt forward with a shout.

The fairies sped towards the walls, dodging arrows, sweeping downwards into the archers on the wall. Arrows followed the fairies, and here and there a figure fell over the wall to land sprawled and broken on the ground. Shaeli waited for the signal, and when it came she aimed the wand and fired at the closed gates. The bolt from the wand hit them with a boom and they burst inwards, the air shrouded with dust and splinters. Inside, the guard scattered, then reformed to defend the shattered gate. On the far flank, Flin was making short work of the archers on the wall, and Shaeli pulled out her quartz finger and began helping him. The fairies buzzed amongst the guard, sweeping down, shooting a tiny poisonous barb and then flashing away.

Jarris and the others met the guard in the opening where the gates had stood only moments before, and for a while Shaeli could not see what was happening there.

The guard defended the gate with gusto, but they were sorely outnumbered, and by the time Shaeli, Tarkoda and Ezebar reached the gate, the guard had been pushed back past the fabled well to the courtyard beneath the turrets where they had created a blockade, holding the forces at bay. As they ran through the gate, Shaeli saw another small pocket fighting at the foot of one of the turrets. The queen's master-at-arms, Sir Azeron, was at their head, and his band cut down all who attacked them. She looked up, saw the dragon perched high above, and then she scanned the melee.

Williver and Llianas were sheltered behind an empty carriage near the base of the turret, and she, Tarkoda and Ezebar ran to join them. Arrows thudded into the ground as they ran across the courtyard, and she looked up to see archers on the balconies above. Shaeli looked around for a fairy, but they were busy dive-bombing the archers around the main fighting, so she aimed her quartz up and fired a bolt at the soldiers on the lowest balcony. The bolt exploded in their midst and they fell screaming to the ground, and she fired another bolt, higher up. These too, fell to their deaths and the soldiers on the other balconies quickly disappeared. Those who had been pinned down by the archers looked at her gratefully, and turned their attention to the soldiers at the foot of the turret.

The guard had set up barrels in the doorway, and she threw a bolt that blew two of the barrels into the sky. The soldiers fell back for a moment and then they rushed out into the courtyard, weapons held high. Their valiant assault was almost pitiful with the forces gathered to meet them and they were disarmed quickly.

Shaeli did not see Sir Azeron amongst them, and she looked back at the doorway they had defended. Azeron was peering out from the shadows, and as his men were defeated, he disappeared.

The last of the guard were throwing down their weapons when Shaeli, Tarkoda, Ezebar, Williver and Llianas followed Azeron through the door.

Across the courtyard, Almarnoch saw them go. He called to Jarris and Flin and they ran across the blood-stained stones and into the tower.

Inside the doorway, they stopped as their eyes adjusted. They were in an entrance hall, wide and elaborate. To their right, a set of stairs ran up. From above they heard the sound of footsteps and they followed them up.

They caught up to them at one end of a long hall. Jarris ducked an arrow as they rounded the corner, leapt back, and saw Shaeli and the others crouched inside a room across the hall.

The walls of the hallway were lined with portraits of long-dead kings and queens, their eyes looking regally down at the arrows flying past them. The arrows thudded into the wall nearby.

Shaeli and the others were sheltered in the doorway of a vast library. At the far end of the long hall, the staircase was barricaded, and two score of soldiers were staunchly defending it.

Flin looked past Jarris, met Shaeli's eye and motioned to her to stay where she was, for his view of the soldiers was broader. He judged the distance, and threw a series of tiny balls at them. The balls flew invisibly along the hall, past the aloof gazes of the monarchs, and zoomed around the edges of the barriers to ignite a few of the bows of the soldiers. There were cries as the burning bows were dropped and then Almarnoch stepped out into the hall.

"Throw down your weapons," he said. "The castle has been taken. There is no need for you to lose your lives also."

There was silence from behind the barricade, and then a dozen arrows were loosed at the old Warlock. Shaeli saw them coming and managed to hit a couple, Flin burned several more and Almarnoch evaded the rest.

Flin looked across the hall. Shaeli shook her head, pursed her lips, and shrugged at him. He nodded, and together they leapt out into the hall and threw a bolt at the barricade.

They threw only one bolt each, but it was enough. The two bolts flew side by side down the hall and blew the barrier at the base of the stairs into pieces. Cries of pain followed as the bolts faded, and a moment later weapons were thrown out and the soldiers stumbled from behind the barriers. Several were wounded, one carried by the others, and they came up the hall with their heads bowed. Almarnoch sent them down to join the others of the guard who had thrown down their weapons at the castle's gates. Sir Azeron lay dead on the floor, the hole in his chest still smoking, his black eyes staring up at nothing, the coldness they had held in life now replaced by the coldness of death.

They watched the soldiers go, and then they went through the shattered barricade and up the stairs.

It was eerie, going through the elaborate empty castle. The sounds of fighting below faded and then ceased altogether. Almarnoch and Jarris led the way, Tarkoda, Shaeli and Llianas behind them, Williver, Ezebar and Flin bringing up the rear.

When they entered the final staircase, the elaborate setting stopped. The walls were faded, the paint was peeling here and there, and there were no rich tapestries or smiling portraits on the walls. They crept up, expecting resistance, yet they met with none. As the top of the staircase loomed, Shaeli recognised the doorway she had shattered from inside the room.

They came out onto a small landing. There were no chairs or tables or anything adorning the space, nothing except for bloodstains on the floor. Shaeli looked away from them to the broken doorway of the Glade Room.

Almarnoch led the way across the stained floor and stepped into the room. Shaeli did not see the queen at first as she followed him, and she looked about the enormous room.

She had seen the room only from the other side, and the magnificence of the mural struck her anew. The trees stretched to the lofty ceiling, the blades of grass seemed to tremble in the shafts of painted sunlight. The faces surrounding the empty glade looked filled with anticipation.

The rest of the room showed old-fashioned, but lovely surroundings. The rugs were a little frayed at the edges, the cushions and curtains were thinning, but the sun shone through the coloured glass and crystal windows and the bay sparkled serenely through the balcony doors.

There was movement on the far side of the room. The queen stepped out from the shadows at the edge of the mural. She was no longer dressed in the sparkling gown she had been flaunting when she'd met them at the gate that morning, but in the garb of a warrior, a hunter; the costume she had worn to the Autumn's Eve Hunt the first year of Shaeli's apprenticeship. One hand was curled into a tight fist, the other held a sword. With a cry, the queen rushed at them, the sword held high above her head.

Shaeli raised her own arm and threw a bolt at the queen. The sword was ripped from her hand and fell to the floor with a clatter. Queen Virrisian screamed in frustration and stopped in the middle of the room.

Somewhere in the distance, a bird called a lilting song, but from the roof above, there was a crash and a thud. Outside the doors of the little balcony, the blue dragon appeared. It hovered in the air, its golden eyes looking in at the queen, and then it roared and the stench of its breath rolled into the room. The queen screamed, and stumbled away from it, back into the shadows beside the mural.

"It's looking for me," she screamed. "Make it go."

The dragon circled outside and came back to hover outside the window. It roared again and the queen screamed with it. The dragon flew away and there were the sounds of it settling on the roof again. A few tiles slid off and fell past the window. One shattered on the balcony and the shards scattered across the floor. The queen screamed again.

"You," she cried, pointing a finger at Shaeli. "You have done this. Take your dragons and leave my city."

"The dragons are not hers to order. They have been restored to the World by the wand," said Almarnoch. His voice was stern, but not unkind, as if talking to a wayward child. "And the city is yours no longer."

"It is mine," the queen snarled. "The Land is mine. Soon all Lands will be mine to rule."

"You are wrong," said Almarnoch, almost gently. "The other Lands have defeated you. Your own people, neglected for so long, have defeated you."

"He will make them listen," said the queen. She raised the clenched fist to the sky. "The black ship will make them all listen."

"The black ship is no more," said Almarnoch. He still spoke quietly, the reasonable words tinged with pity. "It lies empty outside your gates. The dragons have taken their revenge on him. None shall ever listen to him again."

"You lie," she hissed.

"Did you not see?" said Almarnoch.

"I had no need to see his defeat of you," she replied with a haughty toss of her head. "When the black ship rose into the skies, I knew he would be victorious."

"But he was not," said Almarnoch. The words were sterner now. "The dragons downed the black ship, and strength of the wand, of this one girl, was greater than his."

"Again you dare to lie to me," the queen said. "He has always been there. He will always be there. We will live forever."

"You shall see for yourself," Almarnoch said. He strode across the room and grabbed Queen Virrisian by the arm. She was taller than he, much taller, but he propelled her across the room easily. He dragged her to the balcony, her eyes fearfully on the ceiling. "Look," said Almarnoch. "See what has become of the black ship."

Shaeli went and stood behind them as the queen looked out at the scene below.

Far down at the great wall, the gates were sprawled open and the buildings there were surrounded by the scars of battle. Here and there, a wisp of smoke rose into the still air. Bodies were being piled together, the wounded carried away to be tended by the Faunists. The fields were trampled, the downed Trader leaning awkwardly on its side, the remains of the balloon draped across its decks. Purple Leaf was moored at the Landing beside the fields. Groups of scarlet and black were surrounded by the colours of the other Lands.

The black ship lay at the edge of the gardens, the ground around it churned up from the impact of it slamming into the ground. People stood around it, staring up at its ugly lines. In the courtyard beneath the castle, people moved about the great well, yet it was clear they were not fighting, but pushing the defeated soldiers out through the gates, these also laying in ruins.

"Do you see?" said Almarnoch. Again the words were said pityingly. "He has been defeated. He will poison your mind no more."

The queen's face paled as she gazed at the wreckage outside the castle, yet she narrowed her eyes and lifted her chin.

"He will come again," she said. "Always he has risen above defeat. He will return."

Almarnoch shook his head. "Not this time," he said. "The dragons took him. Do you not see what that means?"

The queen shook her arm free. "You are wrong. He will call me to him again." She shook the curled fist. She held a stone in her grasp. "He will speak to me just as he always has. He told me..."

"He told you many things," Almarnoch interrupted. "He filled your life with lies."

Shaeli heard the soft voice of a bird again, and something else. An echo of song, a whisper of melody, yet she had no time to wonder about it, for there came the sound of footsteps on the stairs. Ezebar, Flin, Williver, Llianas and Tarkoda raised their weapons.

"You see?" cried the queen. "He comes to finish you."

She stepped back into the room, and Shaeli edged away from her, the wand held tightly in her fingers, yet no soldiers came to their queen's aid. Ishaan came up the stairs, behind him Olando and Cheval, Jeth and Andos, Blenny led M'zena, and Mareesha came up the stairs behind them. They lowered their weapons with relief as the others came across the barren landing and into the room. The queen backed away from them, her face now etched with fear. Mareesha came and stood beside Shaeli.

"Hello, Virrisian," she said, putting her arm around her daughter's shoulders.

Virrisian's eyes narrowed, and then she sneered. "The little Faunist," she said. "Your age sits heavily upon your face."

"My face shows the joy and tears of the life I have lived," said Mareesha. "I wear my age with pride. Your face is bereft of the lines of one of your age. It looks unnatural."

"Why should one lose years when the Warlocks have the power to make it otherwise?" Virrisian said. "I shall live for a long time, as will he." Her voice rose. The clenched fist rose with it. "We shall rule this Land, and we shall burn every Trader and kill every one of your stupid birds." She came closer, her eyes and voice spitting venom at Mareesha. "We shall find your children and..."

"You will do nothing," cried Shaeli, stepping in front of her mother. "He is gone. The dragons tore him to shreds in the sky above the castle. You have no power over us any more."

Virrisian laughed. "You have your mother's temper," she said. "I will see that it is quelled."

She took a step forward, and the sound of singing came again. She stopped, her brows drawing together. She looked around.

Shaeli heard the melody swell and suddenly she recognised it. The voices blending together in the wordless song grew stronger, and then M'zena's thin voice rose to join it. Shaeli looked at the tiny woman and then she turned towards the mural.

The colours of the painting on the curved wall began to shimmer, softly at first. There came the sound of birdsong again, and the song behind it grew stronger. The leaves on the trees surrounding the silent grass began to move, as if touched by a gentle breeze. The faces entwined in the trees began to move also, the mouths open in song. The faces of the people of the Forest grew clearer.

From between the trees stepped an old lady. Her silver hair was braided to her waist. She stepped onto the grass and three others stepped from the trees behind her. One more step brought the old woman blinking into the room, her feet bare, her eyes scanning the faces looking back at her, coming to rest on Virrisian. Behind the old woman came the twins, looking about them and then squealing and leaping across the room into Mareesha's waiting arms. Kirrit stepped last from the grass of the Glade, Ebony on her shoulder, the packs they had left behind in Forest Village hanging from one hand, M'zena's quilt under her arm. She was frowning as she came, her free hand holding her little crossbow. Behind her, Myrrabilla and Filo took a step from the trees, smiling broadly, yet they came no further, but stayed on the grass of the Glade, singing and smiling. Kirrit shook her head as she stepped out into the crowd of familiar faces, and then she smiled.

"Well, that's a better welcome than the last one I had in this room," she said, with a smile.

Ebony leapt from her shoulder and bounded across the room to Shaeli, who scooped her up and nuzzled her. Ebony chittered and leapt onto Shaeli's shoulder, sniffing the air. Kirrit slipped the bundles to the floor and came and smiled at Shaeli.

"Took you long enough," she said, grinning, then her eyes slid past Shaeli to Tarkoda. Her feet followed a moment later.

"So this is how you did it, Irinesta?" said Virrisian, the queen who was no longer queen. "I knew you were lying about the child. I thought you had smuggled it out somehow, but this," she said, waving a hand at the Glade, "this is something I did not foresee."

"You were not meant to foresee it, Virrisian," said Irinesta. "It is magic like no other in this World."

"We almost found it, you know," Virrisian sneered. "Someone tried to contact you through the calling stones. Virrek caught them, he had the mind snared, he said, and the picture of you and the babe was clear. He saw a small room, a ship surrounded by water, but as he started to probe further, the connection was broken somehow, he knows not why. But for that we would have found the babe and it would not have lived another Moon."

"It was I who used the calling stones," said Mareesha. "The connection was broken by my daughter." She looked at Shaeli. "With a well-aimed kick from a very small girl." She looked back at Virrisian. "And there was no ship, but a Trader, hurrying to Cave in the rain."

"I always suspected," said Virrisian. "But all Traders were gone from the city or far distant." She looked at the Glade. "Now I know how you reached them." Irinesta said nothing, merely stared at Virrisian. "Why do you look at me like that?" she said. "With such pity."

"Because Tenelon was right," said Irinesta. A soft smile lit her face. "The shadow you pulled over the Land will be gone. His child was saved as he said, by its brother and sisters. And the child will rule."

Virrisian's face grew red. She screeched a wordless babble and threw herself across the room. Yet it was not Irinesta she sought, but Shaeli.

Shaeli stood by herself near the balcony, Ebony on her shoulder. Virrisian caught her around the shoulders and shoved her backwards, through the doors and across the balcony. The railing caught Shaeli in the middle of the back and her shoulders went over the void. Virrisian was spitting and screaming in her face, and she felt Ebony clutching her shoulder, the little hands gripping her hair. She grabbed at the railing and the wand dropped to the floor. Virrisian kicked at it, and it skittered across the tiles, went beneath the railing and fell over the edge. Shaeli glanced over her shoulder, saw the wand plummeting downwards, but the sight of the sheer drop beneath her was like a blow to her stomach. As she looked back up into the enraged face, Virrisian grabbed the jevvi off Shaeli's shoulder and threw her out into the air after the wand. Shaeli screamed and grabbed at her, but Ebony was gone, dropping swiftly to the ground below. With one deft movement, Virrisian leant down and grabbed Shaeli's ankle. She picked her up and threw her over the railing after the jevvi.

It had taken only a moment for Virrisian to push Shaeli through the door, and as she shoved Shaeli over the railing she was grabbed from behind by Tarkoda and Williver. Shaeli had one hand still on the rail, but the other flailed in the air as her legs went up and over the edge. Her fingers brushed the railing, her other arm twisted as it took the brunt of her weight, and her feet thudded into the underside of the balcony.

She was vaguely aware of a blue mass streaking past her as her fingers slipped from the railing.

A hand grabbed her wrist just as her fingers left the railing. She looked up and was staring into Ezebar's eyes. He put out his other hand, reaching for her, and she put her hand up, straining for him. She touched his fingers and he grabbed at her. Behind him, her father and Ishaan held his belt, and as he gripped her fingers, they began to pull. She looked down once, saw the ground between her dangling feet, and then Ezebar pulled her up and her legs were over the railing, her feet back on solid ground. She fell against his chest, sobbing.

"There, now," Ezebar soothed her, holding her tightly and stroking her hair, yet his hands were trembling. "You're alright. You're safe now."

He led her inside, her legs shaking, her heart thundering against her ribs. They clustered around her, her parents, Flin, the twins, and Kirrit, and, though she did not want to let him go, Ezebar was pushed into the background.

M'zena came to stand beside him, looking up at him with her mouth curved. "I think I shall like it at the Cave of the Traders," she said.

Ezebar frowned. "What are you talking about?" he asked.

"Nothing, lad," she said, patting his arm. "Just that you'll make a fine trader."

Ezebar shook his head at her, but his eyes turned quickly back to Shaeli. She was drying her eyes now, her head shaking.

"Ebony," she was saying, looking over to where Virrisian struggled between Williver and Tarkoda. "She threw her over."

Ezebar went back out on the balcony and looked over. His head snapped back as the jevvi flew at his face and drifted past him into the room. There was fairy dust fluttering from beneath her, and at first, Ezebar thought she was flying. He heard Shaeli gasp and he followed Ebony back into the room.

The jevvi leapt to the floor and bounded over to Shaeli, who knelt down and scooped her up from the floor, crying anew.

Tish and a dozen other fairies shook out their wings and fluttered over to Shaeli.

When Ebony had been thrown from the balcony she had put out her arms and legs, gliding as she did from tree to tree. But the tower was far too high and even with her limbs splayed wide, the ground rushed up at her far too quickly. She had squealed, and Tish, watching the falling wand and the jevvi following it to the ground, had taken some of her kindred and darted through the air, catching the jevvi before she hit the ground. The jevvi had wriggled a moment, but, seeing her friend Tish, she had relaxed and even enjoyed the flight back up to the Glade Room.

Shaeli hugged her, overjoyed, and thanked the fairies. Within the Glade, the faces of the people of the Forest smiled, their song still floating lightly on the breeze. Virrisian's voice cut through the room like a bloody knife.

"Even if the jevvi survived, the wand did not," she said, her voice as hard and cold as the diamonds she wore. "No stone could survive that fall."

"You are wrong," Tish's voice chimed, even more lovely after Virrisian's cold tones. "The dragon caught the wand before it reached the ground. It waits below, the wand unharmed at its feet."

"Then it is lost, just the same," Virrisian cried. "A dragon would never relinquish such a prize." Her smile was triumphant. "We will return, you'll see, and you will rue this day. I will speak to him and he will tell me what is to be done with your rabble." She spat the words at them, her fist pumped the air. The stone was still in it, a calling stone.

She shoved Tarkoda, grabbing his sword as he fell, and she whirled around and slashed at Williver. The blade struck him on the arm, and he cried out as blood gushed from the wound.

Llianas screamed and dashed to him. Virrisian swung the sword and Llianas caught the blade full in the chest. She staggered as Virrisian withdrew the blade dripping with the little elf's blood. Llianas' face showed only surprise as she crumpled to the floor, her life gone before she hit the cold stones.

Kirrit and Cheval screamed as Llianas was impaled, the screams still echoing through the chamber as Virrisian raised the bloody sword and Llianas' body fell to the floor where she lay in a growing pool of blood.

Shaeli fumbled in her amulet with a scream of denial, but before she could draw a stone, Virrisian rushed across the room and threw herself at the mural. She was gone in an instant and Tarkoda rushed after her. He stopped at the wall and looked back.

"She'll escape," he said. "We have to go after her."

Shaeli looked at the mural. Myrrabilla and Filo still stood on the grass, their faces serene, untroubled. She looked back at her brother and shook her head.

"There is no need," she said.

"What do you mean?" said Tarkoda. "She has my sword. She could go anywhere."

"She won't, Koda," Shaeli said. "The Forest won't let her."

They crowded around where Mareesha was hovering with Williver over the body of Llianas. The young elf who had accompanied them through so much danger was laying in a puddle of blood, her lovely face serene, her eyes closed, dark lashes on ashen cheeks.

Kirrit knelt beside her, holding the lifeless hand. "No, Llianas," she cried over and over. "No, Llianas, no."

Shaeli's tears fell as Williver took a blanket from the bed and tenderly wrapped Llianas in it. Shaeli hugged them both as he lifted the once-lithe body from the ground and carried her to the door where Olando took her. There was silence in the room as he took her down the stairs, a weeping Cheval in his wake. Williver staggered as they left the room and Mareeshas helped him to the bed.

"Is he alright, Mam?" Shaeli asked.

"I'm fine," Williver said, but his face was pale and puckered with pain, his arm covered in blood.

"We must take him down," said Mareesha. "The wound is not deep, but it must be sewn."

As Flin and Ishaan came and helped Williver to his feet, the song from the Glade was still humming through the room, and they turned to gaze at it before they left.

The faces between the trees grew bright, and Tish fluttered forward to hover in front of the mural. Rem came flittering from the shimmering glade to hover beside Tish, taking her hand and smiling out at them.

"It is time," said Rem.

Tish nodded at her and looked back at Shaeli. "We shall be watching," she said.

"Thank you, Tish," she said. "Thank them all."

"I shall," Tish nodded. "And remember, you shall walk within the Forest freely, always," she said.

The two fairies turned and flew towards the shimmering mural. Myrrabilla and Filo raised an arm in farewell as the fairies flew between the lofty trunks, and then they turned and followed them, leaving the Glade empty once again. The song of the Forest grew louder, and M'zena joined in. After a moment, another voice joined in; the voice of the old queen, Irinesta.

The song slowed, faded. The images in the mural stilled, the leaves of the trees stopped swaying in their unfelt breeze. The last faces to shine out at them were those of Myrrabilla and Filo. There was the soft lilac-grey sparkle of a fairy, and then the song sighed to a stop. The echo of it trembled in the room for a moment, and then it was gone. The mural became just a mural once again.

Irinesta and M'zena stopped singing with the last reluctant chord, and now they stood smiling at each other. Mareesha stood with her arms about the twins' shoulders, but she left them and went to stand before Irinesta.

"Come," Mareesha said. She hugged her and then took her hand. "You have spent enough time within these walls."

"I do not regret them," Irinesta said, smiling at the twins. "You have held her safe, and that was ever my only wish."

Neesha stepped forward. "But you didn't have to stay here," she said. "You could have gone long ago. Through the painting."

"No, child," she said. "Then they would have known there was a way out of here, they would have known I could have taken a child out of the castle."

"But they did know, didn't they?" said Neesha.

"No," said Irinesta. "For many years they suspected, but they did not know. Once they did, they found you and your sister and brought you here, and I would have taken you both through the Glade," she shrugged. "But there was no chance. Virrisian removed the door and stationed guard in the room."

"They weren't always here?" said Neesha.

"No," said Irinesta. "For many long Winterings I was left alone with my maid, the door bolted."

"But no more," said Mareesha. "Now you shall join the World again, as mother to the new queen."

Irinesta blinked, her eyes filled with tears. She squeezed Mareesha's hands and nodded.

Flin and Ishaan helped Williver out of the room. The others followed slowly, looking back at the mural, eyes still filled with wonder and sorrow. Kirrit and Tarkoda paused at the door.

"I think that's it," Kirrit said quietly, tears still running down her cheeks at the loss of her friend. She looked up at Tarkoda. "I think maybe it's finished."

Tarkoda looked down at her for a moment, and then he wrapped his arms around her. "Oh, no," he said. "I don't think I've quite finished with you just yet." He took her hand and together they went down the stairs.

Shaeli watched them go. Almarnoch stood beside her, Ezebar and M'zena waited at the door.

"Shaeli?" said Almarnoch, touching her shoulder.

She was staring at the Glade, the colours so rich, the painting so perfect. She shook her head. "I'm alright," she said, pulling Ebony from her shoulder and hugging her to her chest. "It's just, what Kirrit said." She sighed. "It's finished, and I don't have to run anymore. I don't have to fight. The adventure is over."

Almarnoch took her arm. He smiled at her.

"Only this one, child," he said. "Only this one. There is always another adventure."

* * *

When they reached the ground, the guard had been rounded up. Some were corralled in a corner of the courtyard, watched over by the elves. The soldiers sat, heads down, defeat etched on their faces and in the fall of their shoulders.

Also there was Virrisian's treasurer, Orm. He had been found in a small courtyard at the rear of the castle with a few of the young men who had calculated his figures. They had been filling a small carriage with gold and jewels. How they planned to get them out of the castle was a thing to be guessed at, but he and his pasty-faced young men were now sitting with the guard, the gold and gems returned to the vaults for the new queen and her courtiers to deal with.

They went out through the gates, and looked across the castle grounds. The wisps of smoke still rose into the air, the black ship lay at the edge of the road, people gaping up at it. The downed Trader lay in a field, the burnt shell of Golden Eagle out of sight beyond the wall, but above Palveron dozens more Traders were flying victorious circles over the broken city.

Between the castle and the Faunist house lay the blue dragon, its tail stretching out between the beds of a herb garden, the wand on the grass between its feet. From the Faunist and Warlock houses and from the castle walls people watched it and cast fearful eyes at the scores of dragons riding the high winds far overhead.

As Shaeli came through the broken gates the dragon roared. It took up the wand and leapt into the air, circling so close overhead that they could see the gem-dust glittering on its belly. It circled again and then swooped down and landed in front of them. It looked at Shaeli and she bowed her head to it. The others stood around her, weapons drawn.

The dragon came forward, stopping a carriage-length from Shaeli. She could feel the heat of its breath wash over her, yet she was not afraid. The depth of feeling in the golden eyes was unmistakable. It took a step towards her.

The dragon dropped its head, stretching its neck forward. It placed the wand on the ground at Shaeli's feet, and then pulled its head back. She bent over and picked the wand up. She took a step forward, and another, until she could reach out a hand and touch it. She rested her hand upon its great snout for a moment, her blue-grey eyes meeting the huge golden ones, and then she stepped back, smiled, and bowed again to the dragon.

Amazingly, it mirrored her gesture, dropping its head to her. For a moment longer it fixed her with its golden gaze, and then it raised its huge head to the sky, opened its wings, and roared. The sound vibrated about her, and then the dragon took off, leaping into the sky, its great wings washing Shaeli with a wind that pushed her backwards. It flew upwards, streaking through the sky like a bolt of blue lightning, joining its brethren in the skies. They rode the sky above the city for only a moment, and then as one, they roared, and the noise shattered the sky. They streaked away, darting across the skies, splitting up and flying in every direction. Soon only the blue dragon was left. It circled Great Court once more, gave a final mighty roar, and flew off to the north at incredible speed.

Shaeli looked from the sky to the wand in her hand. It was perfect, unmarked and beautiful. She looked up as a familiar voice reached her.

"Oh, my dears, how spectacular."

Arinola came fluttering towards them. Vulcan was easing himself from a tiny carriage behind her. Shaeli looked at the road that the two old people had just traversed, pock-marked and littered with refuse, and she smiled and shook her head. She knew better than to wonder at the Lady Arinola.

"What a wonderful sight they are," she said, looking at the sky. "However did you do it, Shaeli?"

Shaeli shook her head. "I'm not sure," she said. "Arinola, what are you doing here?"

"Well, I had to come, didn't I?" Arinola sniffed. "They said the castle was released, the heir found safe, and I had to…" She stopped, and put a hand to her breast. "Oh, my," she cried, and she rushed forward.

Irinesta's arms were open when Arinola reached her. They clasped each other, and then Arinola pulled back and looked at her friend.

"Look, Vulcan," she cried, dabbing at her eyes. "Irinesta is here, after all these Winterings."

Vulcan came forward, and Irinesta greeted him with more tears and embraces.

"I could hardly wish to see any faces more than yours," Irinesta said to them. "Many times I thought of you both."

"And we of you, my lady," bowed Vulcan.

"And now we shall have a new queen," said Arinola, looking at the twins standing nearby, wide-eyed and stunned by their ordeal.

They held hands, taking strength from each other as they always had. Arinola frowned. She looked from them to Irinesta.

"But which one?" she said loudly. "Which one is the next queen?"

Irinesta looked at Mareesha and smiled.

"I think I know," she said, looking at the girls. Tears long-held pooled in her eyes. "I think I know, for she has her father's smile."

\* \* \*

# EPILOGUE

Autumn's Eve dawned fine and clear. The sky was washed with thick blue strokes, perfect bundles of clouds scudded slowly with the gentlest of breezes, and the thick heat of summer had given way to the more mellow warmth of the approaching autumn.

Palveron woke when the sky to the east was still streaked with peach and pink, eager for the promises of the new day, the new era, for the new queen was to be crowned this day and none would miss it. They dressed in their finest and began milling in the streets before the roosters had ceased to crow.

The city was still scarred with the battles that had been fought between its buildings. Many windows remained glassless, the buildings too damaged by the Qotarr were slowly being pulled down, the sites readied for the rebuilding to begin, yet the mood in the streets was one of gaiety, of renewed hope. Food had flooded into the city with the defeat of Virrisian's guard, and with their strength regained and their fear lifted, the people turned their thoughts to making the city a vibrant place once again. Already the rubble had been sorted beneath the wall, the stones stacked so the fine houses could stand again, even finer than before. Across the city, the people had worked together, yet today none would work; today they readied themselves for the trip to the Royal Parklands, where for days there had been hundreds of people readying the site for the coronation of the new queen.

They gossiped about her as they went to the Parklands, turning the slight bit of information that was known into long, imagined stories, talking of how she'd been hidden with the Traders all these Winterings, how her "sister" was the one who had defeated the black ship and returned the dragons. Tongues clicked against teeth when they thought of the poor old queen, kept prisoner all this time, but how joyful she must feel now that she had been reunited with her lost child. They told each other what a pretty little thing the princess was, with her dark hair and flashing green eyes, how lucky she was to have her mother and Sir Vulcan of Conroi to guide her with the running of the Land until she came of age. She had taken to her role with gusto, they smiled, and her firm young voice was already becoming familiar to those at Court. They gathered early in the Parklands, eager to have a fine view of the coronation later in the afternoon, their spirits held loftily, their laughter tumbling freely across the fields.

*** 

Shaeli also woke early. She lay watching the peach-pink sunrise turn to bright day, and finally she stretched and threw back the covers. She was unwilling to leave its comfort, for she had not yet reached the stage where she took a soft bed for granted, and she sat there for a moment with her feet resting on the cool floor, revelling in the feeling of calm that enveloped her. It had been so long since she had felt at peace that, like the softness of the bed, she was loathe to let it go, but eventually she stood up and padded around the room gathering her clothes for the day. She lay the elegant dress on the bed for later and pulled on another, the blue embroidered dress that Ezebar had stolen for her from the fields to the north. She smoothed the dress and sighed; it seemed so long ago now.

Ebony stretched and yawned as she was tying on her amulet, and she scampered over, waiting eagerly until Shaeli opened the door.

Flin's house was quiet when she stepped out into the hall, but she knew they would all be up and anxious for the day ahead, and she could already smell something good coming from the direction of the kitchen. Though she had tried to hide it, Arinola had been deeply distressed when Yorrow had returned to Flin's when the house had been opened up again.

Flin, of course, had been extremely grateful to Arinola for closing it and taking his people into her home, but Yorrow had returned to Flin's, expressionless as ever, and was now ensconced back in his kitchen. As Shaeli came down the stairs, she saw him come from the kitchen with a large covered platter, and she followed him as he took it out onto the terrace.

There was a long table set beneath the wide eaves, candles burning beneath covered dishes, other platters holding rolls and fruit beside them, a big pot of tezz at one end. Yorrow lay his platter on a stand over a candle, nodded at Shaeli as she came out the door, and disappeared back inside.

Flin smiled at her as she came out. He was standing with Williver and the Ammerr, Ezebar and M'zena near the stairs, each holding a steaming cup. The drell and Spotjaw had been staying at the castle, a thing insisted upon by Irinesta as befitted their royal rank, and Almarnoch was with Purple Leaf. Kirrit and Tarkoda were standing on the throwing platform at the end of the terrace, looking out at the bay. Shaeli poured herself tezz and wandered over to the stairs, not wanting to interrupt the intimacy of the murmured conversation between her brother and Kirrit.

"Beautiful day," she said.

"Lovely," agreed Cheval.

"Did you sleep well, little one?" Williver asked.

She nodded. "I did," she said. "I'm still finding it a bit of a novelty, a big comfortable bed. I keep waking up expecting to roll over onto a rock or a stick or something. I keep expecting to be rained on in my sleep."

Kirrit and Tarkoda came down the stairs and joined them.

"The nights in the Forest were comfortable, but they seem to be fading somehow," said Williver. "I remember the nights in the rain more, too."

"It's odd," said Kirrit. "The days in the Forest seem to run together somehow."

"I know what you mean," said Shaeli, and though it was true, there where some things that she would never forget – a walk across dew-wet grass at dawn; a swim in clear, leafy pool; a long-held gaze. She smiled at Ezebar and knew he was remembering too. "It felt a long time then, I know that, but now it seems as if it was just a few days."

"Remember that awful howl we heard one night? And the day we saw Pizar wandering past on the other side of the creek?" said Kirrit. "Was that when we first arrived, or just before we left?"

Ezebar shook his head. "I don't know," he said. "But I remember the Village clearly, and the song."

"And the Glade," said Shaeli.

Flin looked from one to another. Each face was slack with the remembering, eyes focussed on a distant wonder.

"What do you think happened to her when she reached the Forest?" he asked.

They all knew who he meant. The faces sharpened, the mouths tightened, the eyes grew steely.

"'Tis certain she was not well received," said M'zena. "I think we'll not have to worry about her again."

"And the secret will always be a secret," said Kirrit. "No one who saw such a thing could ever betray it."

"Never," said Shaeli. "And I'll be looking for Tish every time I'm in Zuen." She shook her head and smiled. "I don't think it will be for a while, though. I've promised to stay here until my sister is settled. I know what it's like to spend the Wintering alone, away from Cave, and next year," she shrugged, "we'll see."

"My house will certainly be very boring this Wintering," said Flin. "With you up at Great Court and Illen and Qiren returning to their own lands."

"I don't know, Flin," said Ishaan. "Now that the Ammerr have returned to the World, I'm not anxious to go back to

Qorientae just yet. I'm happy to keep you company, and I think Cheval and Olando might feel the same."

"Oh, indeed we do," said Olando, his arm around Cheval's shoulders.

"And I think we might have many visitors swimming in, too," Cheval said.

"You're not getting rid of us either," said Ezebar. "We're staying too, M'zena, aren't we?"

"Indeed, lad," she smiled. "It seems I have been given yet another life by the grace of Merrom. I shall enjoy the city this Wintering." Here she looked slyly at Shaeli. "And next year I look forward to becoming one of the old ones at the Cave of the Traders."

Flin smiled. "I welcome you all. It seems I've grown used to having companions around me. The years I spent alone in this house seem so wasted now, so lonely. I only wish that our little Llianas was here to enjoy it all with us."

"She would have enjoyed it a great deal, Flin," said Williver with a sad smile. "We will miss her always." They were all silent while they contemplated the loss of the bright young elf. "I'm inclined to stay too," he said at last. "At least for the Wintering."

"And we'll come down for a visit," said Shaeli, a blush fading on her cheeks at M'zena's words and all they implied. "And Arinola has promised to give another ball. The twins are already looking forward to it." She rolled her eyes. "It's really hard to stop saying that."

"They're still your sisters, Shaeli," said Ishaan. "Even if one of them is to be crowned this afternoon."

"Crowned," said Shaeli, shaking her head again. "My sister, the queen. How odd."

The past days had all seemed odd to her; back in Flin's house; Red Arrow and others moored safely in the main square and other Landings throughout the city; Purple Leaf moored in the castle grounds; preparations for her sister's coronation – a thing still almost unbelievable.

Her sister had picked the colours for her new regime, and green flags with purple stars fluttered above the castle, the colours chosen to reflect her upbringing on Purple Leaf.

So, too, were the colours worn proudly by the new guard eager to serve their queen; green uniforms with purple stars across their breasts. Tailors worked day and night on the new colours, and every day more of the green-and-purple was seen, replacing the scarlet-and-black that had terrified the Land for so long.

Of the old guard, those still alive, they had been given a choice: pledge allegiance to the crown or rot in the dungeons. People had come forward and pointed fingers at those who had committied the worst atrocities throughout the Land, and they were held in the dungeons, awaiting trial. Most of the common soldiers had bent the knee, some had stubbornly chosen the dungeons, but there were many who returned to homes they had longed for, unable to leave Virrisian's service on pain of death. There were those too, who sought to make amends by joining the new guard.

The Traders had been on many flights from the time of the defeat of the black ship. The bodies of Taffka, Renn, Rennan and other traders who had died during the battle had been taken to Cave to be mourned over and buried overlooking the Long Lea.

They had also returned battle-weary fighters to their homes, brought supplies into the city, and they had flown to Lythnori, taking the elves home, the bodies of Llianas and other elves with them, and bringing Xyrrol and Mithrina back to Palveron for the coronation, Ky and Jocovar as their happy escorts.

So too, had Traders flown up the Nebillonia Straits and zig-zagged their way up and over the great cliffs into Qorientae. The Ammerr had turned wondrous faces to the sky as two Traders filled with their brethren circled the lake and landed on a sandy beach below. Rizar had collected Aneris and brought her back to the city, and they were also attending the coronation.

Traders had also flown to the south, to the island of the Qotarr off Wokk. Mahra told them that this was where Virrek had hidden for many years, where he taken the drell, enslaved their minds, and had them build the black ship. Mahra remembered only snatches of her time there, but she knew they had been kept in a deep cavern, high above the Qotarr on the plateau, and the metal had been dug from the bowels of the old volcano. There were others there, drell and people, even a few elves, enslaved by Virrek, and these were freed with the arrival of the Traders. The whole Fleet was overjoyed to find Bic's mother and his brother, Tam, there, and finally the riddle of the missing Trader was solved; the black ship had fired on them as they crossed to Zirrus, all the others on board, and all but two Zoi who had returned to Cave had perished, but Bic was there to free what remained of his family.

Why the Wokkii had chosen to aid Virrek was also something soon explained. It seemed he had never lost hold of some of his old ties there, and as his old allies had bred sons and grandsons, these too had been aiding Virrek in secret; a society that had spent decades capturing young Qotarr and training them. They had built ships and gone first to take the castle of the King of Wokk, using the great lizards and a pointed visit from the black ship to keep those on Wokk who would protest in their place. The ships had then taken the great lizards on to wreak destruction in Palveron, leaving two Qotarr to control the Wokkii monarchy. The King of Wokk and his family had now been freed, the remaining Qotarr, too, had been returned to their island to roam untethered with their brethren, and all those who had been found on the plateau had been returned to the World.

As for the black ship, it still lay in the gardens below the castle, eyed suspiciously, skirted warily, but completely harmless. The drell would fly it to their home, vowing to reshape it and use it to visit new friends. Wendll had proudly flown with a Trader into the Drell Mountains to bring Orbanna to the city to be reunited with Blenny and Mahra, watching with shining eyes as the tiny old woman hugged the queen of the drell. They would return to drell lands straight after the coronation, yet Wendll would not accompany them; he enjoyed seeing the World outside the mountains and would now accompany Spotjaw on his travels as Blenny's replacement.

Most of the people from the other Lands had already returned to their homes, but some had stayed to witness the coronation of the new Queen of Zirrus. As the morning passed, they, too, gathered to partake of the Hunts and await the arrival of the royal party.

When the sun reached its zenith, Shaeli and the others went to their rooms to dress. She took off the blue dress and put on the more elaborate one she had laid out earlier. She brushed her hair and Ebony's until both shone, and then she tied a deep purple velvet collar patterned with tiny crystals around the jevvi's neck. The collar matched her own dress and she smiled and the jevvi grinned back, preening. As she picked up Ebony, there was a knock on the door.

Ezebar stood outside. He was dressed in new clothes, his beard neatly trimmed, his hair tied at the nape, his eyes shining.

"You're beautiful," he said, and she closed her eyes as he leant to kiss her.

"You look pretty fancy yourself," she smiled.

They stood smiling at each other for a while, and then he took her hand, wrapped it through his arm and squeezed it.

"Come on," he said. "They're all waiting."

They went down the stairs to where the others waited; Flin, Ishaan, Cheval and Olando, Williver, Tarkoda and Kirrit,

M'zena, and they all boarded Flin's carriage and drove down through the city and out to the Royal Parklands.

A large, open pavilion had been set up across the water beside the forest, yet there would be no hunting there this year, in memory of King Tenelon, father of the new queen, poisoned by a barb at a Hunt so long before. There was an avenue of people leading up to the pavilion, and Shaeli and the others walked along it, seeing familiar faces at every step.

There were the two rebels, Fezzik and Fozar with their families, Fozar missing a leg from wounds sustained as they stormed Palveron; Dorkit standing proudly with them, the Warlock Bekerra and the ex-soldier, Bithani, behind them. There were the elves, Qiren and Illen with them, the drell, the Ammerr; people from other Lands, Captain Mahi, Crissita and Brudloc among them. Next came the members of the Fleet; Rafi in the place his parents would have been, their loss still plain to see on his face. Delphi and the rest of Baroz's family were beside him, the children of her Cave year, Sahli'en and Navez, Wyshka and Olver with them, brought from the Long Lea with Illen and Llevvis to witness the coronation. Next was Jeth and Eenis, both beaming, Andos with his arm proudly around a blushing S'resh, the two just betrothed. There, too, was Dari, in a chair, pale and bent from his wound, but alive, his face free of the anguish which had coloured it, and Shaeli stopped to kiss him before she went on. Here was Almarnoch, his brows quivering with the brightness of his smile, Spotjaw and Wendll all grinning broadly with Orbanna, and then Blenny and Mahra. The sight of them brought tears to Shaeli's eyes, and she stopped at the top of the avenue, looking back at the smiling people from every race looking at her.

Ezebar took her hand, and she looked up at him, the tears turning to shimmering joy. A trumpet sounded, and she turned her face to the sky.

Purple Leaf was flying from the castle. It rose high over the city and flew down to the Parklands with every eye upon it.

The Zoi glowed in the sunlight, the rainbows beneath their wings shimmering as they circled the waiting crowd, the voice of the lead female chiming above the fields as the Trader flew down to the newly-built Landing.

Rhubic and Tajindi moored the ship, and then stood, shoulders squared and heads high, either side of the stairs as the party descended.

Jarris and Mareesha came first, their faces beaming.

Next came Irinesta, escorted by the tall, proud Sir Vulcan, and greeted with resounding cheers. Lady Arinola attended Irinesta, her face awash with tears.

The found princess came last, walking alone, her sister behind, holding the long glittering train she wore.

Roshanna held her head high, a soft smile playing about her lips, her shining eyes on the faces lining the avenue. Behind her, Reneesha glowed, her smile caught by the crowd and returned to her twofold.

They came slowly down the avenue, and, though Shaeli was fairly sure she wasn't supposed to, when they reached the place where Shaeli stood beside Ezebar, Shanna came over and kissed her. Neesha would not be left out, and the three of them hugged together while the people looked smilingly on. They kissed Tarkoda too, before returning to walk the final steps to where the appointed officials waited to begin.

The crown that the new Queen Roshanna would wear sat on a pedestal, glowing with the many gems it held, and later, there would be skylights more beautiful than anyone could dream.

Shaeli looked from her sisters into Ezebar's eyes, and then she turned her face to the sky.

High above, in the endless blue, a dragon circled, a cobalt-blue dragon. As the crown was placed on the new queen's head, the dragon roared.

THE END

## *ABOUT THE AUTHOR*

R.L. Aiken lives on the eastern coast of Australia in a small town with the ocean out the front and kangaroos out the back. She has been writing this very big story in this very small town for a very long time, and is very happy to finally put it in your hands to be read. Thanks for holding it.

www.ingramcontent.com/pod-product-compliance
Ingram Content Group UK Ltd.
Pitfield, Milton Keynes, MK11 3LW, UK
UKHW041303180426
11947UKWH00009B/662